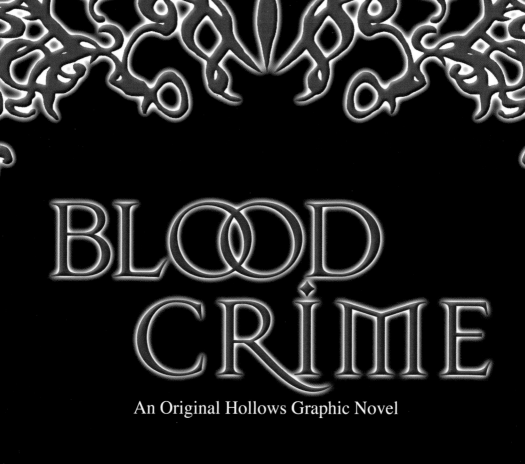

BLOOD CRIME

An Original Hollows Graphic Novel

Kim Harrison

Illustrations by
Gemma Magno

Ballantine Books • New York

Published in the United States by Del Rey, an imprint of The Random House Publishing Group, a division of Random House, Inc., New York.

DEL REY is a registered trademark and the Del Rey colophon is a trademark of Random House, Inc.

ISBN 978-0-345-52102-6
eBook ISBN 978-0-345-53529-0

Illustrations by Gemma Magno

Colors and lettering by Mae Hao

Design by Zach Matheny

Printed in the United States of America on acid-free paper.

www.delreybooks.com

2 4 6 8 9 7 5 3 1

Contents

Other Books by Kim Harrison

The Hollows Original Graphic Novels
Blood Work

The Hollows Series
Dead Witch Walking
The Good, the Bad, and the Undead
Every Which Way but Dead
A Fistful of Charms
For a Few Demons More
The Outlaw Demon Wails
White Witch, Black Curse
Black Magic Sanction
Pale Demon

The Madison Avery Series
Prom Nights from Hell
Once Dead, Twice Shy
Early to Death, Early to Rise
Something Deadly This Way Comes

Writing as Dawn Cook
First Truth
Hidden Truth
Forgotten Truth
Lost Truth
The Decoy Princess
Princess at Sea

Other Del Rey Graphic Novels

From Dean Koontz
Dean Koontz's Frankenstein: Prodigal Son
In Odd We Trust
Odd Is on Our Side
House of Odd

From Patricia Briggs
Mercy Thompson: Homecoming

From Jim Butcher
Dresden Files: Welcome to the Jungle
Dresden Files: Storm Front Vol. 1: The Gathering Storm

From Diana Gabaldon
The Exile: An Outlander Graphic Novel

From Naomi Novik
Will Supervillains Be on the Final?

From Terry Brooks
Dark Wraith of Shannara

From Jason Thompson
King of RPGs 1
King of RPGs 2

From Karin Marie Moning
Fever Moon

From Scott Westerfeld
Uglies: Shay's Story

BLOOD CRIME

Introduction

When there's time enough for everything, there's no reason to survive. Boredom is the primary cause of death among the undead. The power they wield, their control over others, results in a paler world where little can stimulate or surprise and that which does is prized beyond gold. Surviving the tricky forty-year barrier into a longer undead existence is not a given for the Hollows vampire, and it's only the most clever, most inventive who manage it. It's not that it's harder to make those around you love you when you have no soul, but that tedium is the enemy when time no longer is.

Piscary long ago became skilled enough at mimicking life to convince his "children" that he loved them, ensuring himself a steady supply of blood, but with that challenge gone boredom threatened until he began searching for, and then attempting to create, the perfect soul mate: a person who could stand up to him and say no, someone who had the potential to surprise him, outthink him, keep him stimulated, whether this person be a friend or foe—someone who could keep him from walking out into the sun when the boredom became too great.

Ivy knows that her mother and grandmother were part of Piscary's search for the perfect distraction and that they died when he decided they were not suitable, not strong enough to withstand the agonies of eternity. She knows that every time she defies him she's closer to becoming what he wants, every time she plans around him that she is doing his bidding, and yet she can't help but resist him in her own search for control and freedom.

It is an ugly circle of mental abuse, and Ivy is willing to risk death and her sanity to save the only person she believes can give her the strength to outwit and outlive the man she both loves and hates. Undead vampires don't love, but they *remember* love with a fierce loyalty, and love is the only thing that might save her.

In *Blood Crime*, the tortured relationship between Ivy and her master vampire reaches a fever pitch. Caught between them as a point of contention, Rachel is ill-equipped to survive, much less understand, the passions that pull Ivy both to Piscary and to herself. The strength and sense of strong will that Ivy sees in Rachel are the same qualities that Piscary sees in Ivy, and even as Ivy fights to be free of Piscary, she finds herself beginning to prey upon Rachel in the same way, wanting what Rachel can give her—not just blood, but the will to survive.

Rachel, of course, is oblivious, making Ivy's long hunt for the powerful witch all the sweeter, more heartbreaking, as in her realization that only Rachel can set her free, she knows that one wrong move, one slide into temptation, and she will become exactly what Piscary wants.

Kim Harrison
December 2012

CHAPTER I

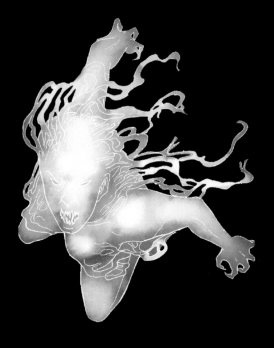

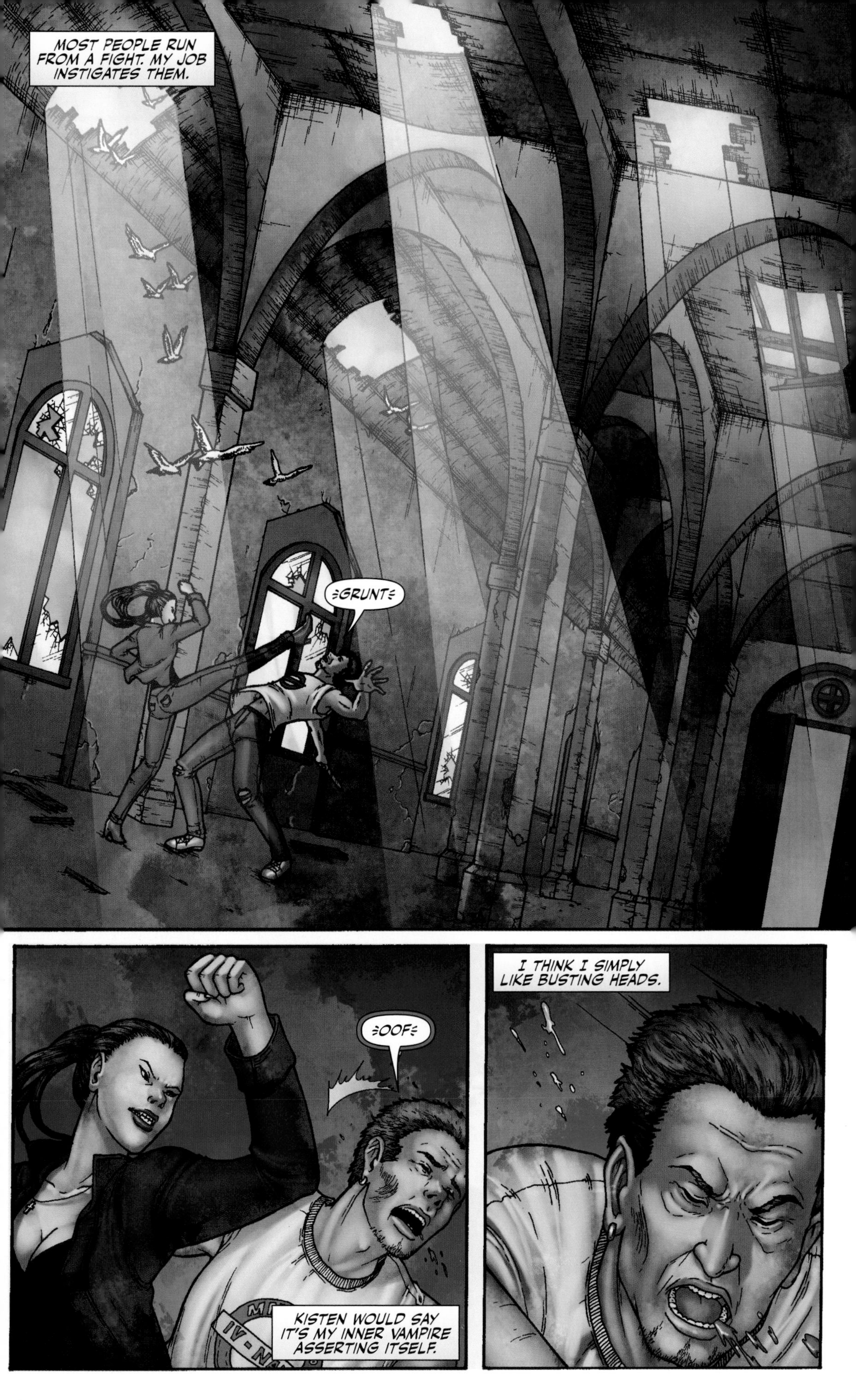
MOST PEOPLE RUN FROM A FIGHT. MY JOB INSTIGATES THEM.
GRUNT
OOF
KISTEN WOULD SAY IT'S MY INNER VAMPIRE ASSERTING ITSELF.
I THINK I SIMPLY LIKE BUSTING HEADS.

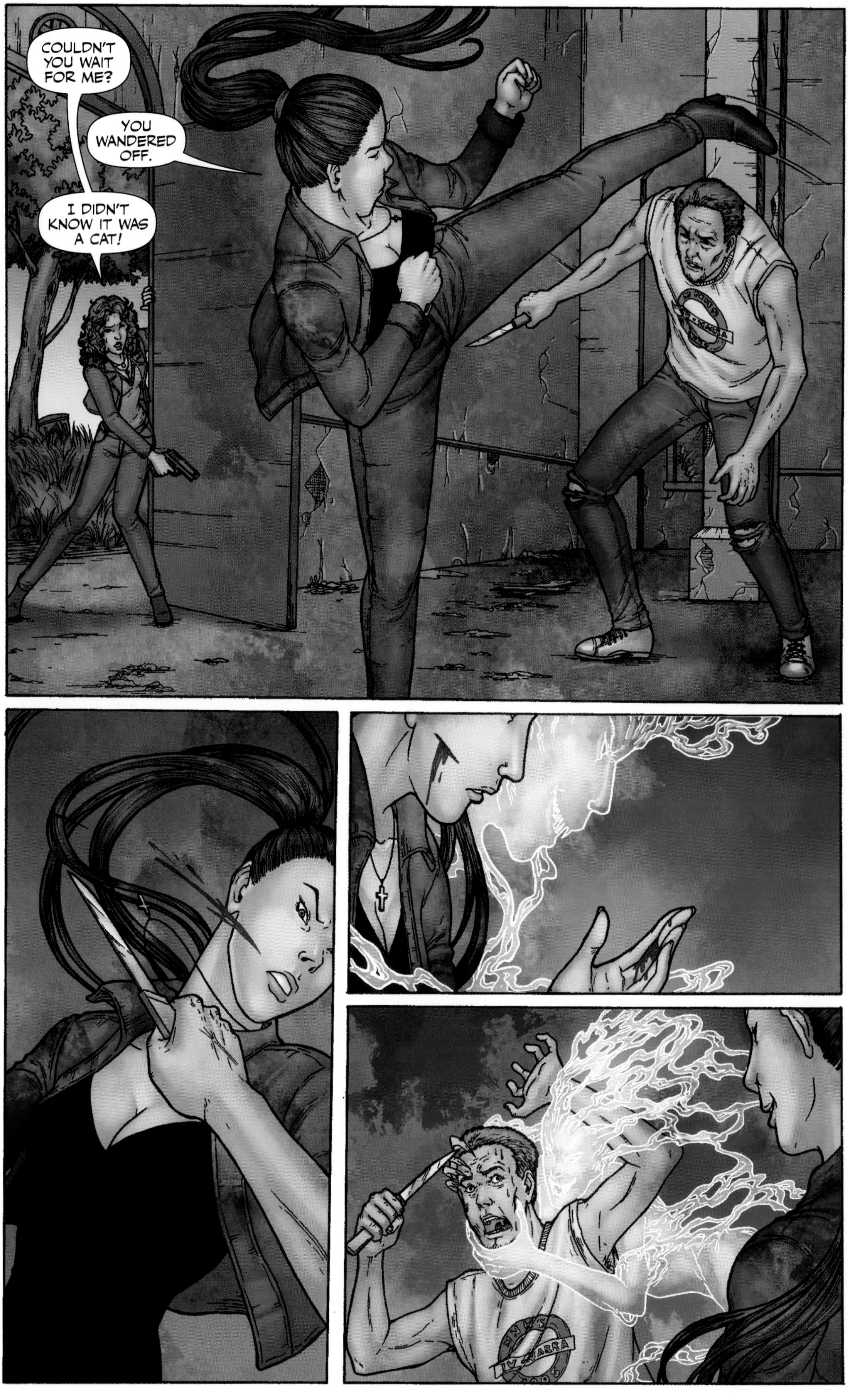
COULDN'T YOU WAIT FOR ME?
YOU WANDERED OFF.
I DIDN'T KNOW IT WAS A CAT!

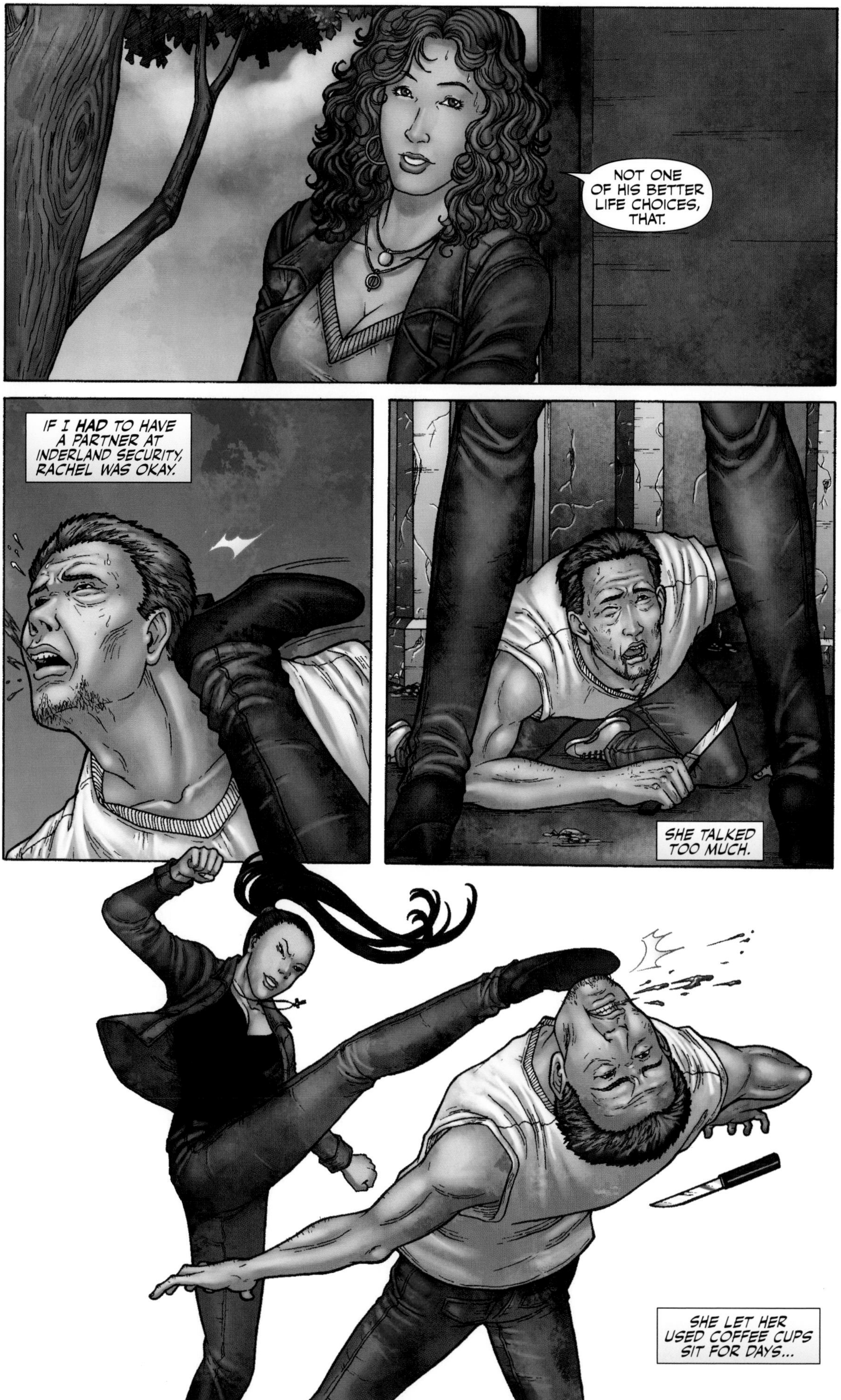
NOT ONE OF HIS BETTER LIFE CHOICES, THAT.
IF I HAD TO HAVE A PARTNER AT INDERLAND SECURITY, RACHEL WAS OKAY.
SHE TALKED TOO MUCH.
SHE LET HER USED COFFEE CUPS SIT FOR DAYS...

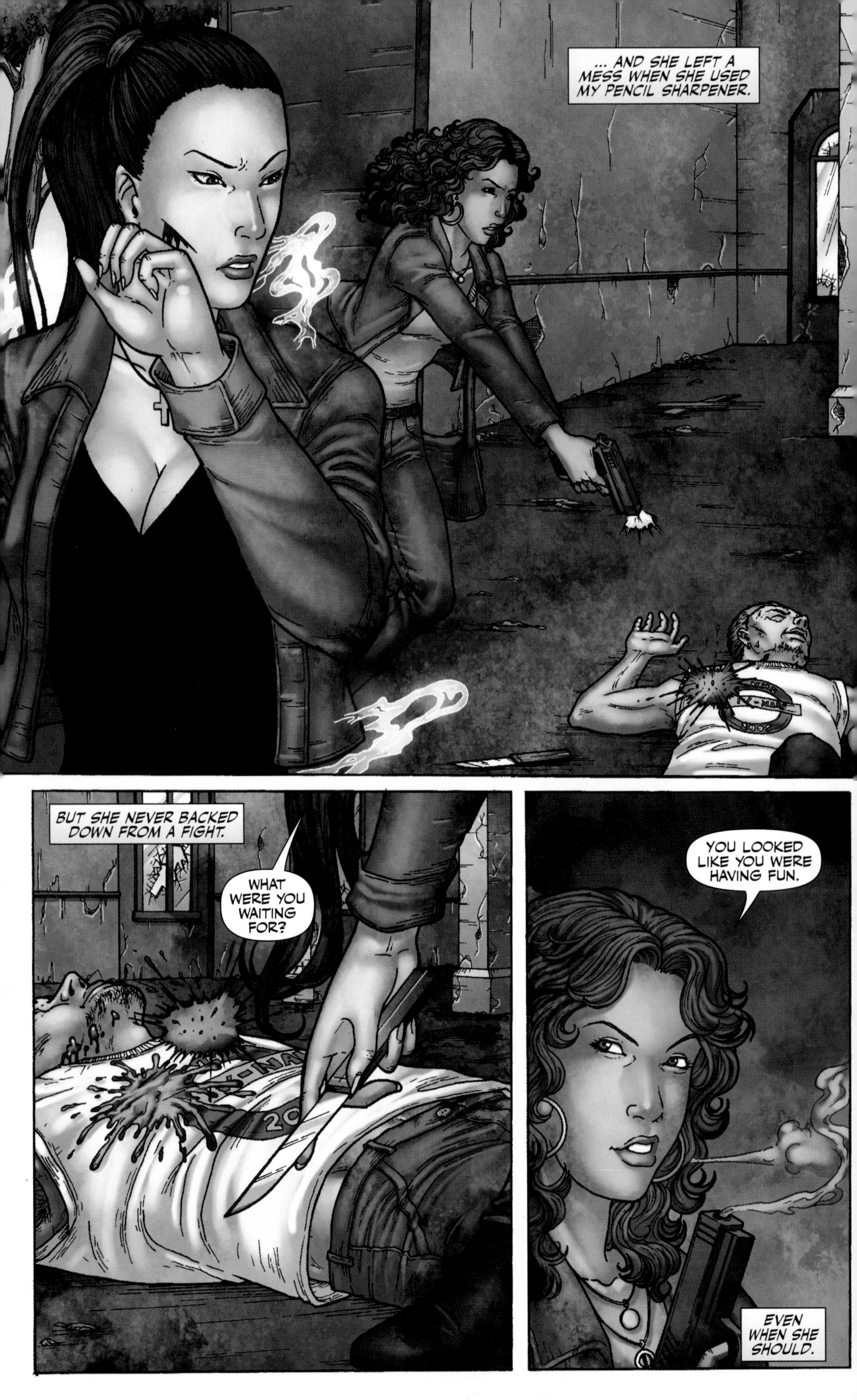
... AND SHE LEFT A MESS WHEN SHE USED MY PENCIL SHARPENER.
BUT SHE NEVER BACKED DOWN FROM A FIGHT.
WHAT WERE YOU WAITING FOR?
YOU LOOKED LIKE YOU WERE HAVING FUN.
EVEN WHEN SHE SHOULD.

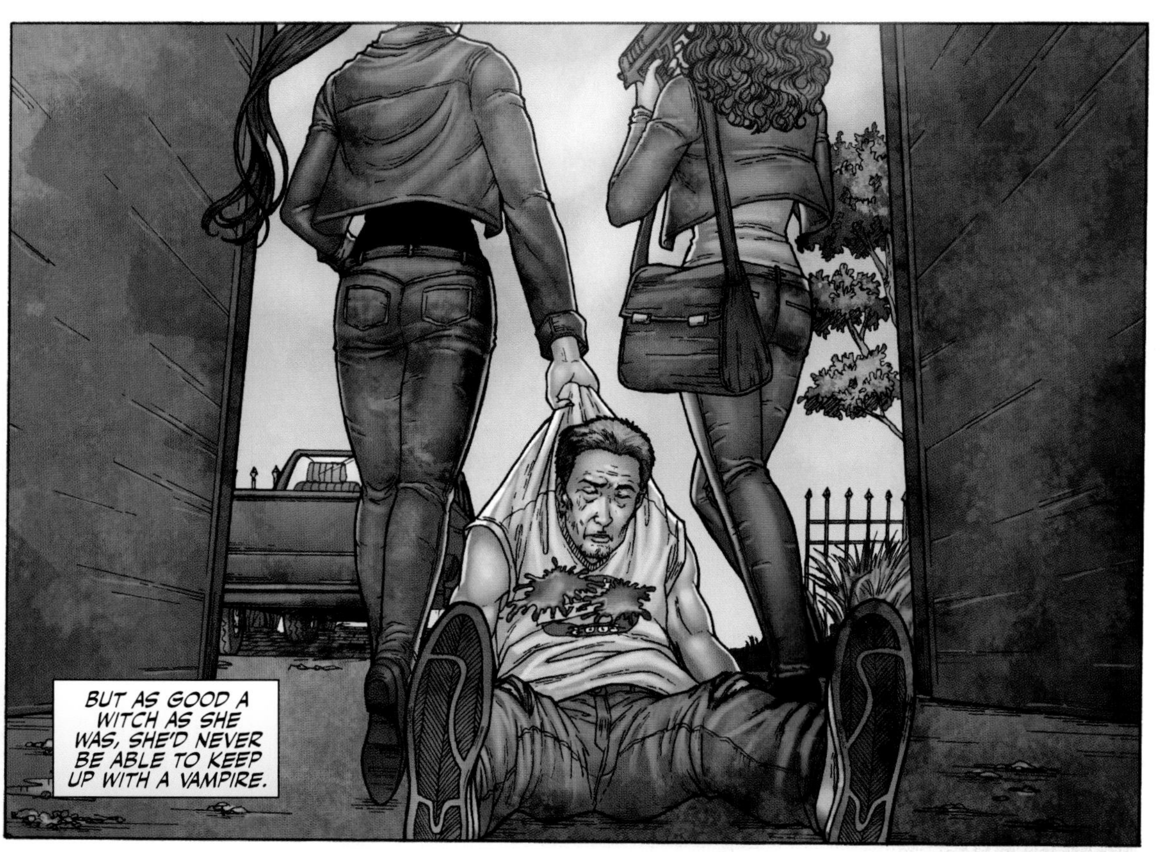
BUT AS GOOD A WITCH AS SHE WAS, SHE'D NEVER BE ABLE TO KEEP UP WITH A VAMPIRE.

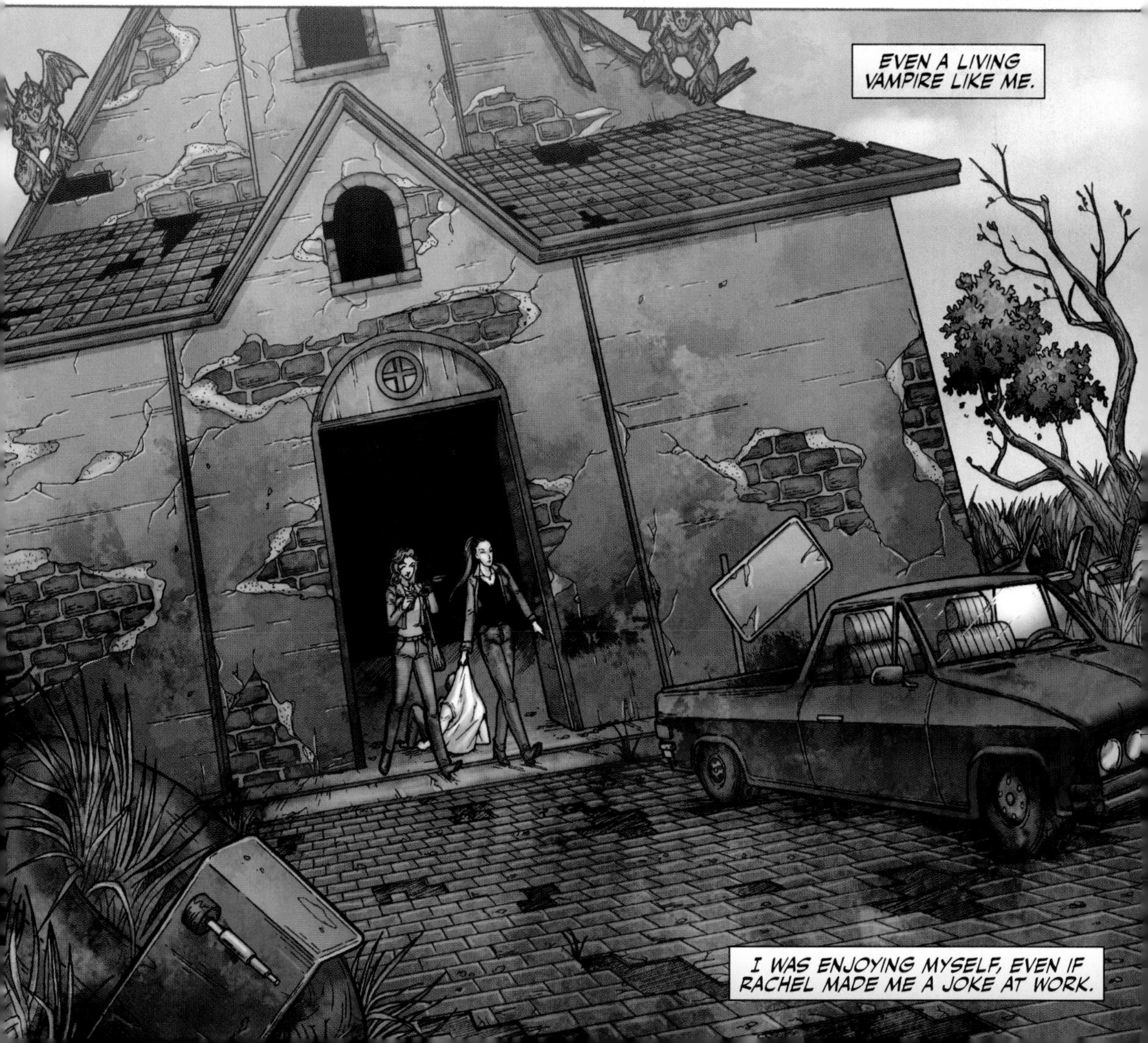
EVEN A LIVING VAMPIRE LIKE ME.
I WAS ENJOYING MYSELF, EVEN IF RACHEL MADE ME A JOKE AT WORK.

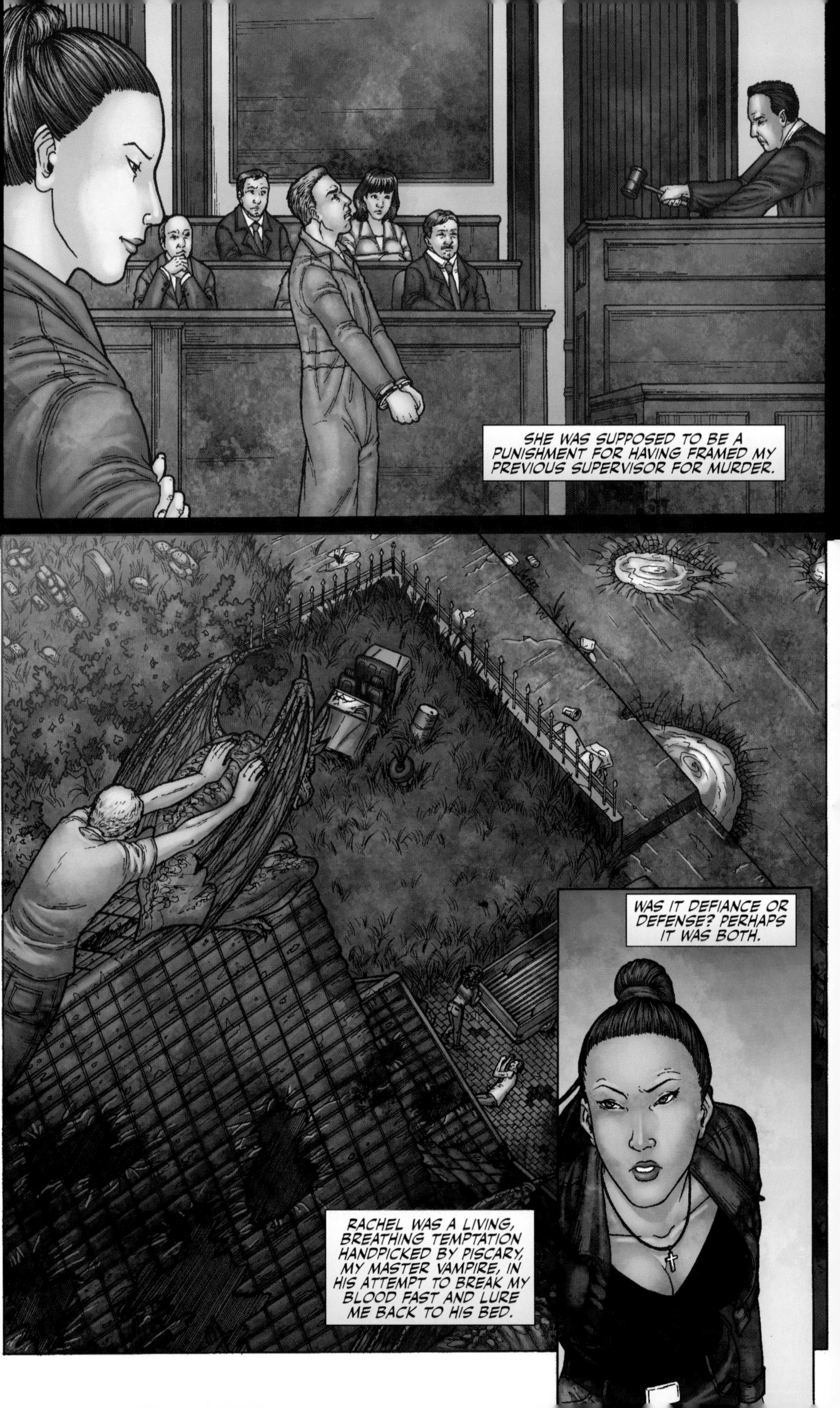
SHE WAS SUPPOSED TO BE A PUNISHMENT FOR HAVING FRAMED MY PREVIOUS SUPERVISOR FOR MURDER.
WAS IT DEFIANCE OR DEFENSE? PERHAPS IT WAS BOTH.
RACHEL WAS A LIVING, BREATHING TEMPTATION HANDPICKED BY PISCARY, MY MASTER VAMPIRE, IN HIS ATTEMPT TO BREAK MY BLOOD FAST AND LURE ME BACK TO HIS BED.

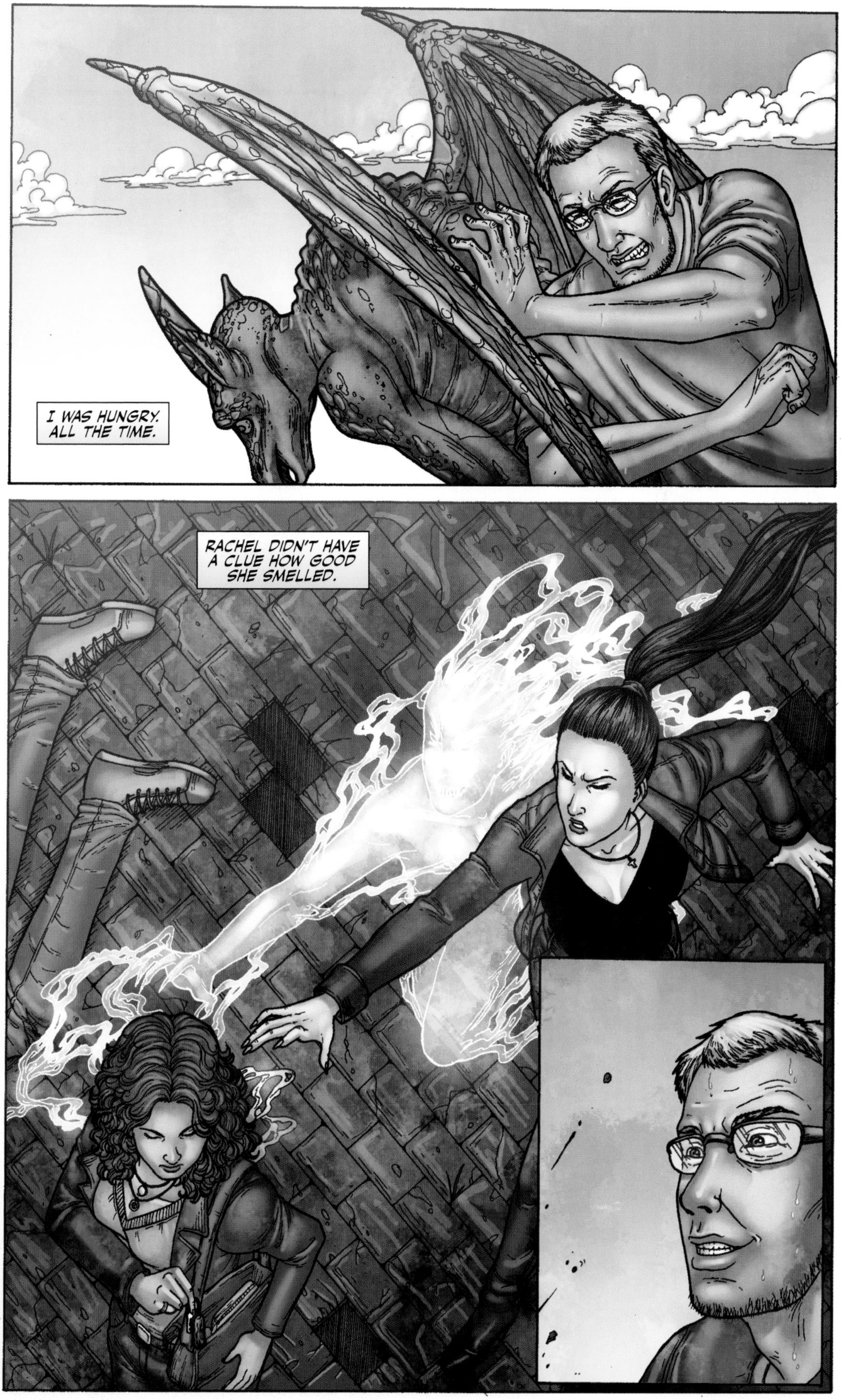
I WAS HUNGRY. ALL THE TIME.
RACHEL DIDN'T HAVE A CLUE HOW GOOD SHE SMELLED.

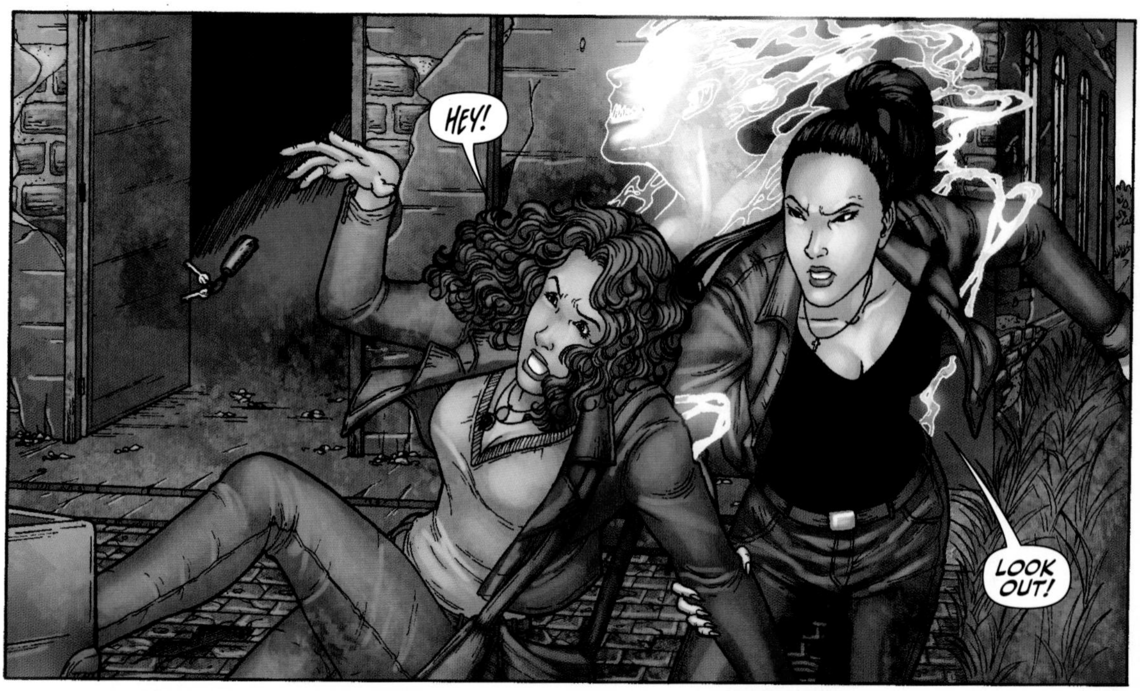
HEY!
LOOK OUT!

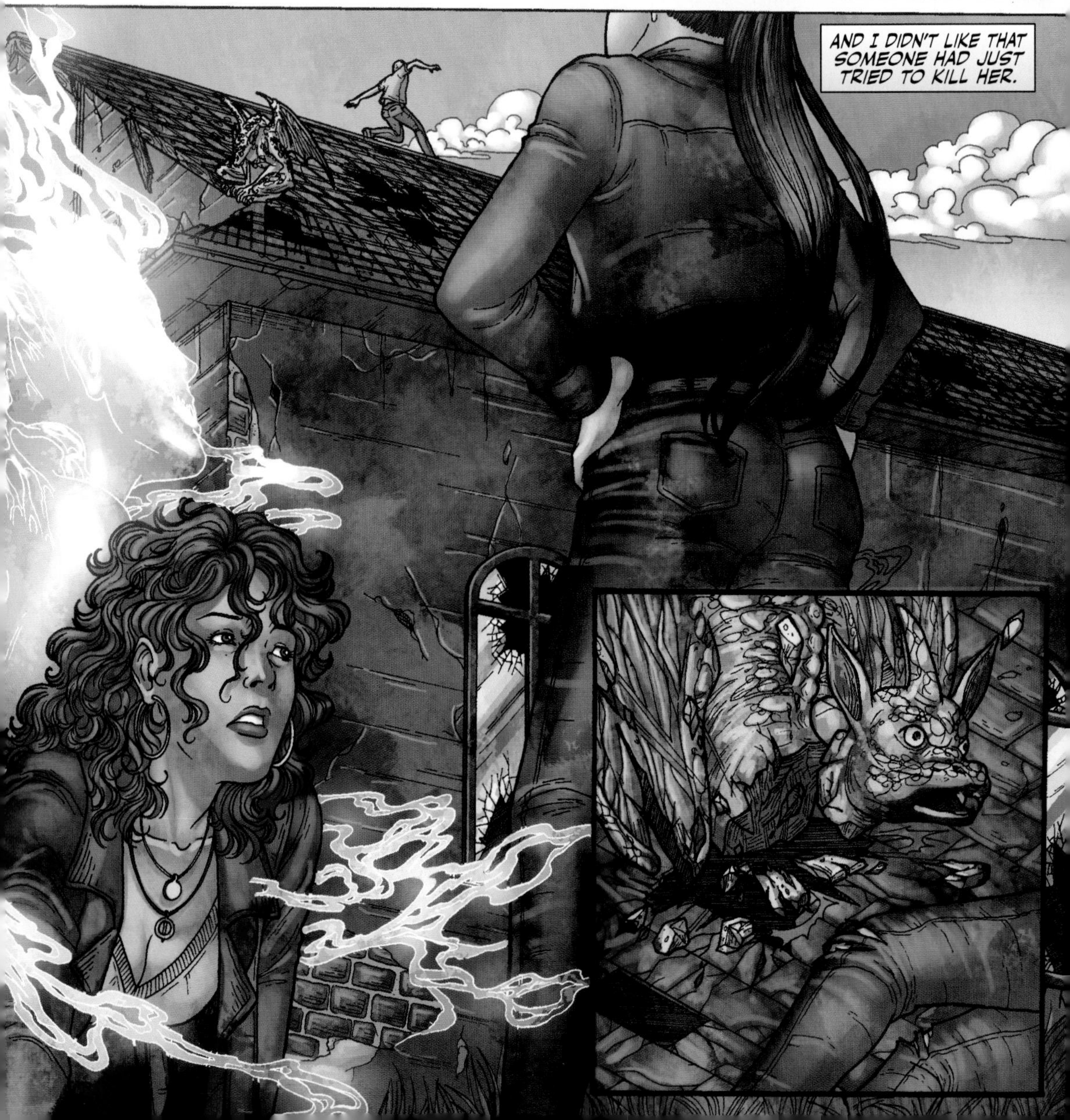
AND I DIDN'T LIKE THAT SOMEONE HAD JUST TRIED TO KILL HER.

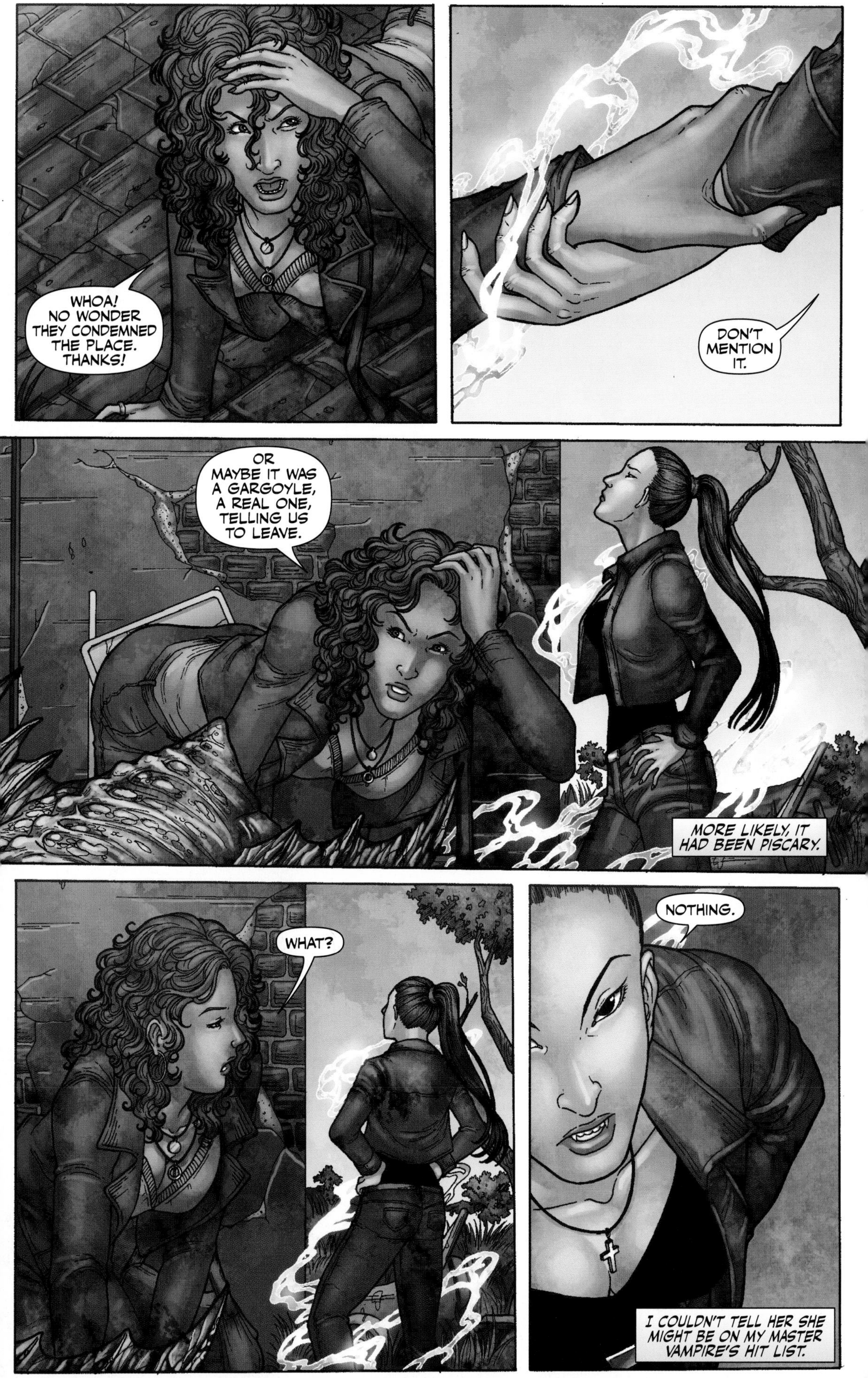
WHOA! NO WONDER THEY CONDEMNED THE PLACE. THANKS!
DON'T MENTION IT.
OR MAYBE IT WAS A GARGOYLE, A REAL ONE, TELLING US TO LEAVE.
MORE LIKELY, IT HAD BEEN PISCARY.
WHAT?
NOTHING.
I COULDN'T TELL HER SHE MIGHT BE ON MY MASTER VAMPIRE'S HIT LIST.

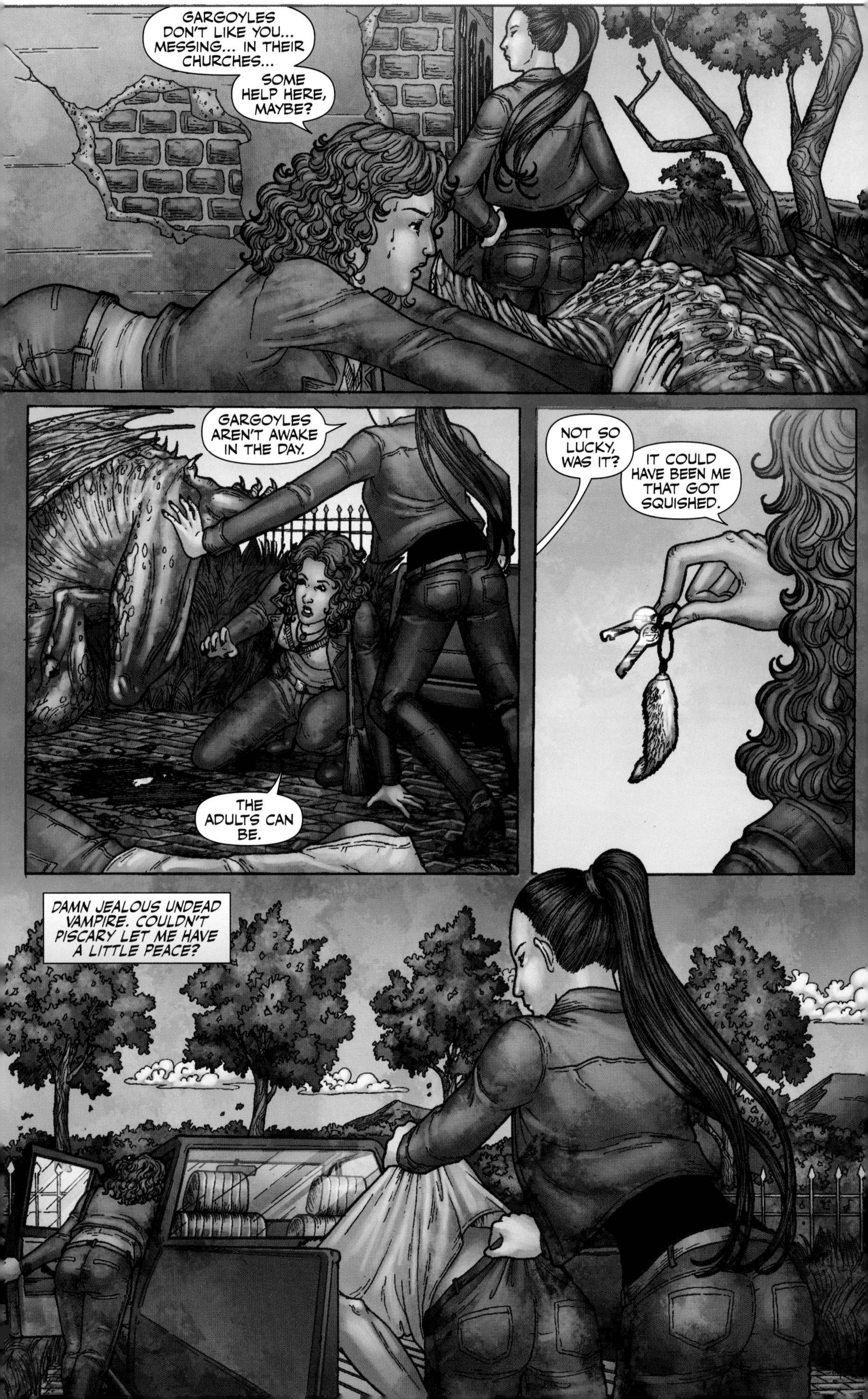
GARGOYLES DON'T LIKE YOU... MESSING... IN THEIR CHURCHES...
SOME HELP HERE, MAYBE?
GARGOYLES AREN'T AWAKE IN THE DAY.
THE ADULTS CAN BE.
NOT SO LUCKY, WAS IT?
IT COULD HAVE BEEN ME THAT GOT SQUISHED.
DAMN JEALOUS UNDEAD VAMPIRE. COULDN'T PISCARY LET ME HAVE A LITTLE PEACE?

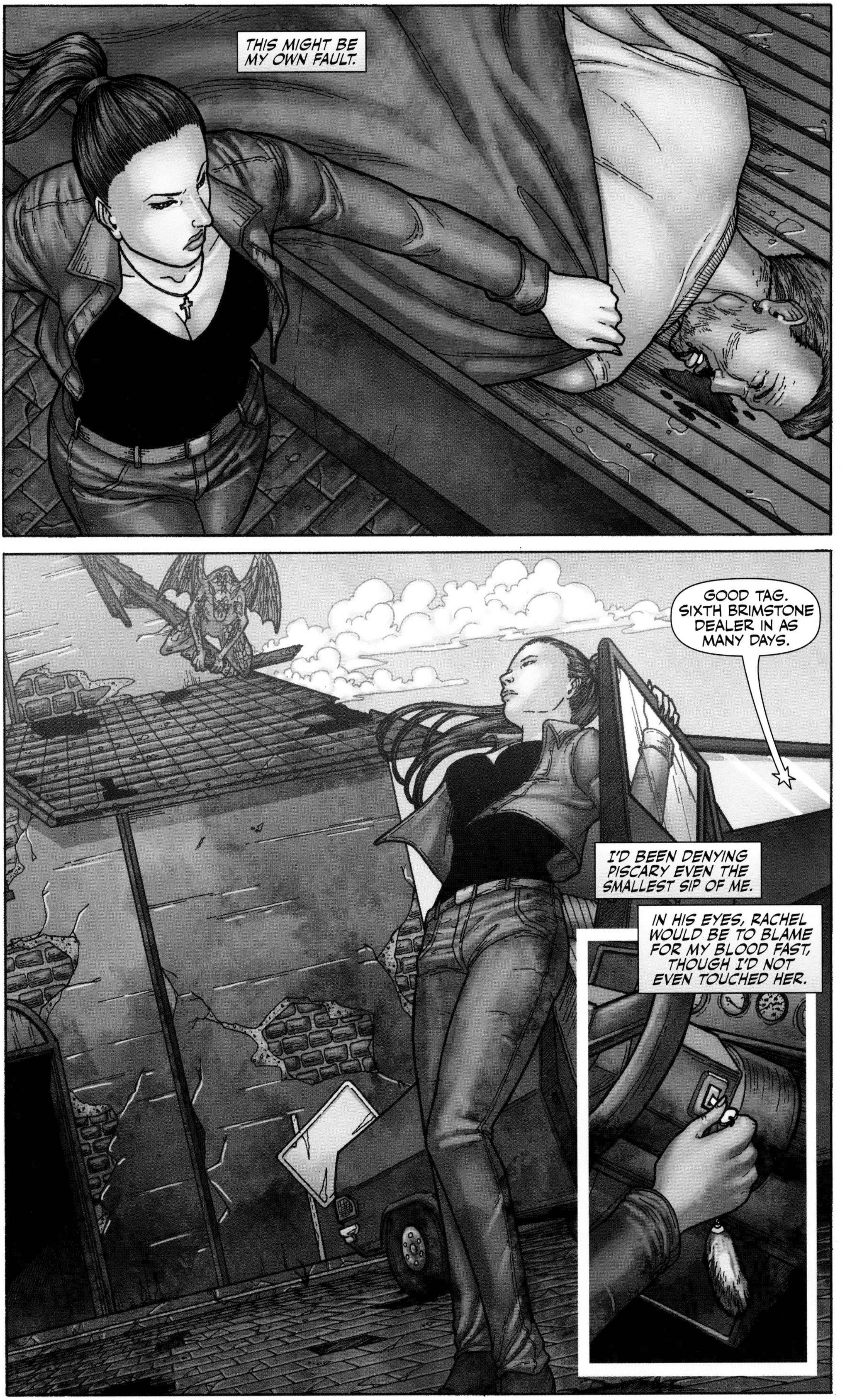
THIS MIGHT BE MY OWN FAULT.
GOOD TAG. SIXTH BRIMSTONE DEALER IN AS MANY DAYS.
I'D BEEN DENYING PISCARY EVEN THE SMALLEST SIP OF ME.
IN HIS EYES, RACHEL WOULD BE TO BLAME FOR MY BLOOD FAST, THOUGH I'D NOT EVEN TOUCHED HER.

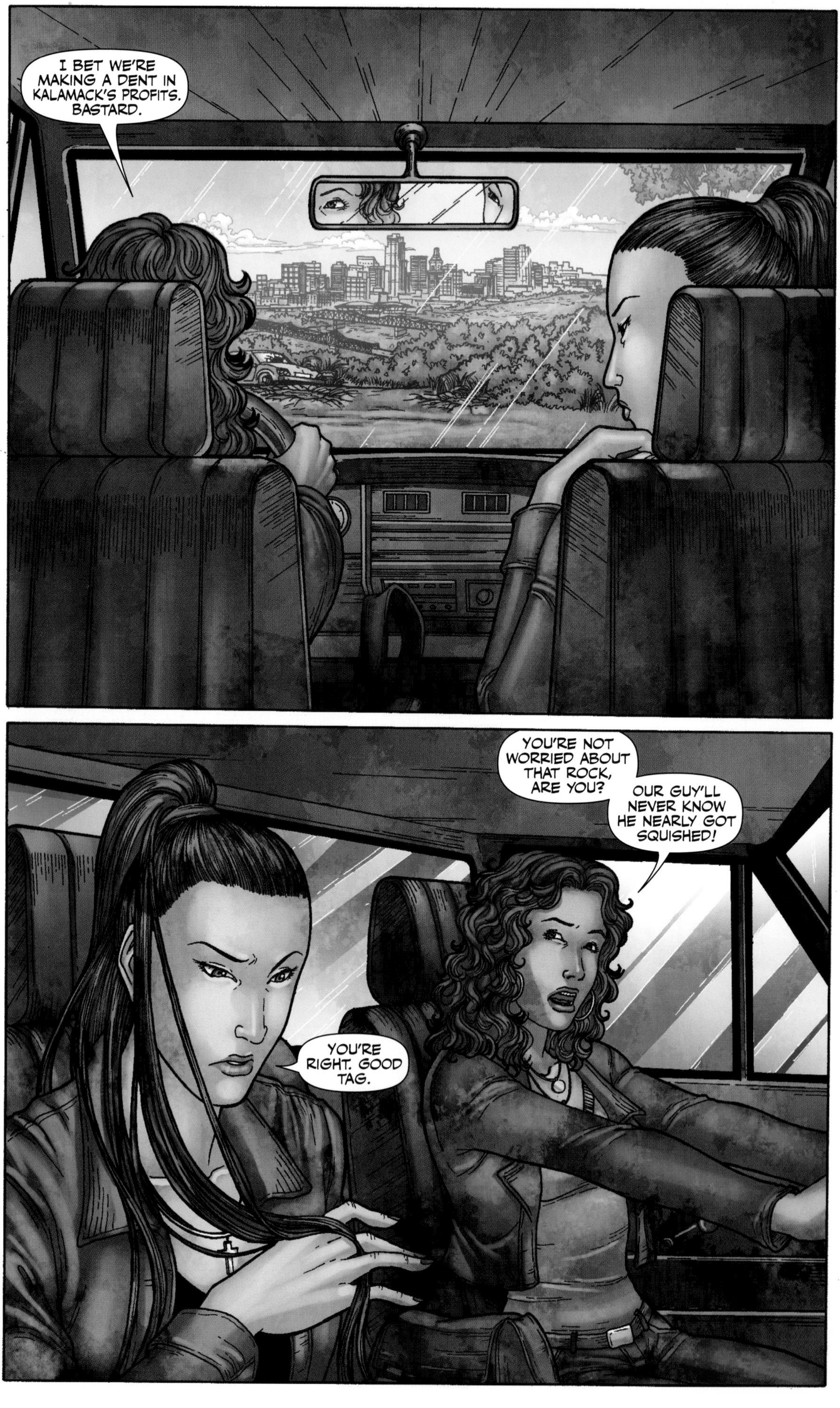
I BET WE'RE MAKING A DENT IN KALAMACK'S PROFITS. BASTARD.
YOU'RE NOT WORRIED ABOUT THAT ROCK, ARE YOU?
OUR GUY'LL NEVER KNOW HE NEARLY GOT SQUISHED!
YOU'RE RIGHT. GOOD TAG.

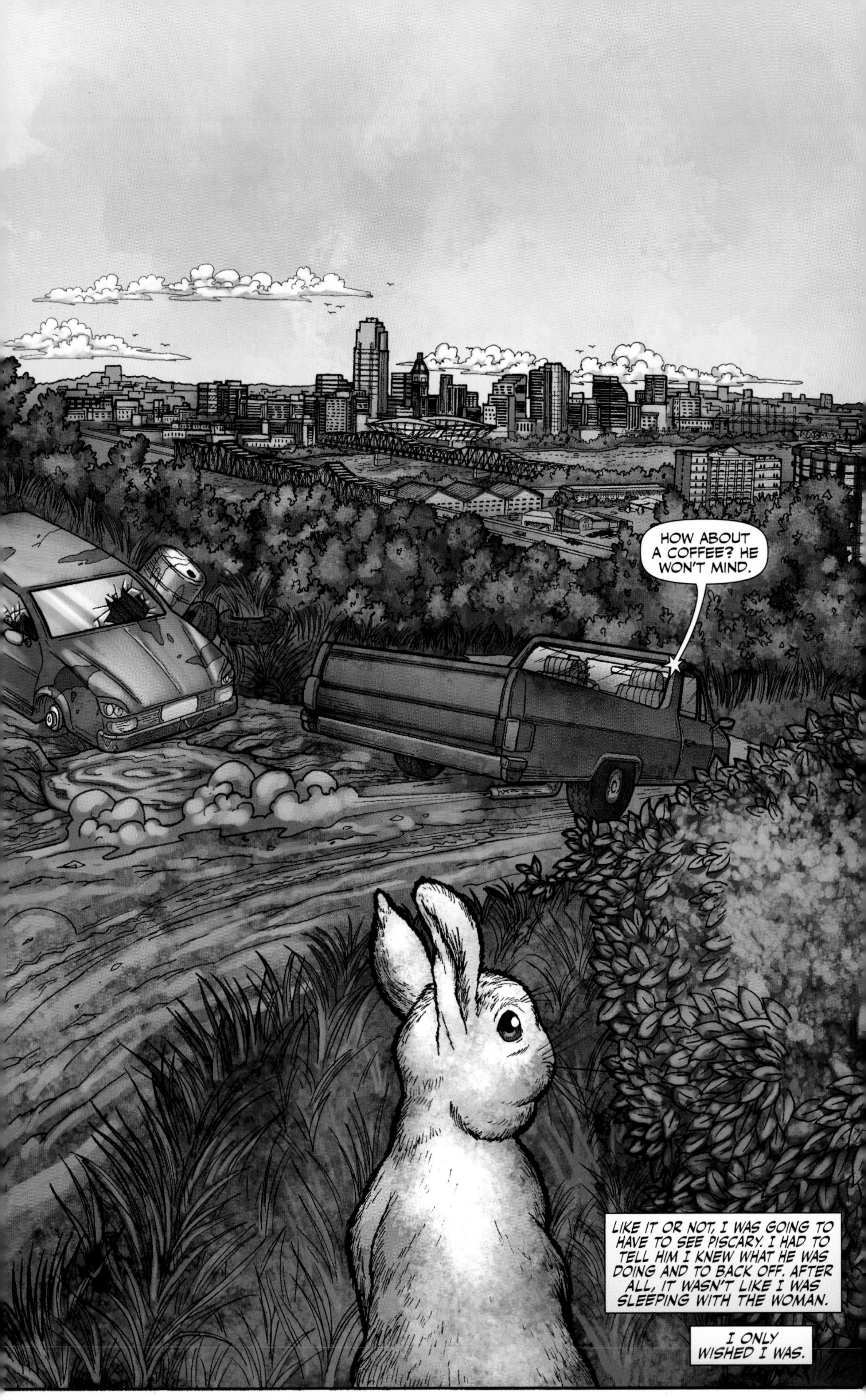
HOW ABOUT A COFFEE? HE WON'T MIND.
LIKE IT OR NOT, I WAS GOING TO HAVE TO SEE PISCARY. I HAD TO TELL HIM I KNEW WHAT HE WAS DOING AND TO BACK OFF. AFTER ALL, IT WASN'T LIKE I WAS SLEEPING WITH THE WOMAN.
I ONLY WISHED I WAS.

CHAPTER 2

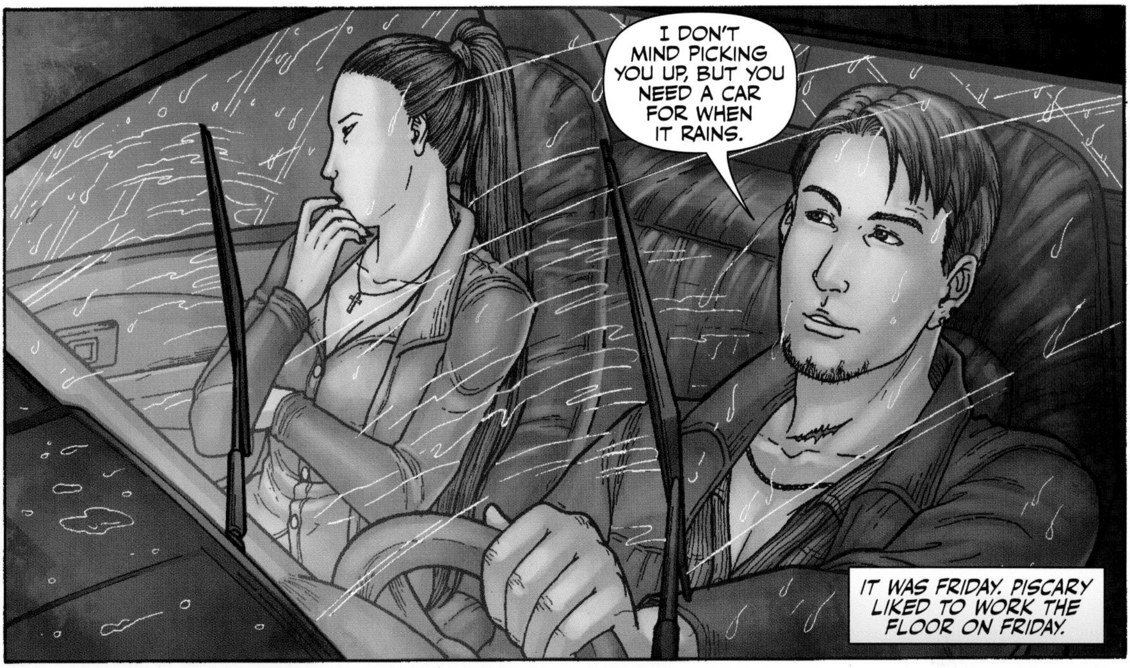
I DON'T MIND PICKING YOU UP, BUT YOU NEED A CAR FOR WHEN IT RAINS.
IT WAS FRIDAY. PISCARY LIKED TO WORK THE FLOOR ON FRIDAY.

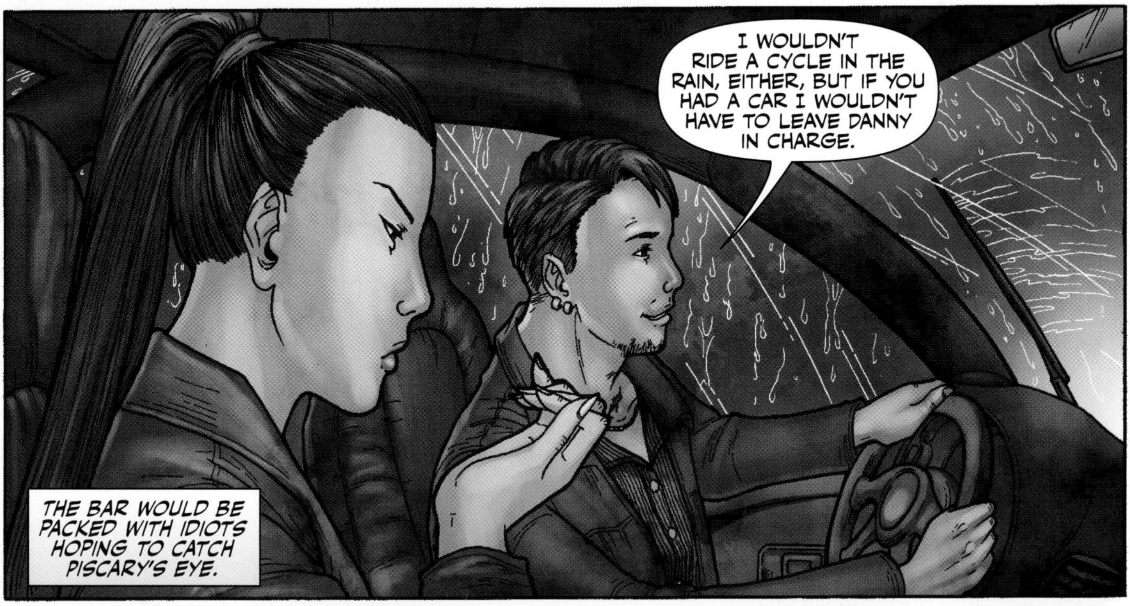
I WOULDN'T RIDE A CYCLE IN THE RAIN, EITHER, BUT IF YOU HAD A CAR I WOULDN'T HAVE TO LEAVE DANNY IN CHARGE.
THE BAR WOULD BE PACKED WITH IDIOTS HOPING TO CATCH PISCARY'S EYE.

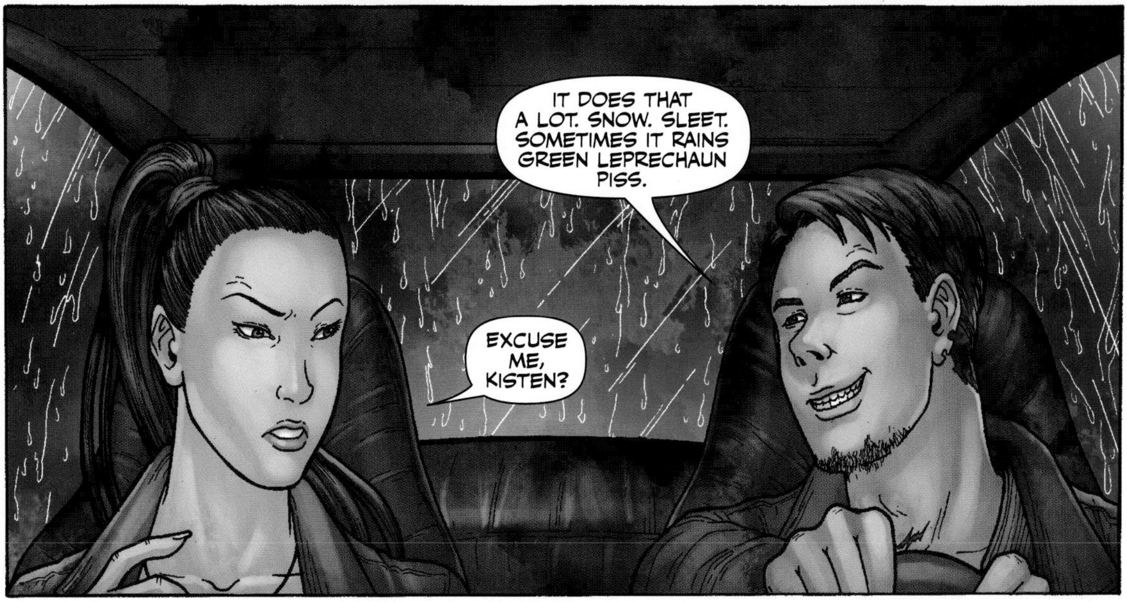
IT DOES THAT A LOT. SNOW. SLEET. SOMETIMES IT RAINS GREEN LEPRECHAUN PISS.
EXCUSE ME, KISTEN?

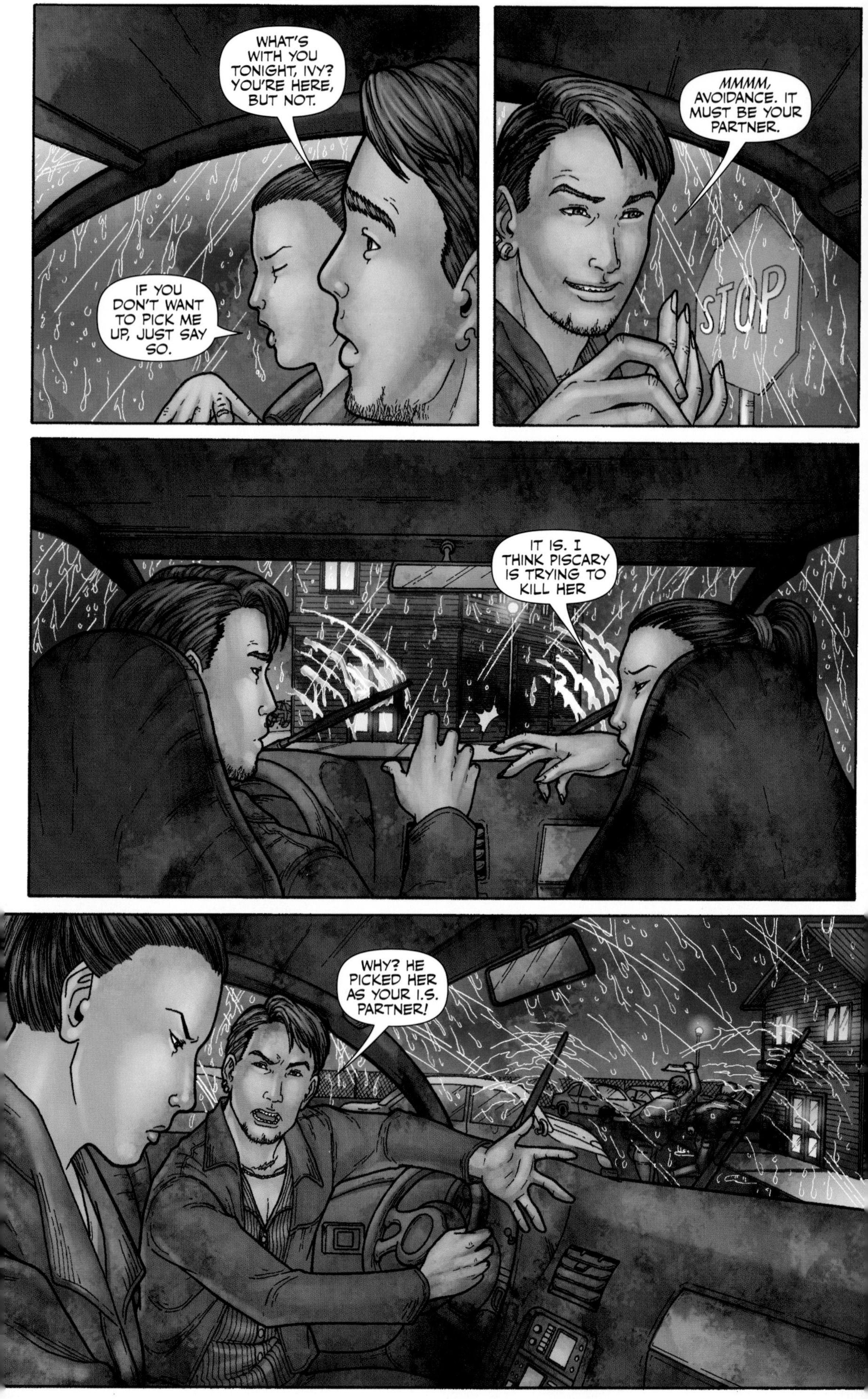
WHAT'S WITH YOU TONIGHT, IVY? YOU'RE HERE, BUT NOT.
IF YOU DON'T WANT TO PICK ME UP, JUST SAY SO.
MMMM, AVOIDANCE. IT MUST BE YOUR PARTNER.
STOP
IT IS. I THINK PISCARY IS TRYING TO KILL HER
WHY? HE PICKED HER AS YOUR I.S. PARTNER!

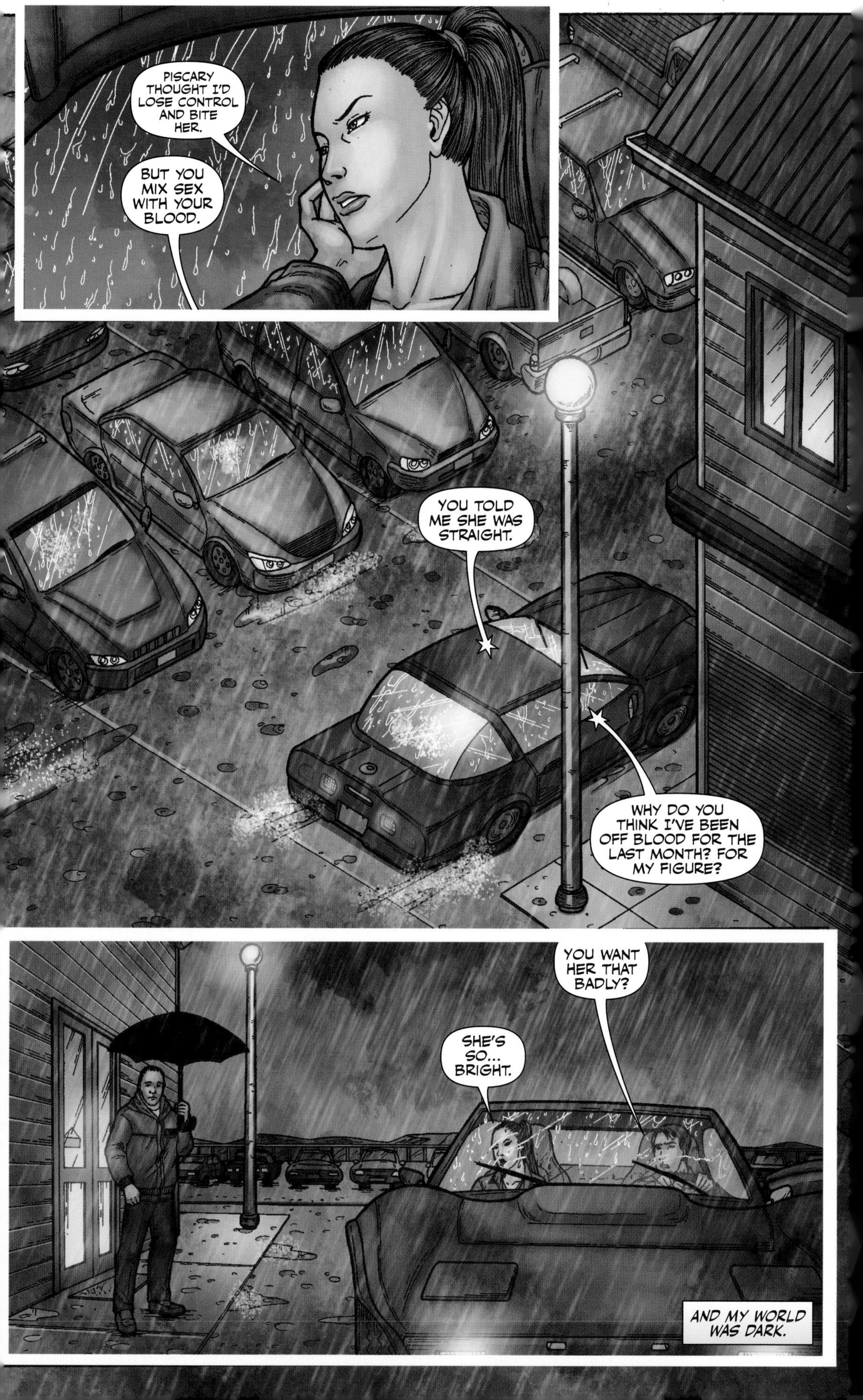
PISCARY THOUGHT I'D LOSE CONTROL AND BITE HER.
BUT YOU MIX SEX WITH YOUR BLOOD.
YOU TOLD ME SHE WAS STRAIGHT.
WHY DO YOU THINK I'VE BEEN OFF BLOOD FOR THE LAST MONTH? FOR MY FIGURE?
YOU WANT HER THAT BADLY?
SHE'S SO... BRIGHT.
AND MY WORLD WAS DARK.

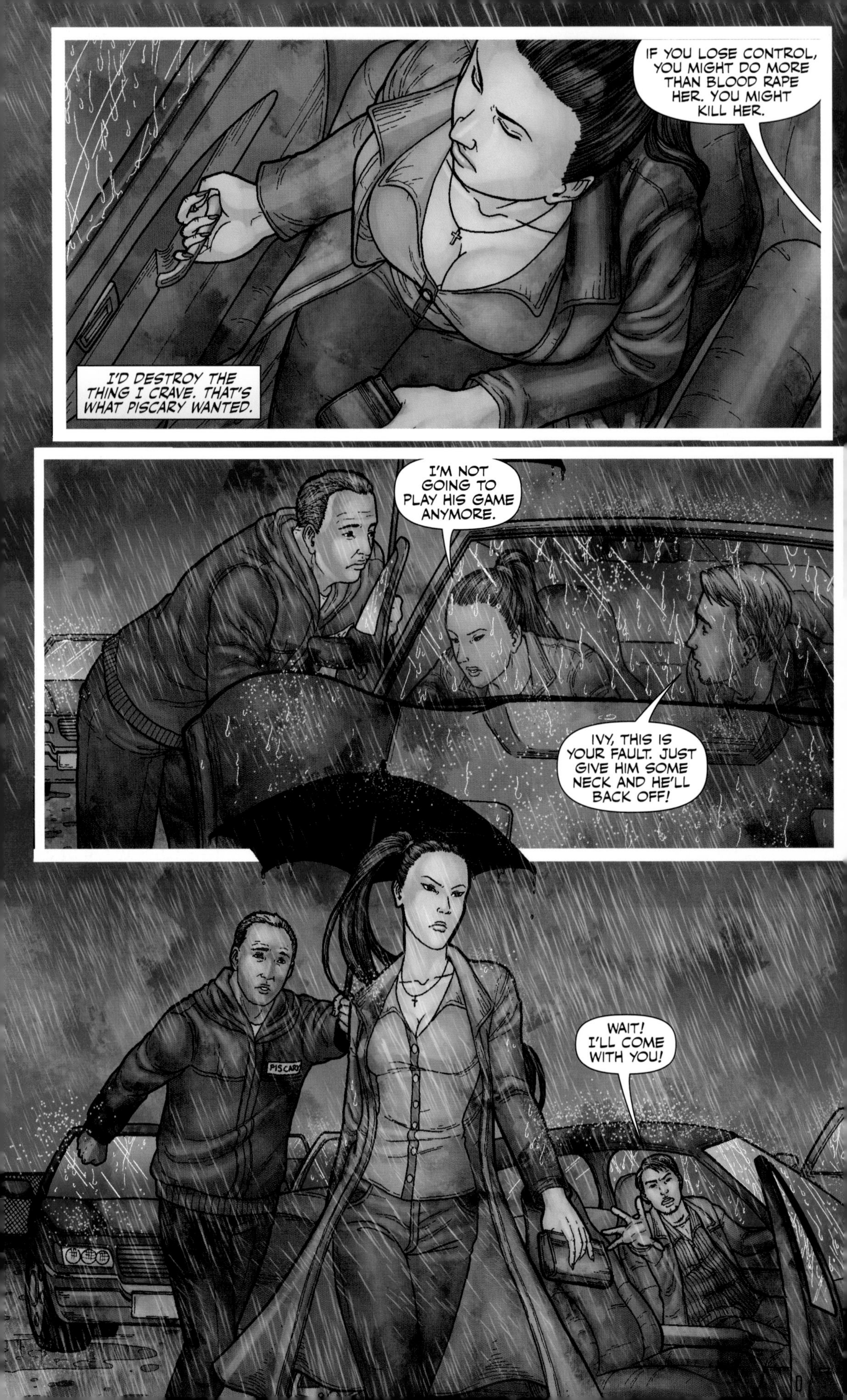
IF YOU LOSE CONTROL, YOU MIGHT DO MORE THAN BLOOD RAPE HER. YOU MIGHT KILL HER.
I'D DESTROY THE THING I CRAVE. THAT'S WHAT PISCARY WANTED.
I'M NOT GOING TO PLAY HIS GAME ANYMORE.
IVY, THIS IS YOUR FAULT. JUST GIVE HIM SOME NECK AND HE'LL BACK OFF!
PISCARY
WAIT! I'LL COME WITH YOU!

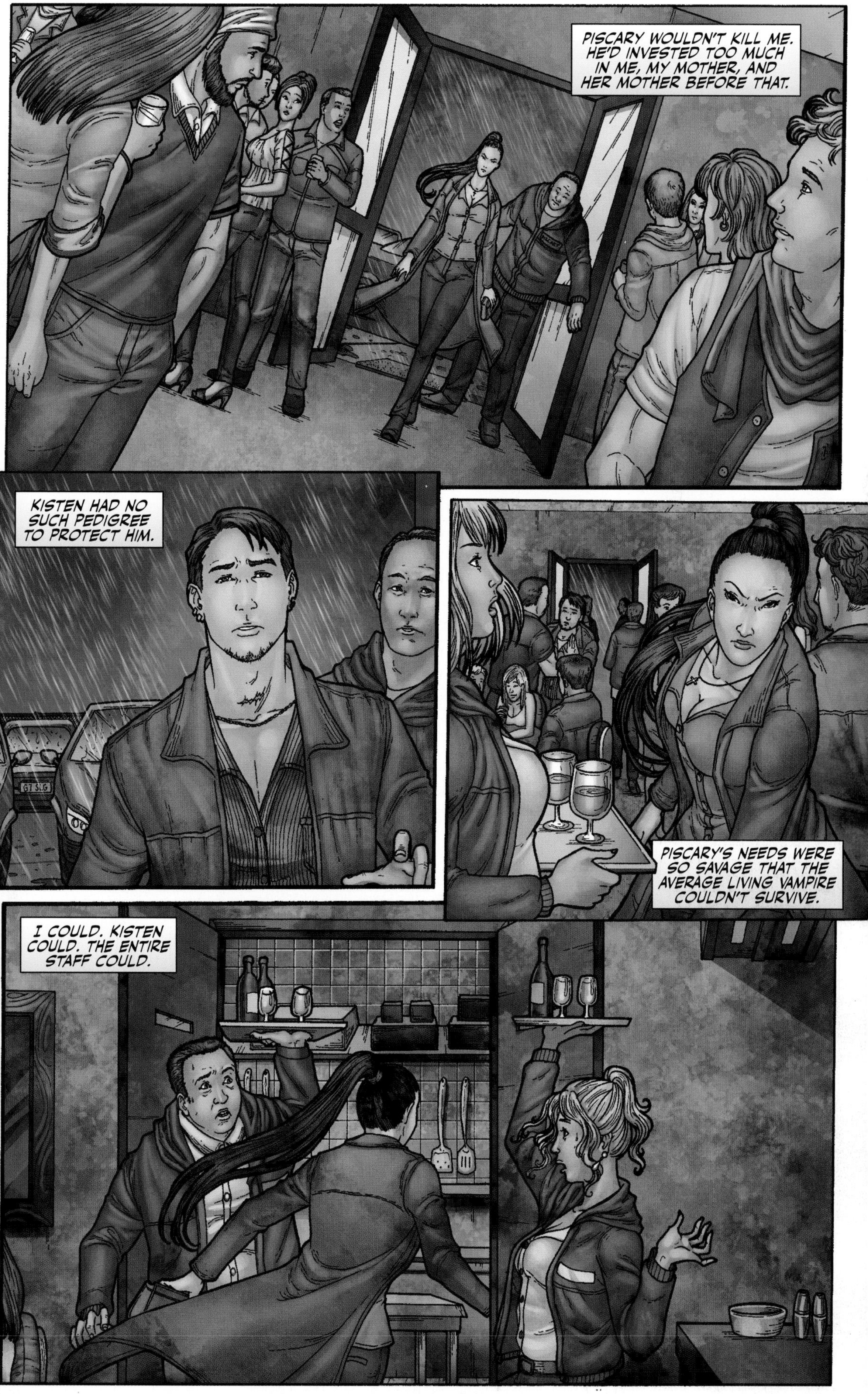
PISCARY WOULDN'T KILL ME. HE'D INVESTED TOO MUCH IN ME, MY MOTHER, AND HER MOTHER BEFORE THAT.
KISTEN HAD NO SUCH PEDIGREE TO PROTECT HIM.
PISCARY'S NEEDS WERE SO SAVAGE THAT THE AVERAGE LIVING VAMPIRE COULDN'T SURVIVE.
I COULD. KISTEN COULD. THE ENTIRE STAFF COULD.

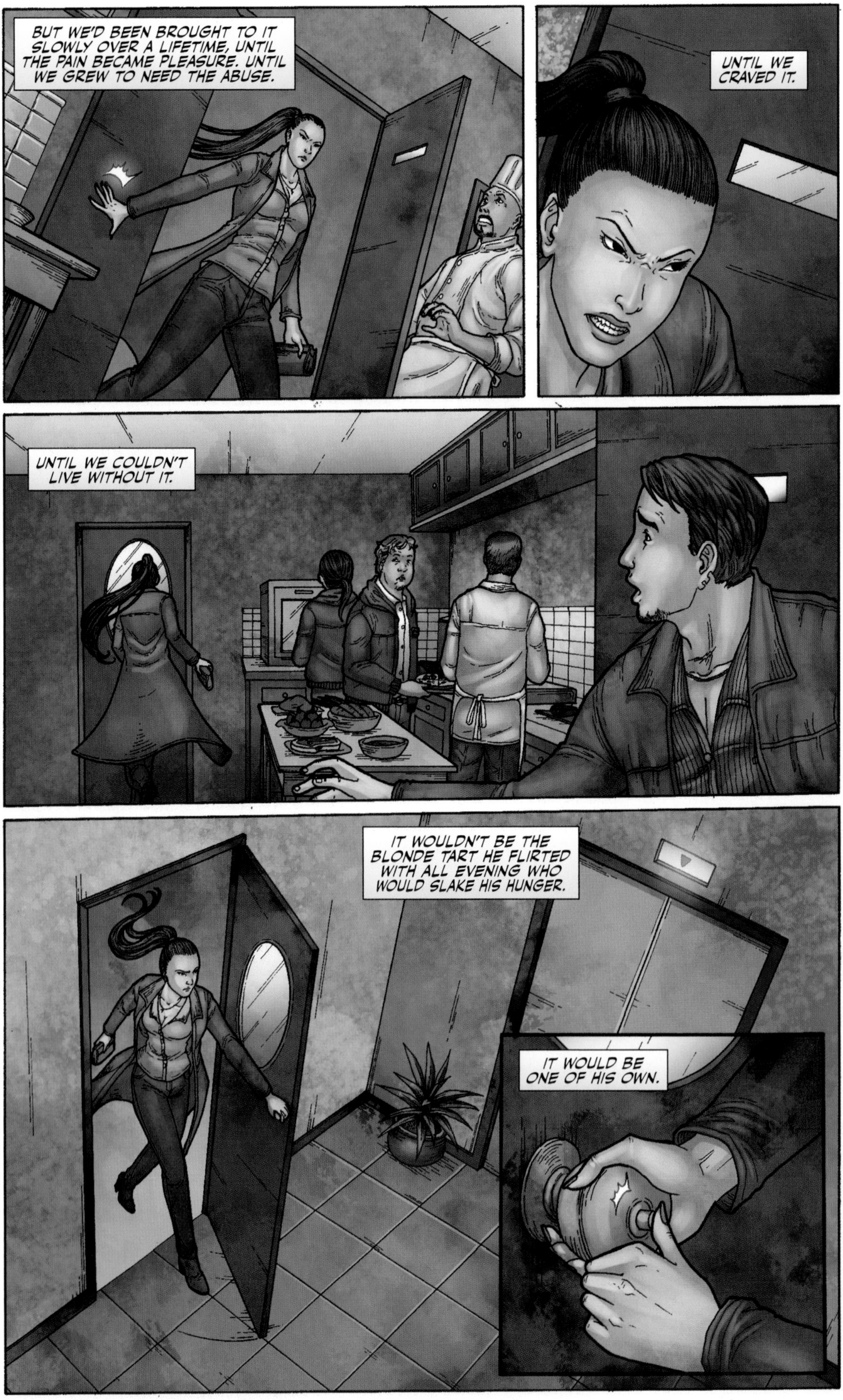
BUT WE'D BEEN BROUGHT TO IT SLOWLY OVER A LIFETIME, UNTIL THE PAIN BECAME PLEASURE. UNTIL WE GREW TO NEED THE ABUSE.
UNTIL WE CRAVED IT.
UNTIL WE COULDN'T LIVE WITHOUT IT.
IT WOULDN'T BE THE BLONDE TART HE FLIRTED WITH ALL EVENING WHO WOULD SLAKE HIS HUNGER.
IT WOULD BE ONE OF HIS OWN.

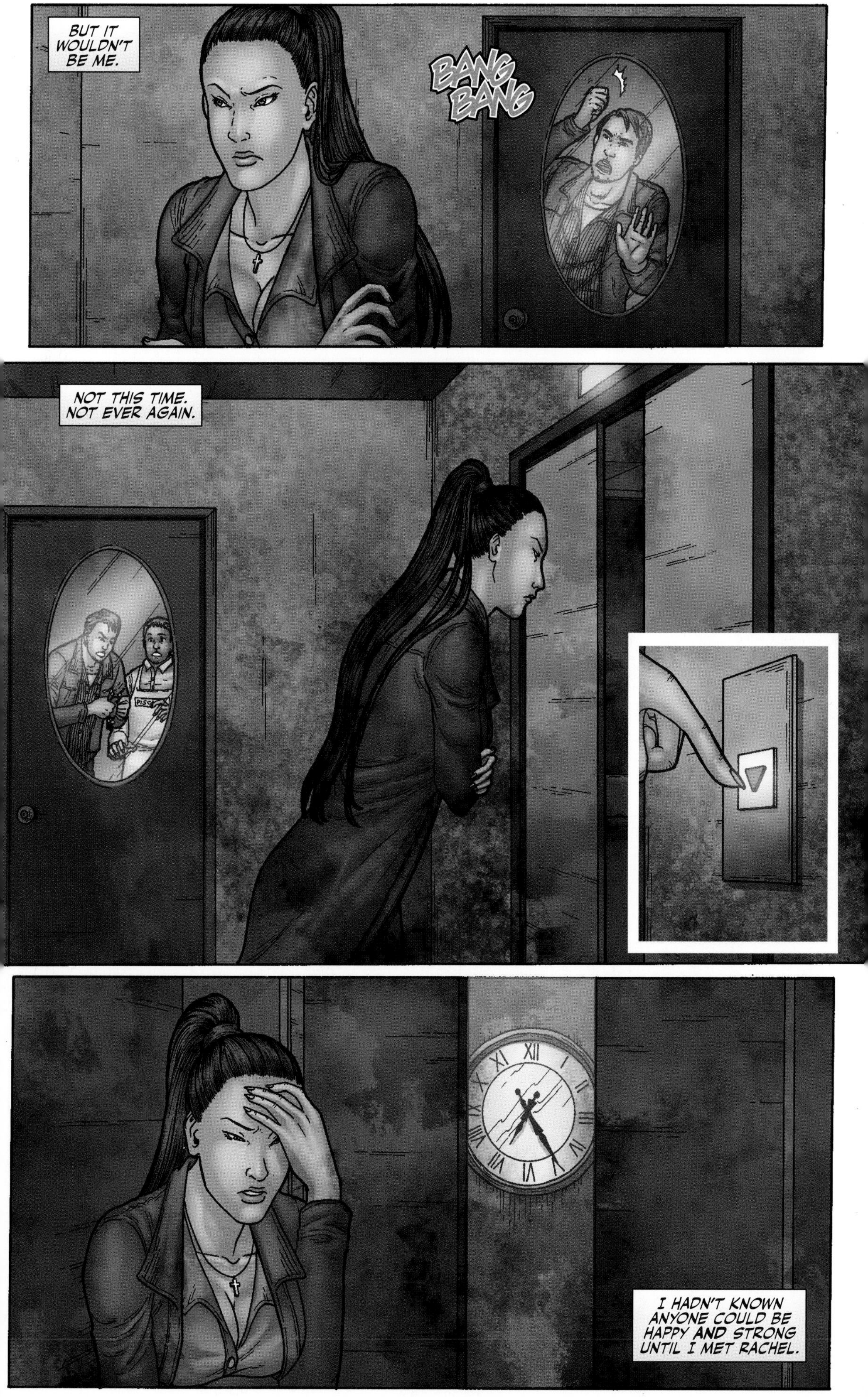

BUT IT WOULDN'T BE ME.
BANG BANG
NOT THIS TIME. NOT EVER AGAIN.
I HADN'T KNOWN ANYONE COULD BE HAPPY AND STRONG UNTIL I MET RACHEL.

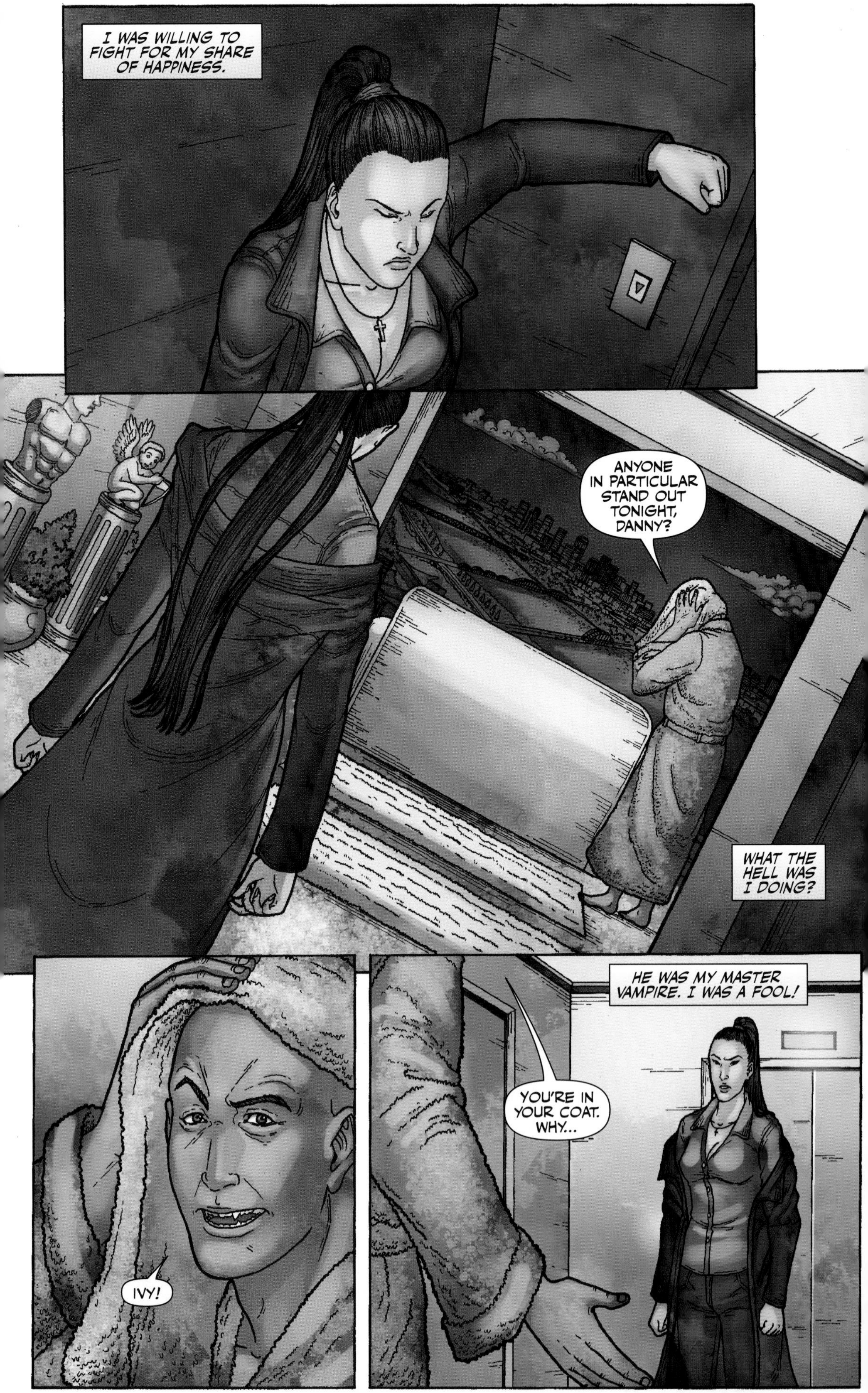
I WAS WILLING TO FIGHT FOR MY SHARE OF HAPPINESS.
ANYONE IN PARTICULAR STAND OUT TONIGHT, DANNY?
WHAT THE HELL WAS I DOING?
IVY!
HE WAS MY MASTER VAMPIRE. I WAS A FOOL!
YOU'RE IN YOUR COAT. WHY...

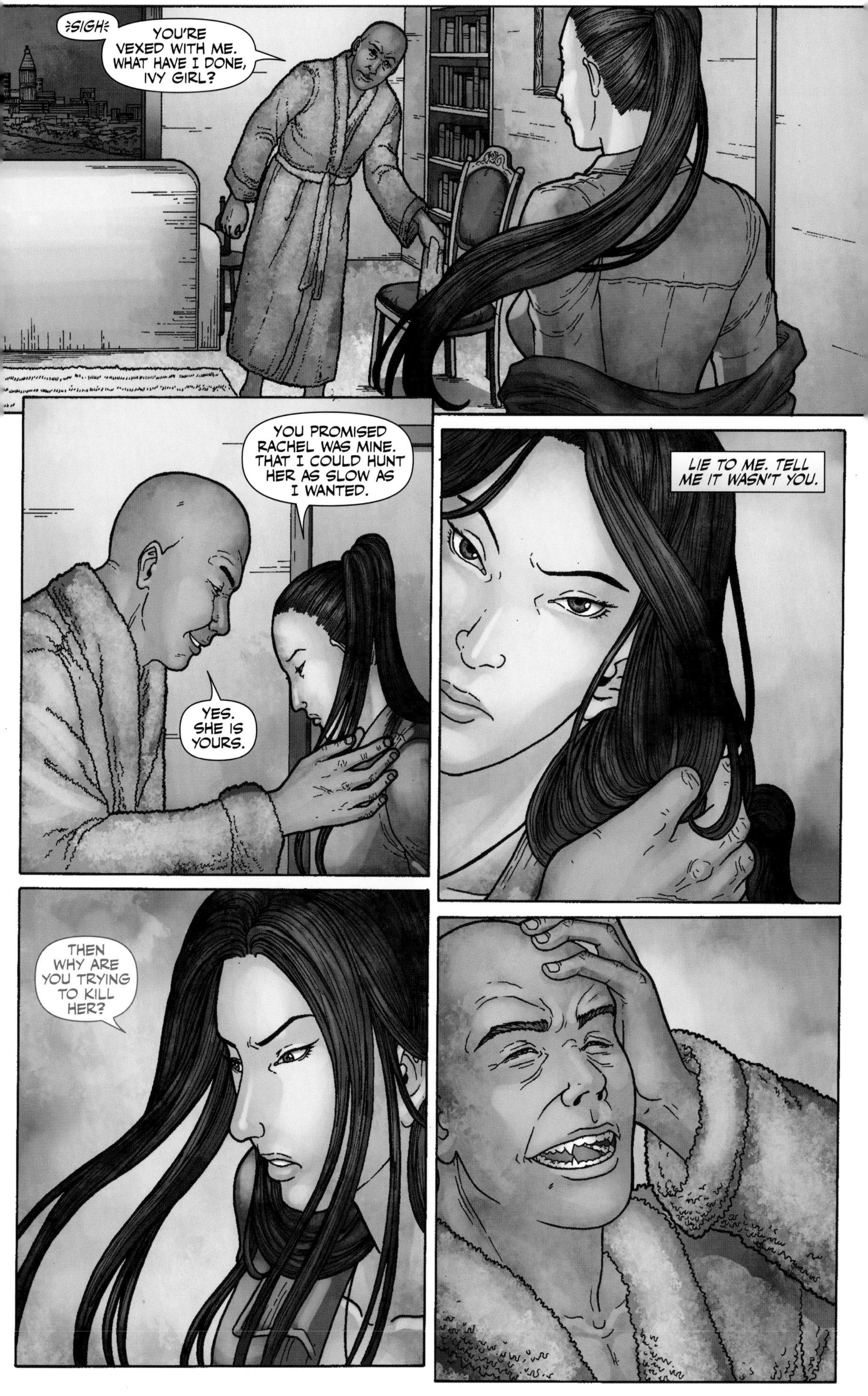
SIGH
YOU'RE VEXED WITH ME. WHAT HAVE I DONE, IVY GIRL?
YOU PROMISED RACHEL WAS MINE. THAT I COULD HUNT HER AS SLOW AS I WANTED.
YES. SHE IS YOURS.
LIE TO ME. TELL ME IT WASN'T YOU.
THEN WHY ARE YOU TRYING TO KILL HER?

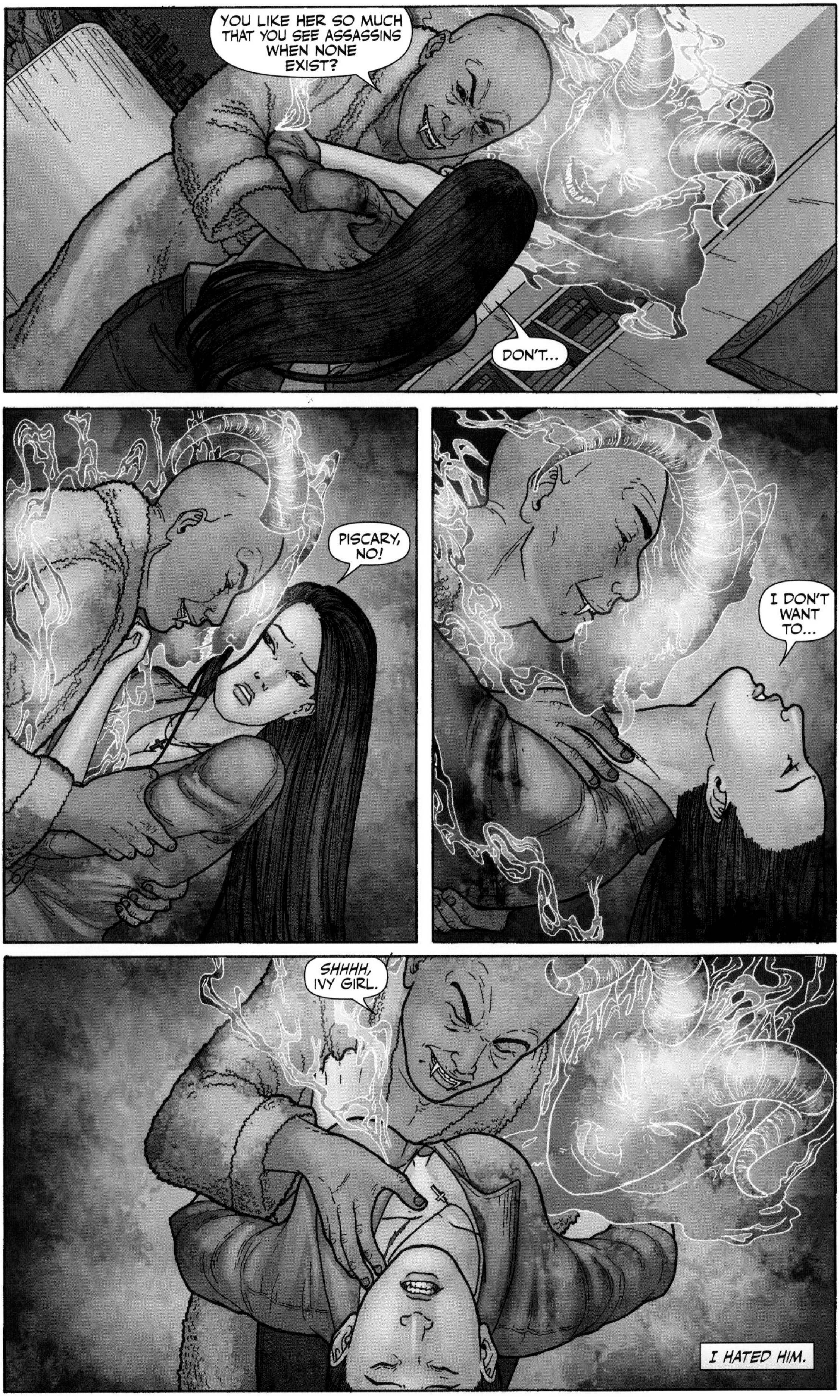
YOU LIKE HER SO MUCH THAT YOU SEE ASSASSINS WHEN NONE EXIST?
DON'T...
PISCARY, NO!
I DON'T WANT TO...
SHHHH, IVY GIRL.
I HATED HIM.

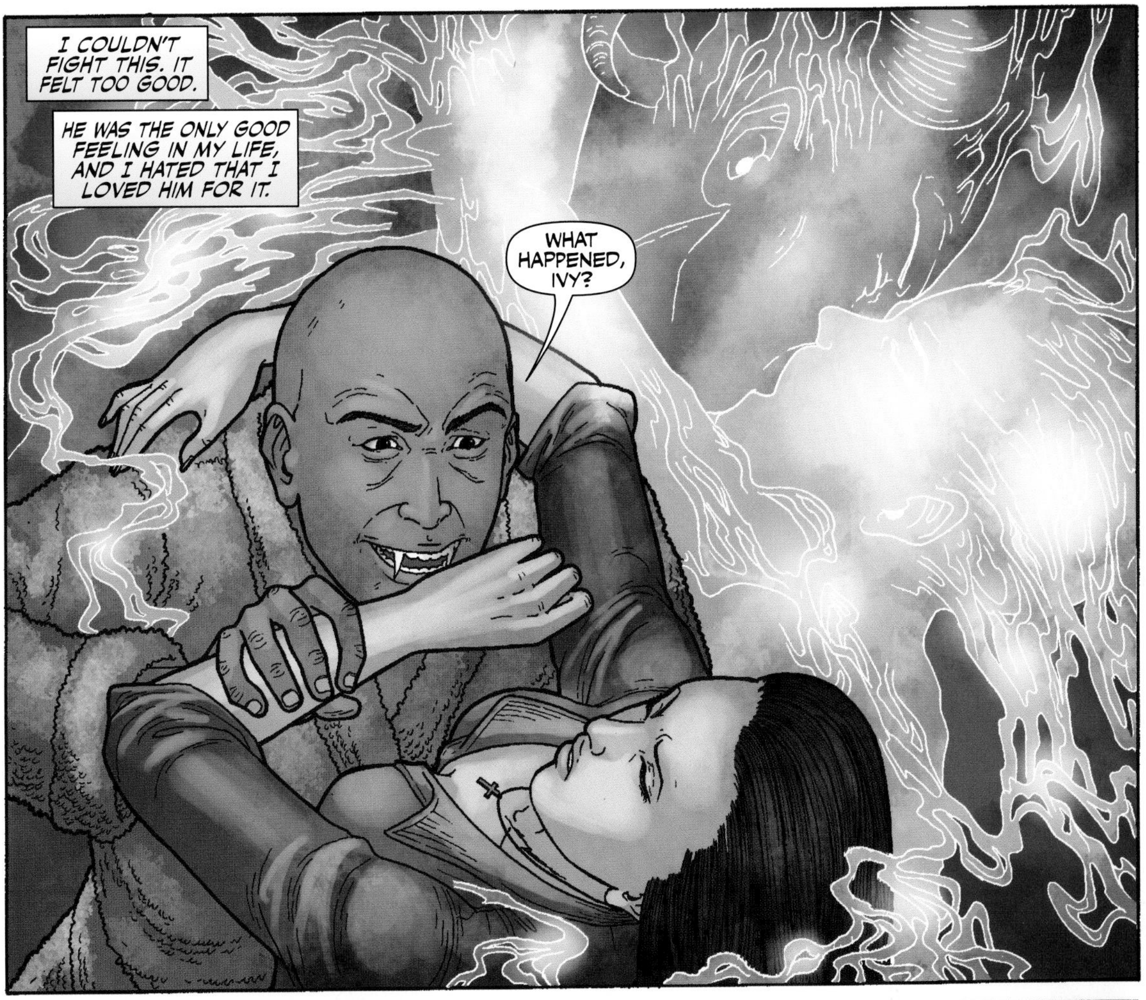
I COULDN'T FIGHT THIS. IT FELT TOO GOOD.
HE WAS THE ONLY GOOD FEELING IN MY LIFE, AND I HATED THAT I LOVED HIM FOR IT.
WHAT HAPPENED, IVY?

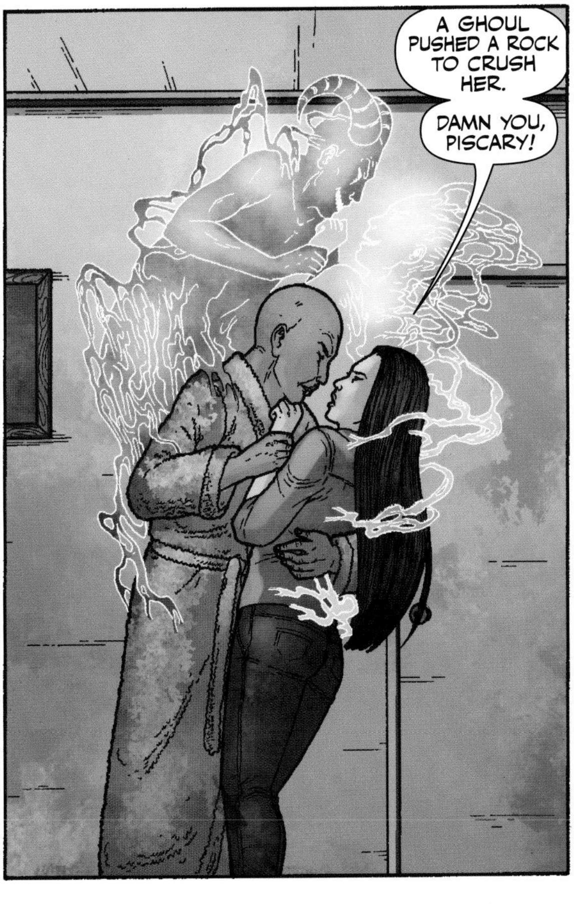
A GHOUL PUSHED A ROCK TO CRUSH HER.
DAMN YOU, PISCARY!

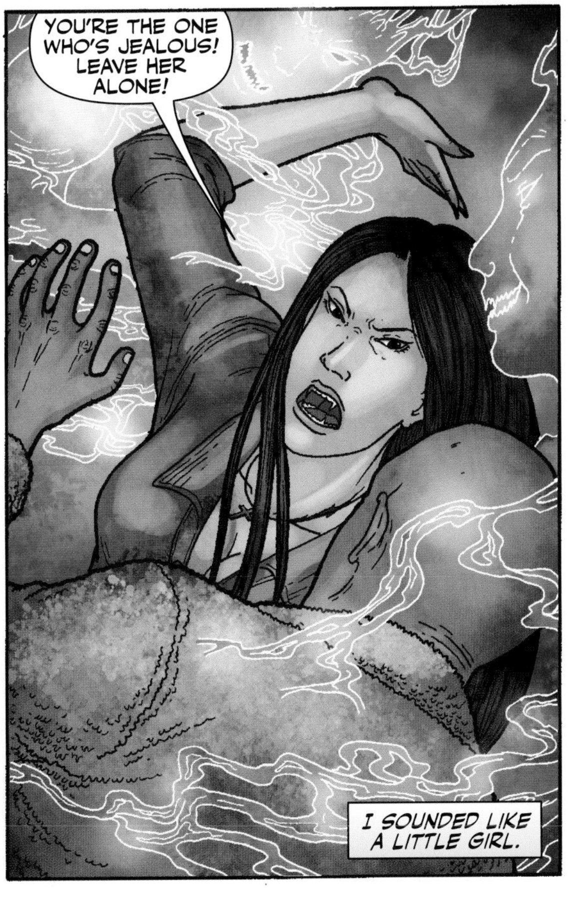
YOU'RE THE ONE WHO'S JEALOUS! LEAVE HER ALONE!
I SOUNDED LIKE A LITTLE GIRL.

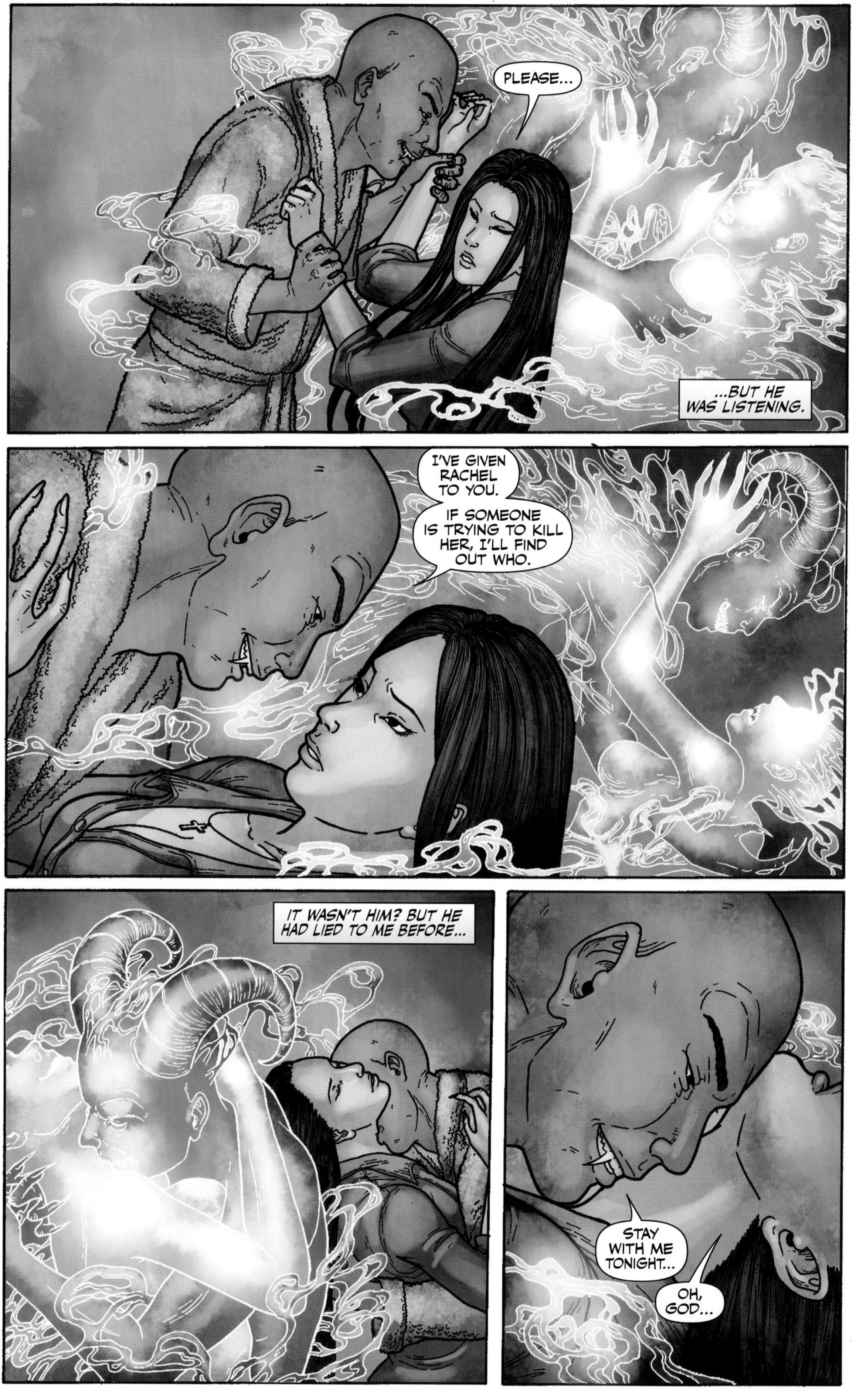
PLEASE...
...BUT HE WAS LISTENING.
I'VE GIVEN RACHEL TO YOU.
IF SOMEONE IS TRYING TO KILL HER, I'LL FIND OUT WHO.
IT WASN'T HIM? BUT HE HAD LIED TO ME BEFORE...
STAY WITH ME TONIGHT...
OH, GOD...

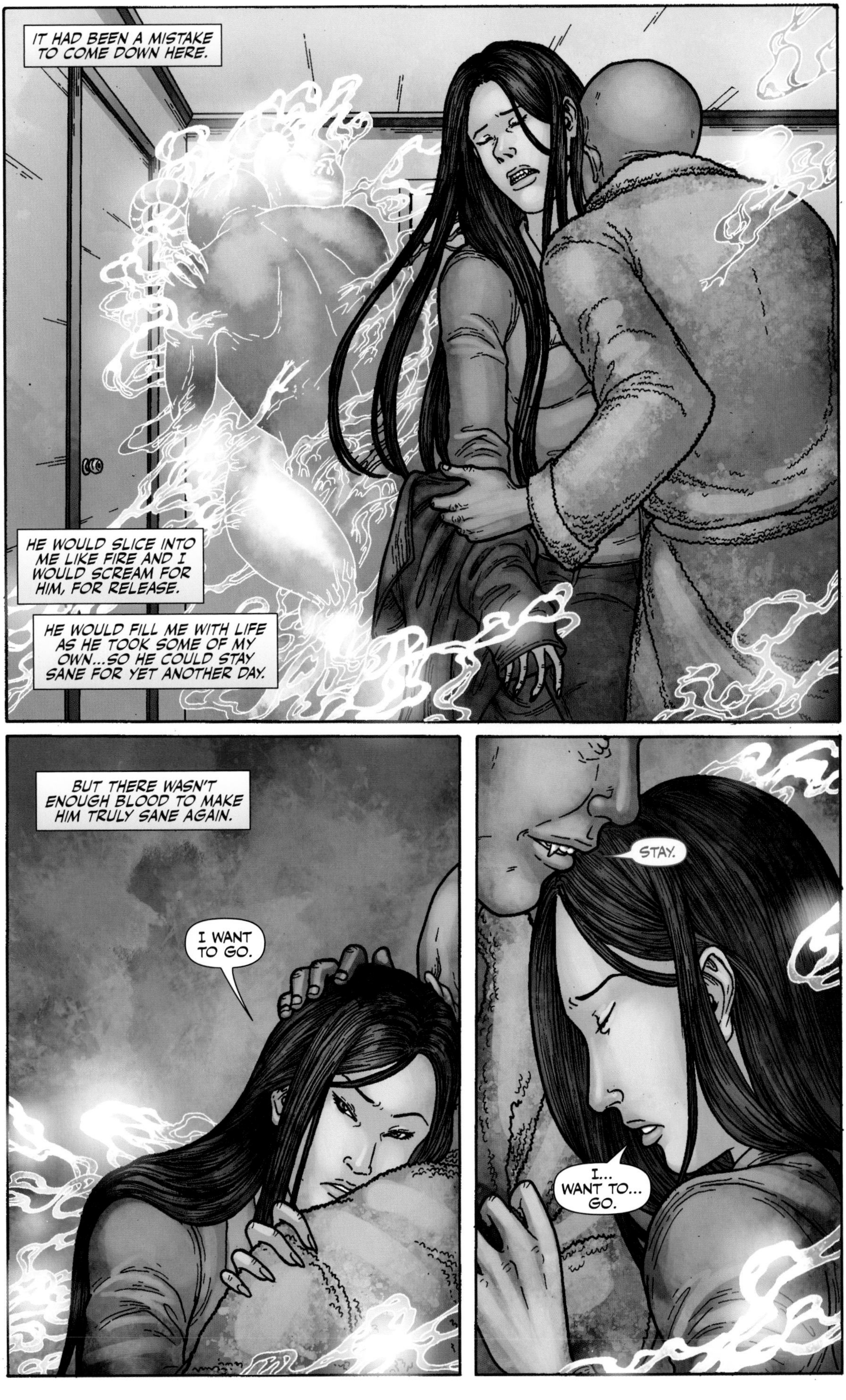
IT HAD BEEN A MISTAKE TO COME DOWN HERE.
HE WOULD SLICE INTO ME LIKE FIRE AND I WOULD SCREAM FOR HIM, FOR RELEASE.
HE WOULD FILL ME WITH LIFE AS HE TOOK SOME OF MY OWN...SO HE COULD STAY SANE FOR YET ANOTHER DAY.
BUT THERE WASN'T ENOUGH BLOOD TO MAKE HIM TRULY SANE AGAIN.
I WANT TO GO.
STAY.
I... WANT TO... GO.

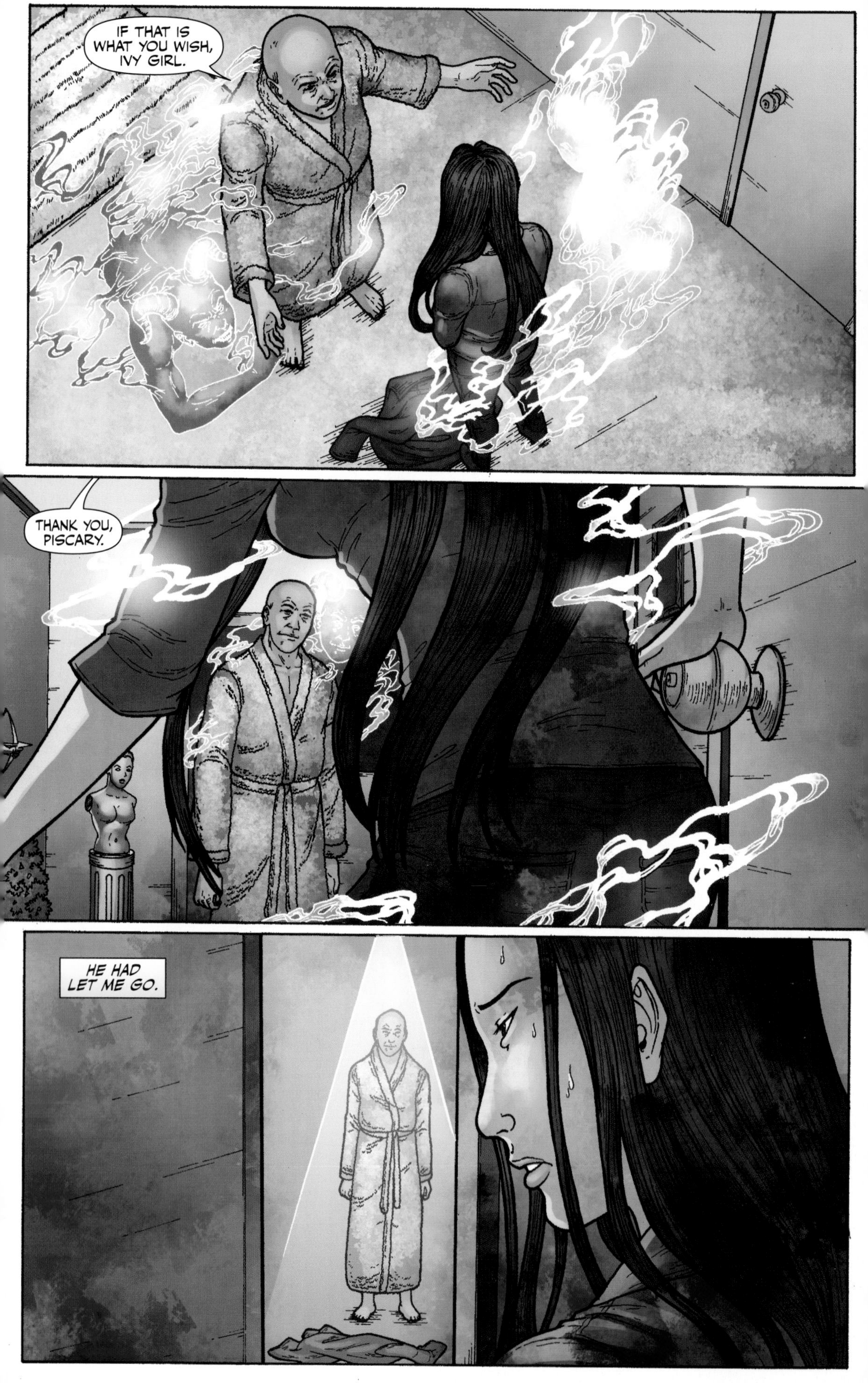
IF THAT IS WHAT YOU WISH, IVY GIRL.
THANK YOU, PISCARY.
HE HAD LET ME GO.

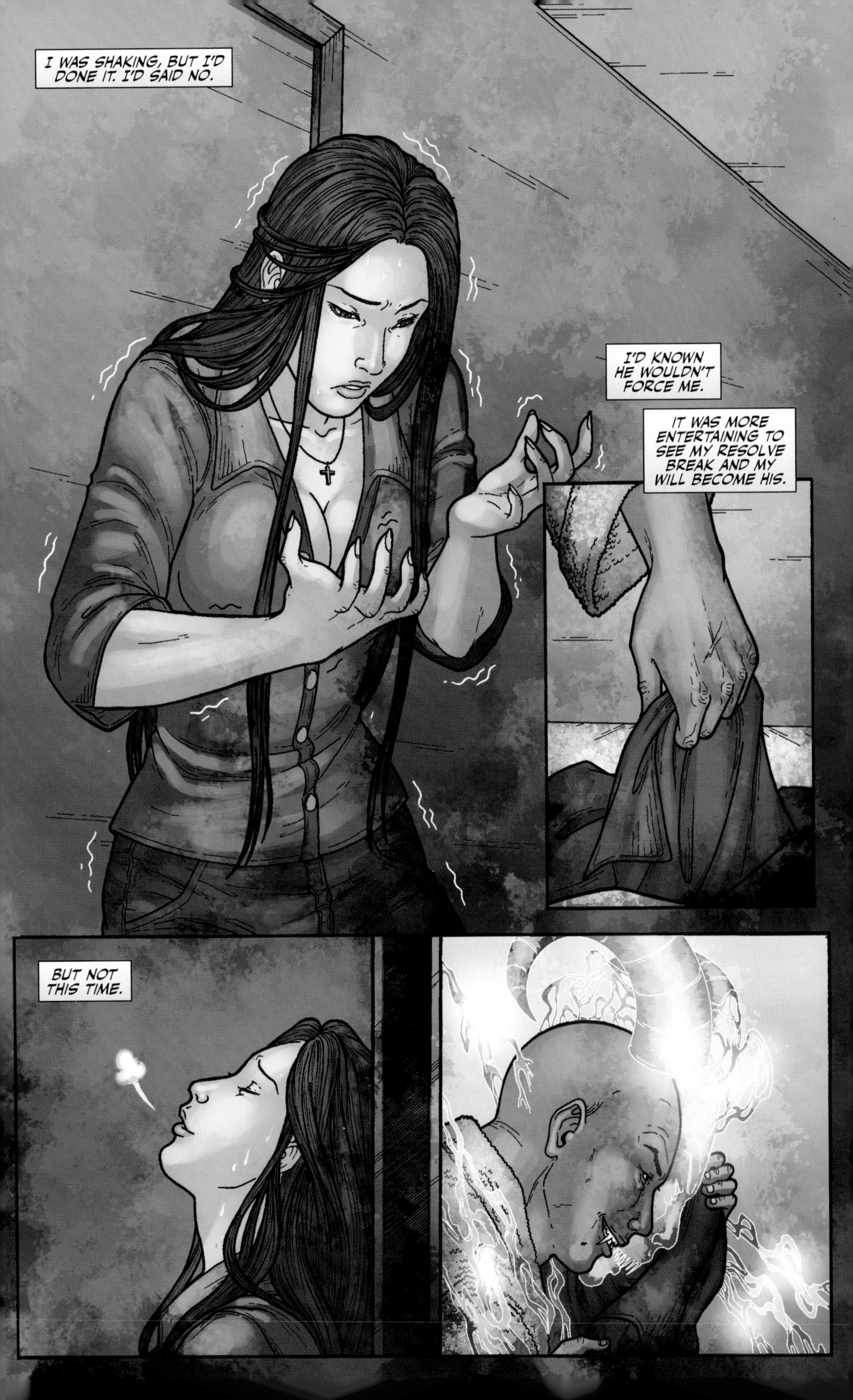
I WAS SHAKING, BUT I'D DONE IT. I'D SAID NO.
I'D KNOWN HE WOULDN'T FORCE ME.
IT WAS MORE ENTERTAINING TO SEE MY RESOLVE BREAK AND MY WILL BECOME HIS.
BUT NOT THIS TIME.

CHAPTER 3

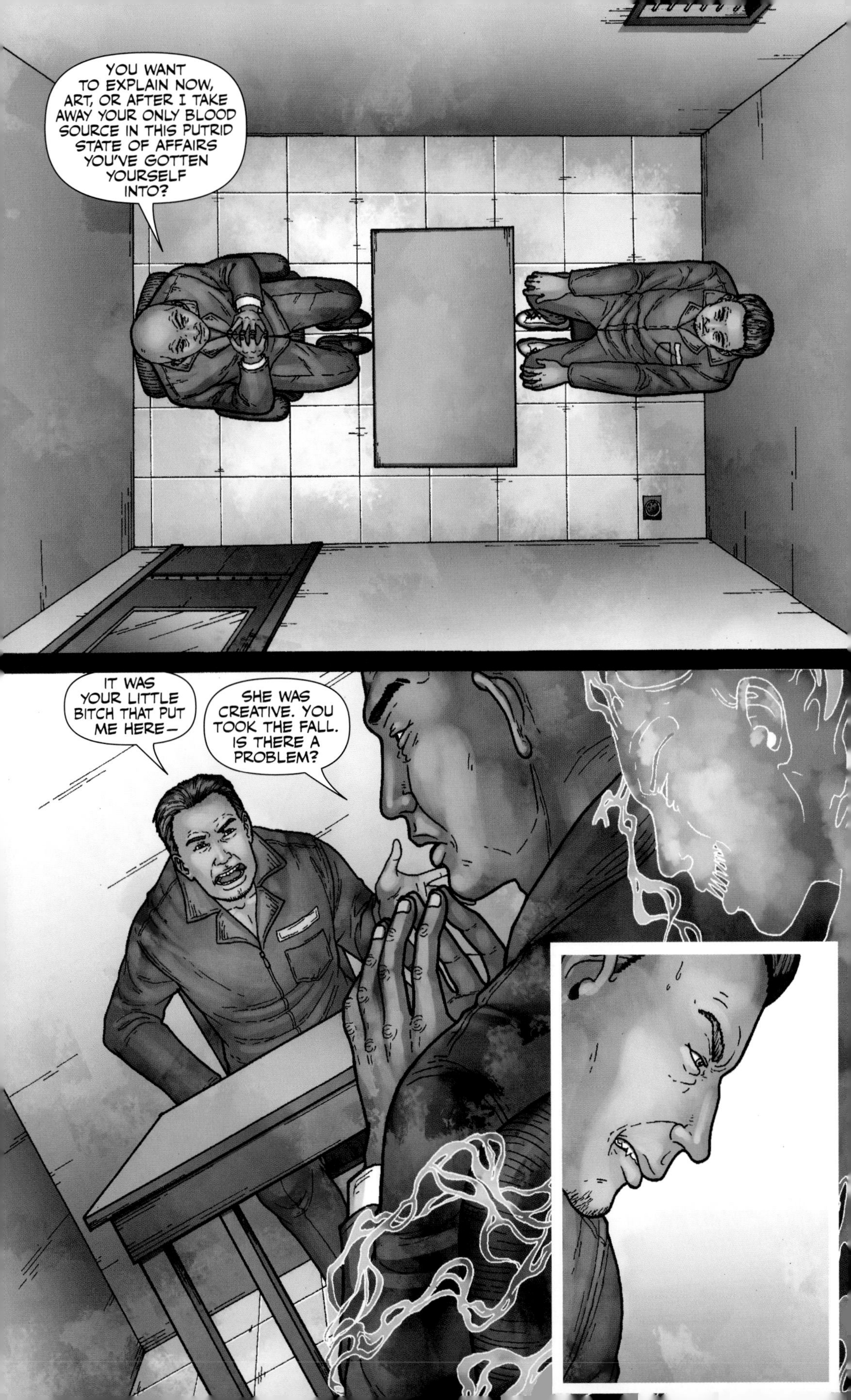
YOU WANT TO EXPLAIN NOW, ART, OR AFTER I TAKE AWAY YOUR ONLY BLOOD SOURCE IN THIS PUTRID STATE OF AFFAIRS YOU'VE GOTTEN YOURSELF INTO?
IT WAS YOUR LITTLE BITCH THAT PUT ME HERE—
SHE WAS CREATIVE. YOU TOOK THE FALL. IS THERE A PROBLEM?

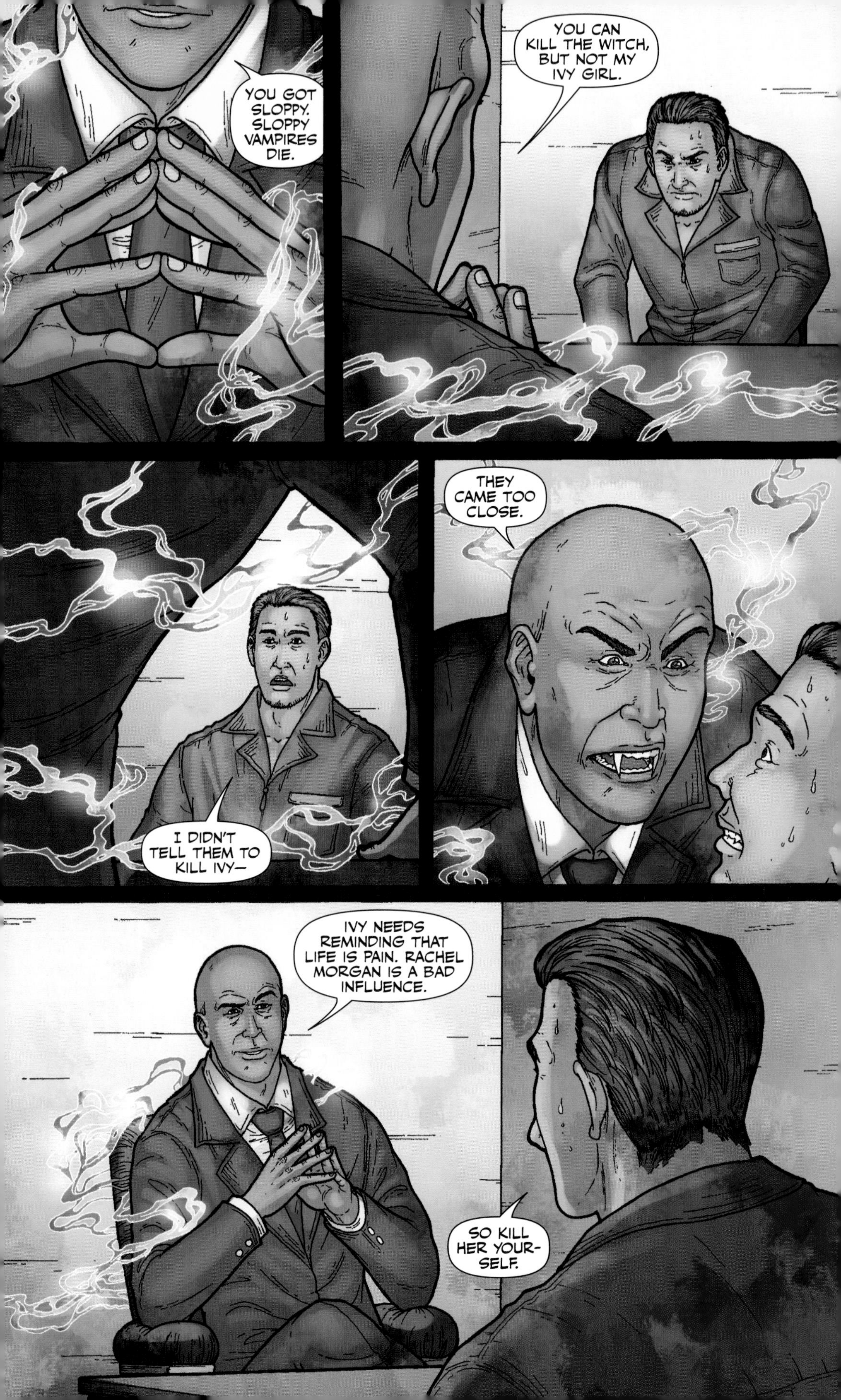
YOU GOT SLOPPY. SLOPPY VAMPIRES DIE.
YOU CAN KILL THE WITCH, BUT NOT MY IVY GIRL.
I DIDN'T TELL THEM TO KILL IVY—
THEY CAME TOO CLOSE.
IVY NEEDS REMINDING THAT LIFE IS PAIN. RACHEL MORGAN IS A BAD INFLUENCE.
SO KILL HER YOUR-SELF.

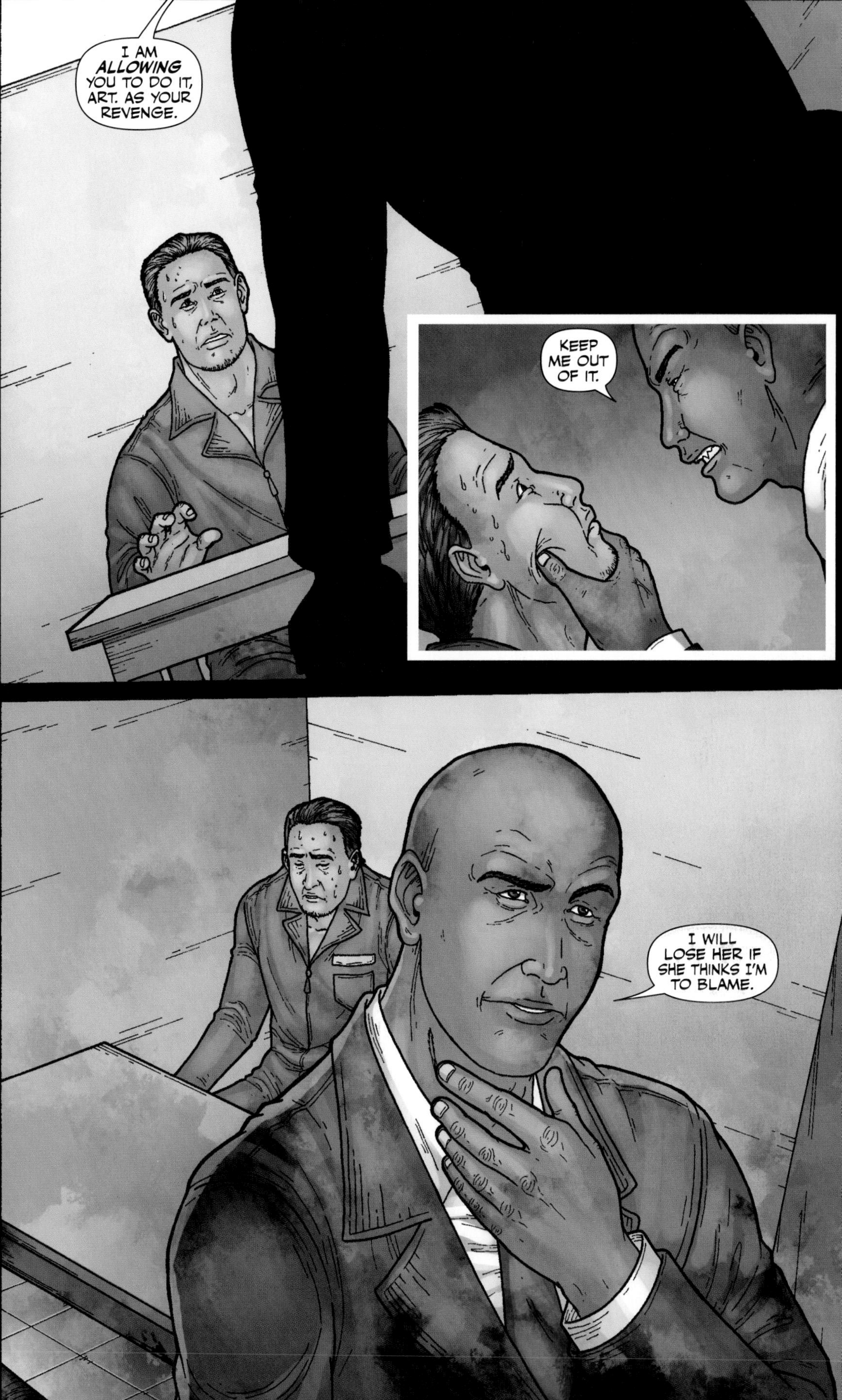
I AM *ALLOWING* YOU TO DO IT, ART. AS YOUR REVENGE.
KEEP ME OUT OF IT.
I WILL LOSE HER IF SHE THINKS I'M TO BLAME.

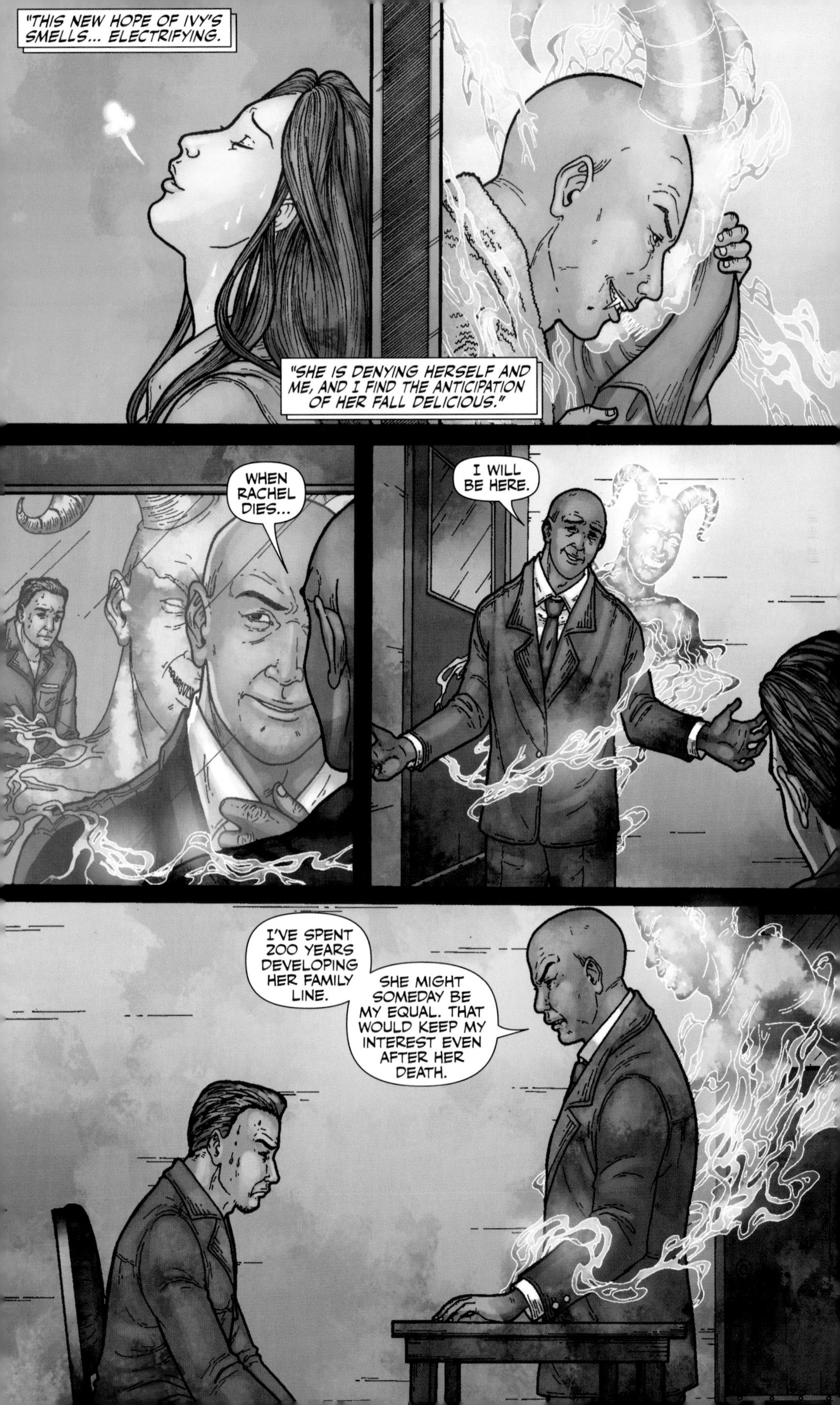
"THIS NEW HOPE OF IVY'S SMELLS... ELECTRIFYING.
"SHE IS DENYING HERSELF AND ME, AND I FIND THE ANTICIPATION OF HER FALL DELICIOUS."
WHEN RACHEL DIES...
I WILL BE HERE.
I'VE SPENT 200 YEARS DEVELOPING HER FAMILY LINE.
SHE MIGHT SOMEDAY BE MY EQUAL. THAT WOULD KEEP MY INTEREST EVEN AFTER HER DEATH.

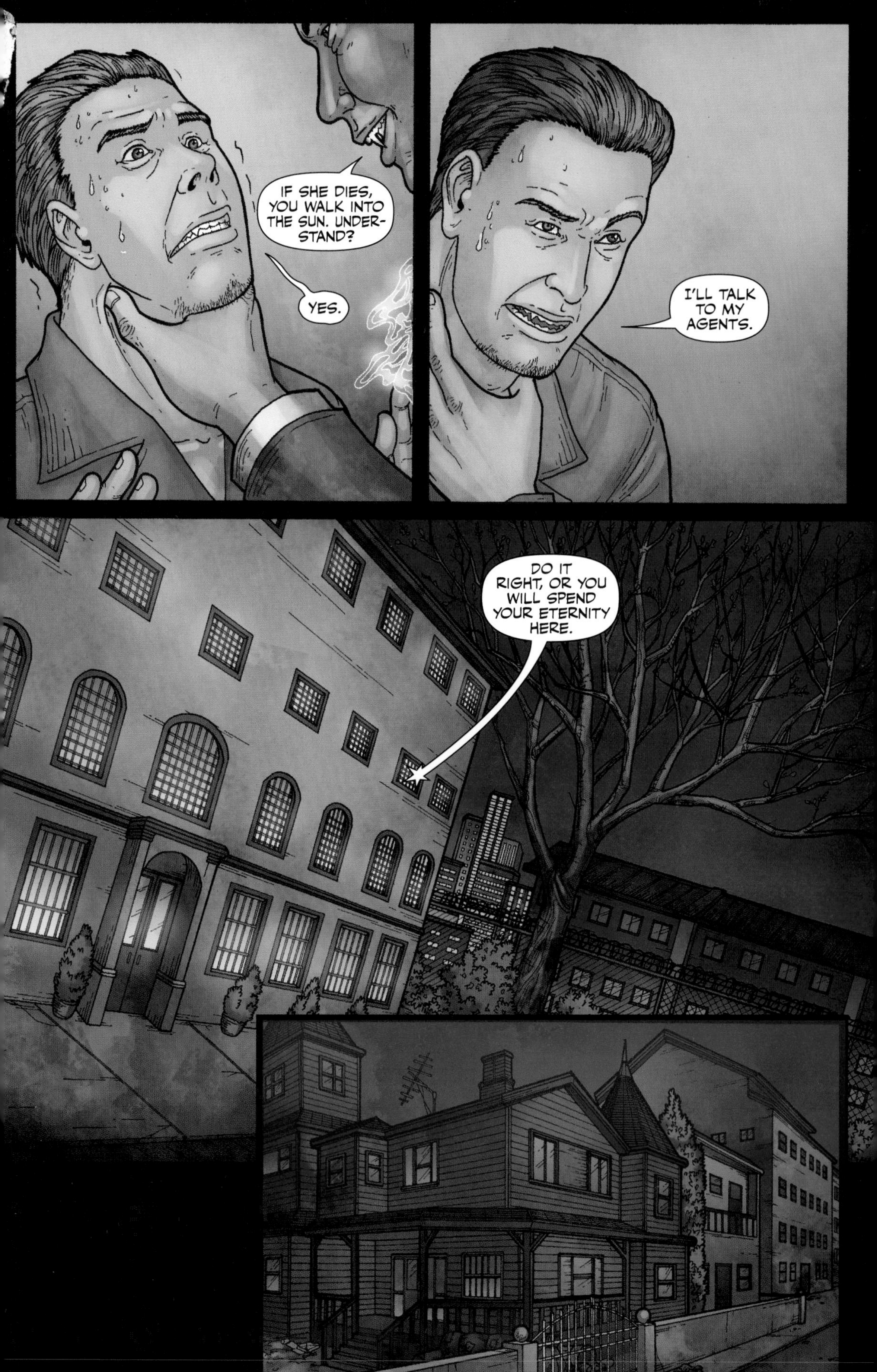
IF SHE DIES, YOU WALK INTO THE SUN. UNDER-STAND?
YES.
I'LL TALK TO MY AGENTS.
DO IT RIGHT, OR YOU WILL SPEND YOUR ETERNITY HERE.

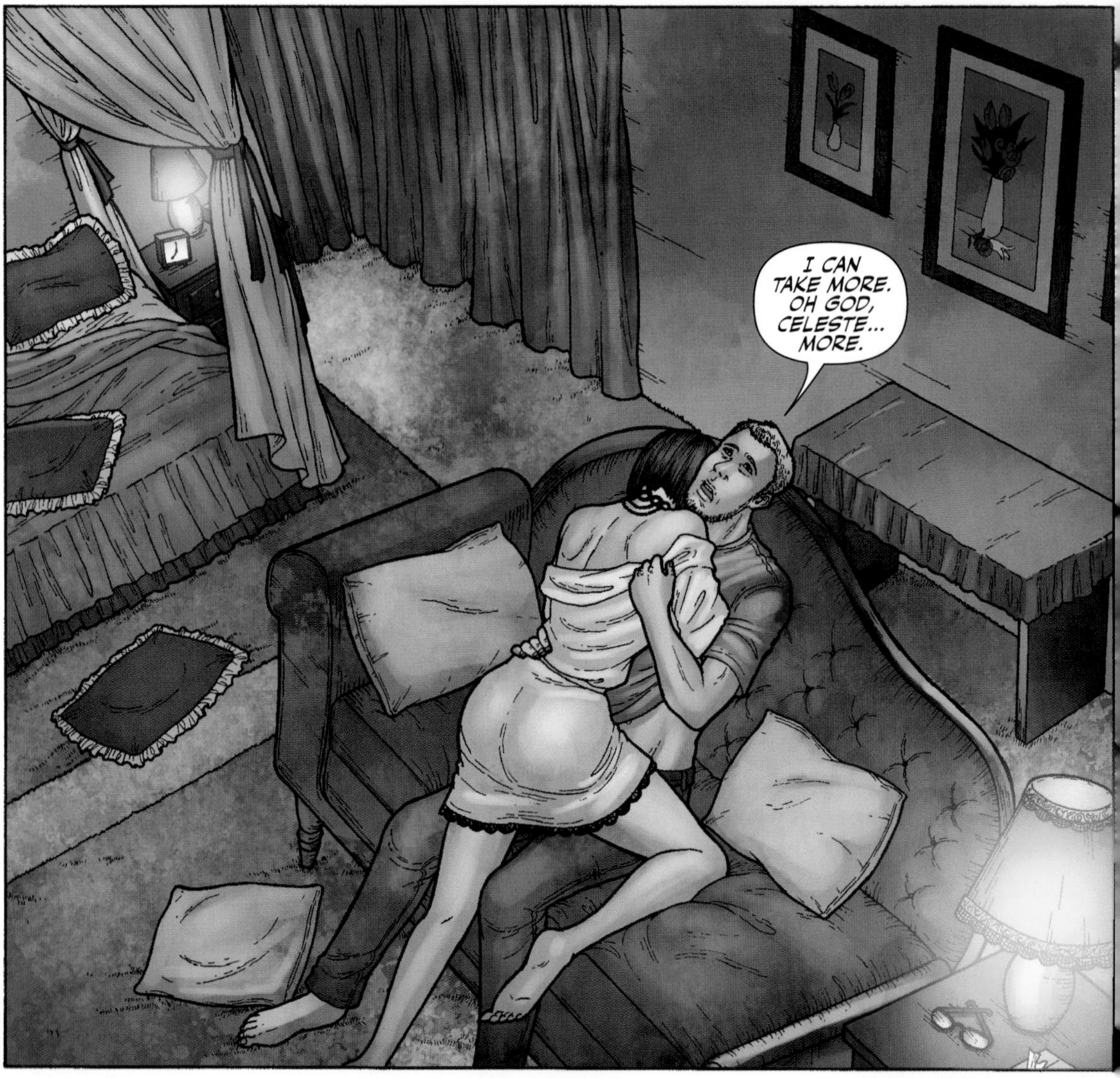
I CAN TAKE MORE. OH GOD, CELESTE... MORE.

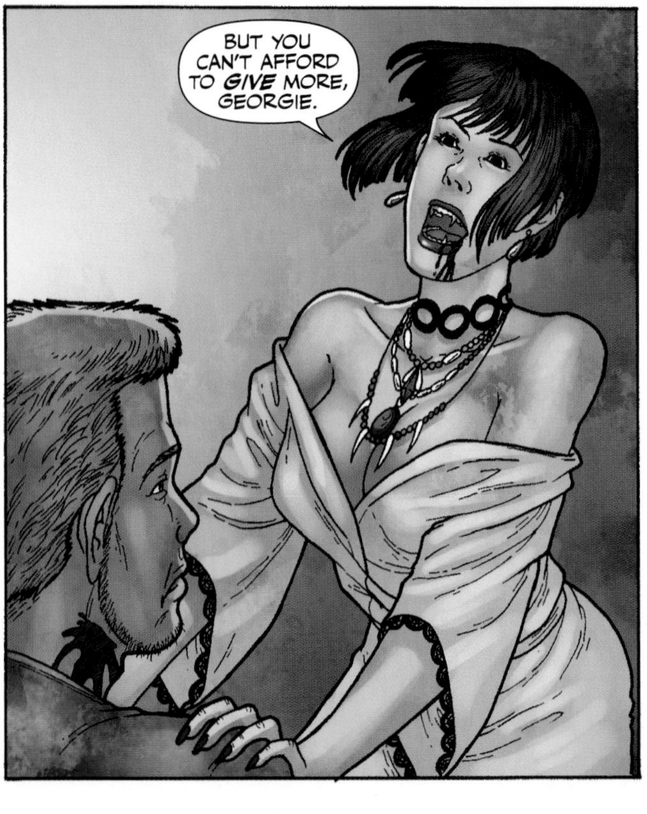
BUT YOU CAN'T AFFORD TO GIVE MORE, GEORGIE.

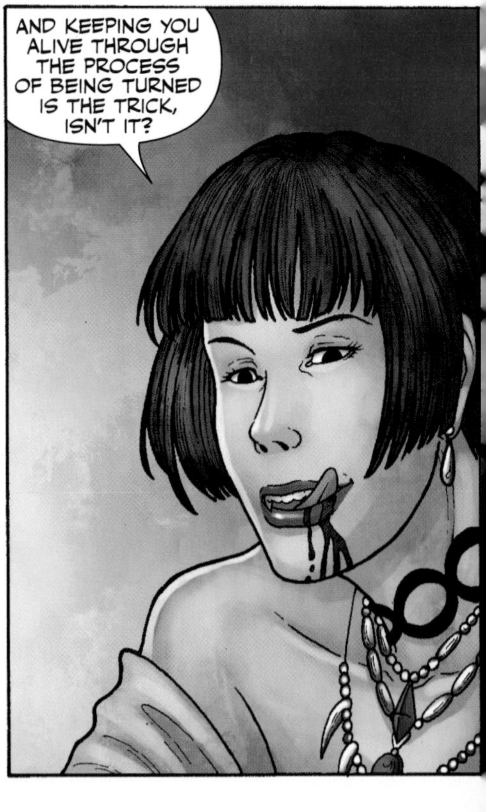
AND KEEPING YOU ALIVE THROUGH THE PROCESS OF BEING TURNED IS THE TRICK, ISN'T IT?

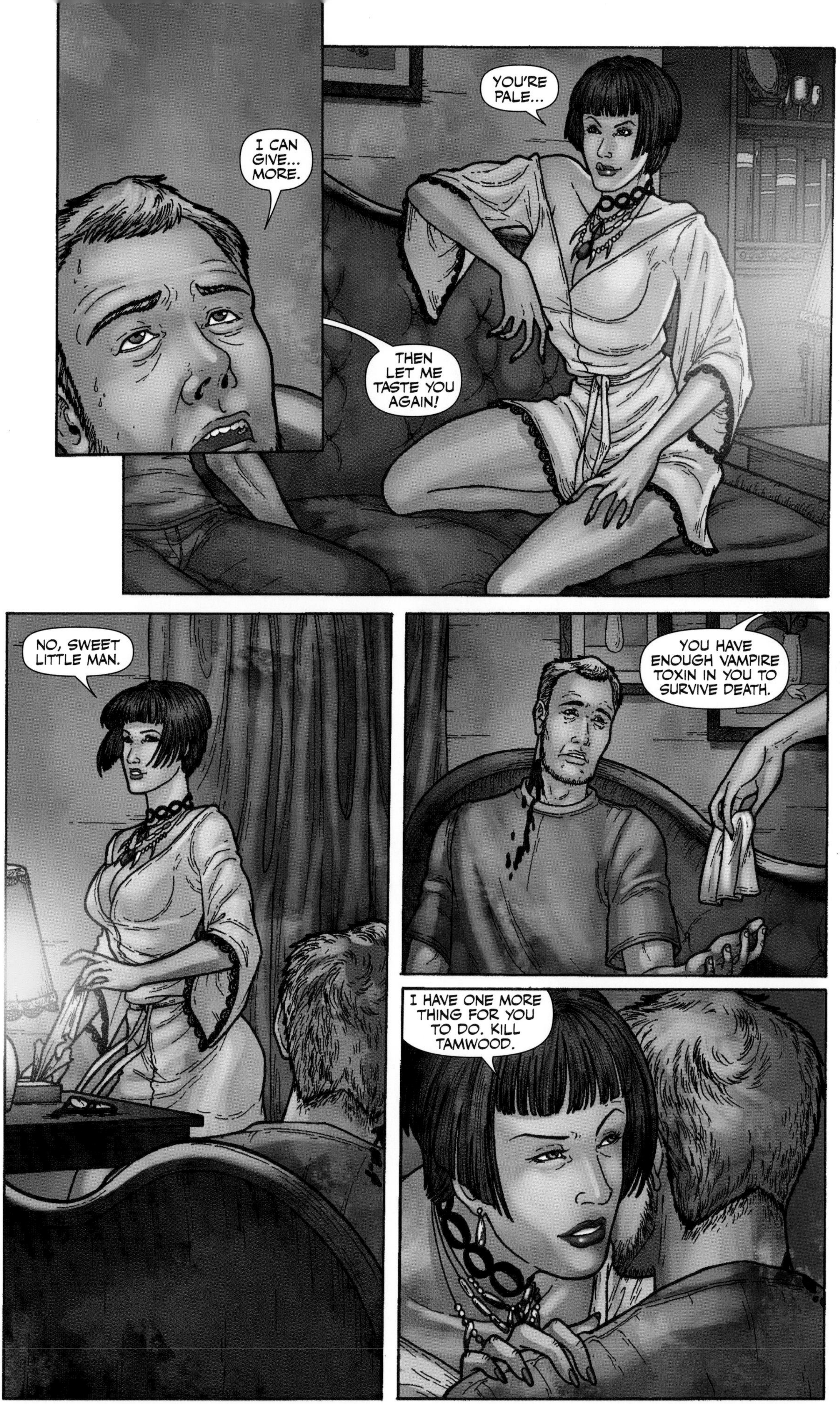
YOU'RE PALE...
I CAN GIVE... MORE.
THEN LET ME TASTE YOU AGAIN!
NO, SWEET LITTLE MAN.
YOU HAVE ENOUGH VAMPIRE TOXIN IN YOU TO SURVIVE DEATH.
I HAVE ONE MORE THING FOR YOU TO DO. KILL TAMWOOD.

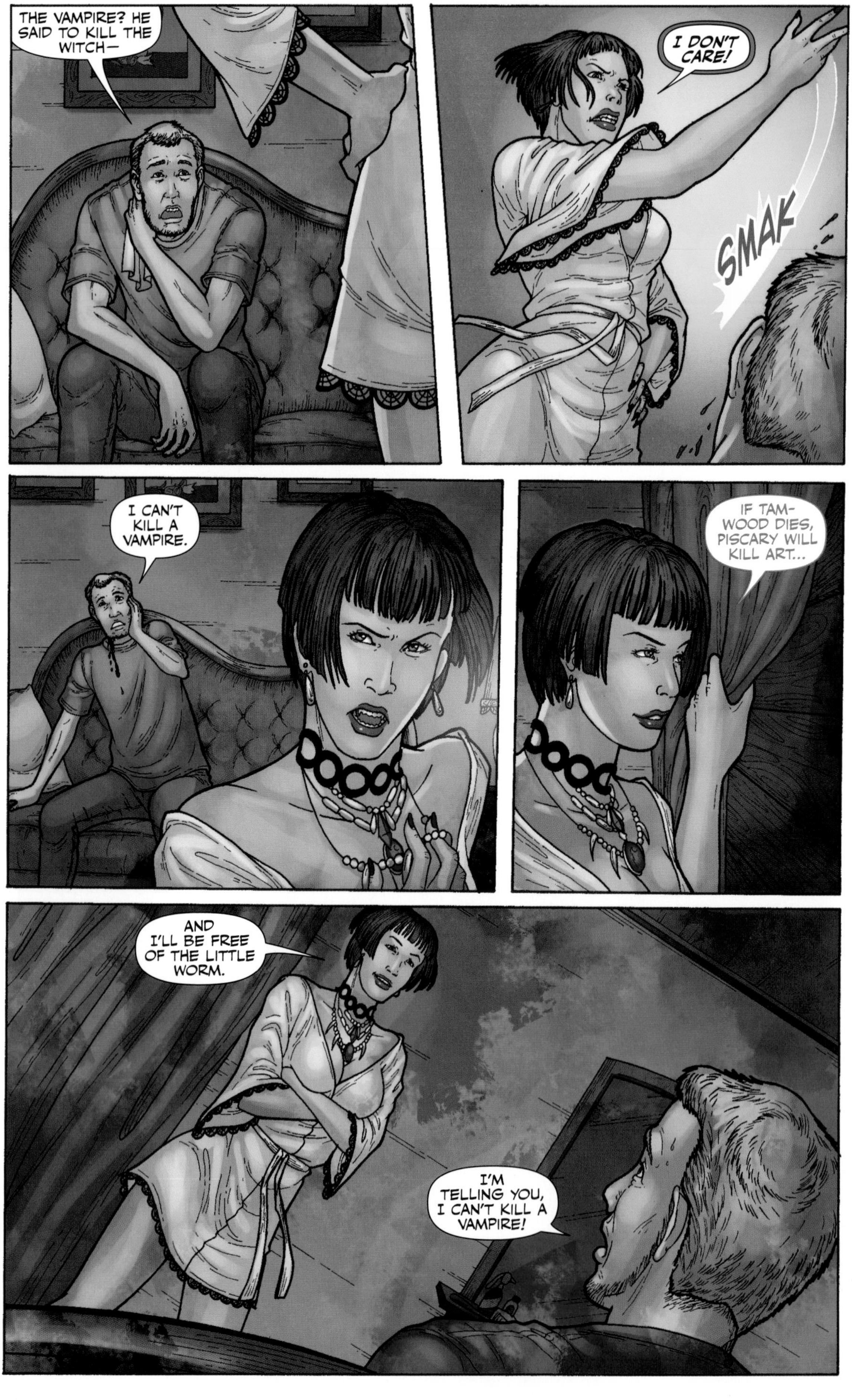
THE VAMPIRE? HE SAID TO KILL THE WITCH—
I DON'T CARE!
SMAK
I CAN'T KILL A VAMPIRE.
IF TAMWOOD DIES, PISCARY WILL KILL ART...
AND I'LL BE FREE OF THE LITTLE WORM.
I'M TELLING YOU, I CAN'T KILL A VAMPIRE!

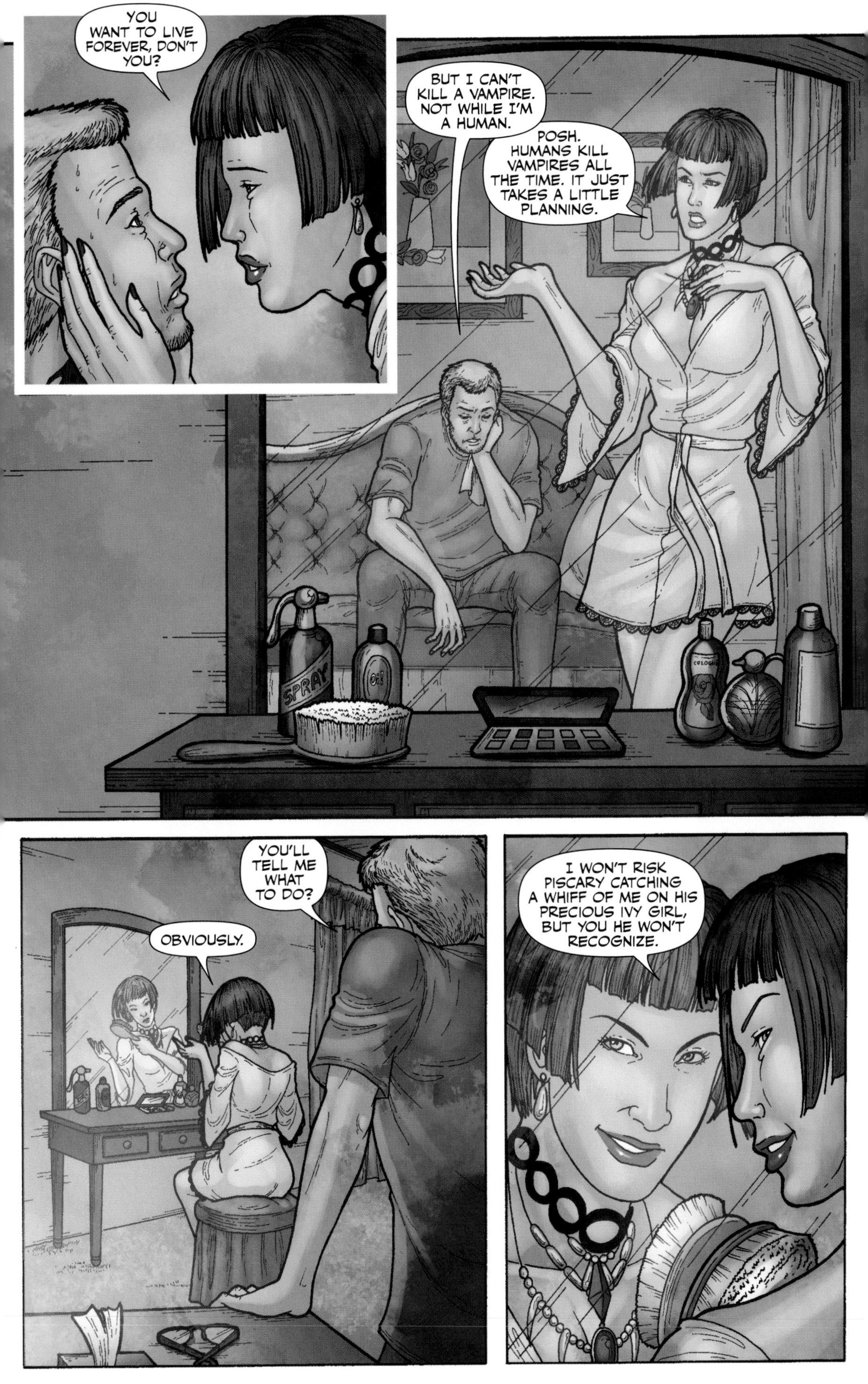

YOU WANT TO LIVE FOREVER, DON'T YOU?
BUT I CAN'T KILL A VAMPIRE. NOT WHILE I'M A HUMAN.
POSH. HUMANS KILL VAMPIRES ALL THE TIME. IT JUST TAKES A LITTLE PLANNING.
SPRAY
Oil
COLOGNE
YOU'LL TELL ME WHAT TO DO?
OBVIOUSLY.
I WON'T RISK PISCARY CATCHING A WHIFF OF ME ON HIS PRECIOUS IVY GIRL, BUT YOU HE WON'T RECOGNIZE.

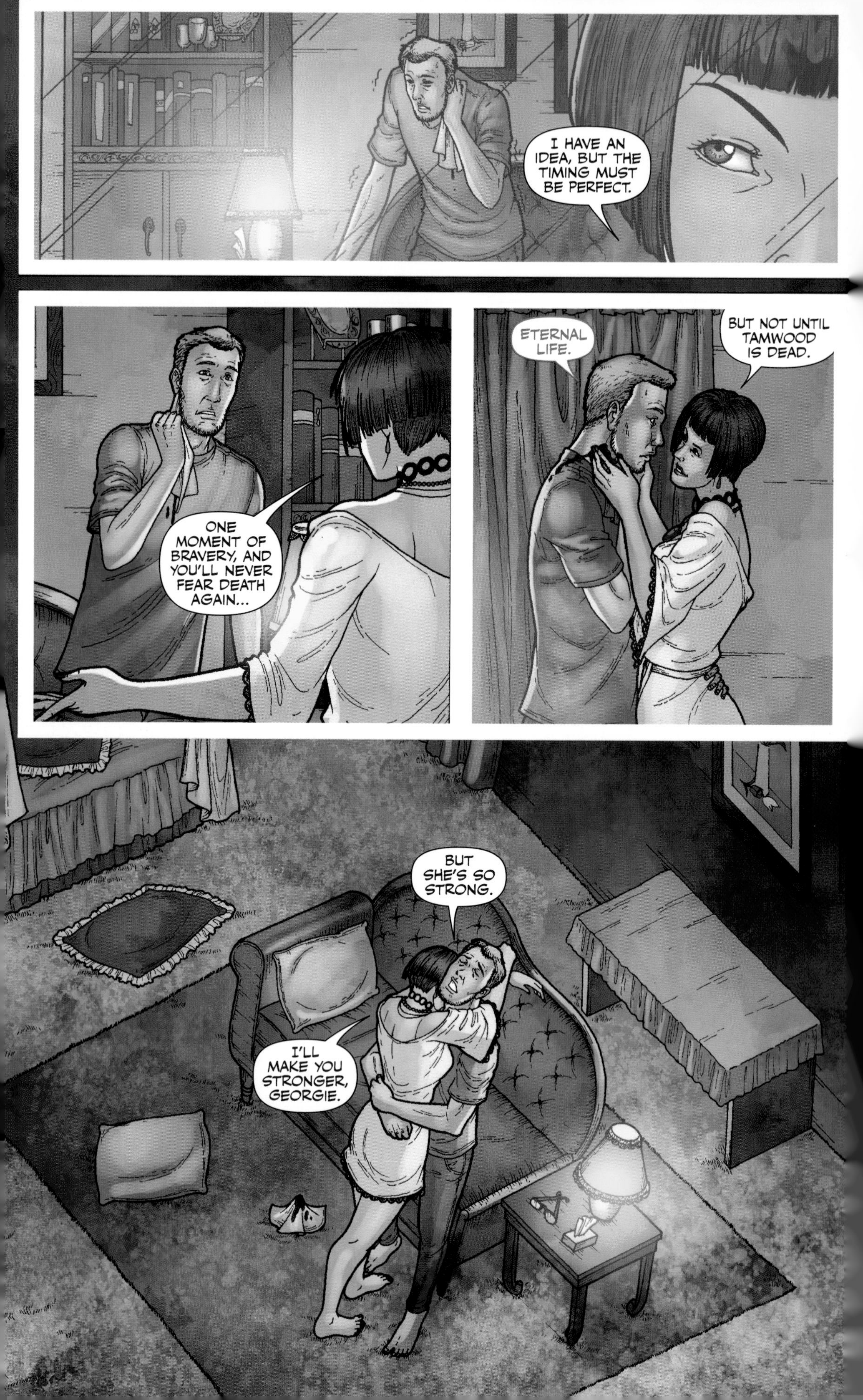
I HAVE AN IDEA, BUT THE TIMING MUST BE PERFECT.
ONE MOMENT OF BRAVERY, AND YOU'LL NEVER FEAR DEATH AGAIN...
ETERNAL LIFE.
BUT NOT UNTIL TAMWOOD IS DEAD.
BUT SHE'S SO STRONG.
I'LL MAKE YOU STRONGER, GEORGIE.

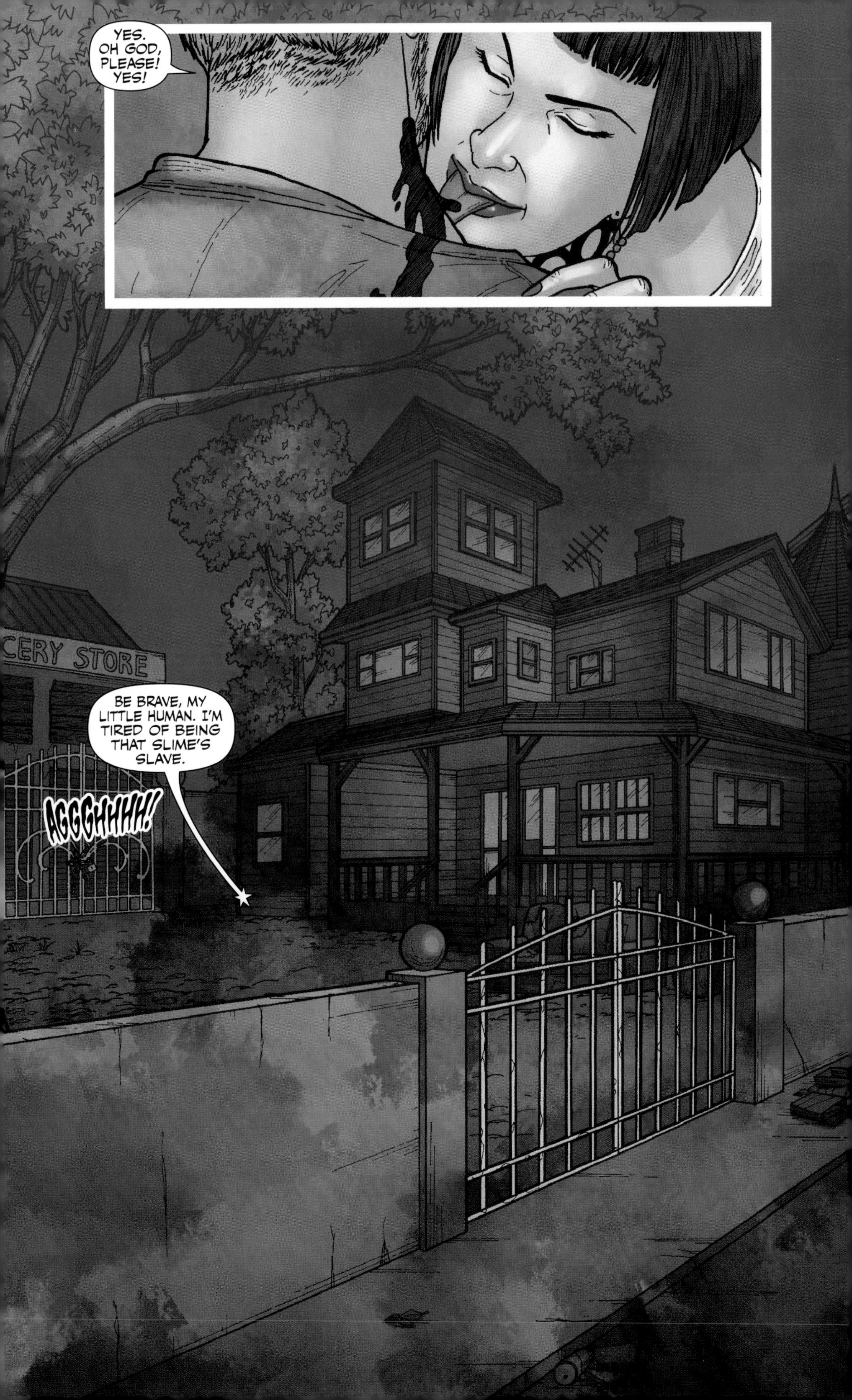
YES. OH GOD, PLEASE! YES!
CERY STORE
BE BRAVE, MY LITTLE HUMAN. I'M TIRED OF BEING THAT SLIME'S SLAVE.
AGGGHHHH!

CHAPTER 4

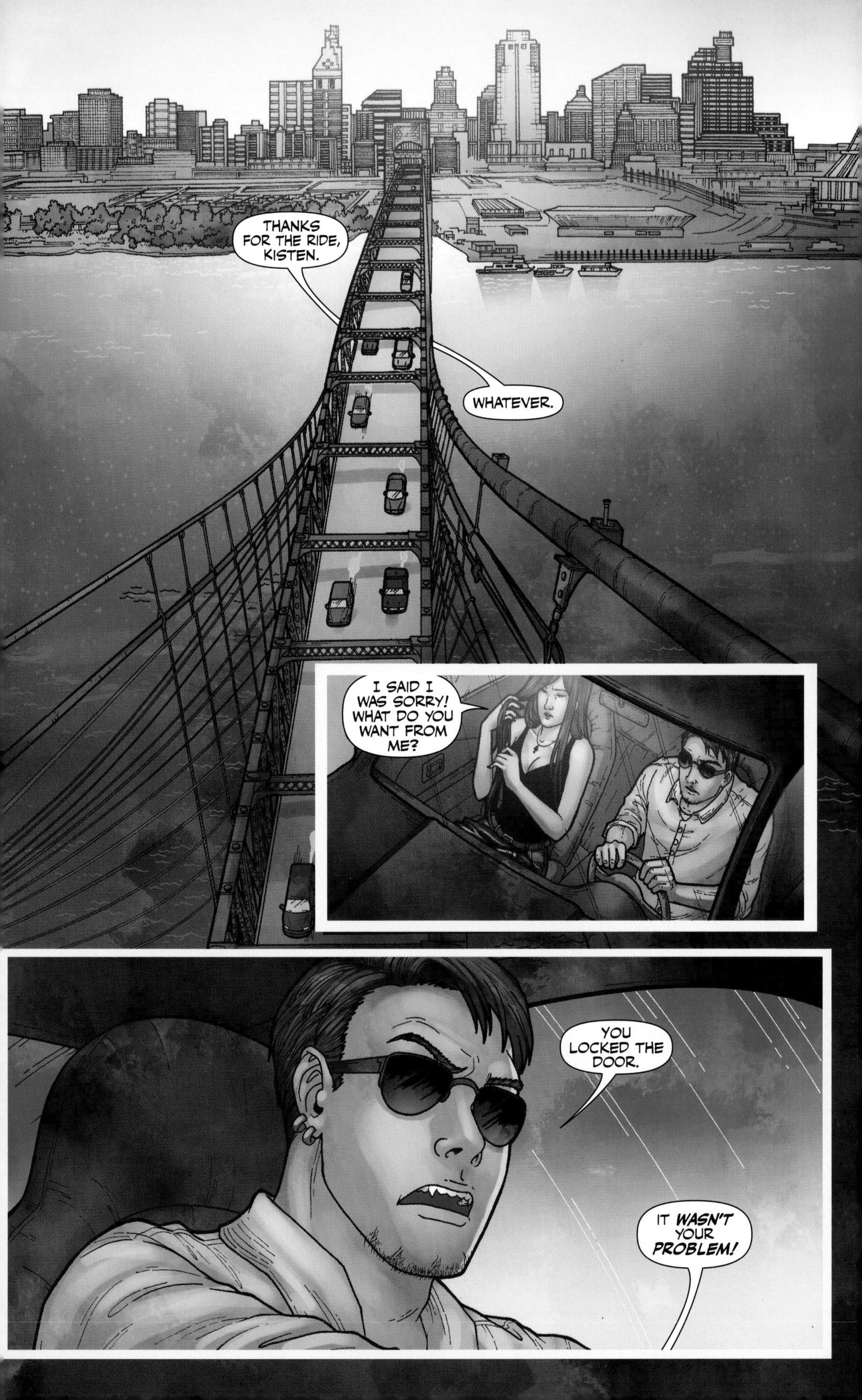
THANKS FOR THE RIDE, KISTEN.
WHATEVER.
I SAID I WAS SORRY! WHAT DO YOU WANT FROM ME?
YOU LOCKED THE DOOR.
IT *WASN'T* YOUR *PROBLEM!*

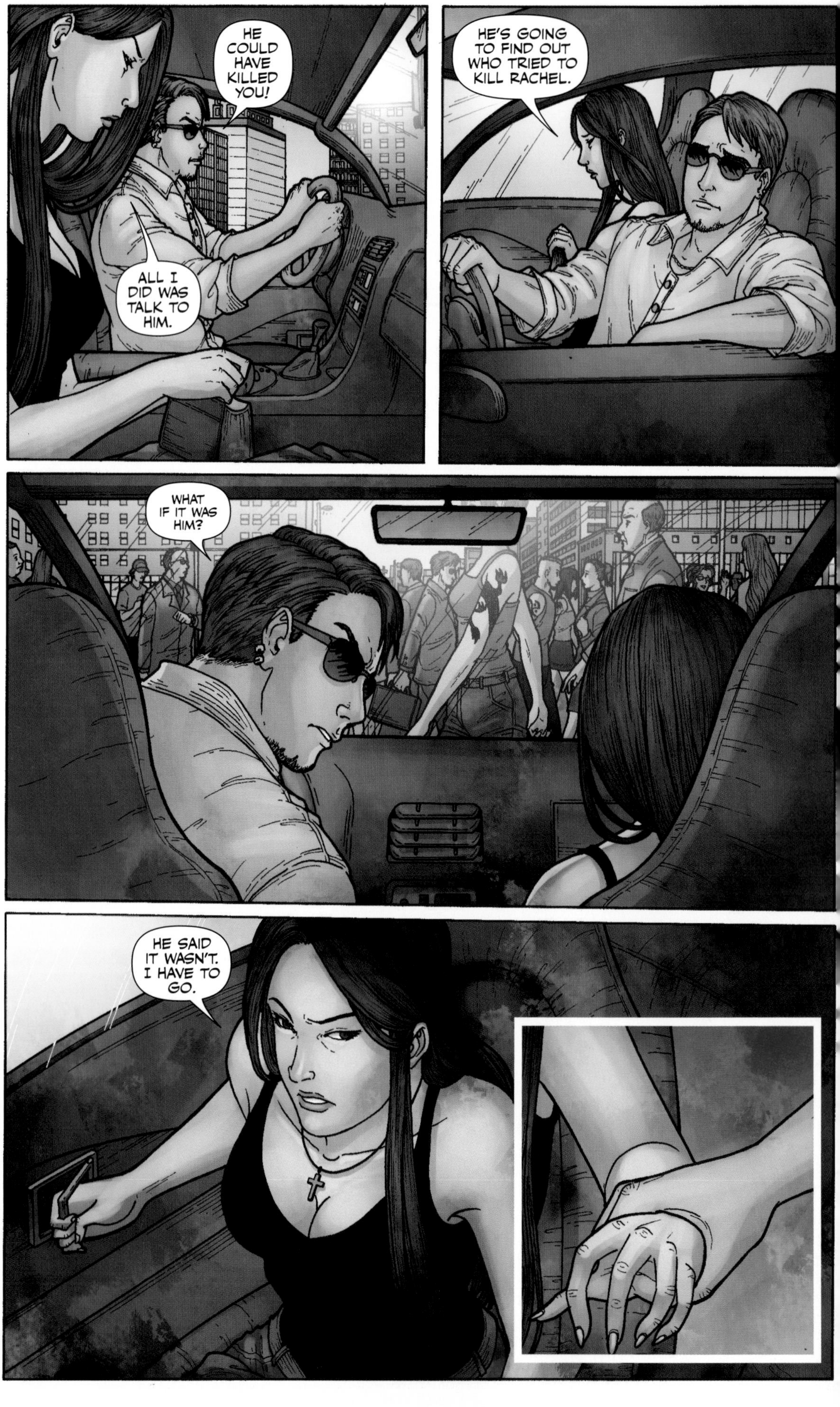
HE COULD HAVE KILLED YOU!
ALL I DID WAS TALK TO HIM.
HE'S GOING TO FIND OUT WHO TRIED TO KILL RACHEL.
WHAT IF IT WAS HIM?
HE SAID IT WASN'T. I HAVE TO GO.

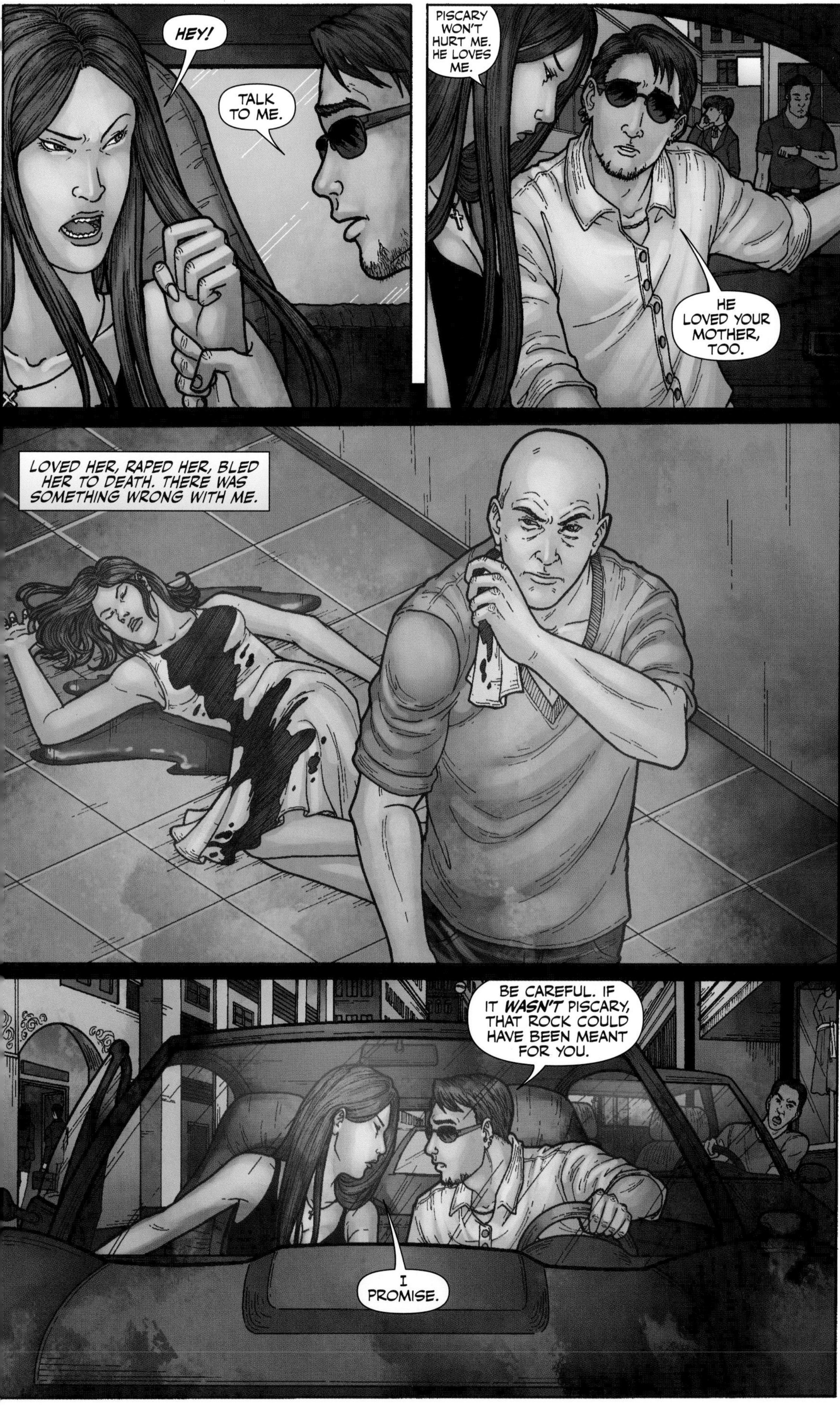
HEY!
TALK TO ME.
PISCARY WON'T HURT ME. HE LOVES ME.
HE LOVED YOUR MOTHER, TOO.
LOVED HER, RAPED HER, BLED HER TO DEATH. THERE WAS SOMETHING WRONG WITH ME.
BE CAREFUL. IF IT *WASN'T* PISCARY, THAT ROCK COULD HAVE BEEN MEANT FOR YOU.
I PROMISE.

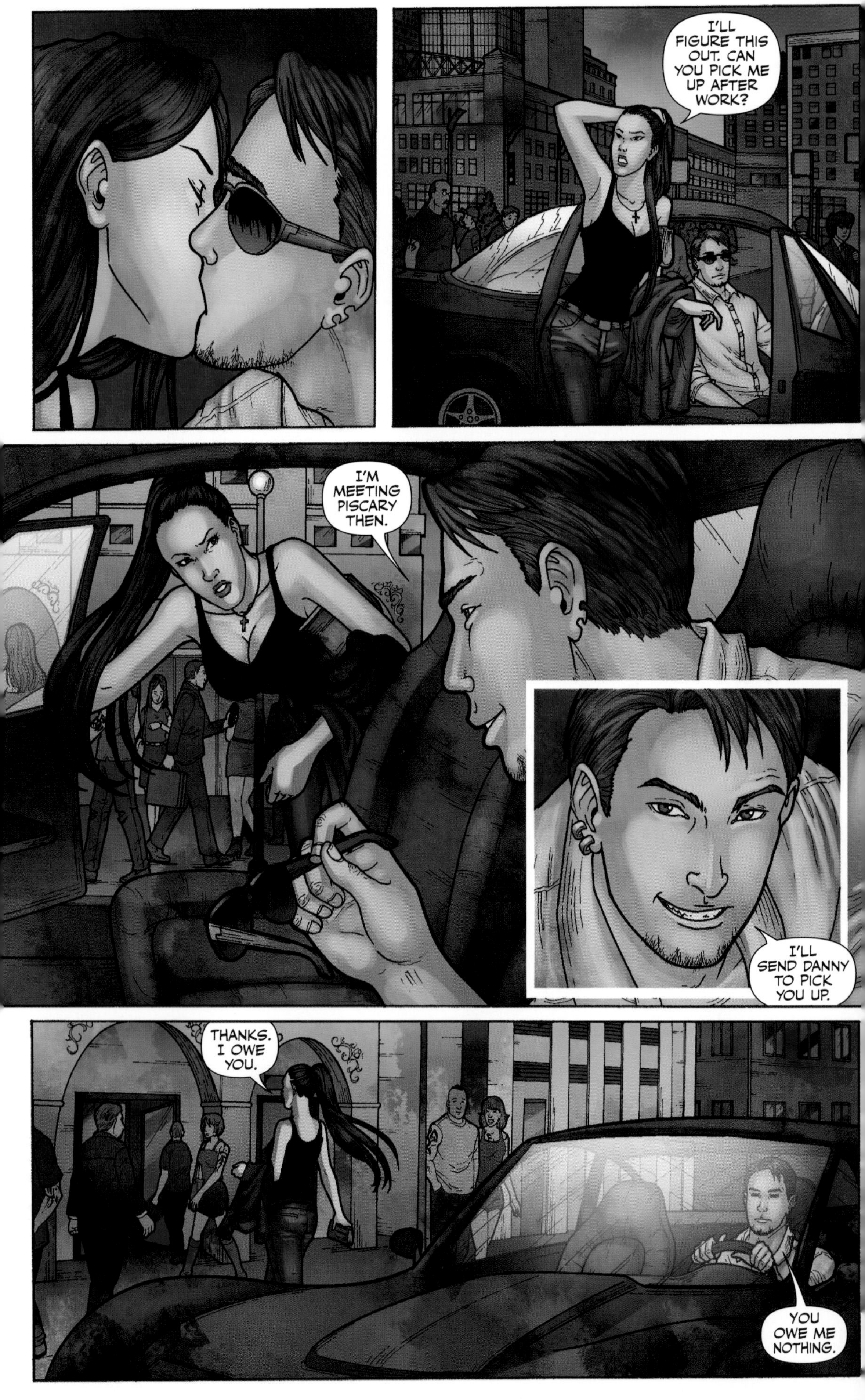
I'LL FIGURE THIS OUT. CAN YOU PICK ME UP AFTER WORK?
I'M MEETING PISCARY THEN.
I'LL SEND DANNY TO PICK YOU UP.
THANKS. I OWE YOU.
YOU OWE ME NOTHING.

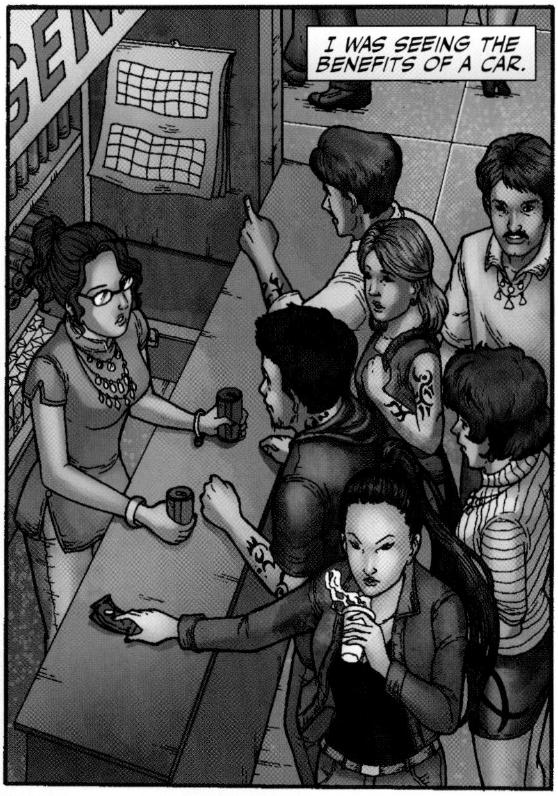
I WAS SEEING THE BENEFITS OF A CAR.

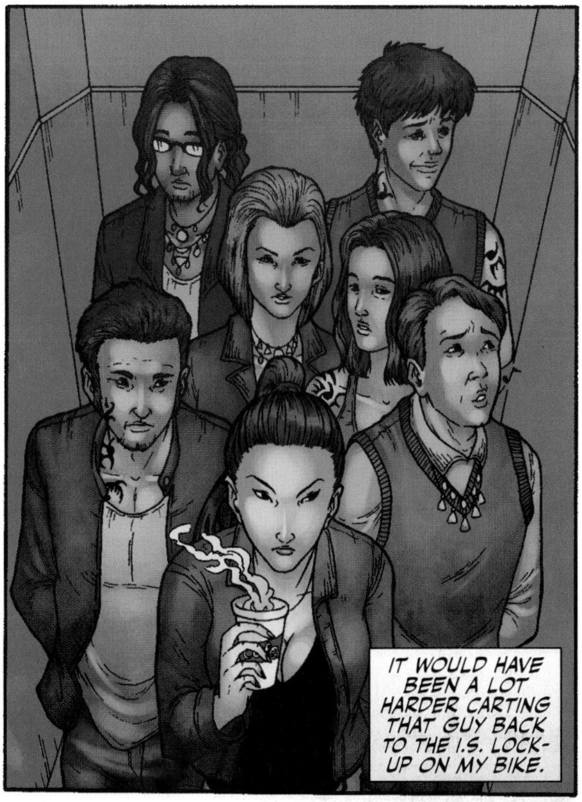
IT WOULD HAVE BEEN A LOT HARDER CARTING THAT GUY BACK TO THE I.S. LOCK-UP ON MY BIKE.

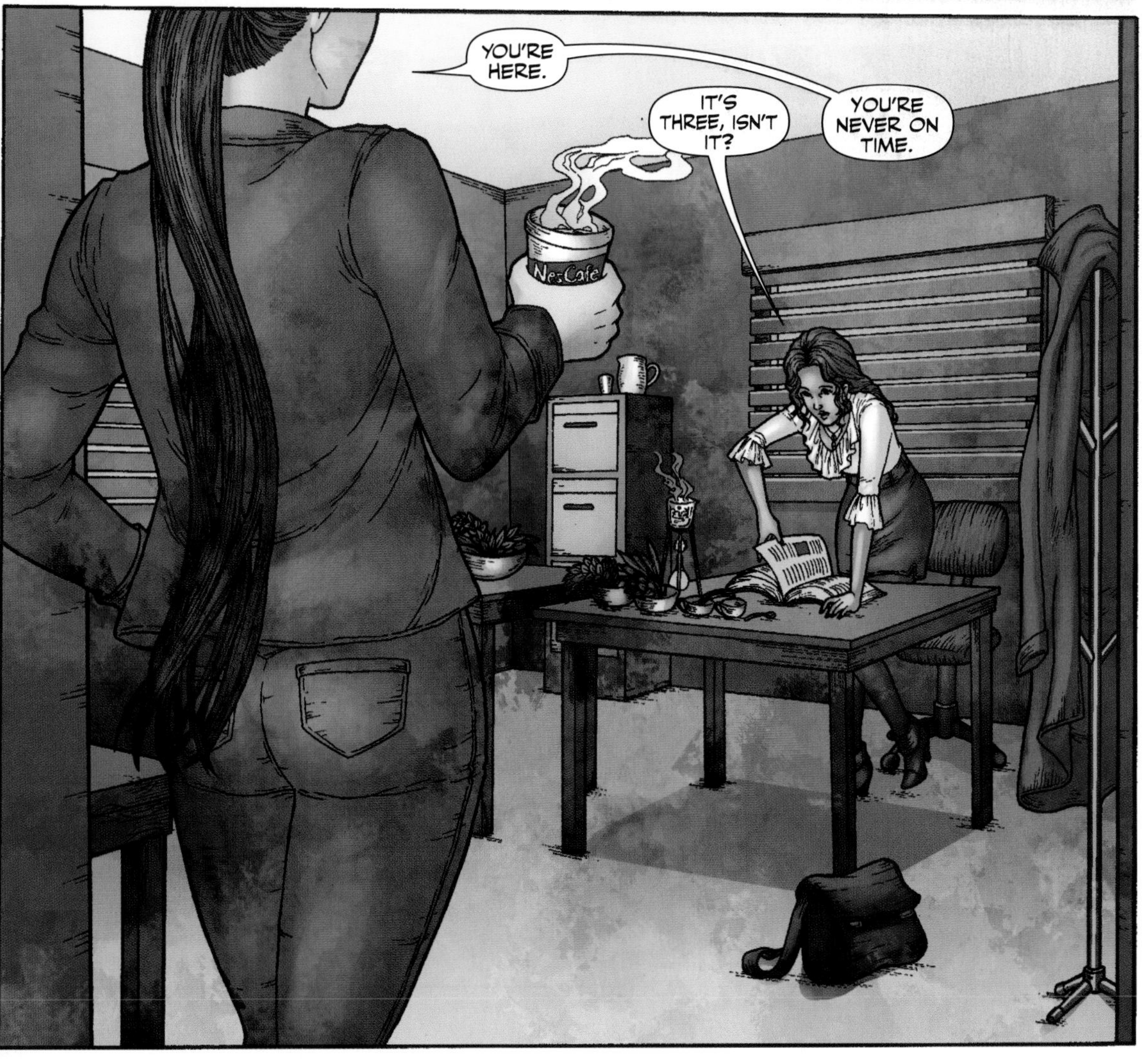
YOU'RE HERE.
IT'S THREE, ISN'T IT?
YOU'RE NEVER ON TIME.
NesCafe

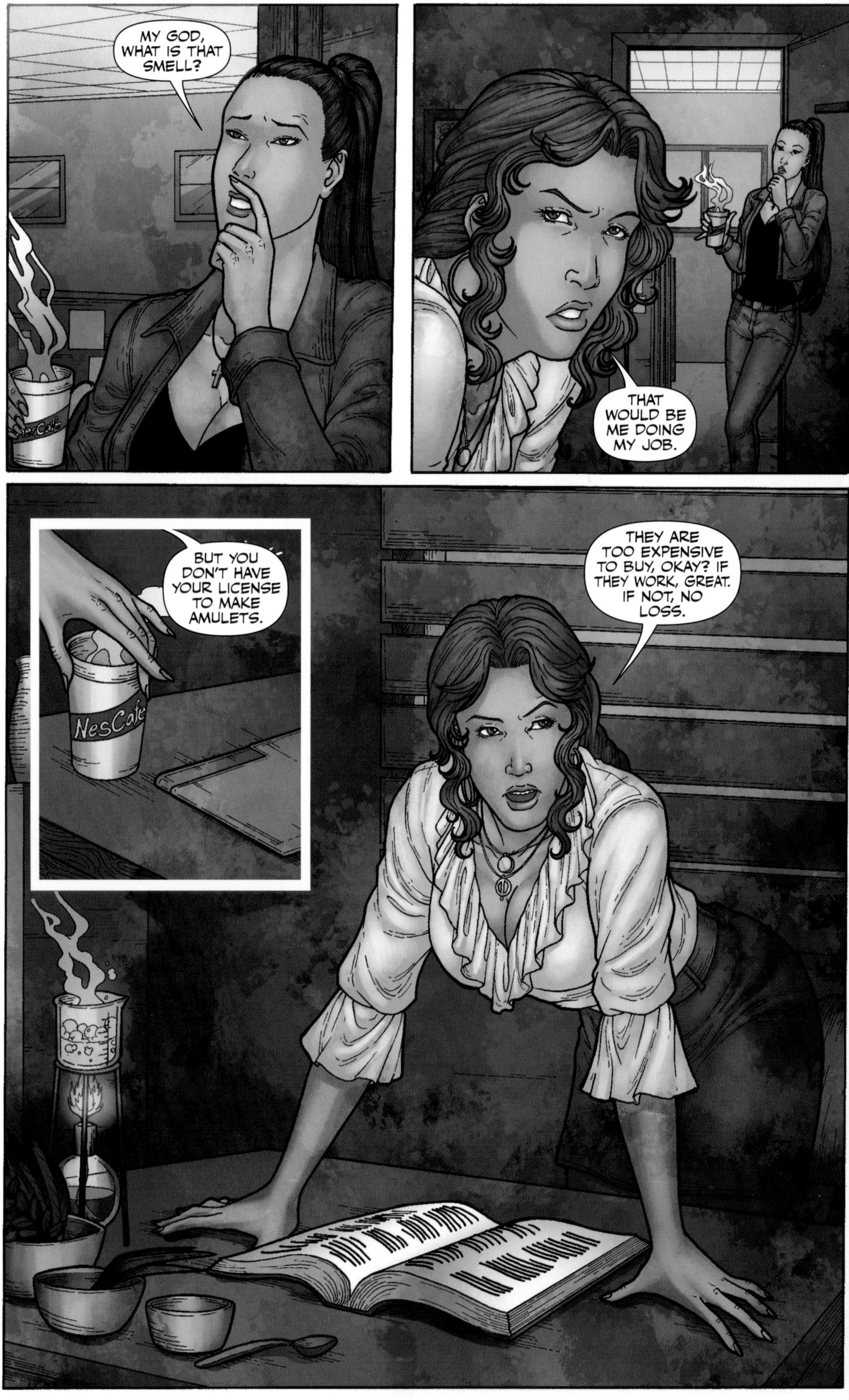
MY GOD, WHAT IS THAT SMELL?
THAT WOULD BE ME DOING MY JOB.
BUT YOU DON'T HAVE YOUR LICENSE TO MAKE AMULETS.
NesCafe
THEY ARE TOO EXPENSIVE TO BUY, OKAY? IF THEY WORK, GREAT. IF NOT, NO LOSS.

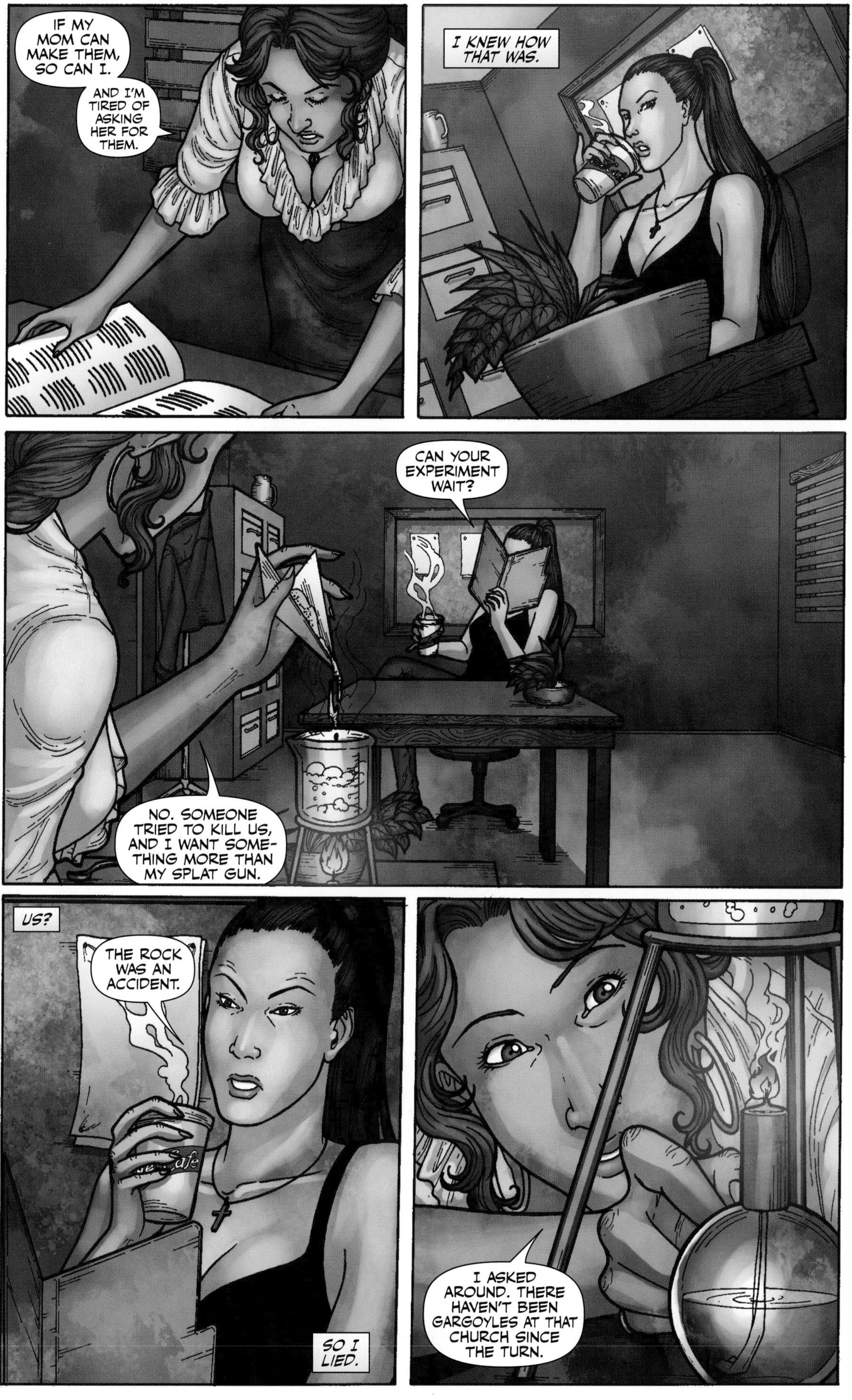
IF MY MOM CAN MAKE THEM, SO CAN I.
AND I'M TIRED OF ASKING HER FOR THEM.
I KNEW HOW THAT WAS.
CAN YOUR EXPERIMENT WAIT?
NO. SOMEONE TRIED TO KILL US, AND I WANT SOME-THING MORE THAN MY SPLAT GUN.
US?
THE ROCK WAS AN ACCIDENT.
SO I LIED.
I ASKED AROUND. THERE HAVEN'T BEEN GARGOYLES AT THAT CHURCH SINCE THE TURN.

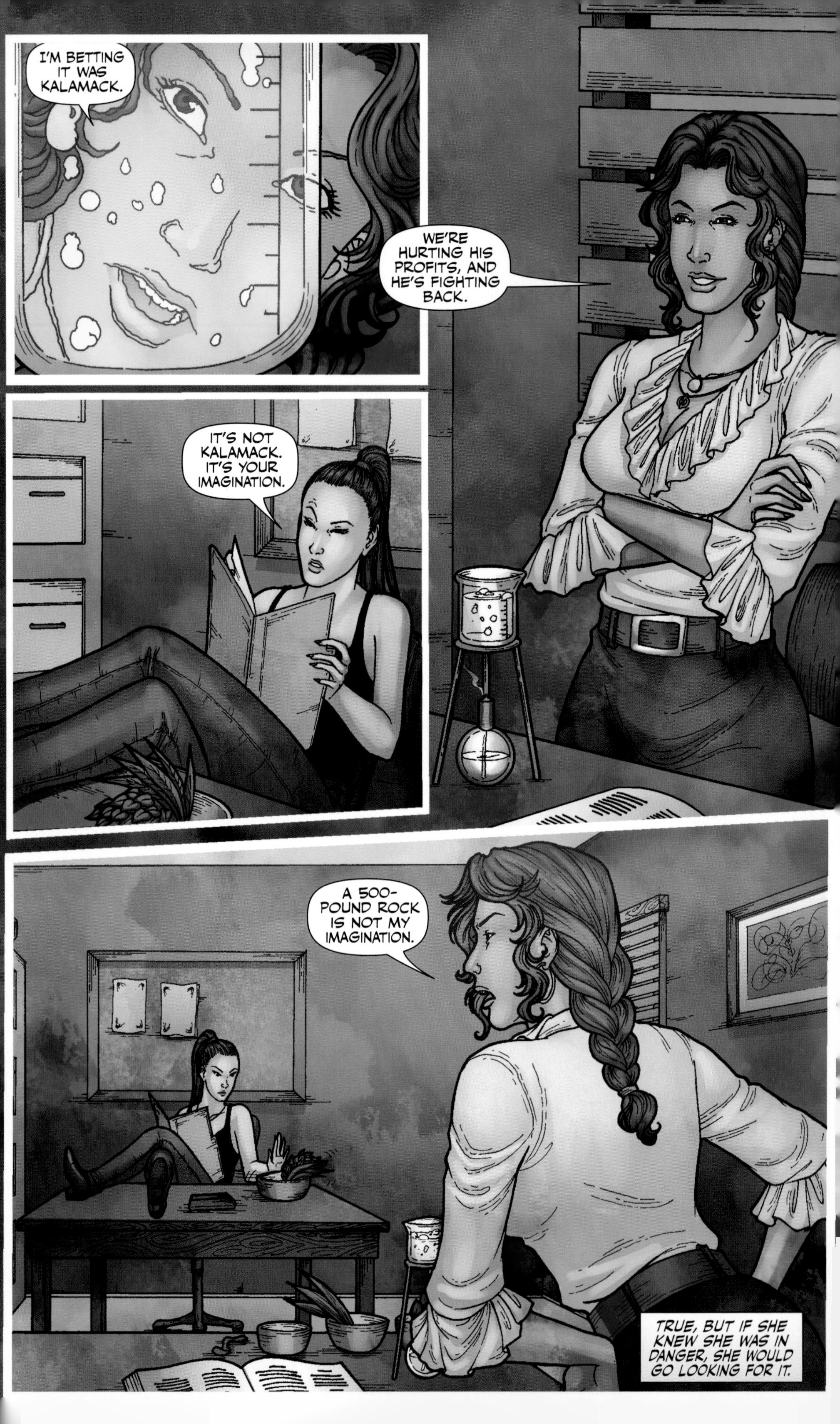
I'M BETTING IT WAS KALAMACK.
WE'RE HURTING HIS PROFITS, AND HE'S FIGHTING BACK.
IT'S NOT KALAMACK. IT'S YOUR IMAGINATION.
A 500-POUND ROCK IS NOT MY IMAGINATION.
TRUE, BUT IF SHE KNEW SHE WAS IN DANGER, SHE WOULD GO LOOKING FOR IT.

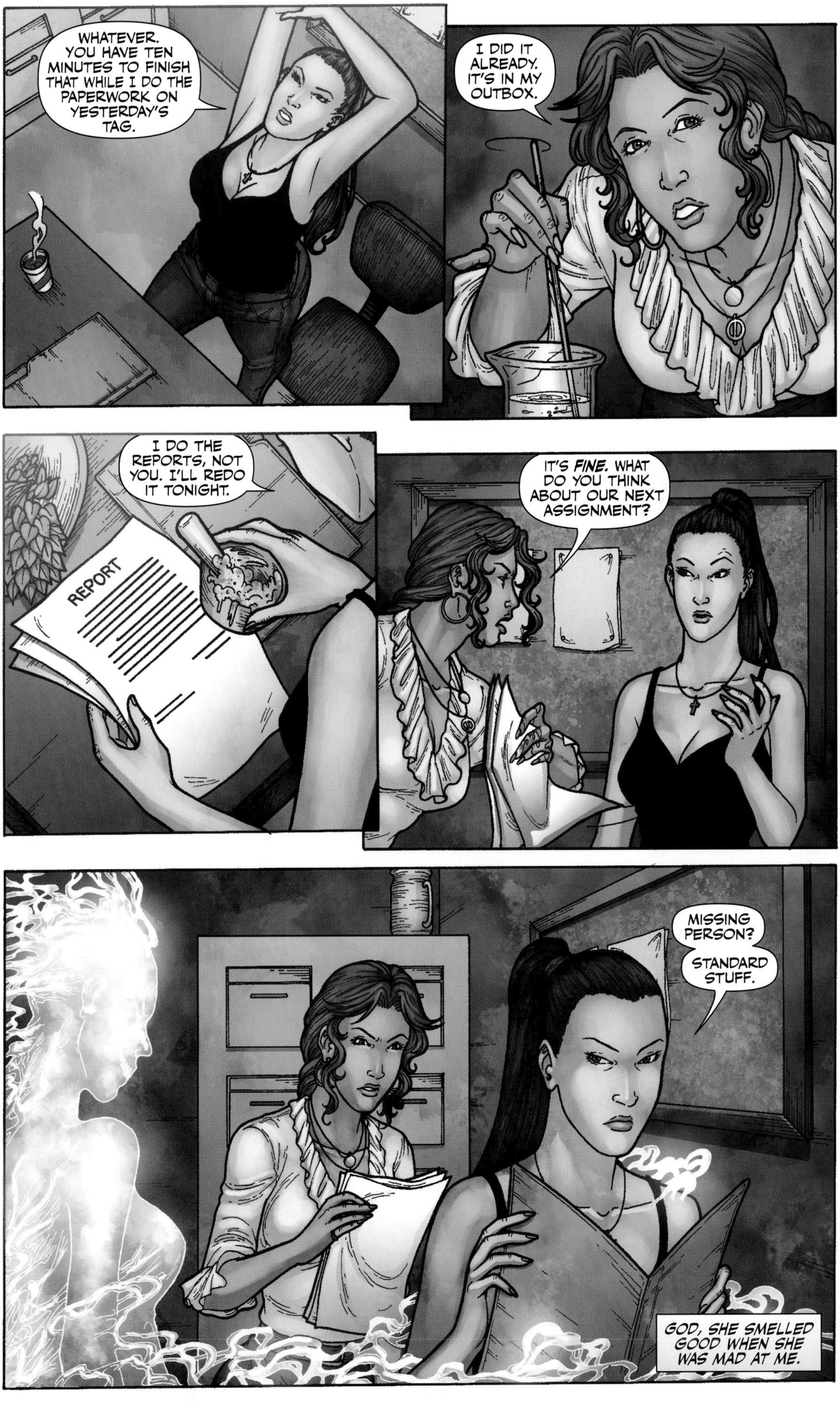
WHATEVER. YOU HAVE TEN MINUTES TO FINISH THAT WHILE I DO THE PAPERWORK ON YESTERDAY'S TAG.
I DID IT ALREADY. IT'S IN MY OUTBOX.
I DO THE REPORTS, NOT YOU. I'LL REDO IT TONIGHT.
REPORT
IT'S *FINE.* WHAT DO YOU THINK ABOUT OUR NEXT ASSIGNMENT?
MISSING PERSON?
STANDARD STUFF.
GOD, SHE SMELLED GOOD WHEN SHE WAS MAD AT ME.

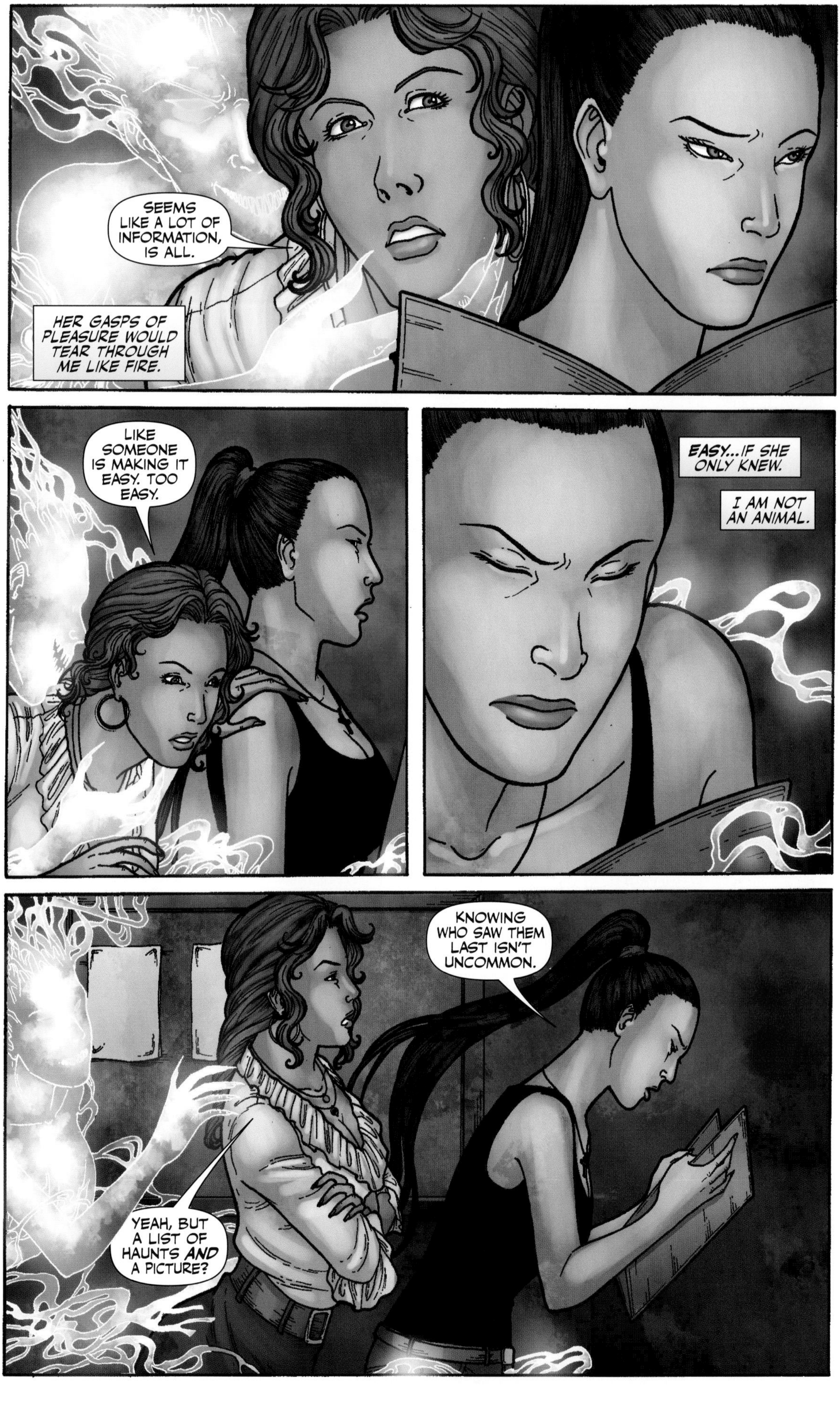
SEEMS LIKE A LOT OF INFORMATION, IS ALL.
HER GASPS OF PLEASURE WOULD TEAR THROUGH ME LIKE FIRE.
LIKE SOMEONE IS MAKING IT EASY. TOO EASY.
EASY...IF SHE ONLY KNEW.
I AM NOT AN ANIMAL.
KNOWING WHO SAW THEM LAST ISN'T UNCOMMON.
YEAH, BUT A LIST OF HAUNTS AND A PICTURE?

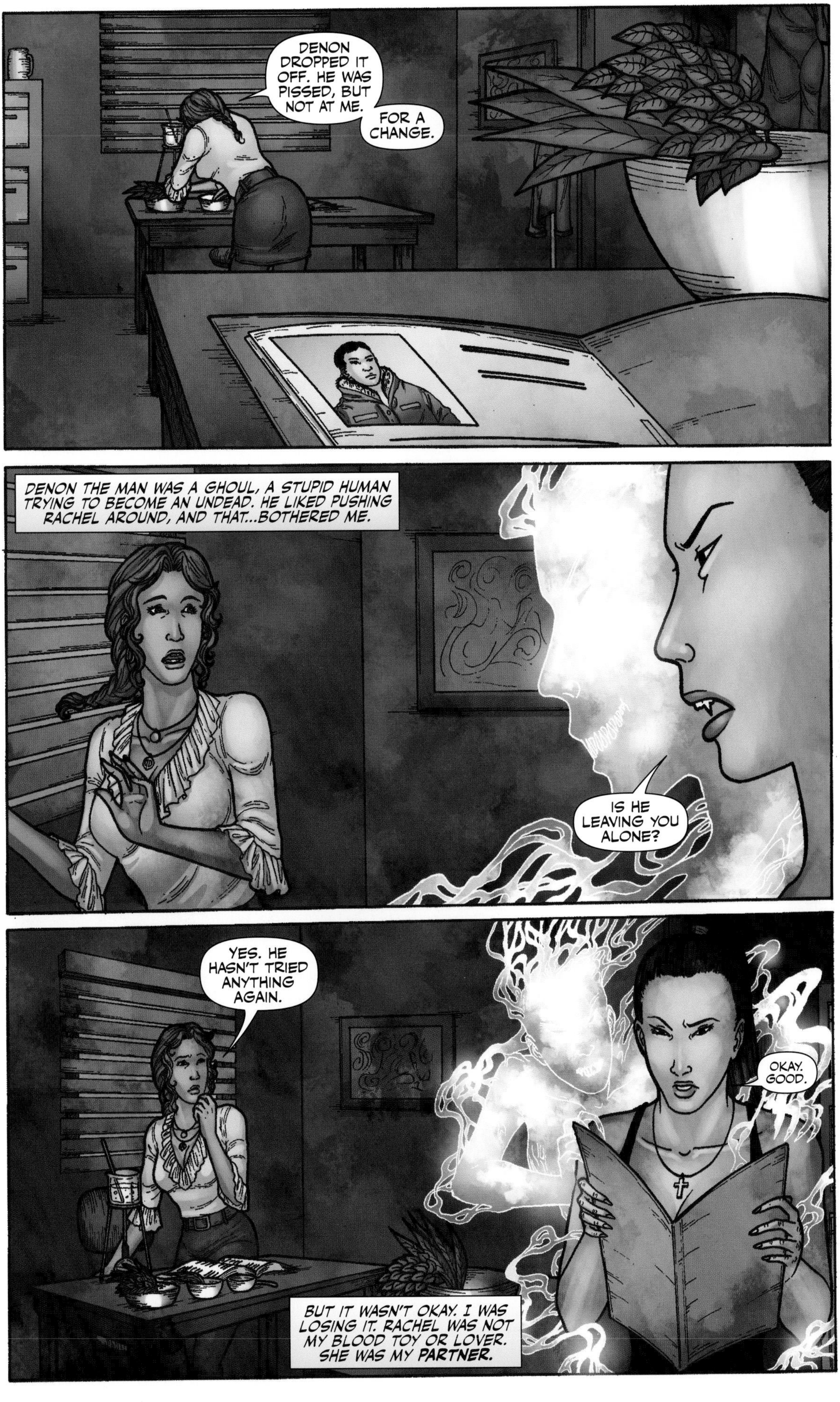
DENON DROPPED IT OFF. HE WAS PISSED, BUT NOT AT ME.
FOR A CHANGE.
DENON THE MAN WAS A GHOUL, A STUPID HUMAN TRYING TO BECOME AN UNDEAD. HE LIKED PUSHING RACHEL AROUND, AND THAT...BOTHERED ME.
IS HE LEAVING YOU ALONE?
YES. HE HASN'T TRIED ANYTHING AGAIN.
OKAY. GOOD.
BUT IT WASN'T OKAY. I WAS LOSING IT. RACHEL WAS NOT MY BLOOD TOY OR LOVER. SHE WAS MY PARTNER.

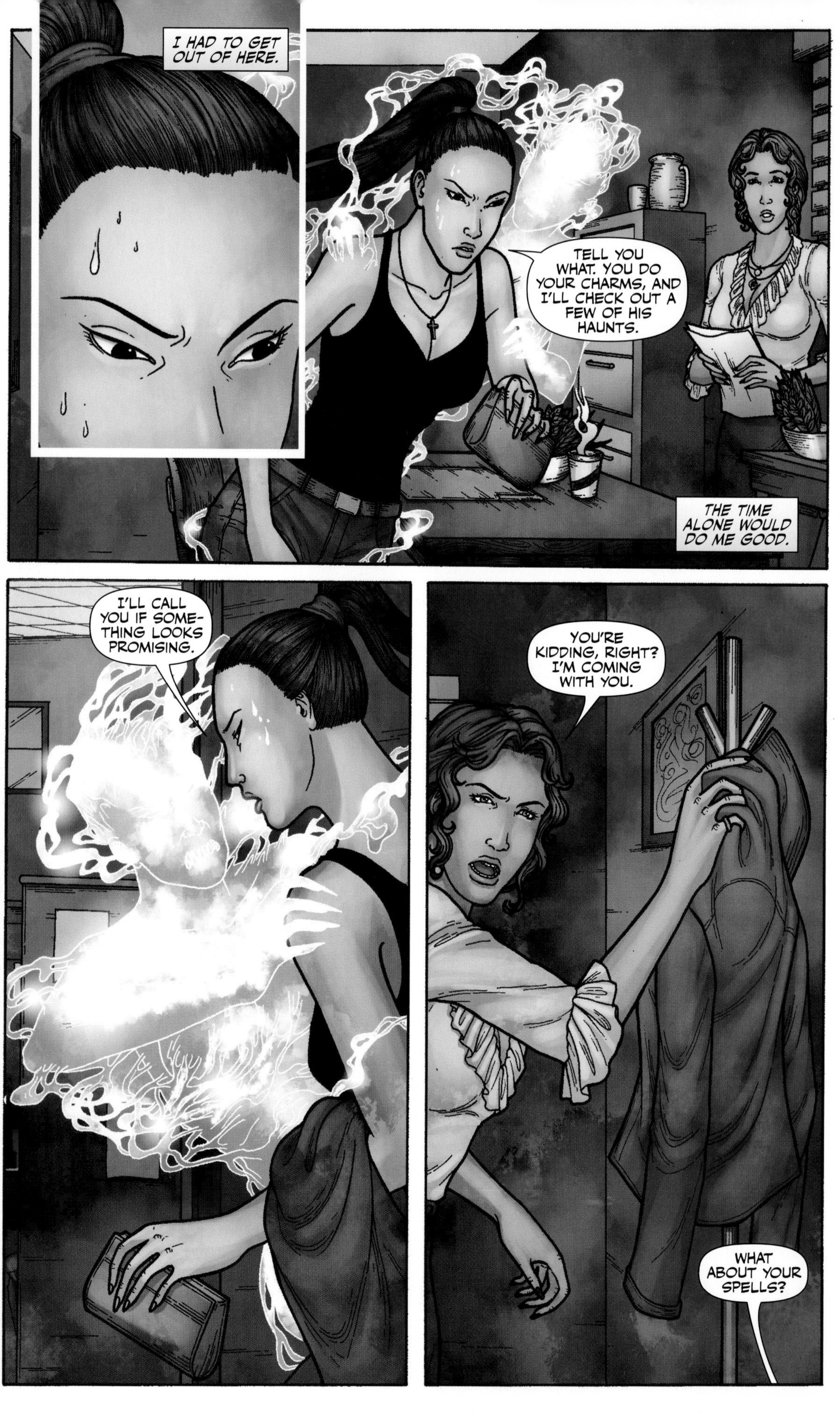
I HAD TO GET OUT OF HERE.
TELL YOU WHAT. YOU DO YOUR CHARMS, AND I'LL CHECK OUT A FEW OF HIS HAUNTS.
THE TIME ALONE WOULD DO ME GOOD.
I'LL CALL YOU IF SOMETHING LOOKS PROMISING.
YOU'RE KIDDING, RIGHT? I'M COMING WITH YOU.
WHAT ABOUT YOUR SPELLS?

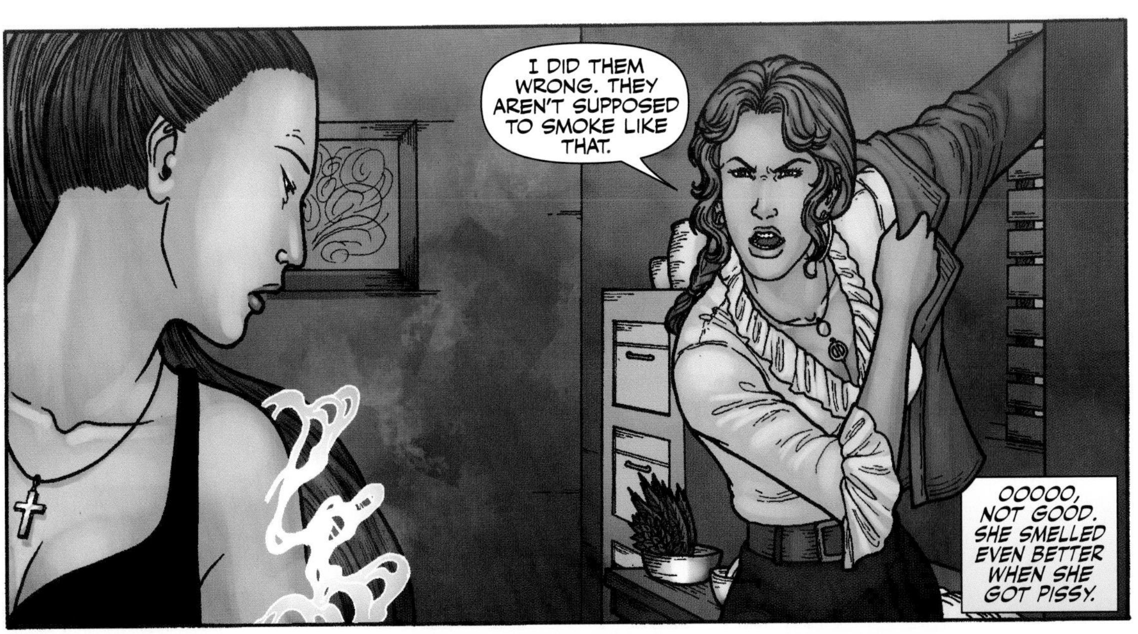
I DID THEM WRONG. THEY AREN'T SUPPOSED TO SMOKE LIKE THAT.
OOOOO, NOT GOOD. SHE SMELLED EVEN BETTER WHEN SHE GOT PISSY.

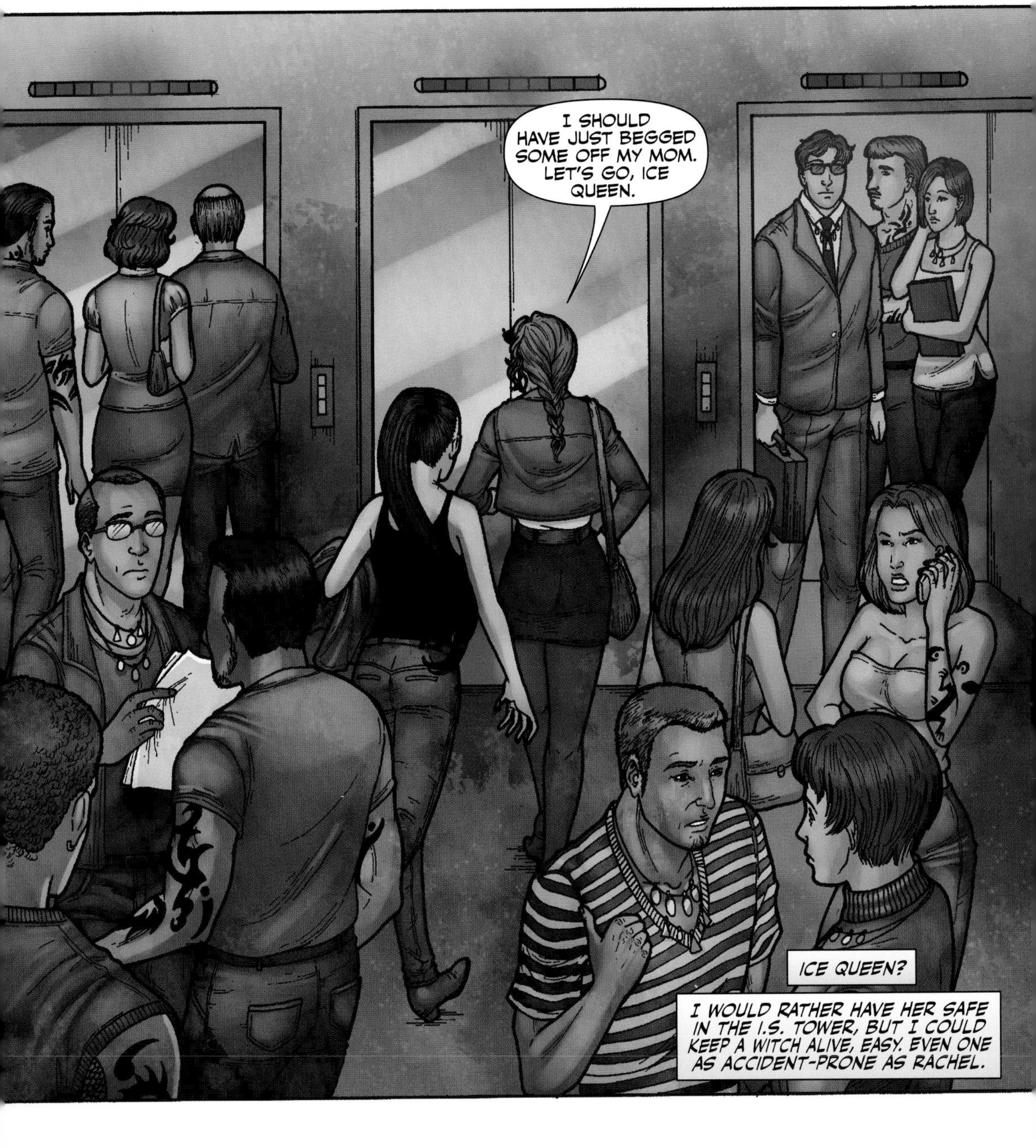
I SHOULD HAVE JUST BEGGED SOME OFF MY MOM. LET'S GO, ICE QUEEN.
ICE QUEEN?
I WOULD RATHER HAVE HER SAFE IN THE I.S. TOWER, BUT I COULD KEEP A WITCH ALIVE, EASY. EVEN ONE AS ACCIDENT-PRONE AS RACHEL.

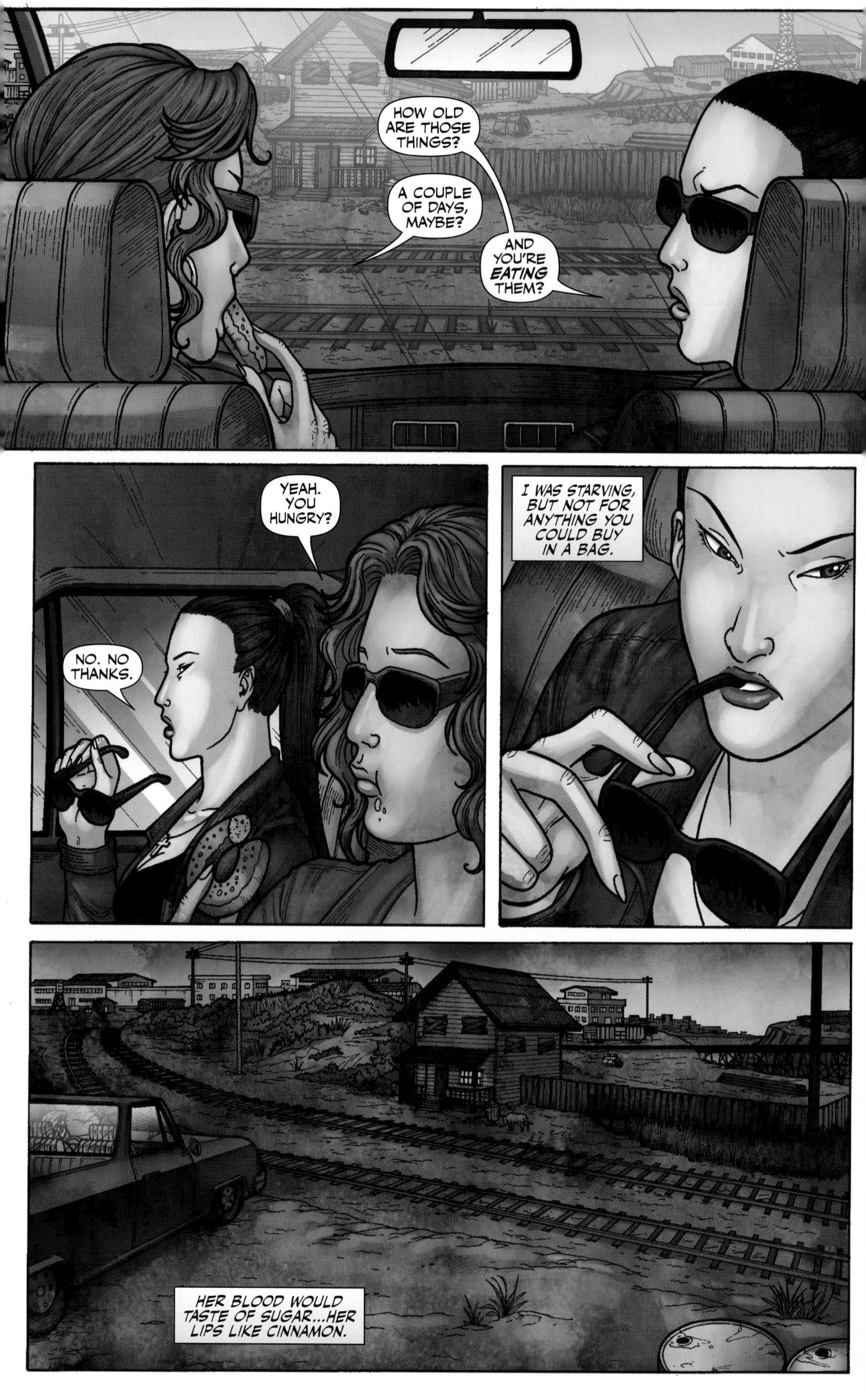
HOW OLD ARE THOSE THINGS?
A COUPLE OF DAYS, MAYBE?
AND YOU'RE *EATING* THEM?
YEAH. YOU HUNGRY?
NO. NO THANKS.
I WAS STARVING, BUT NOT FOR ANYTHING YOU COULD BUY IN A BAG.
HER BLOOD WOULD TASTE OF SUGAR...HER LIPS LIKE CINNAMON.

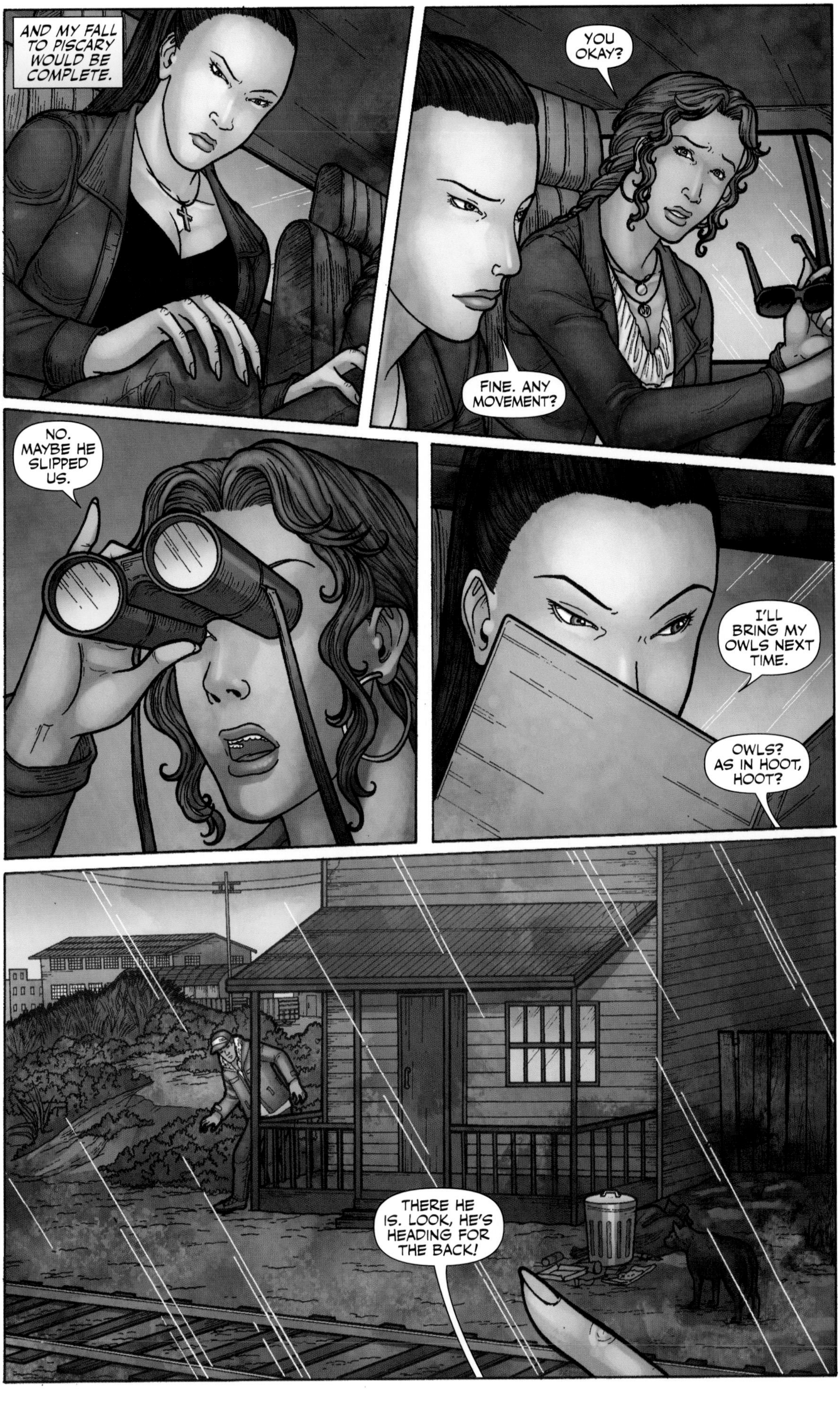
AND MY FALL TO PISCARY WOULD BE COMPLETE.
YOU OKAY?
FINE. ANY MOVEMENT?
NO. MAYBE HE SLIPPED US.
I'LL BRING MY OWLS NEXT TIME.
OWLS? AS IN HOOT, HOOT?
THERE HE IS. LOOK, HE'S HEADING FOR THE BACK!

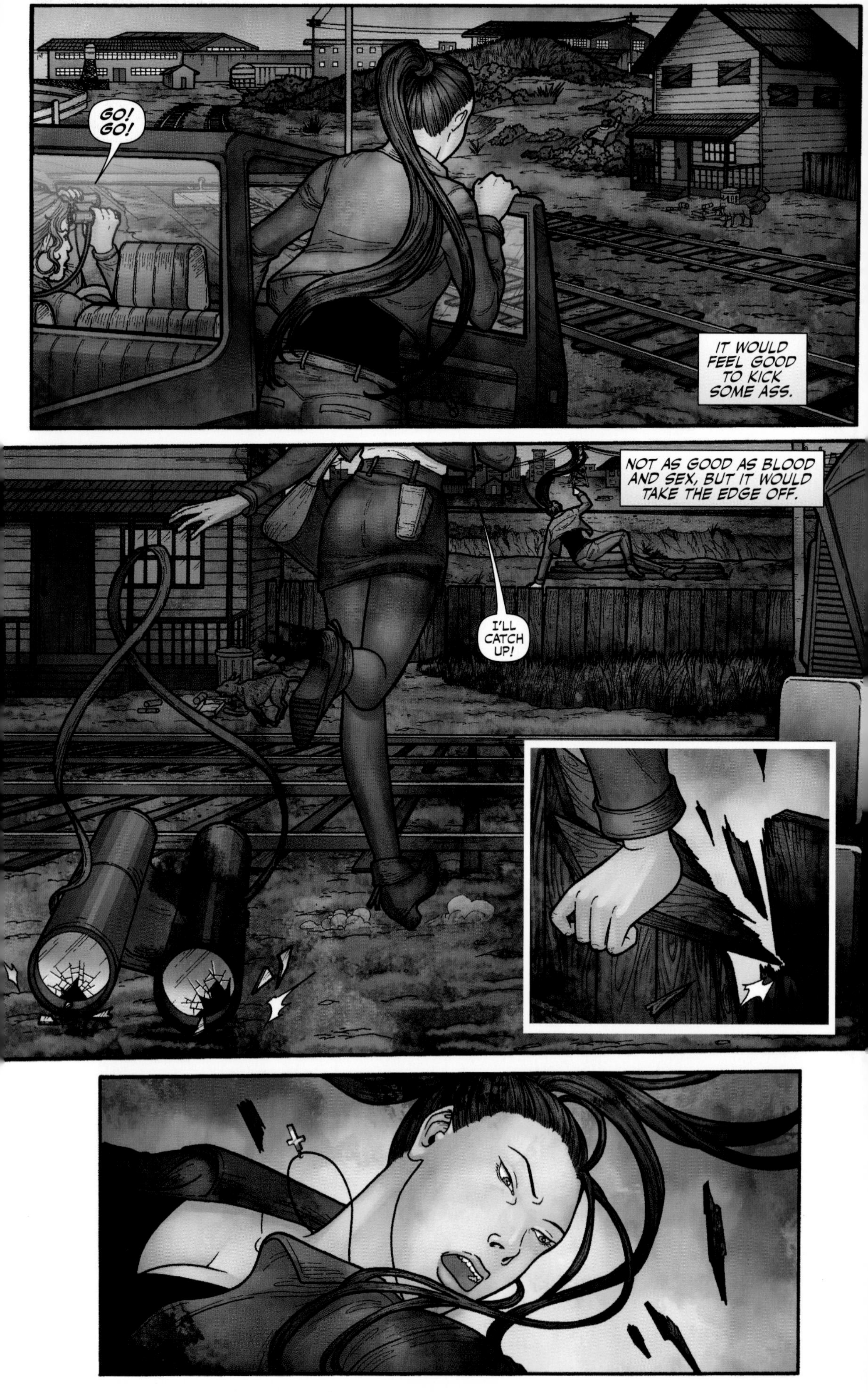
GO! GO!
IT WOULD FEEL GOOD TO KICK SOME ASS.
NOT AS GOOD AS BLOOD AND SEX, BUT IT WOULD TAKE THE EDGE OFF.
I'LL CATCH UP!

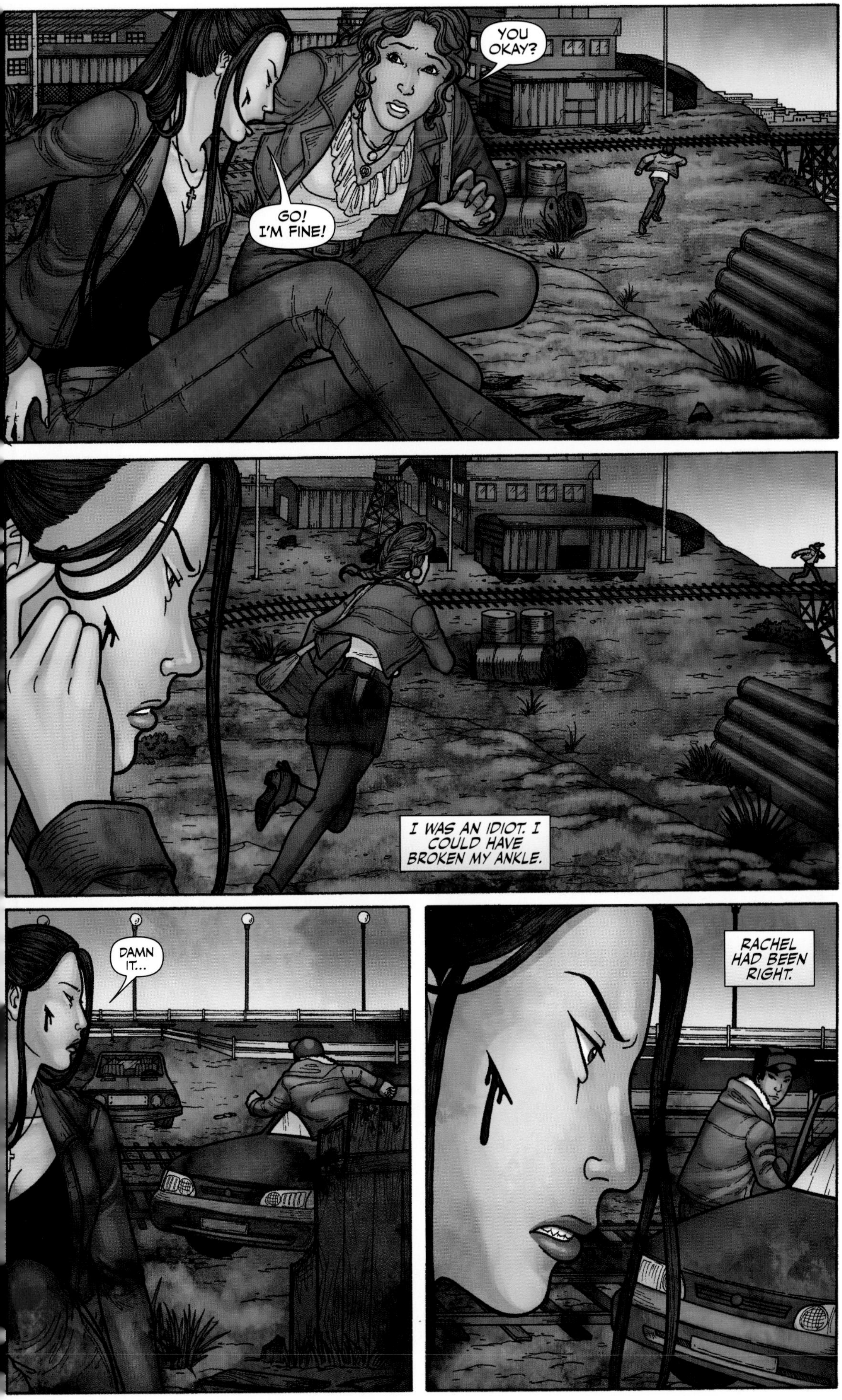

YOU OKAY?
GO! I'M FINE!
I WAS AN IDIOT. I COULD HAVE BROKEN MY ANKLE.
DAMN IT...
RACHEL HAD BEEN RIGHT.

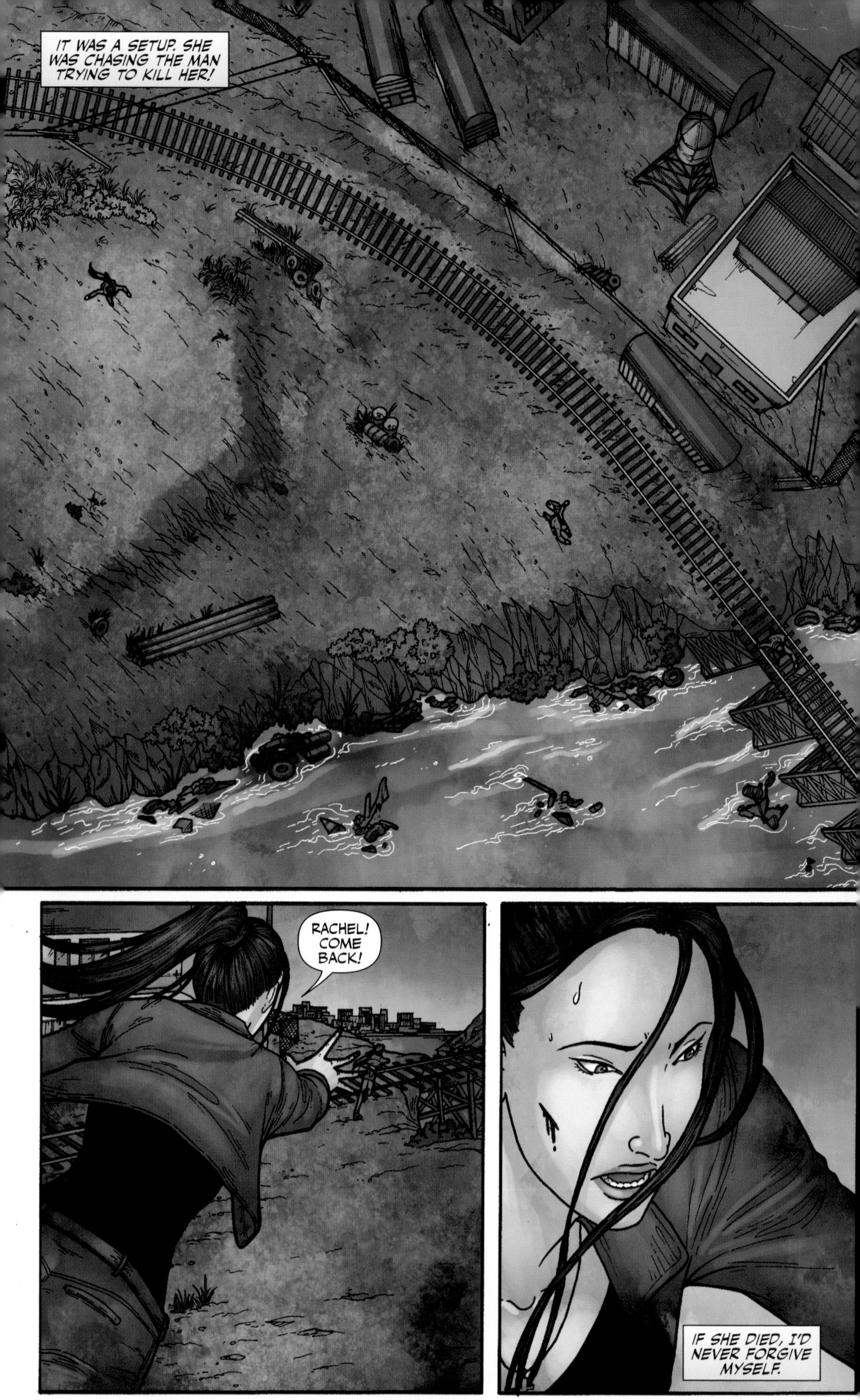
IT WAS A SETUP. SHE WAS CHASING THE MAN TRYING TO KILL HER!
RACHEL! COME BACK!
IF SHE DIED, I'D NEVER FORGIVE MYSELF.

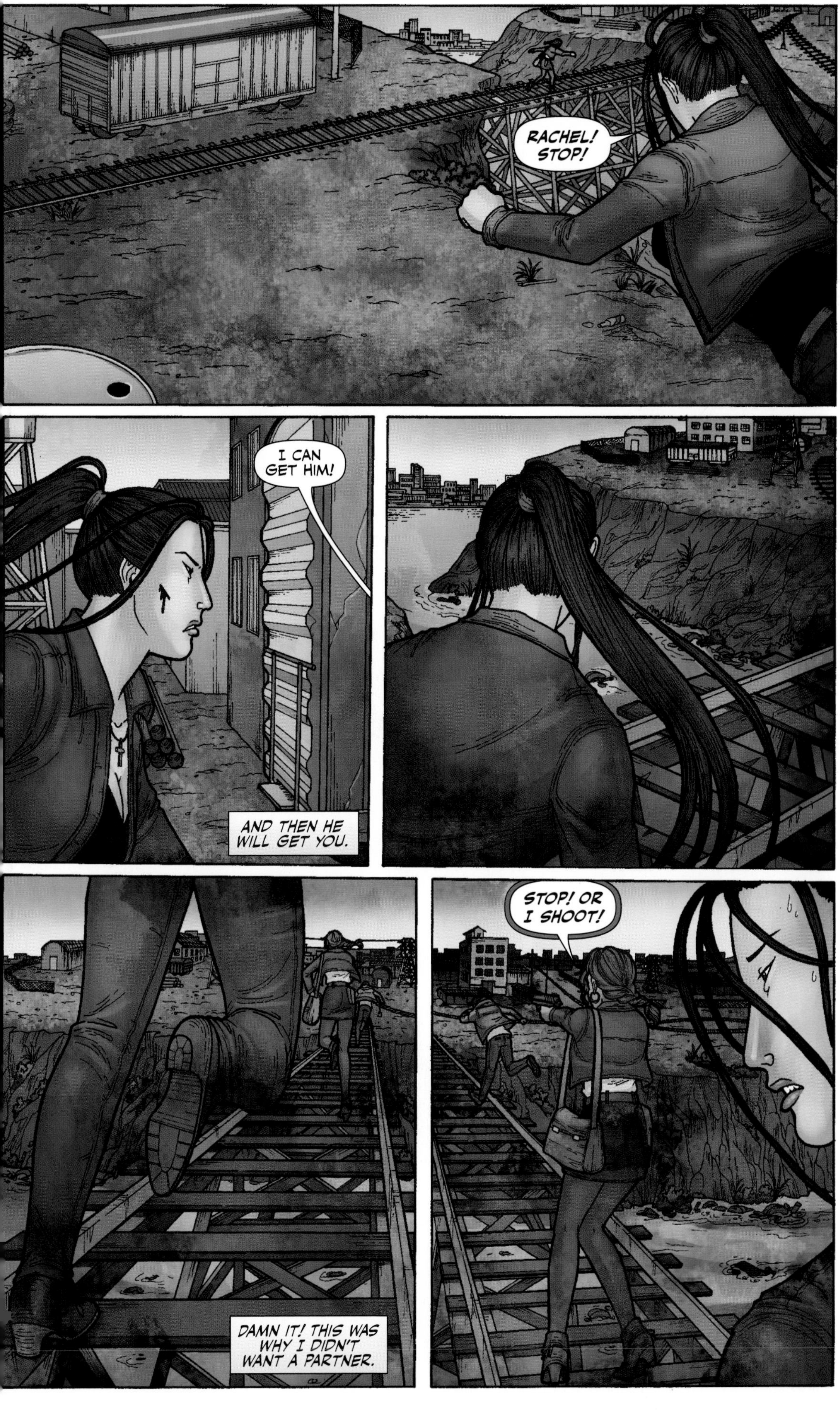

RACHEL! STOP!
I CAN GET HIM!
AND THEN HE WILL GET YOU.
DAMN IT! THIS WAS WHY I DIDN'T WANT A PARTNER.
STOP! OR I SHOOT!

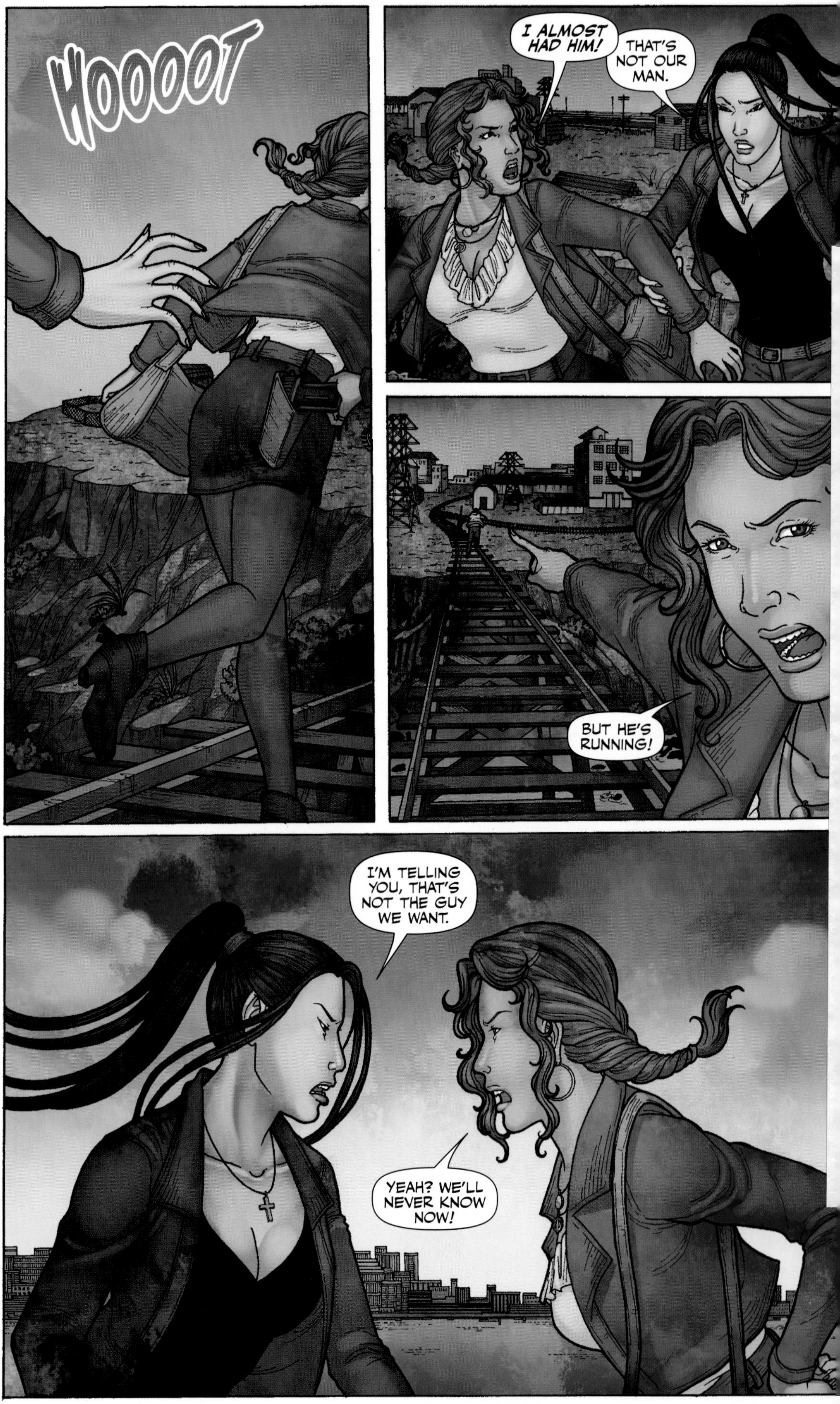
HOOOOT
I ALMOST HAD HIM!
THAT'S NOT OUR MAN.
BUT HE'S RUNNING!
I'M TELLING YOU, THAT'S NOT THE GUY WE WANT.
YEAH? WE'LL NEVER KNOW NOW!

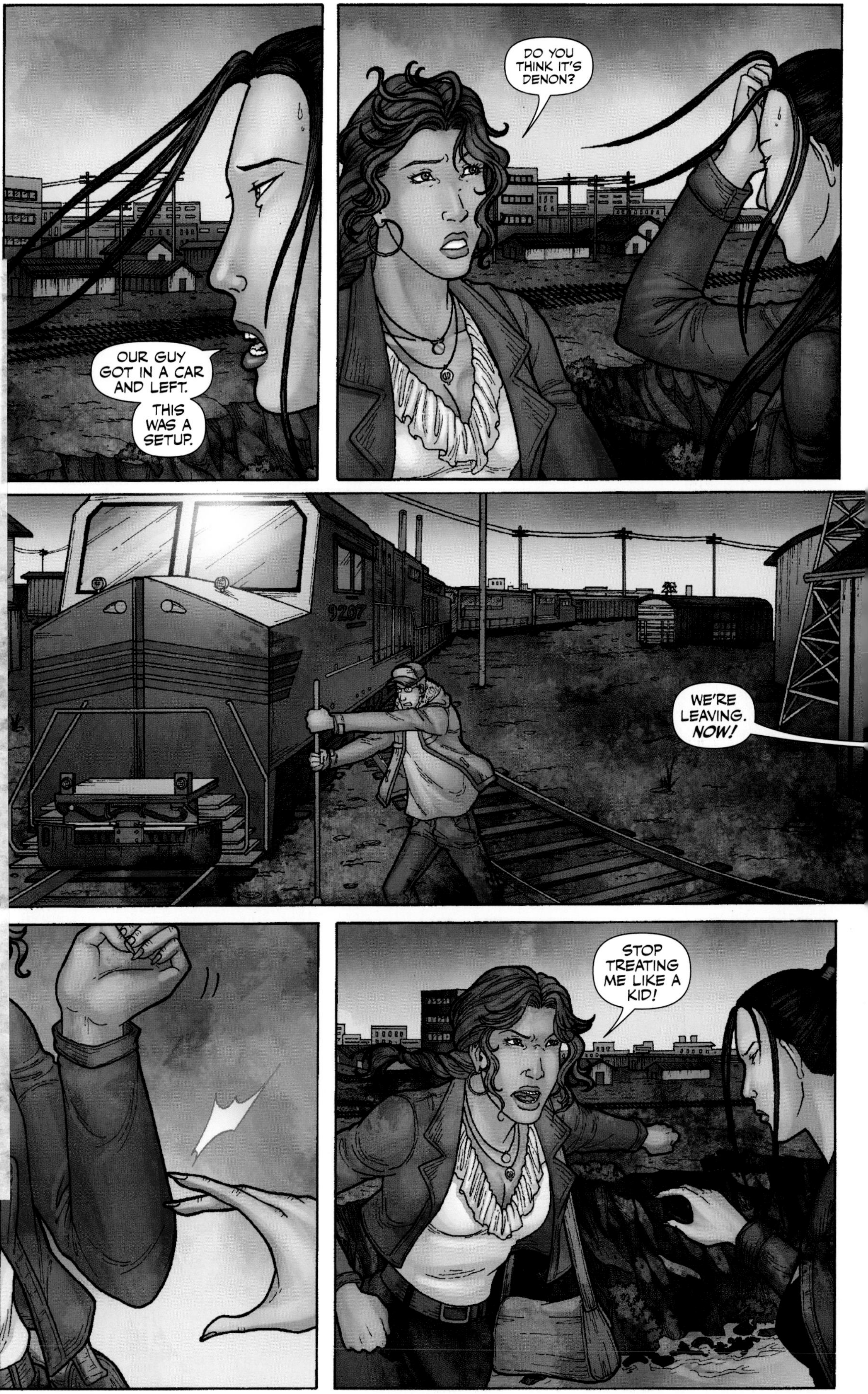
OUR GUY GOT IN A CAR AND LEFT.
THIS WAS A SETUP.
DO YOU THINK IT'S DENON?
WE'RE LEAVING. NOW!
STOP TREATING ME LIKE A KID!

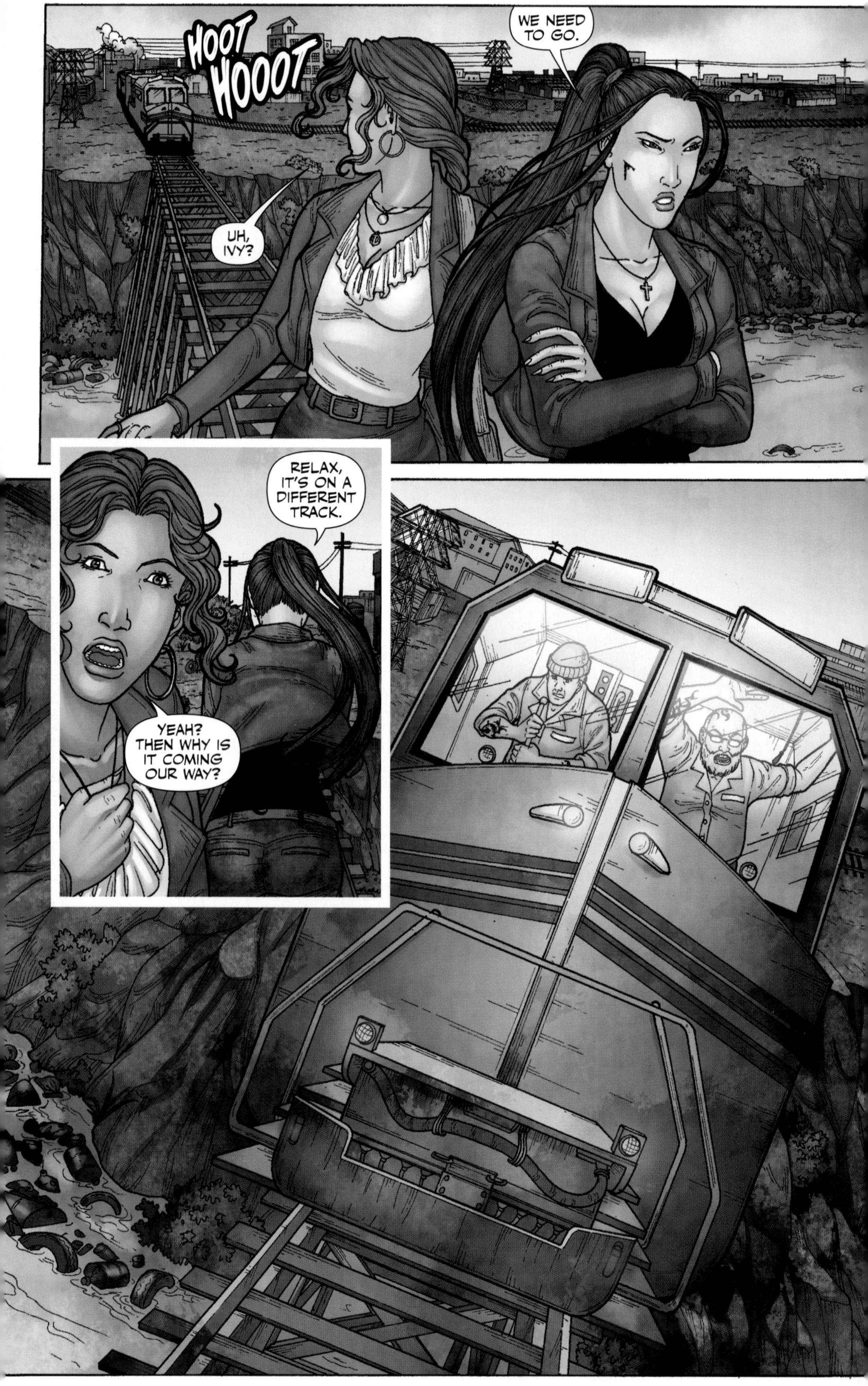
HOOT HOOOT
WE NEED TO GO.
UH, IVY?
RELAX, IT'S ON A DIFFERENT TRACK.
YEAH? THEN WHY IS IT COMING OUR WAY?

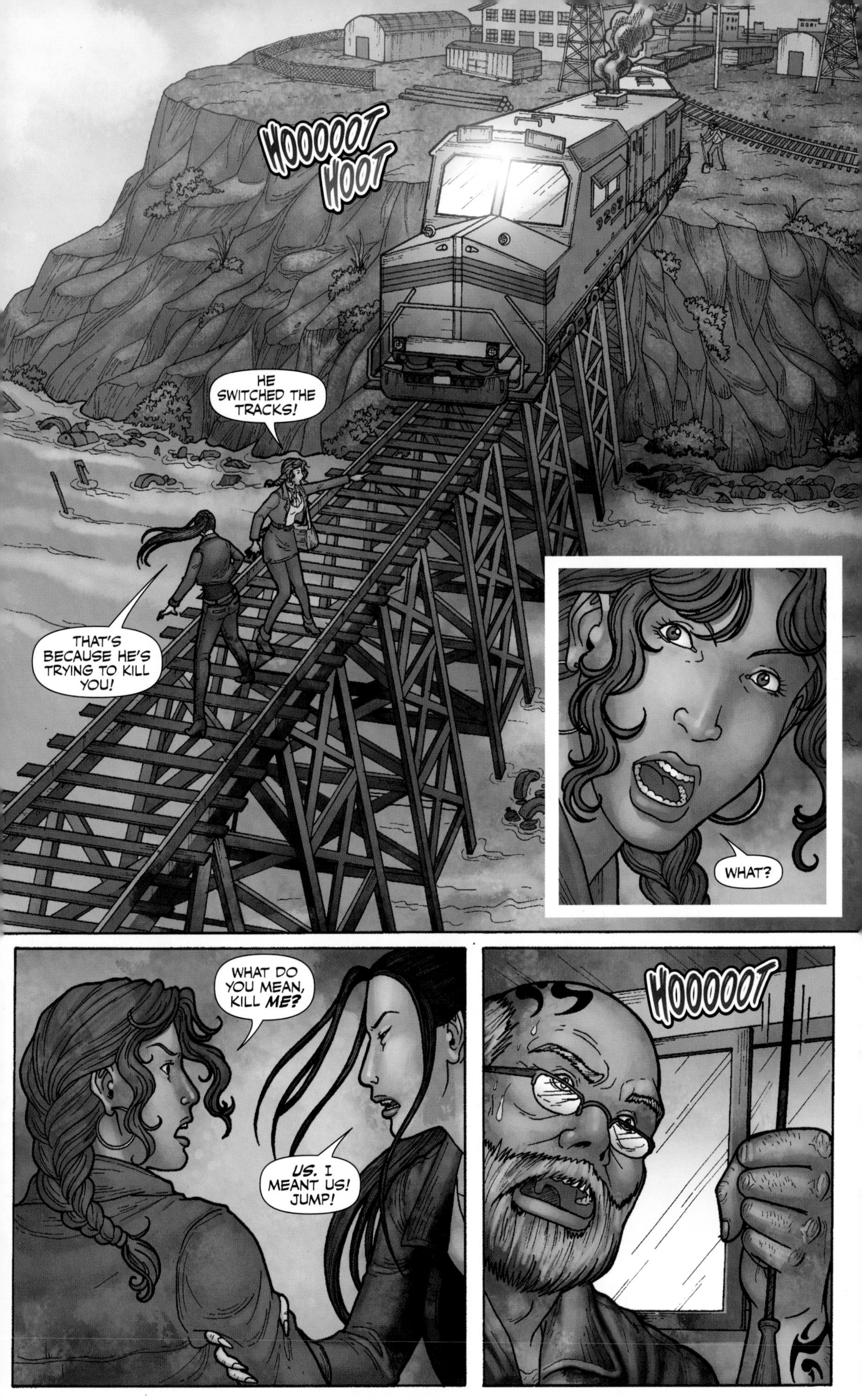
HOOOOOT HOOT
HE SWITCHED THE TRACKS!
THAT'S BECAUSE HE'S TRYING TO KILL YOU!
WHAT?
WHAT DO YOU MEAN, KILL ME?
US. I MEANT US! JUMP!
HOOOOOT

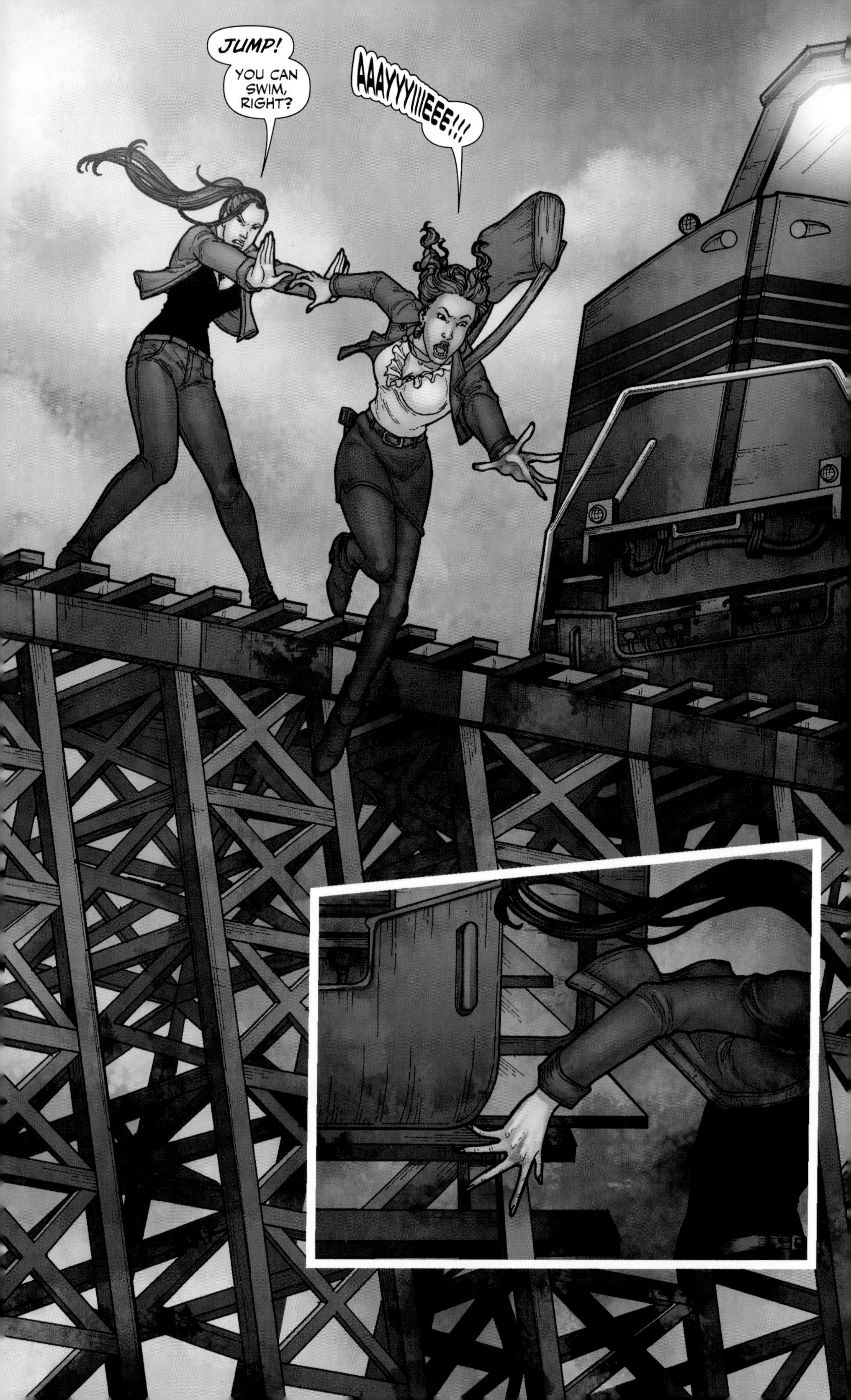
JUMP!
YOU CAN SWIM, RIGHT?
AAAYYYIIIIEEE!!!

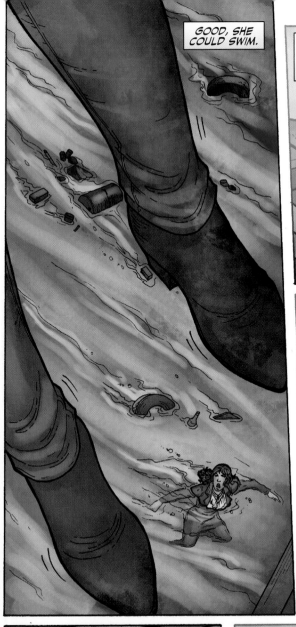

GOOD, SHE COULD SWIM.

I COULD SWIM TOO, WHEN THE OCCASION DEMANDED IT.

BUT I DIDN'T WANT TO END THIS RUN SOAKING WET LIKE OUR FIRST ONE.

SHIT...

YOU OKAY?!

YOU STUPID-ASS VAMPIRE...

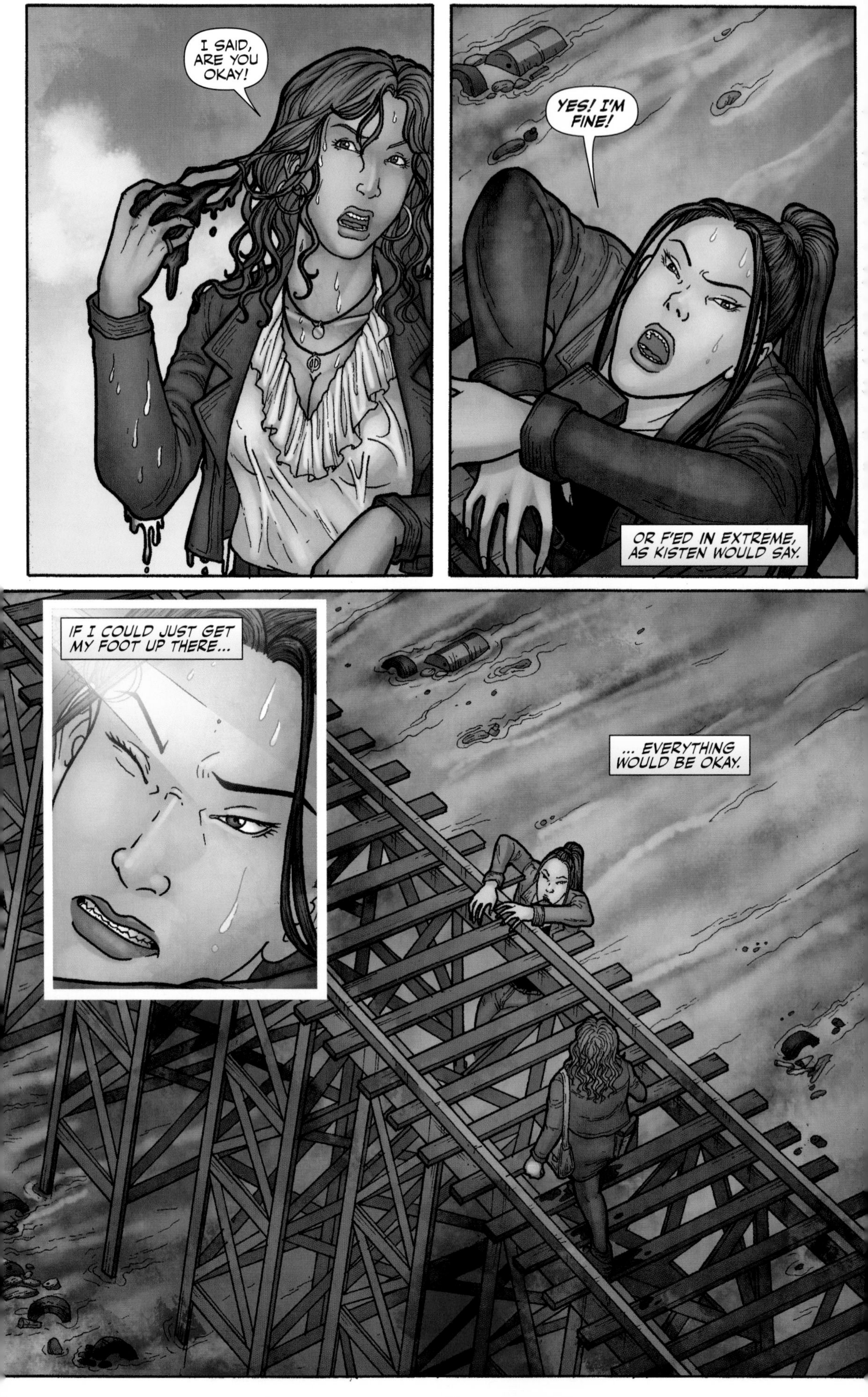
I SAID, ARE YOU OKAY!
YES! I'M FINE!
OR F'ED IN EXTREME, AS KISTEN WOULD SAY.
IF I COULD JUST GET MY FOOT UP THERE...
... EVERYTHING WOULD BE OKAY.

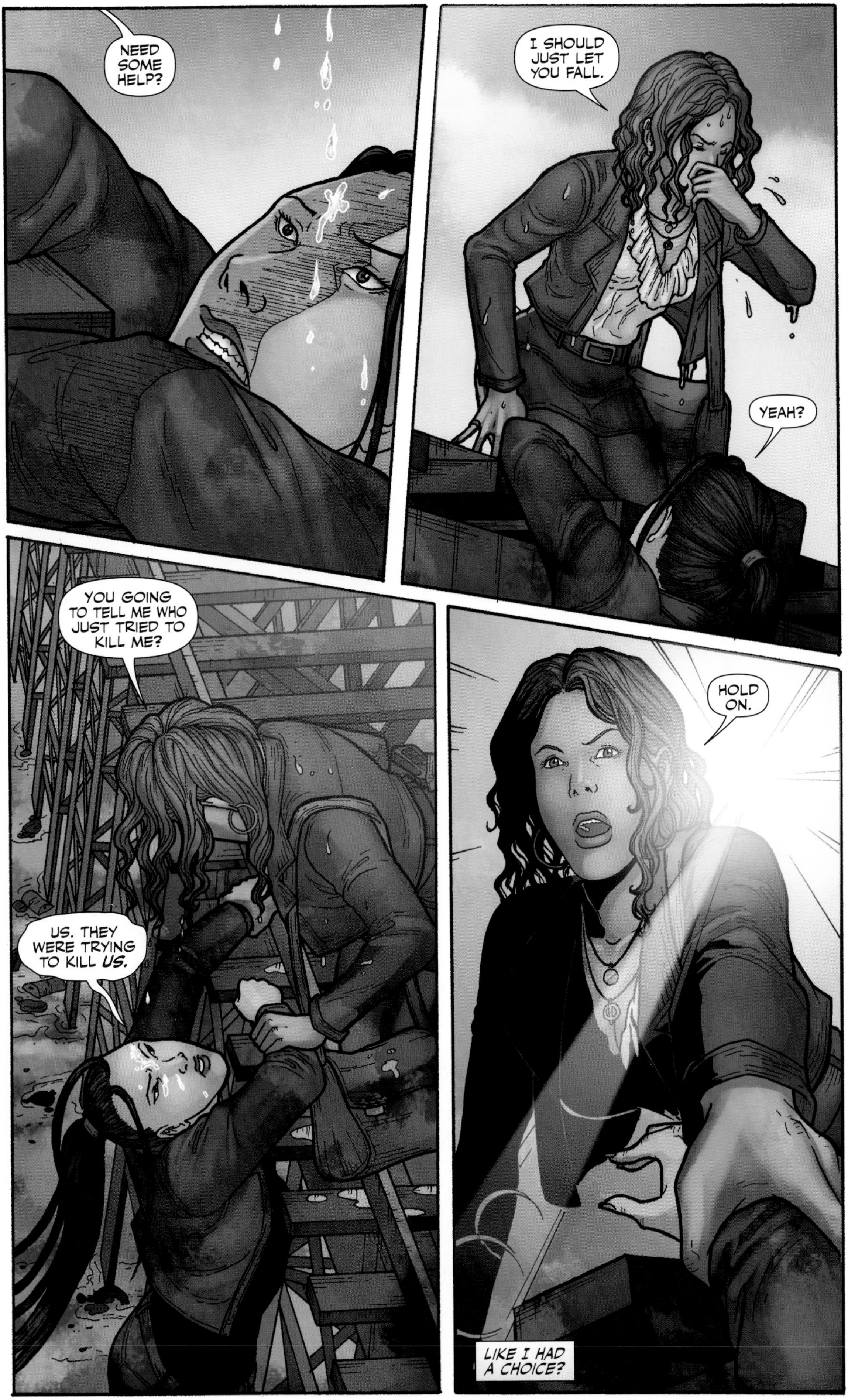
NEED SOME HELP?
I SHOULD JUST LET YOU FALL.
YEAH?
YOU GOING TO TELL ME WHO JUST TRIED TO KILL ME?
US. THEY WERE TRYING TO KILL *US.*
HOLD ON.
LIKE I HAD A CHOICE?

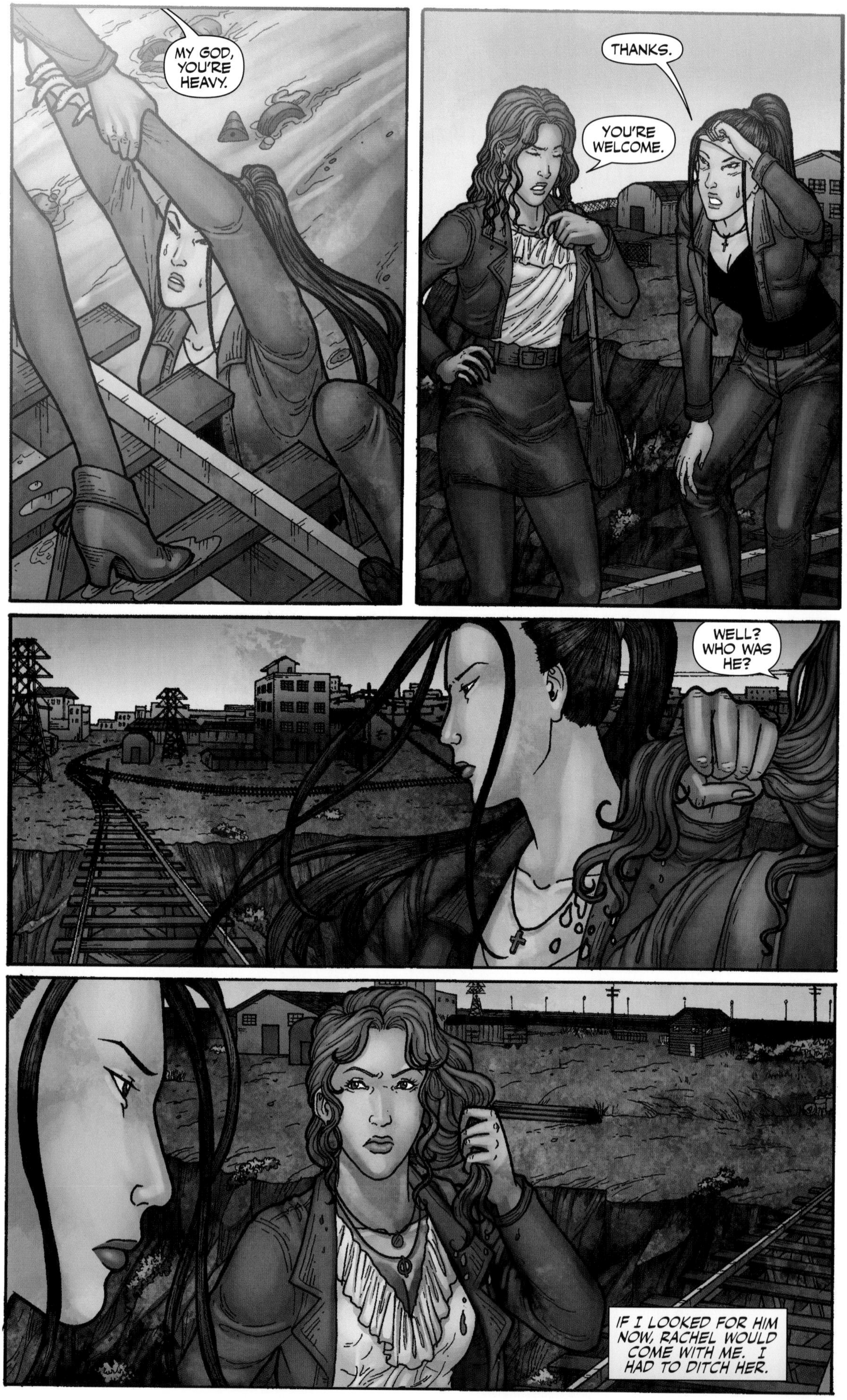
MY GOD, YOU'RE HEAVY.
THANKS.
YOU'RE WELCOME.
WELL? WHO WAS HE?
IF I LOOKED FOR HIM NOW, RACHEL WOULD COME WITH ME. I HAD TO DITCH HER.

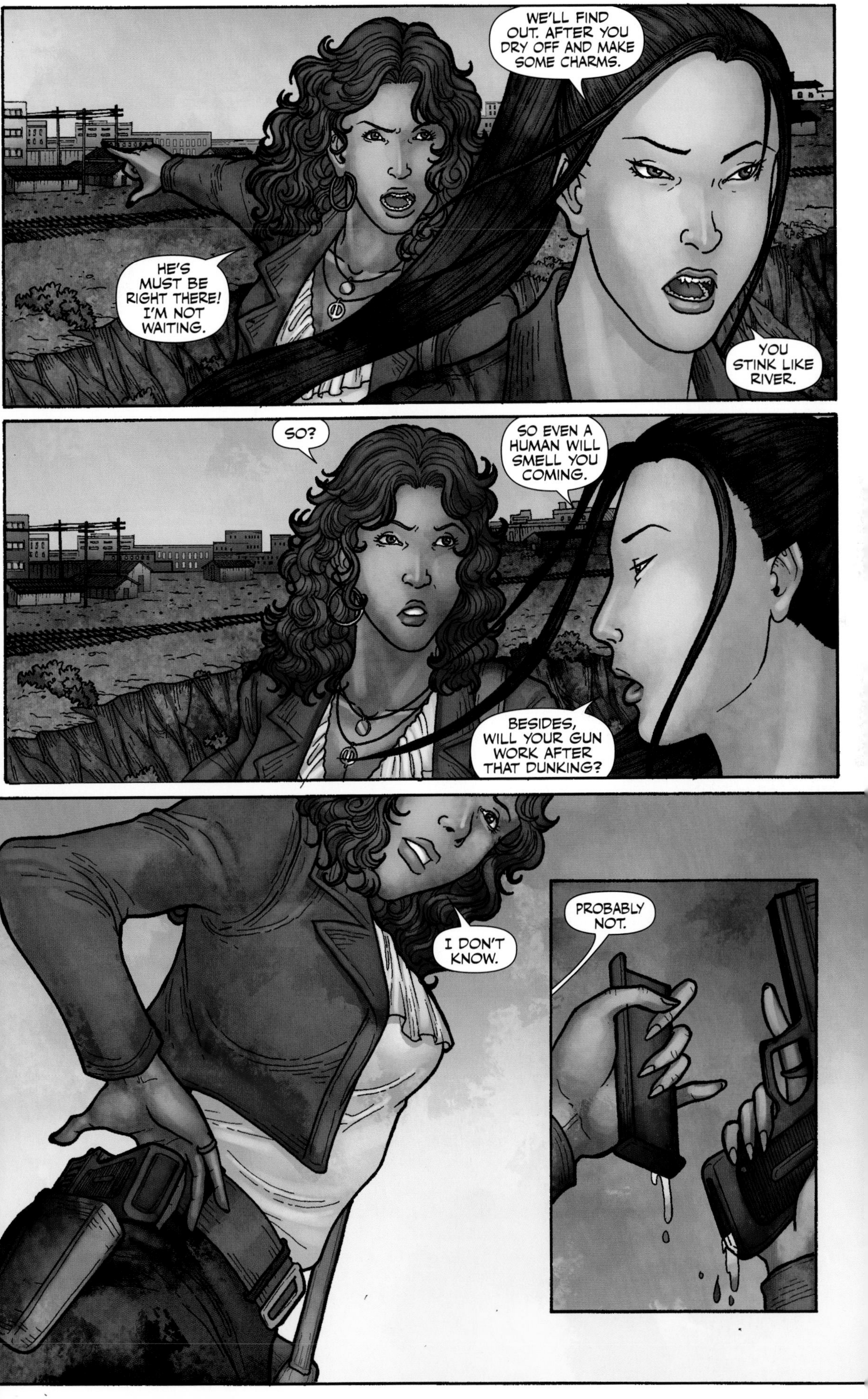
HE'S MUST BE RIGHT THERE! I'M NOT WAITING.
WE'LL FIND OUT. AFTER YOU DRY OFF AND MAKE SOME CHARMS.
YOU STINK LIKE RIVER.
SO?
SO EVEN A HUMAN WILL SMELL YOU COMING.
BESIDES, WILL YOUR GUN WORK AFTER THAT DUNKING?
I DON'T KNOW.
PROBABLY NOT.

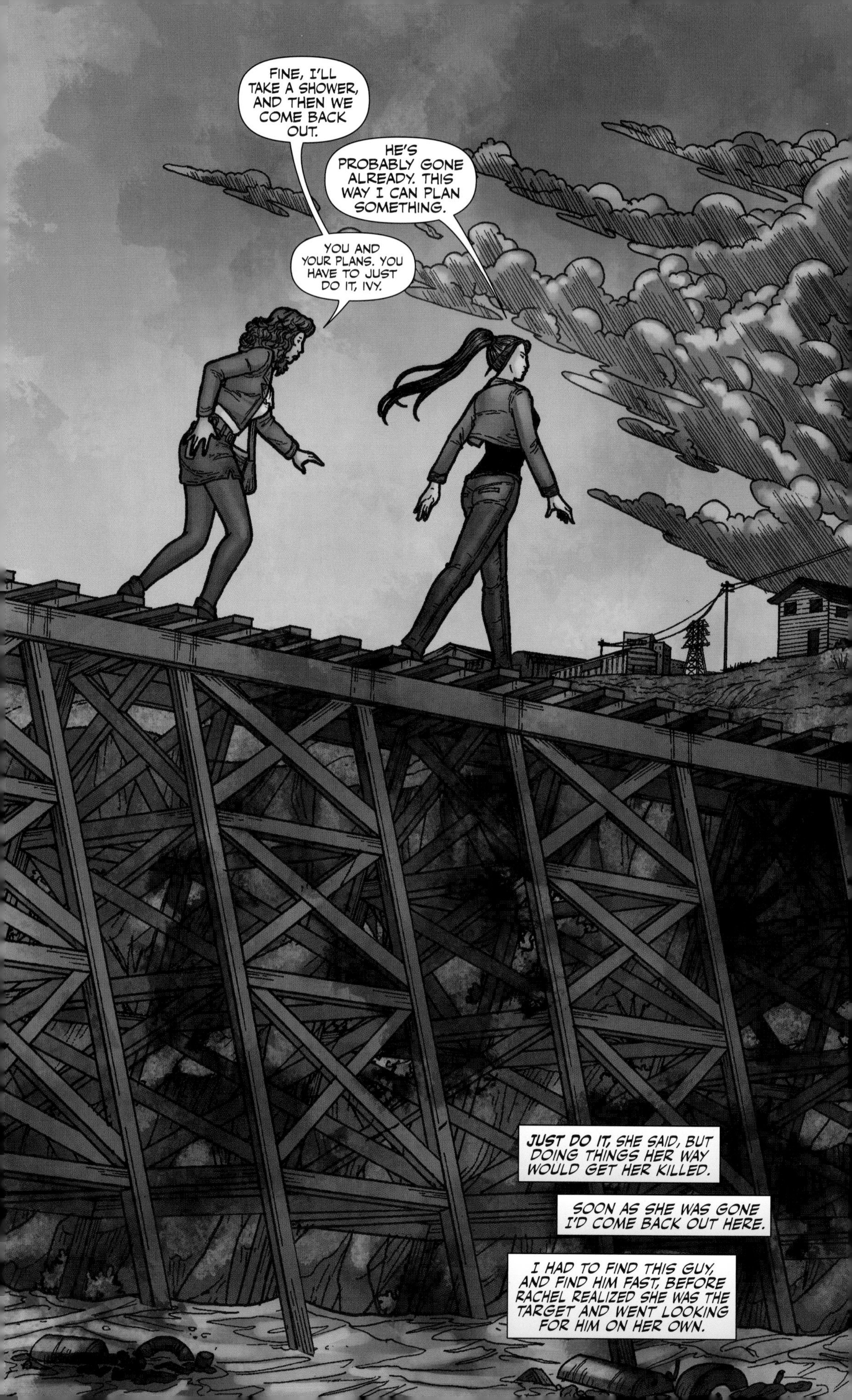
FINE, I'LL TAKE A SHOWER, AND THEN WE COME BACK OUT.
HE'S PROBABLY GONE ALREADY. THIS WAY I CAN PLAN SOMETHING.
YOU AND YOUR PLANS. YOU HAVE TO JUST DO IT, IVY.
JUST DO IT, SHE SAID, BUT DOING THINGS HER WAY WOULD GET HER KILLED.
SOON AS SHE WAS GONE I'D COME BACK OUT HERE.
I HAD TO FIND THIS GUY, AND FIND HIM FAST, BEFORE RACHEL REALIZED SHE WAS THE TARGET AND WENT LOOKING FOR HIM ON HER OWN.

CHAPTER 5

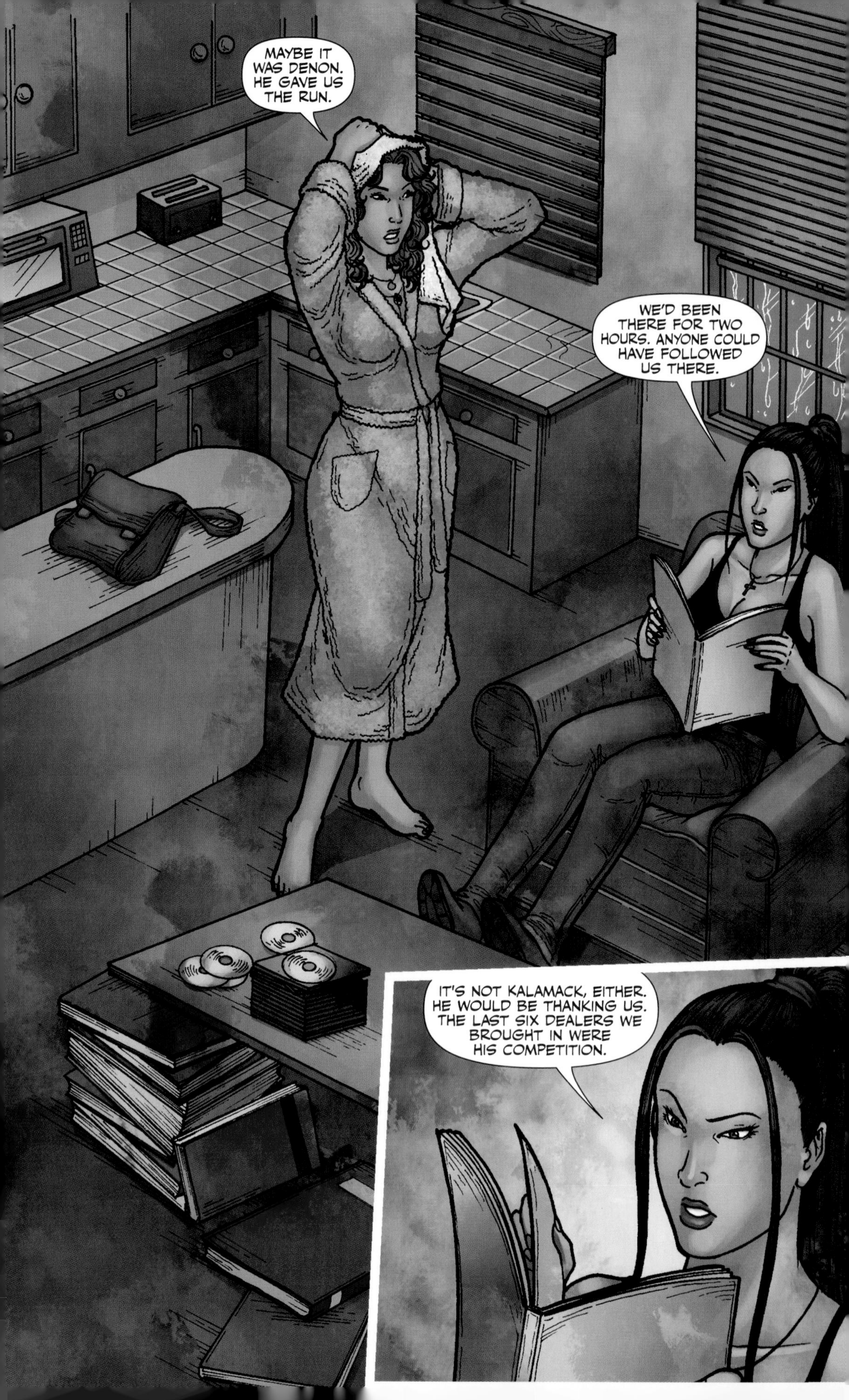
MAYBE IT WAS DENON. HE GAVE US THE RUN.
WE'D BEEN THERE FOR TWO HOURS. ANYONE COULD HAVE FOLLOWED US THERE.
IT'S NOT KALAMACK, EITHER. HE WOULD BE THANKING US. THE LAST SIX DEALERS WE BROUGHT IN WERE HIS COMPETITION.

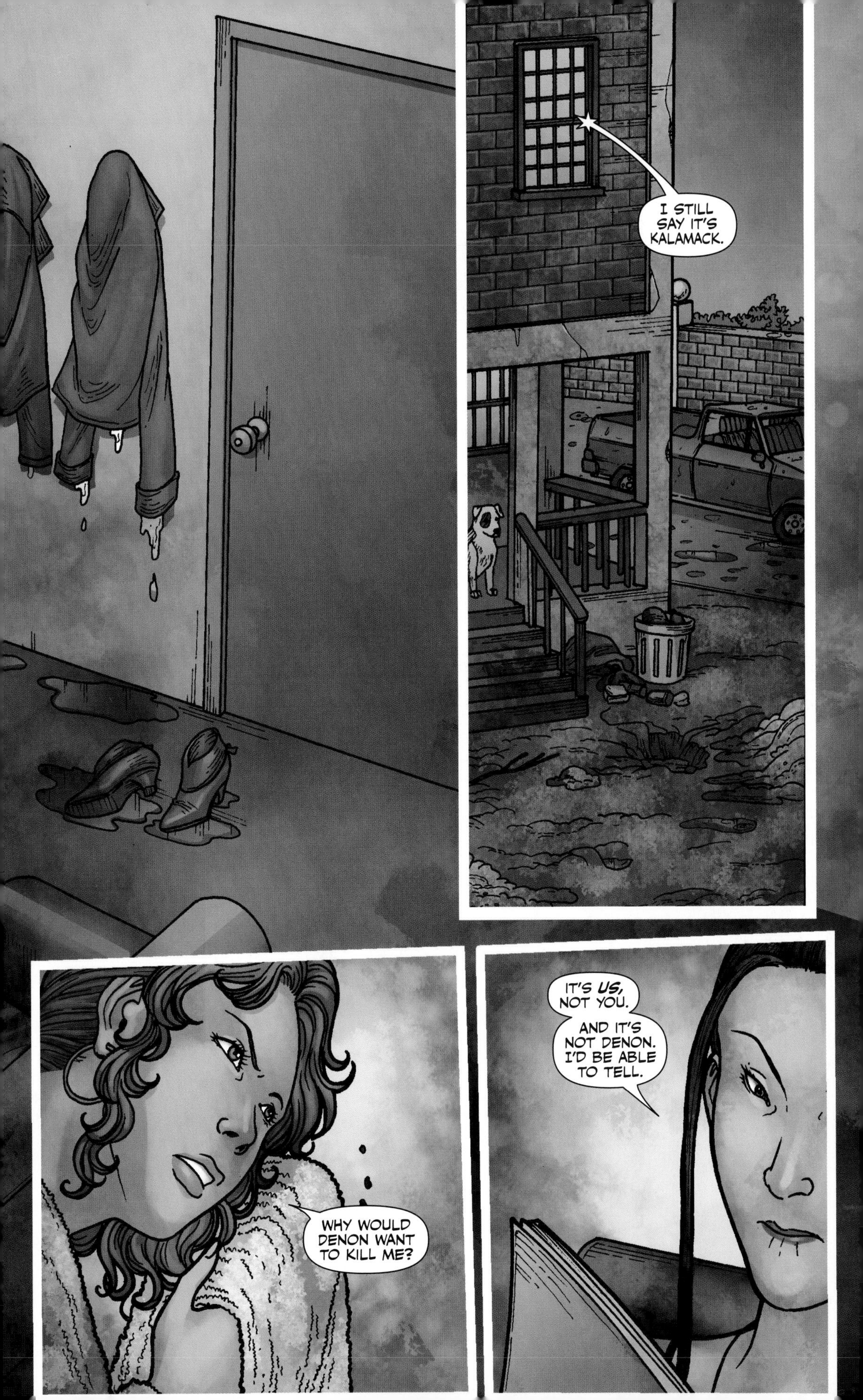
I STILL SAY IT'S KALAMACK.
WHY WOULD DENON WANT TO KILL ME?
IT'S *US,* NOT YOU.
AND IT'S NOT DENON. I'D BE ABLE TO TELL.

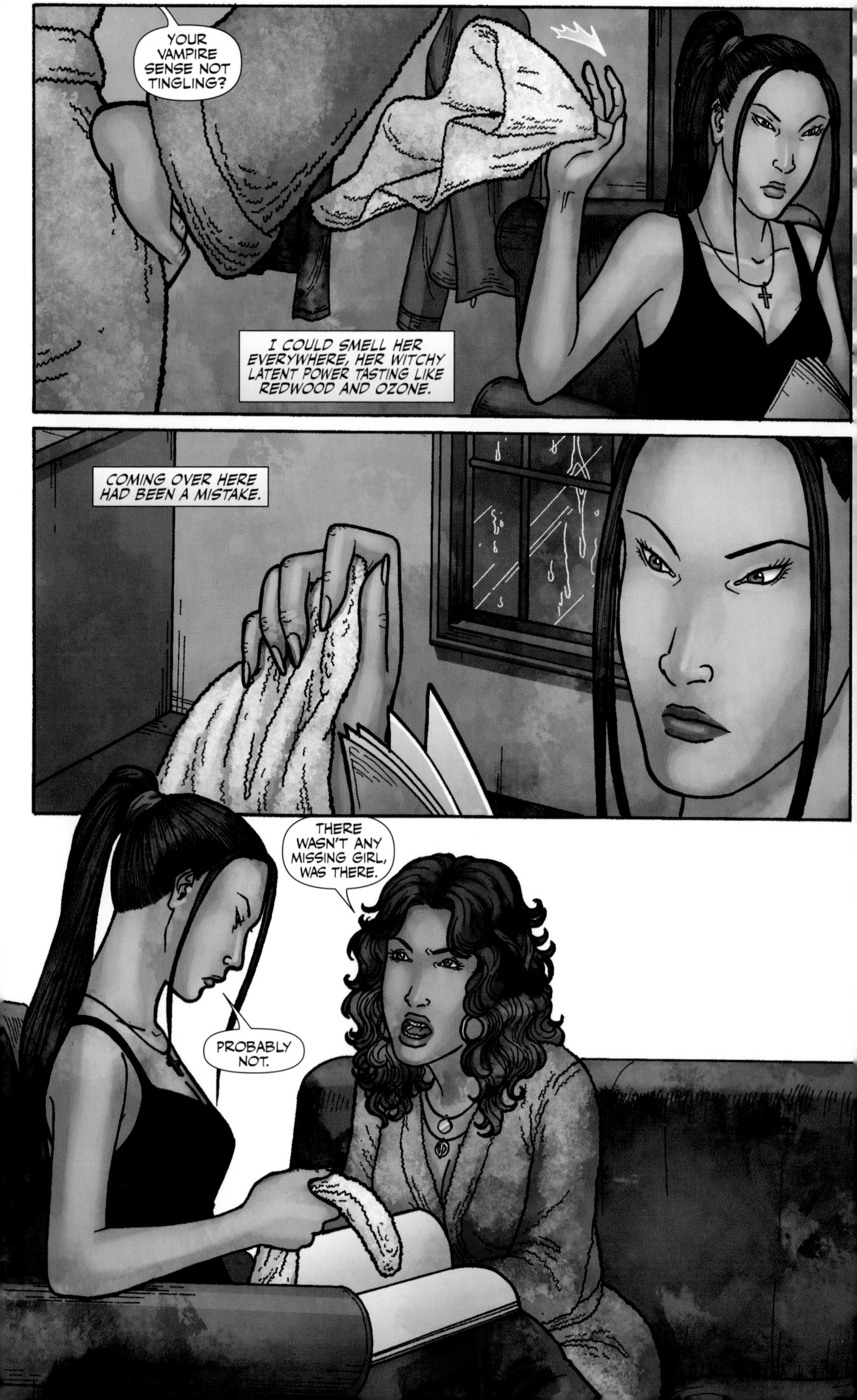
YOUR VAMPIRE SENSE NOT TINGLING?
I COULD SMELL HER EVERYWHERE, HER WITCHY LATENT POWER TASTING LIKE REDWOOD AND OZONE.
COMING OVER HERE HAD BEEN A MISTAKE.
THERE WASN'T ANY MISSING GIRL, WAS THERE.
PROBABLY NOT.

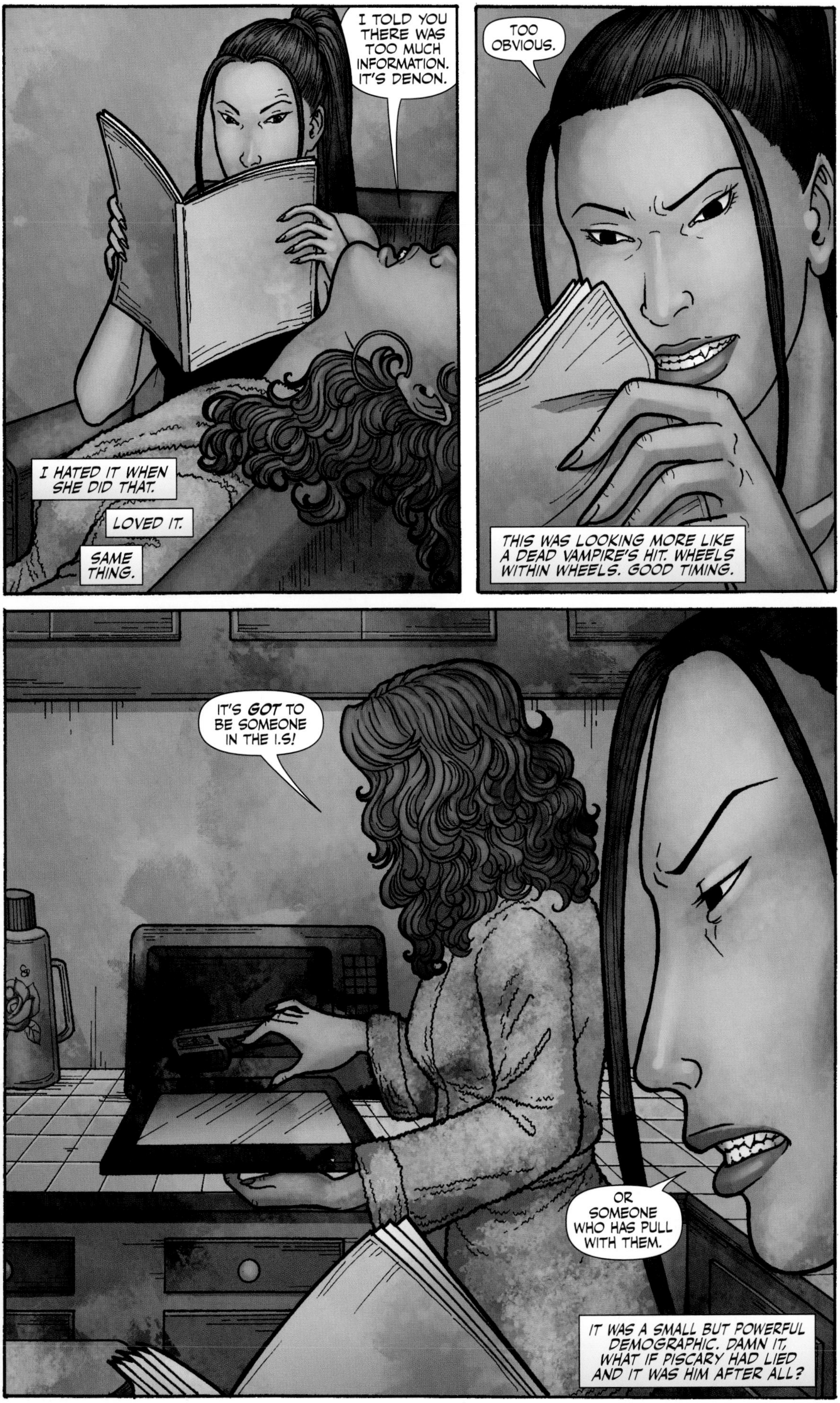
I TOLD YOU THERE WAS TOO MUCH INFORMATION. IT'S DENON.
I HATED IT WHEN SHE DID THAT.
LOVED IT.
SAME THING.
TOO OBVIOUS.
THIS WAS LOOKING MORE LIKE A DEAD VAMPIRE'S HIT. WHEELS WITHIN WHEELS. GOOD TIMING.
IT'S *GOT* TO BE SOMEONE IN THE I.S!
OR SOMEONE WHO HAS PULL WITH THEM.
IT WAS A SMALL BUT POWERFUL DEMOGRAPHIC. DAMN IT, WHAT IF PISCARY HAD LIED AND IT WAS HIM AFTER ALL?

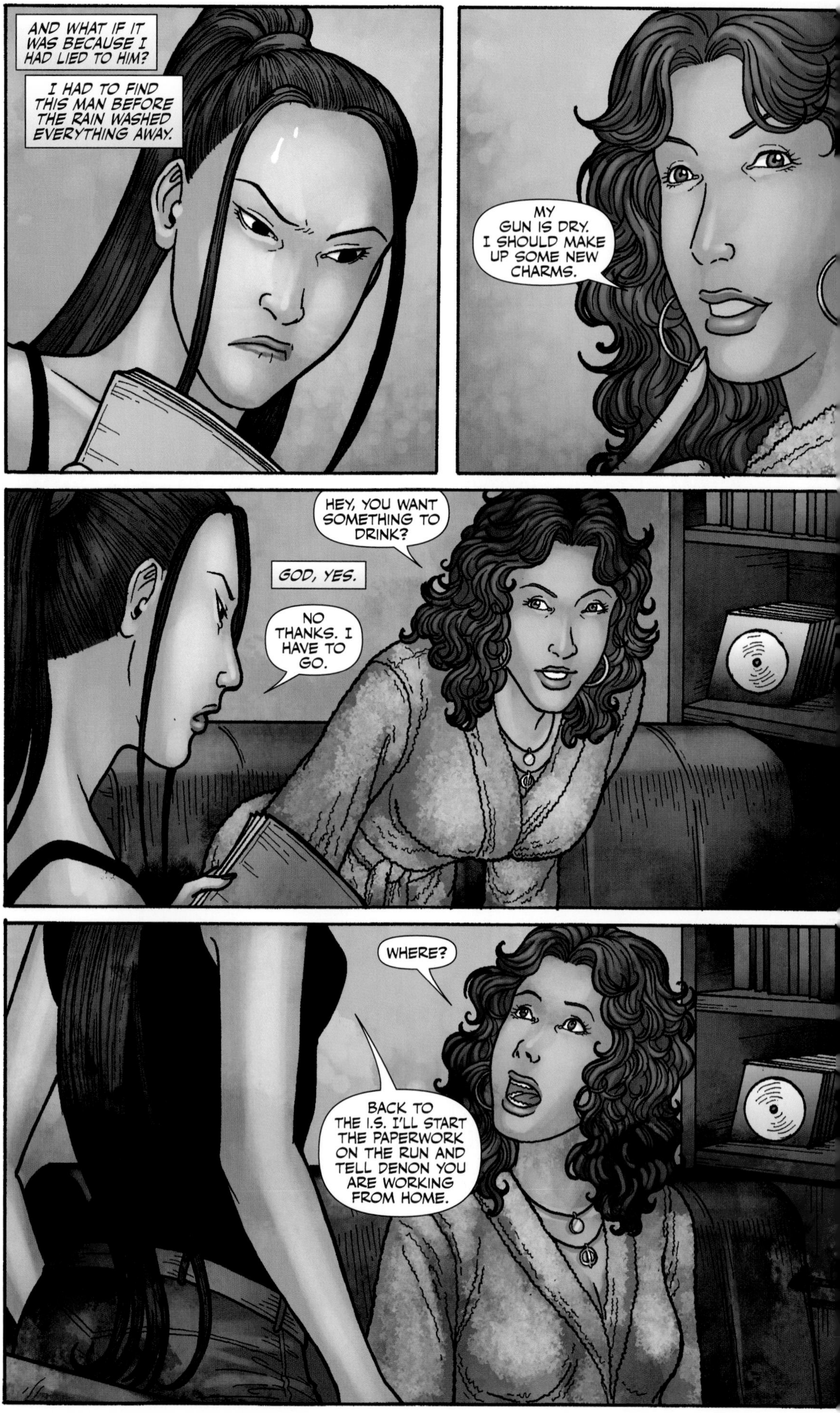
AND WHAT IF IT WAS BECAUSE I HAD LIED TO HIM?
I HAD TO FIND THIS MAN BEFORE THE RAIN WASHED EVERYTHING AWAY.
MY GUN IS DRY. I SHOULD MAKE UP SOME NEW CHARMS.
HEY, YOU WANT SOMETHING TO DRINK?
GOD, YES.
NO THANKS. I HAVE TO GO.
WHERE?
BACK TO THE I.S. I'LL START THE PAPERWORK ON THE RUN AND TELL DENON YOU ARE WORKING FROM HOME.

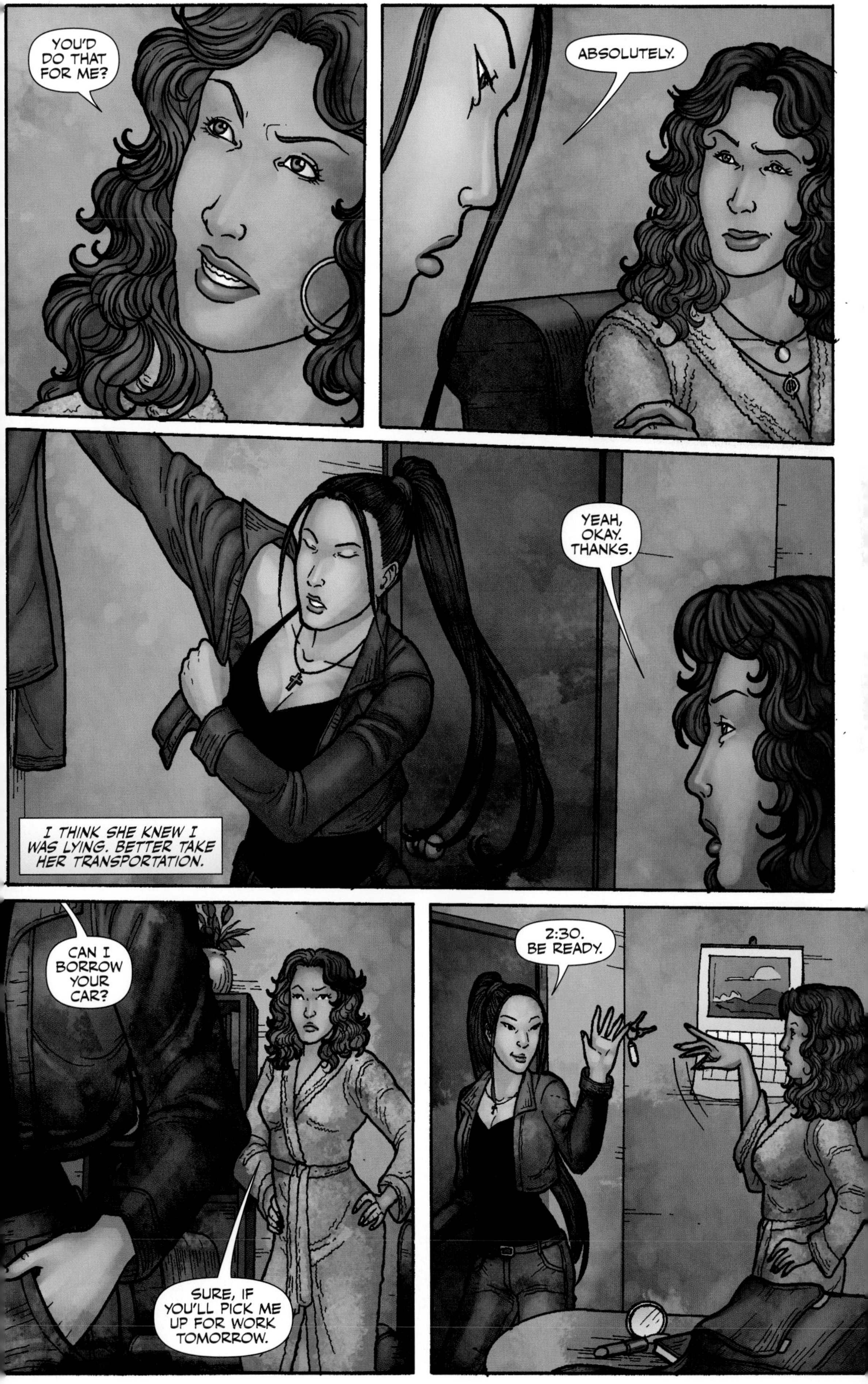
YOU'D DO THAT FOR ME?
ABSOLUTELY.
YEAH, OKAY. THANKS.
I THINK SHE KNEW I WAS LYING. BETTER TAKE HER TRANSPORTATION.
CAN I BORROW YOUR CAR?
SURE, IF YOU'LL PICK ME UP FOR WORK TOMORROW.
2:30. BE READY.

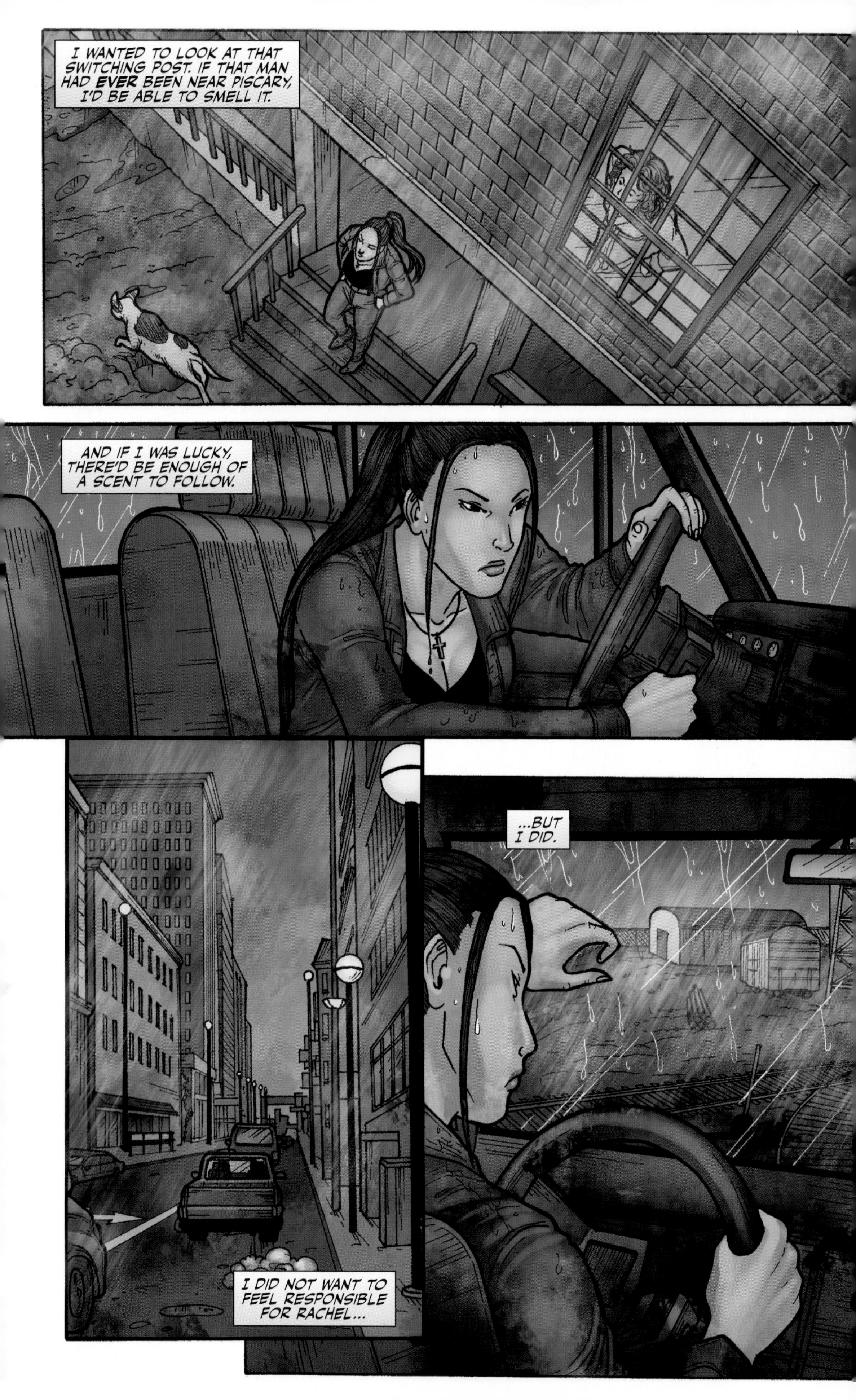
I WANTED TO LOOK AT THAT SWITCHING POST. IF THAT MAN HAD EVER BEEN NEAR PISCARY, I'D BE ABLE TO SMELL IT.
AND IF I WAS LUCKY, THERE'D BE ENOUGH OF A SCENT TO FOLLOW.
I DID NOT WANT TO FEEL RESPONSIBLE FOR RACHEL...
...BUT I DID.

...FEMALE...

THERE WAS VAMPIRE HERE...

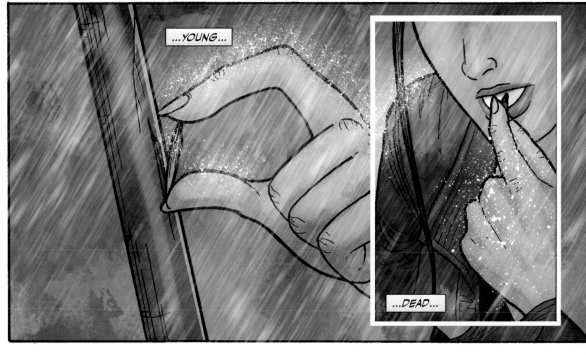

...YOUNG...

...DEAD...

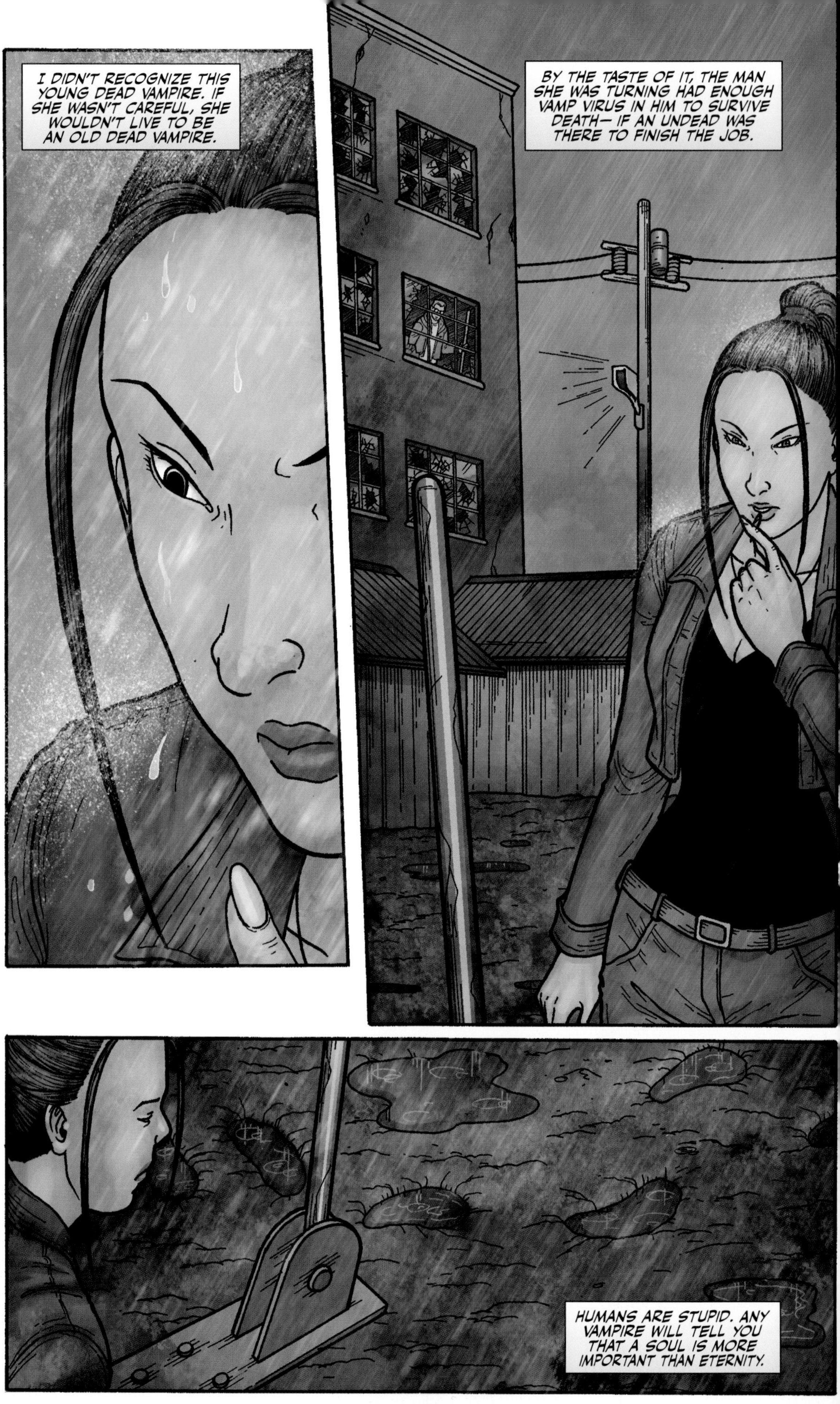
I DIDN'T RECOGNIZE THIS YOUNG DEAD VAMPIRE. IF SHE WASN'T CAREFUL, SHE WOULDN'T LIVE TO BE AN OLD DEAD VAMPIRE.
BY THE TASTE OF IT, THE MAN SHE WAS TURNING HAD ENOUGH VAMP VIRUS IN HIM TO SURVIVE DEATH— IF AN UNDEAD WAS THERE TO FINISH THE JOB.
HUMANS ARE STUPID. ANY VAMPIRE WILL TELL YOU THAT A SOUL IS MORE IMPORTANT THAN ETERNITY.

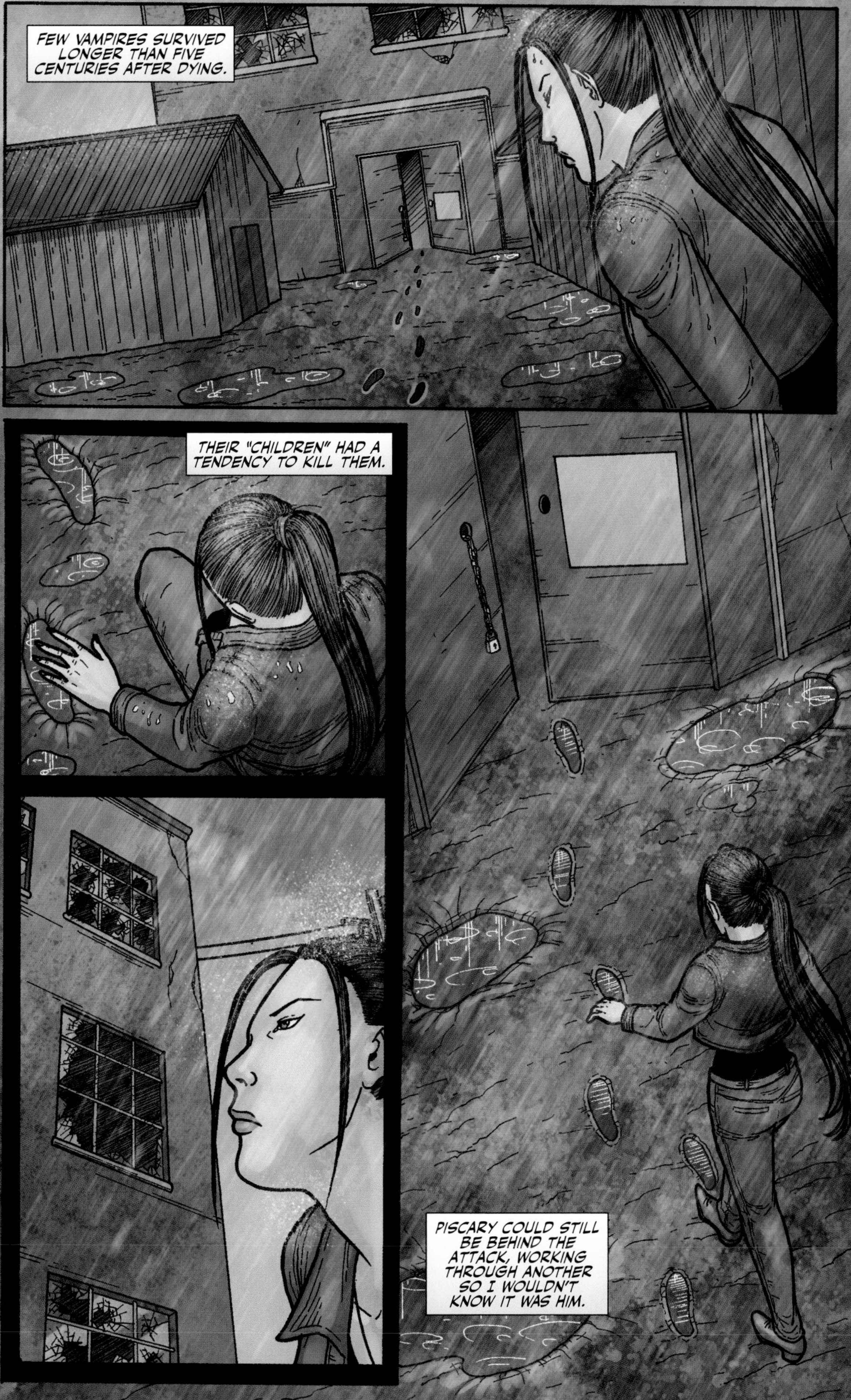
FEW VAMPIRES SURVIVED LONGER THAN FIVE CENTURIES AFTER DYING.
THEIR "CHILDREN" HAD A TENDENCY TO KILL THEM.
PISCARY COULD STILL BE BEHIND THE ATTACK, WORKING THROUGH ANOTHER SO I WOULDN'T KNOW IT WAS HIM.

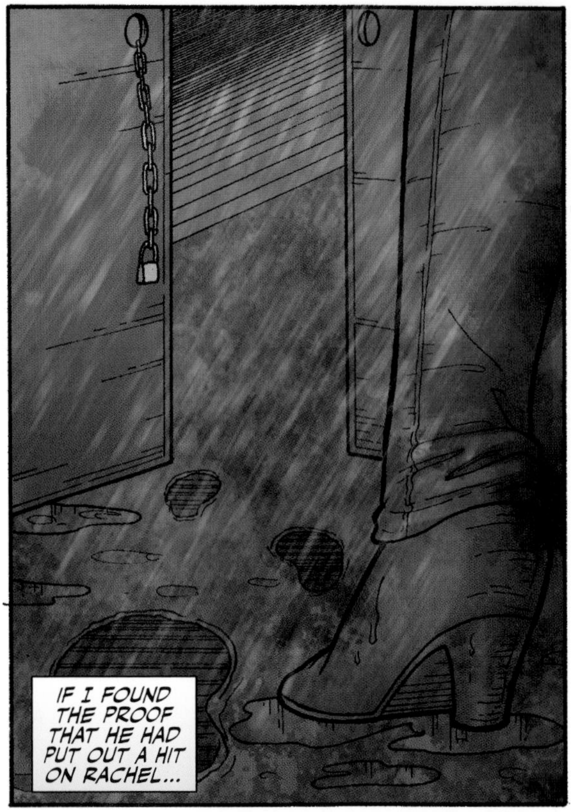
IF I FOUND THE PROOF THAT HE HAD PUT OUT A HIT ON RACHEL...

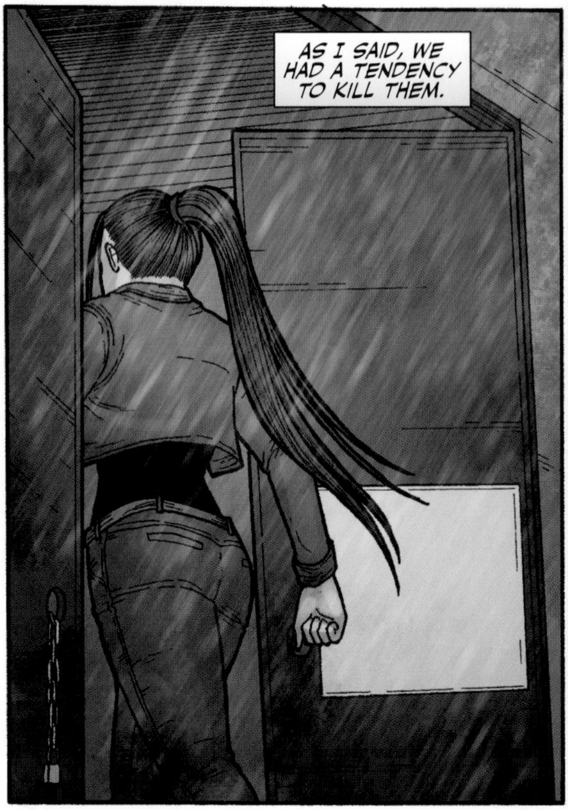
AS I SAID, WE HAD A TENDENCY TO KILL THEM.

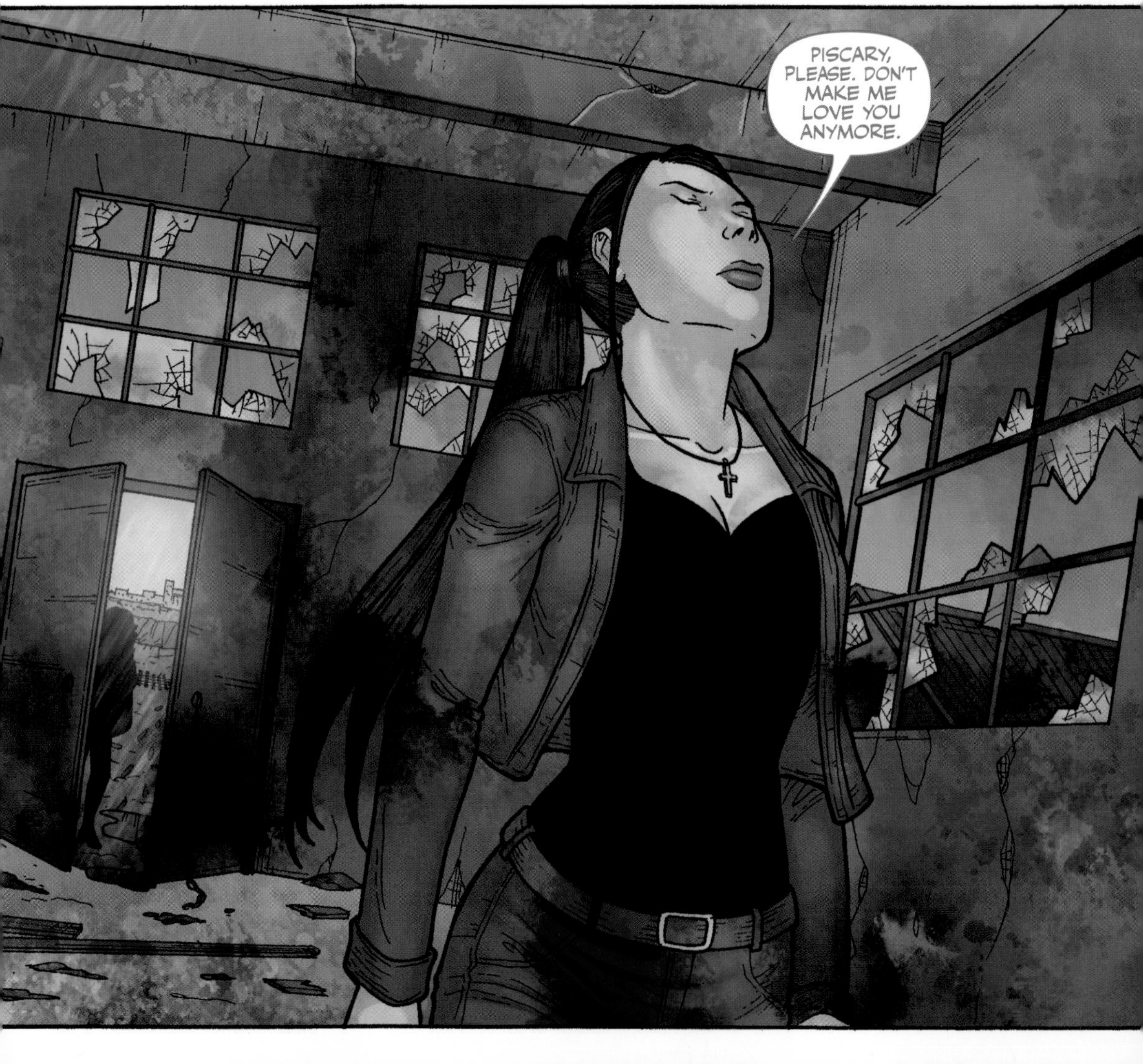
PISCARY, PLEASE. DON'T MAKE ME LOVE YOU ANYMORE.

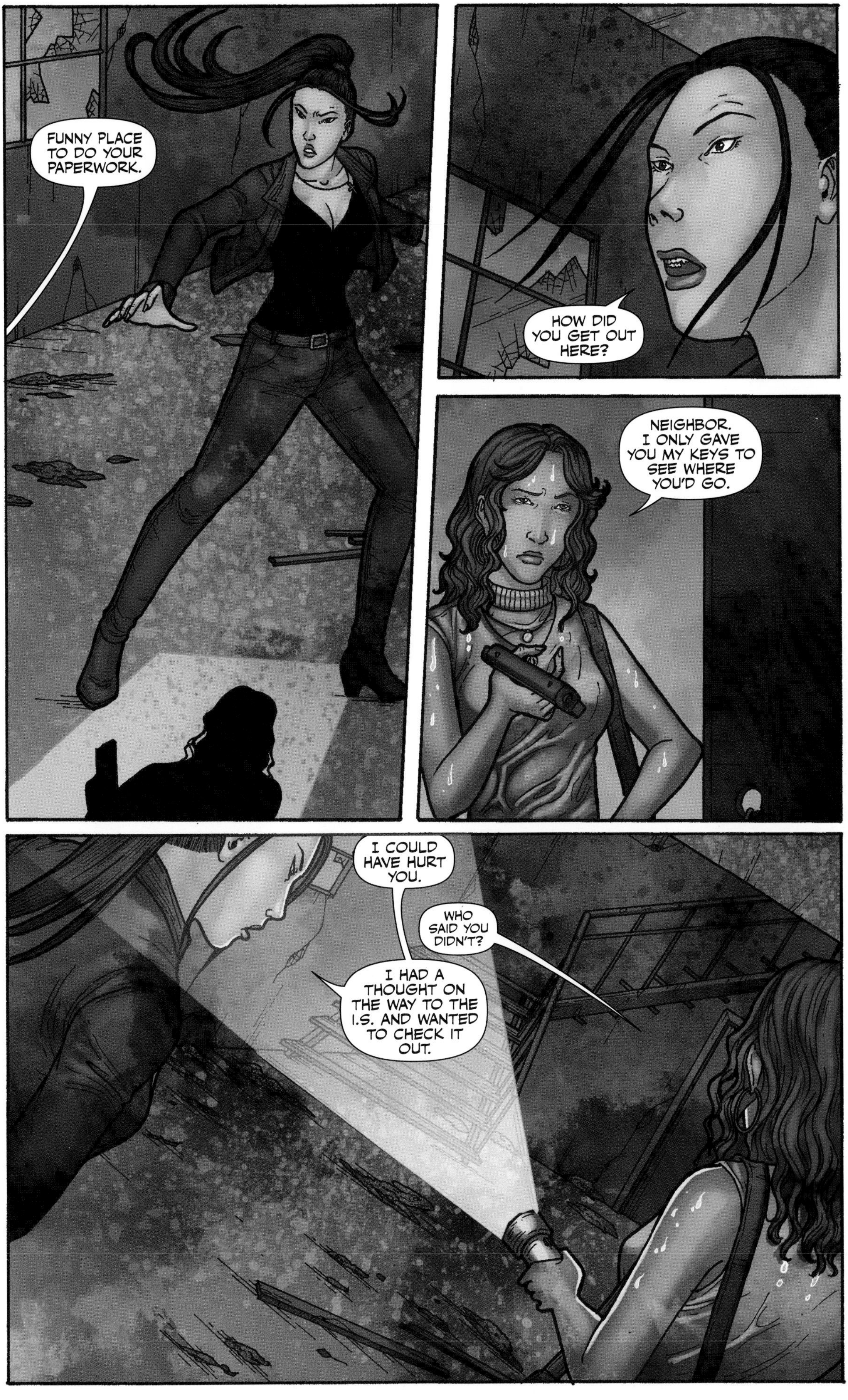
FUNNY PLACE TO DO YOUR PAPERWORK.
HOW DID YOU GET OUT HERE?
NEIGHBOR. I ONLY GAVE YOU MY KEYS TO SEE WHERE YOU'D GO.
I COULD HAVE HURT YOU.
WHO SAID YOU DIDN'T?
I HAD A THOUGHT ON THE WAY TO THE I.S. AND WANTED TO CHECK IT OUT.

DID YOU KNOW YOU PUT YOUR HANDS IN YOUR POCKETS WHEN YOU LIE?

I'LL WORK ON THAT. THANKS.

STUPID VAMP! I OUGHT TO JUST—

LOOK OUT!

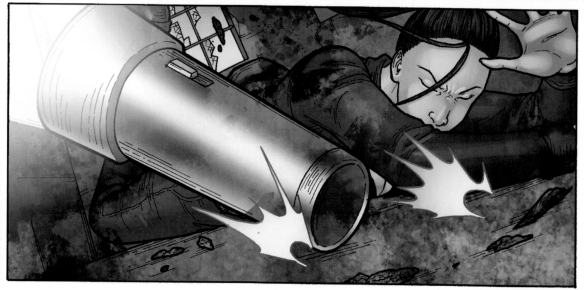

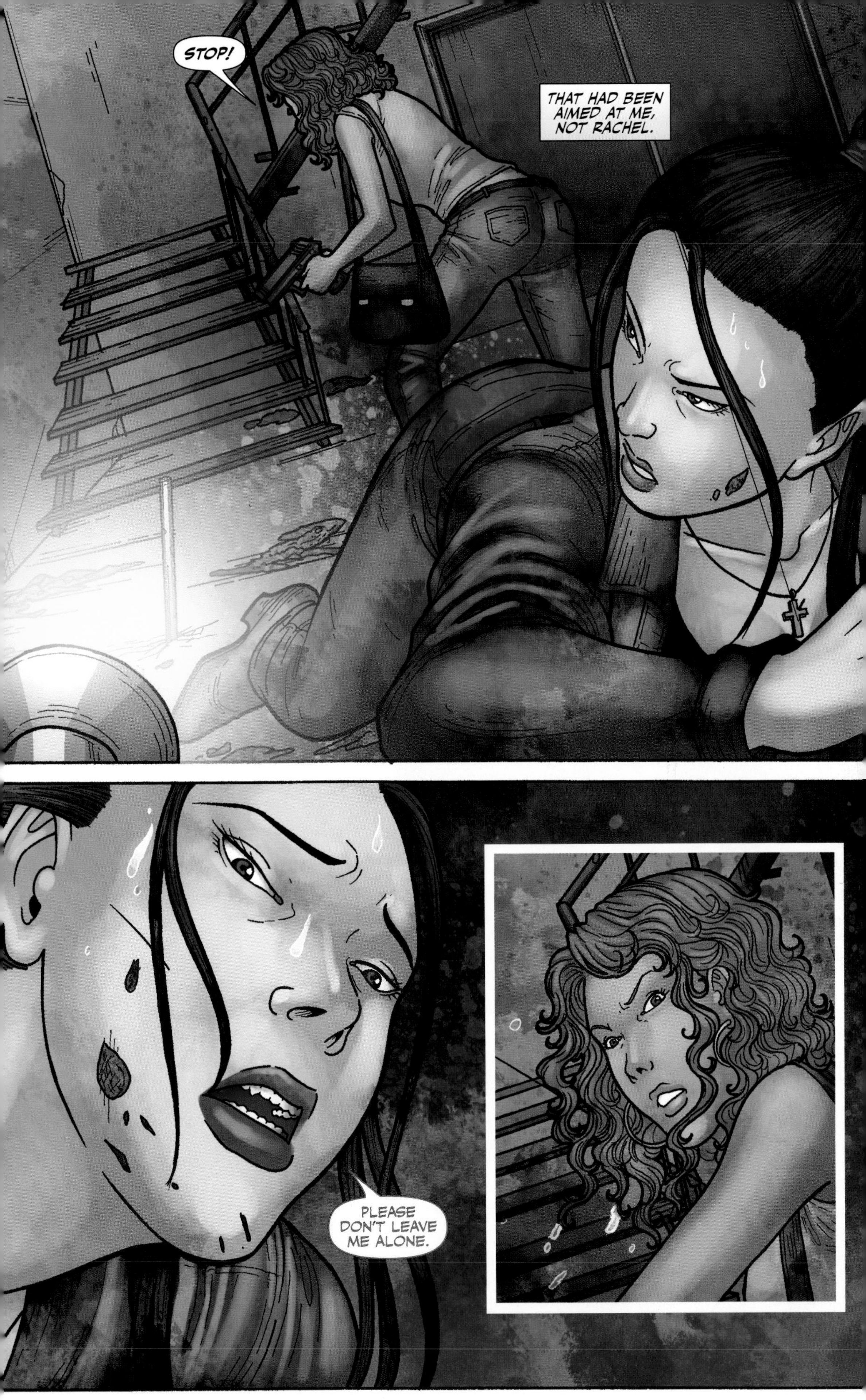
STOP!
THAT HAD BEEN AIMED AT ME, NOT RACHEL.
PLEASE DON'T LEAVE ME ALONE.

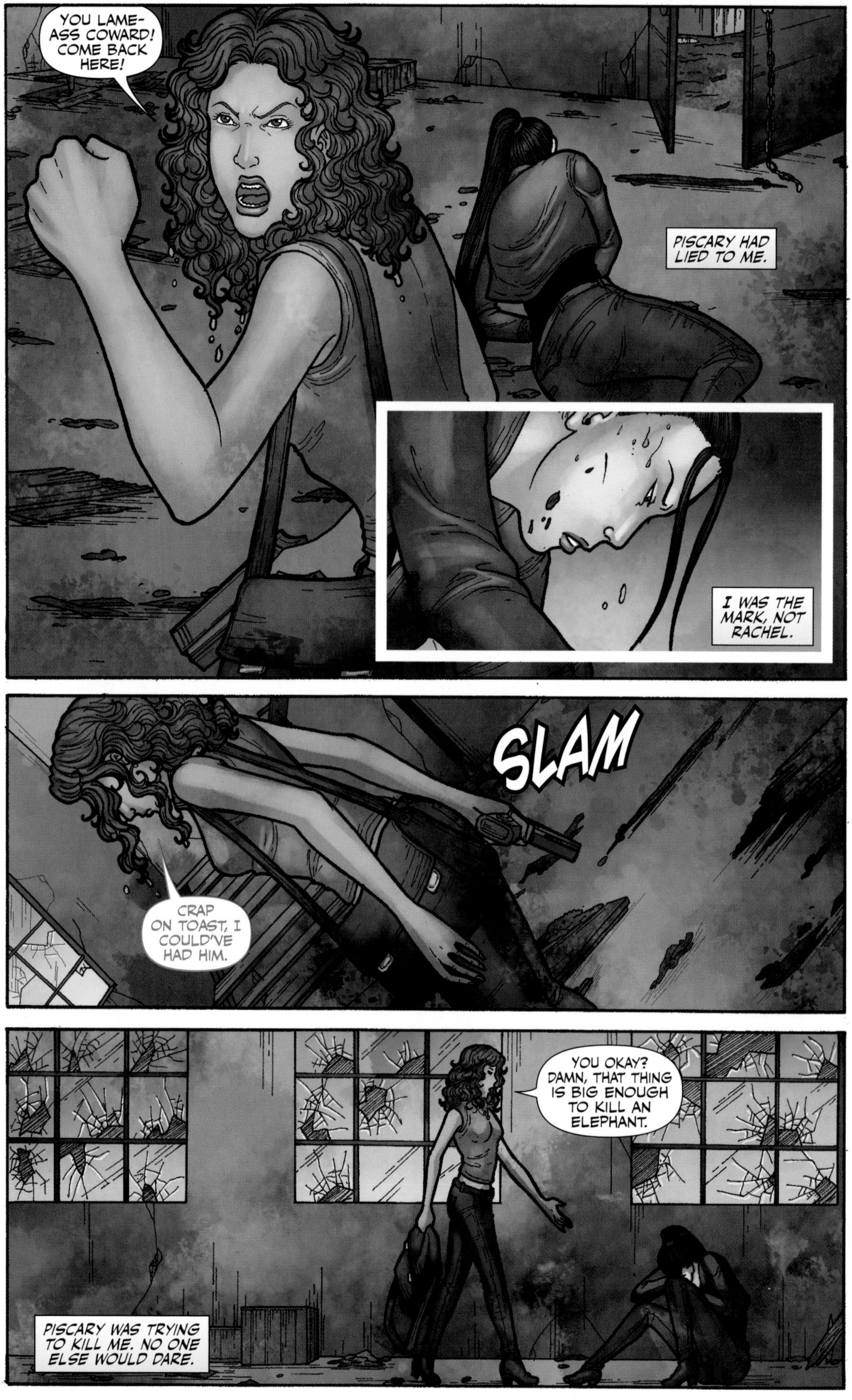
YOU LAME-ASS COWARD! COME BACK HERE!
PISCARY HAD LIED TO ME.
I WAS THE MARK, NOT RACHEL.
SLAM
CRAP ON TOAST, I COULD'VE HAD HIM.
YOU OKAY? DAMN, THAT THING IS BIG ENOUGH TO KILL AN ELEPHANT.
PISCARY WAS TRYING TO KILL ME. NO ONE ELSE WOULD DARE.

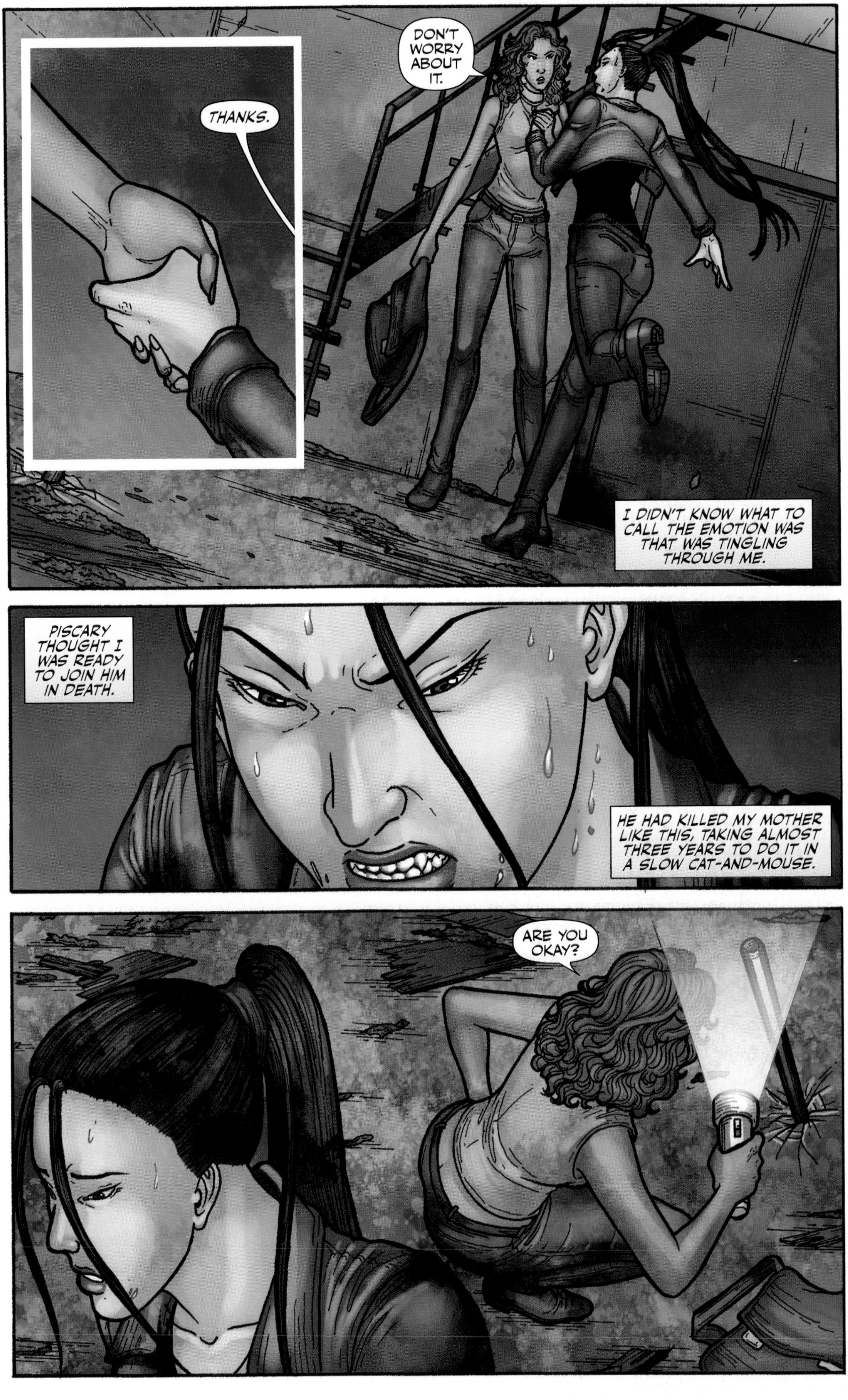
THANKS.
DON'T WORRY ABOUT IT.
I DIDN'T KNOW WHAT TO CALL THE EMOTION WAS THAT WAS TINGLING THROUGH ME.
PISCARY THOUGHT I WAS READY TO JOIN HIM IN DEATH.
HE HAD KILLED MY MOTHER LIKE THIS, TAKING ALMOST THREE YEARS TO DO IT IN A SLOW CAT-AND-MOUSE.
ARE YOU OKAY?

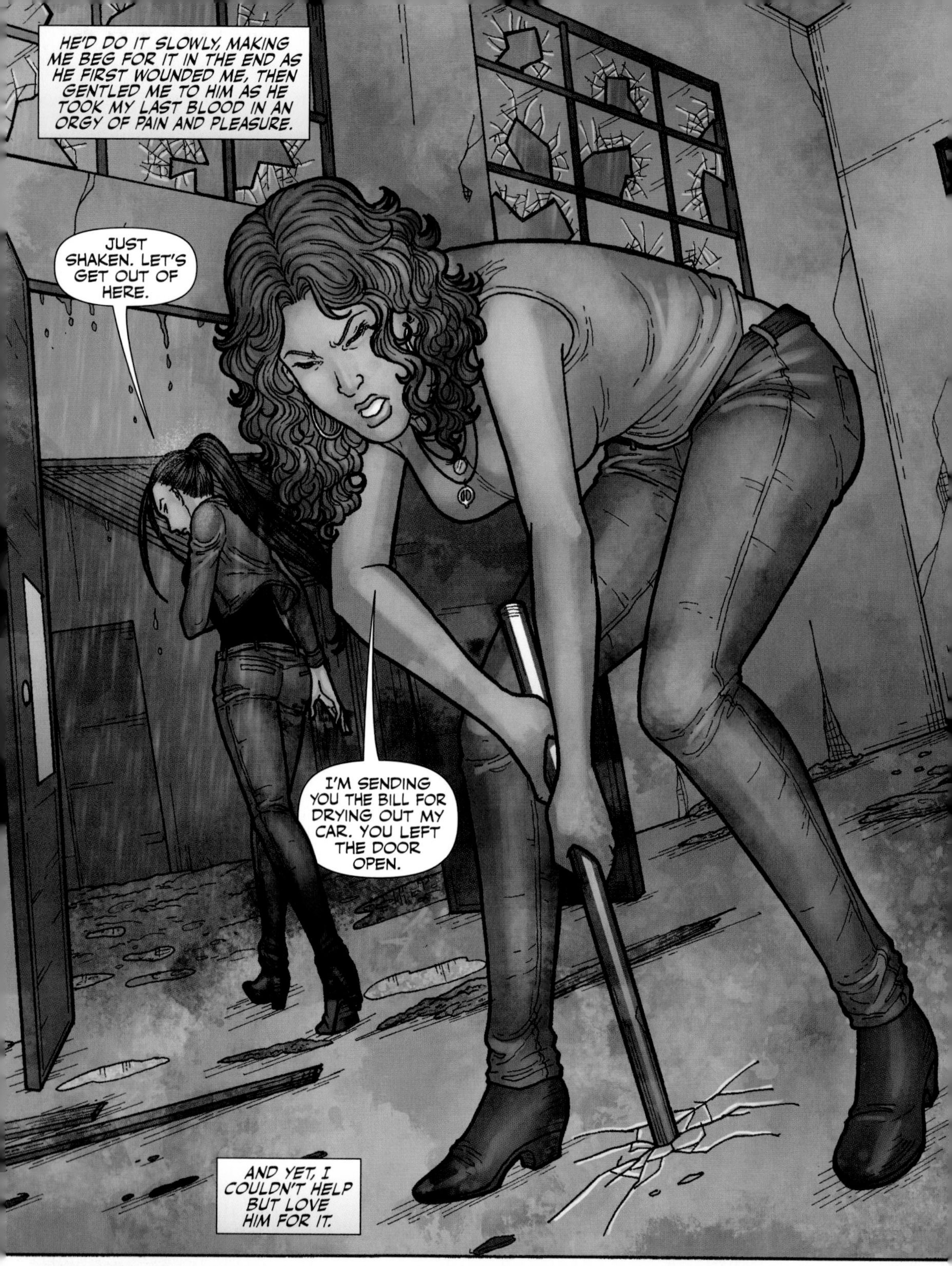
HE'D DO IT SLOWLY, MAKING ME BEG FOR IT IN THE END AS HE FIRST WOUNDED ME, THEN GENTLED ME TO HIM AS HE TOOK MY LAST BLOOD IN AN ORGY OF PAIN AND PLEASURE.
JUST SHAKEN. LET'S GET OUT OF HERE.
I'M SENDING YOU THE BILL FOR DRYING OUT MY CAR. YOU LEFT THE DOOR OPEN.
AND YET, I COULDN'T HELP BUT LOVE HIM FOR IT.

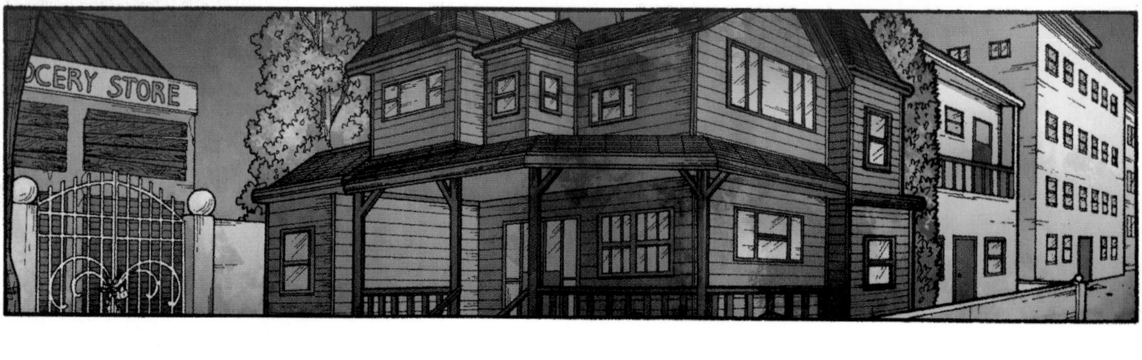
OCERY STORE

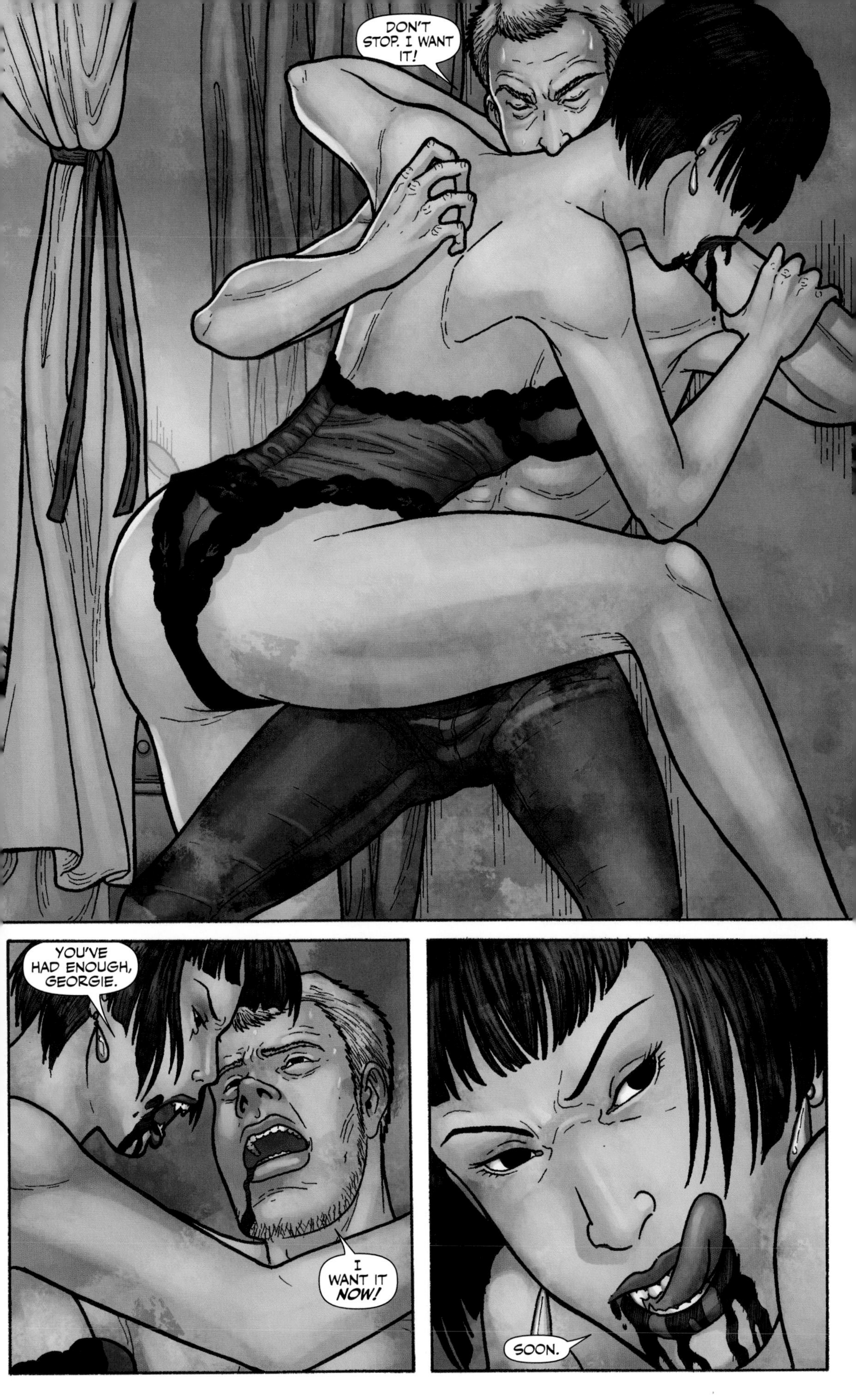
DON'T STOP. I WANT IT!
YOU'VE HAD ENOUGH, GEORGIE.
I WANT IT *NOW!*
SOON.

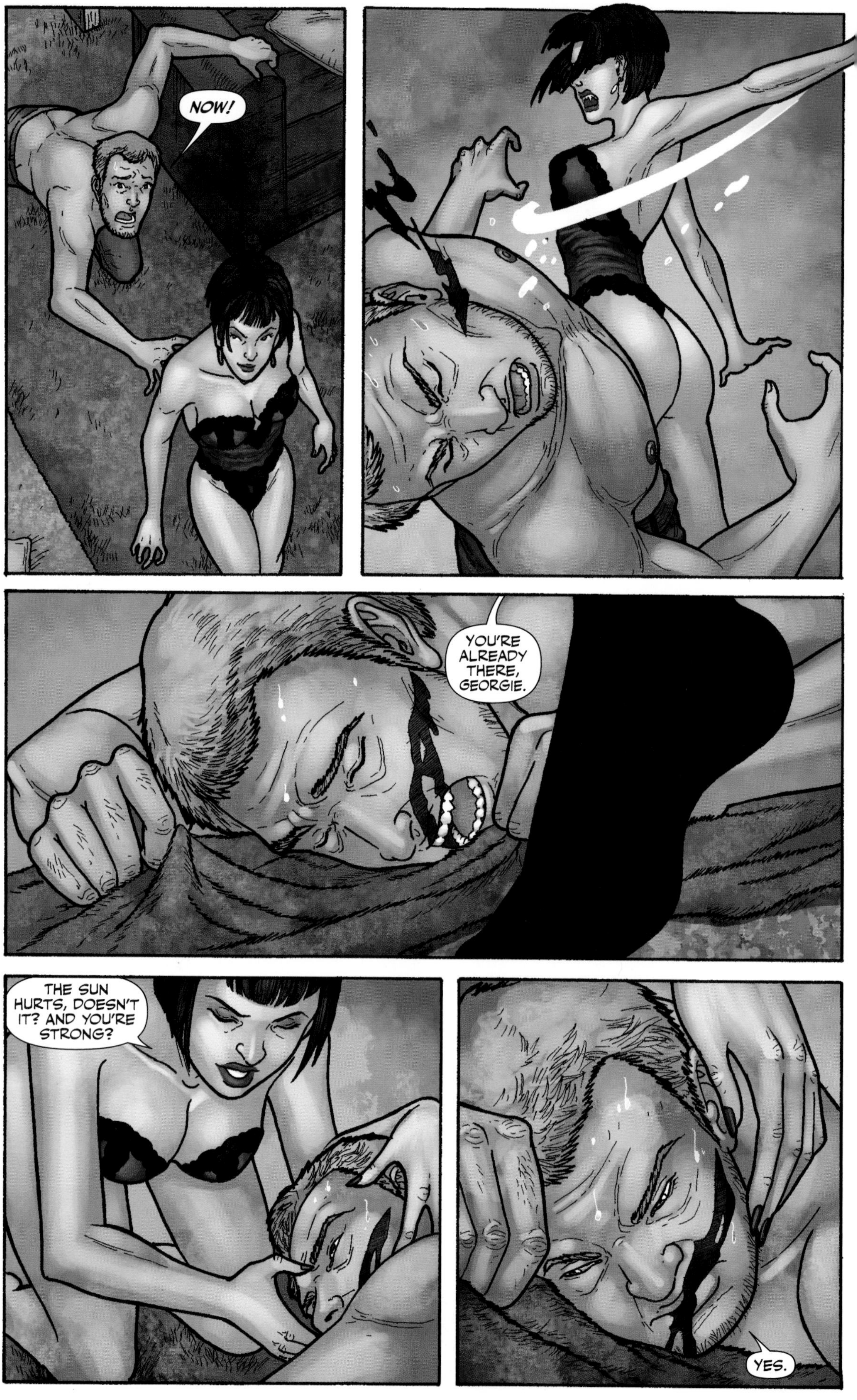
NOW!
YOU'RE ALREADY THERE, GEORGIE.
THE SUN HURTS, DOESN'T IT? AND YOU'RE STRONG?
YES.

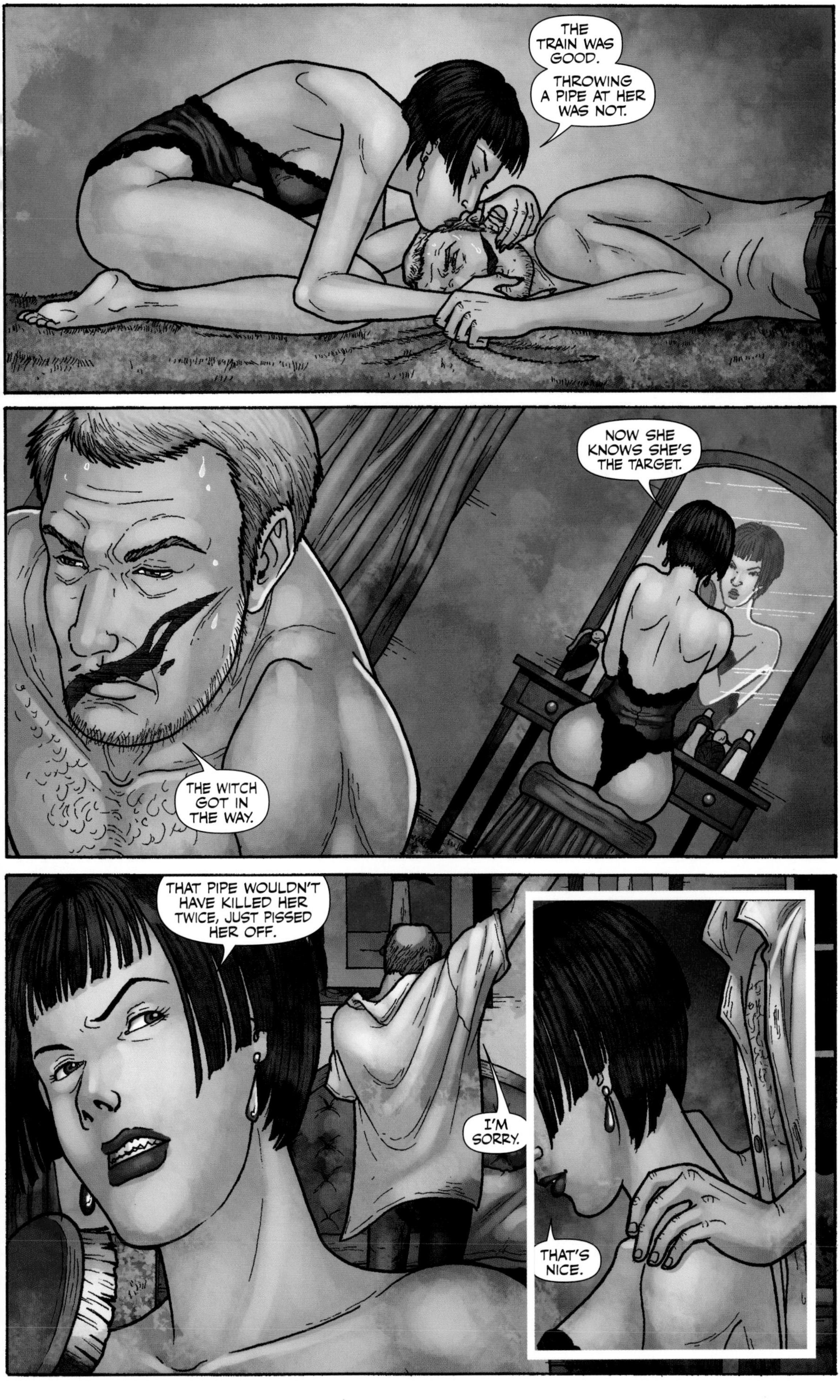
THE TRAIN WAS GOOD.
THROWING A PIPE AT HER WAS NOT.
NOW SHE KNOWS SHE'S THE TARGET.
THE WITCH GOT IN THE WAY.
THAT PIPE WOULDN'T HAVE KILLED HER TWICE, JUST PISSED HER OFF.
I'M SORRY.
THAT'S NICE.

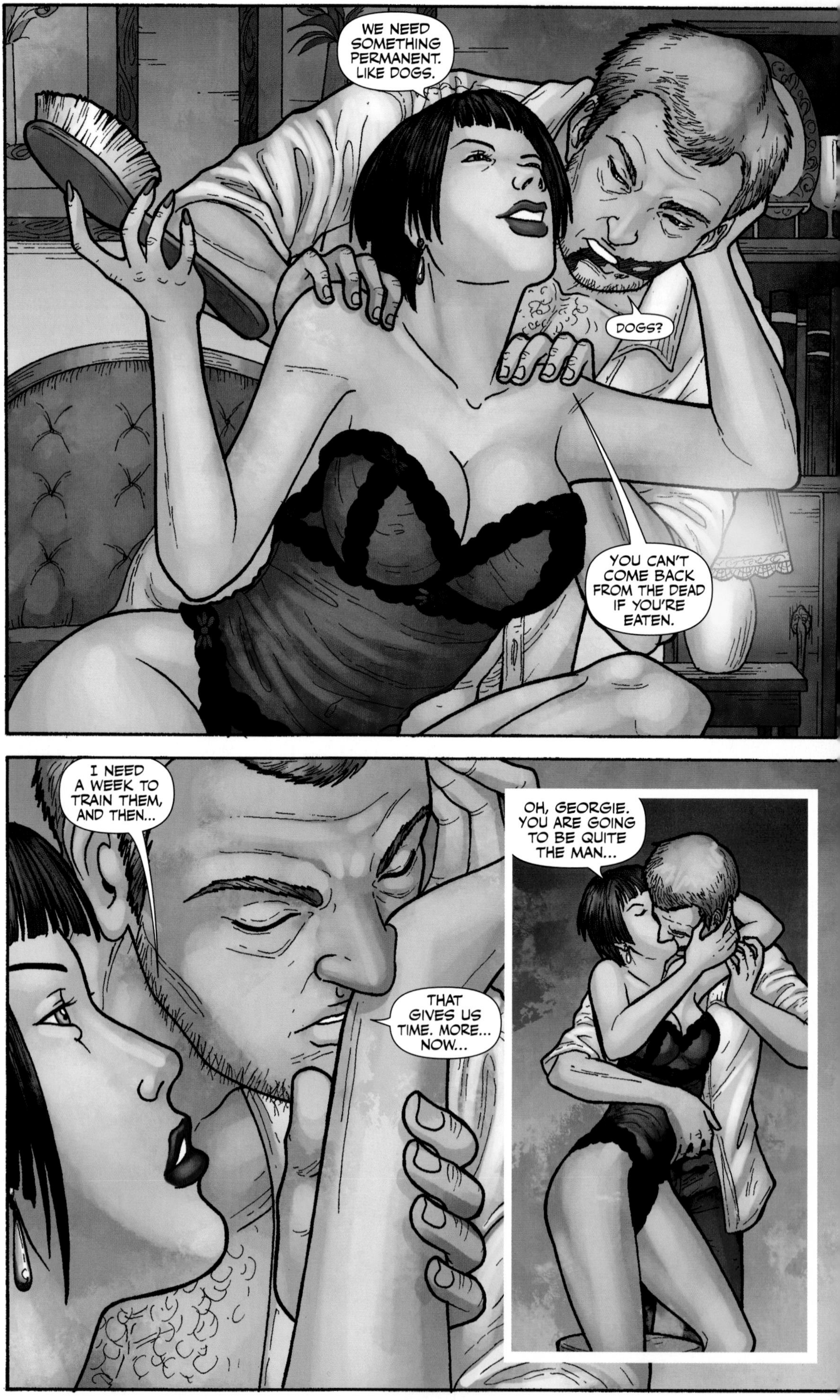
WE NEED SOMETHING PERMANENT. LIKE DOGS.
DOGS?
YOU CAN'T COME BACK FROM THE DEAD IF YOU'RE EATEN.
I NEED A WEEK TO TRAIN THEM, AND THEN...
THAT GIVES US TIME. MORE... NOW...
OH, GEORGIE. YOU ARE GOING TO BE QUITE THE MAN...

Chapter 6

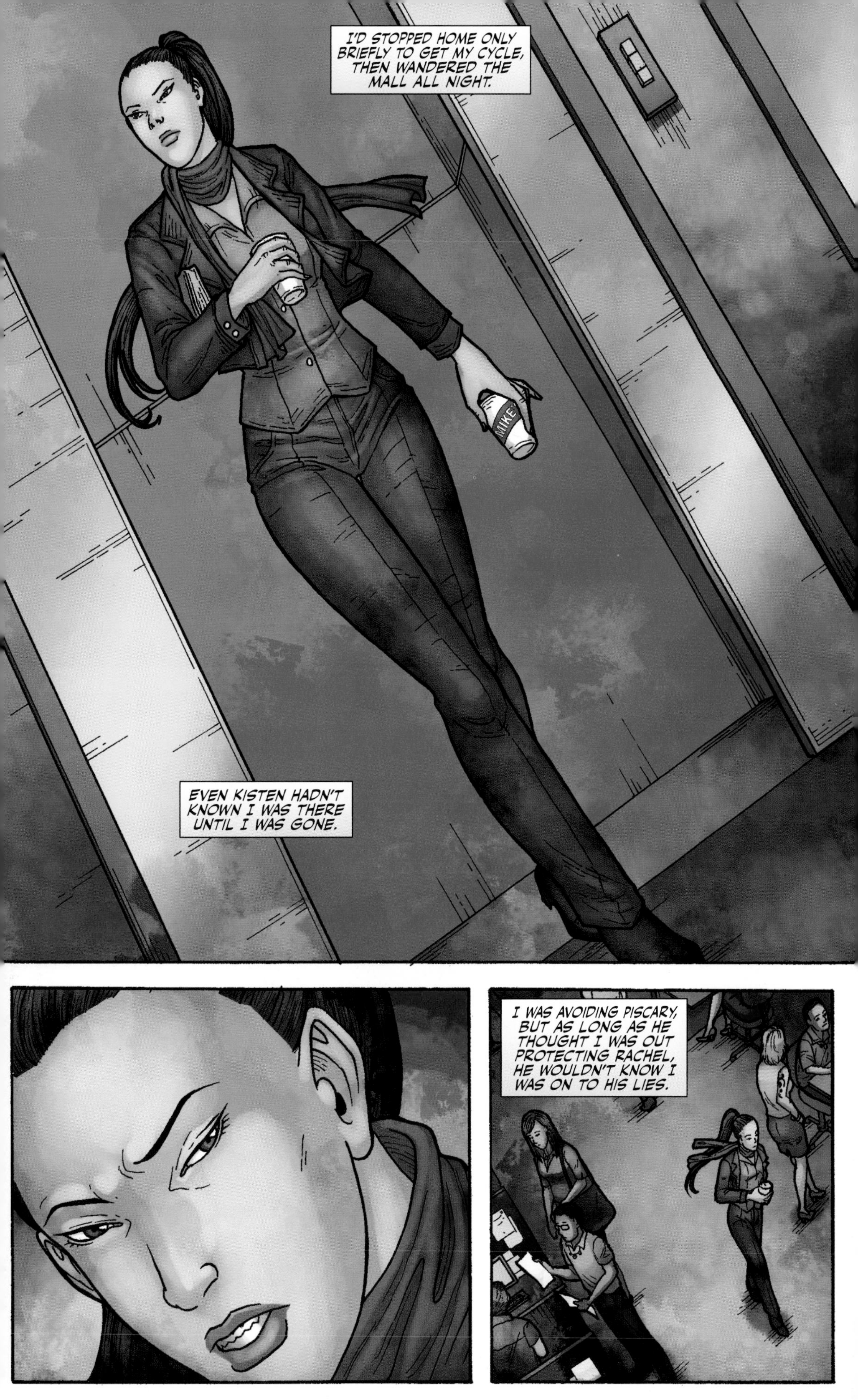
I'D STOPPED HOME ONLY BRIEFLY TO GET MY CYCLE, THEN WANDERED THE MALL ALL NIGHT.
EVEN KISTEN HADN'T KNOWN I WAS THERE UNTIL I WAS GONE.
I WAS AVOIDING PISCARY, BUT AS LONG AS HE THOUGHT I WAS OUT PROTECTING RACHEL, HE WOULDN'T KNOW I WAS ON TO HIS LIES.

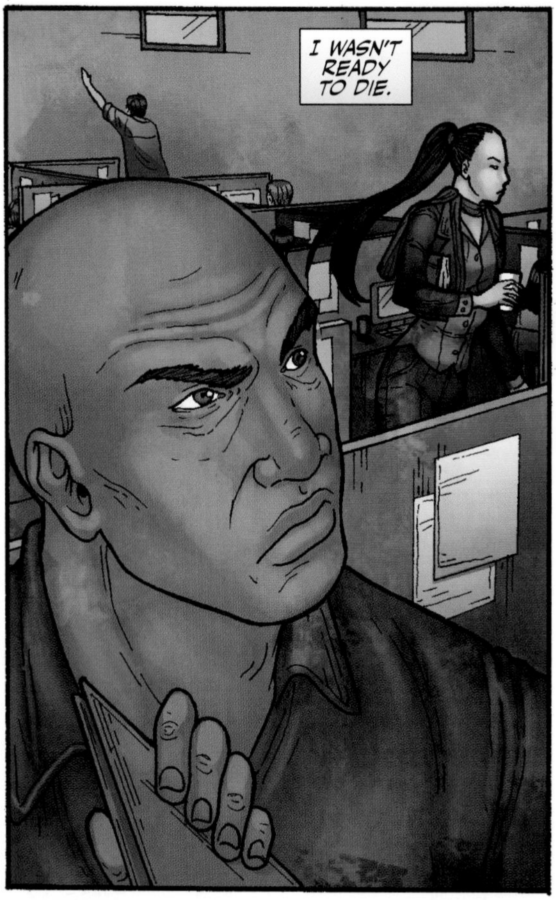
I WASN'T READY TO DIE.

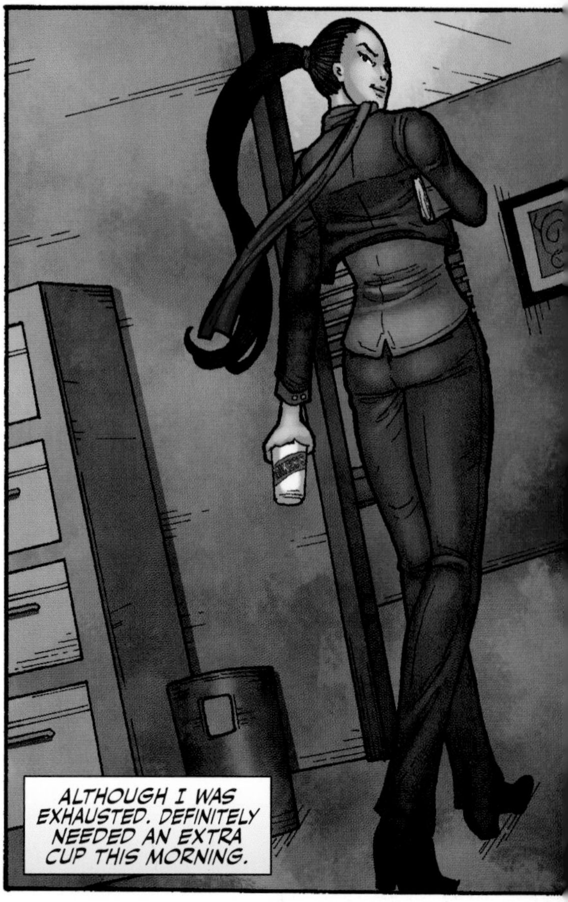
ALTHOUGH I WAS EXHAUSTED. DEFINITELY NEEDED AN EXTRA CUP THIS MORNING.

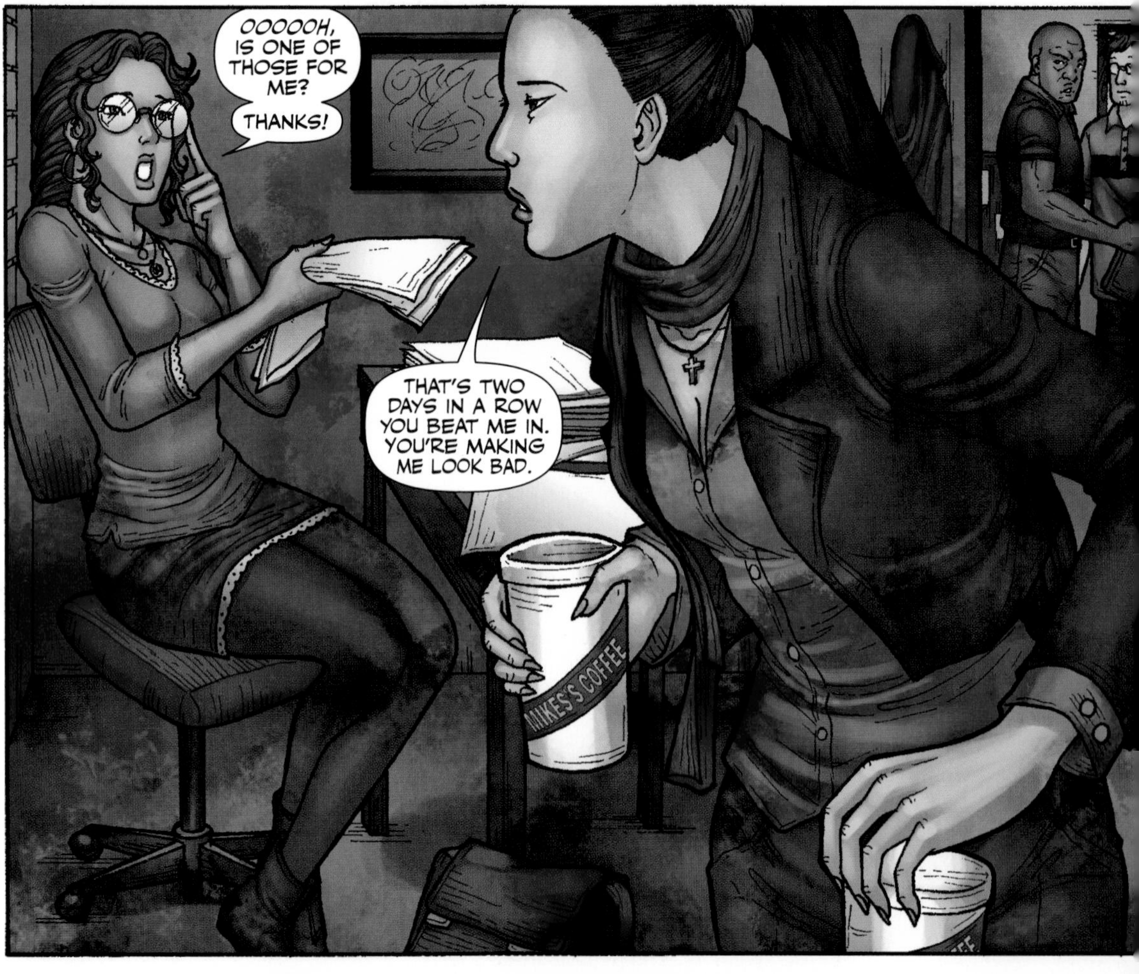
OOOOOH, IS ONE OF THOSE FOR ME?
THANKS!
THAT'S TWO DAYS IN A ROW YOU BEAT ME IN. YOU'RE MAKING ME LOOK BAD.
MIKE'S COFFEE

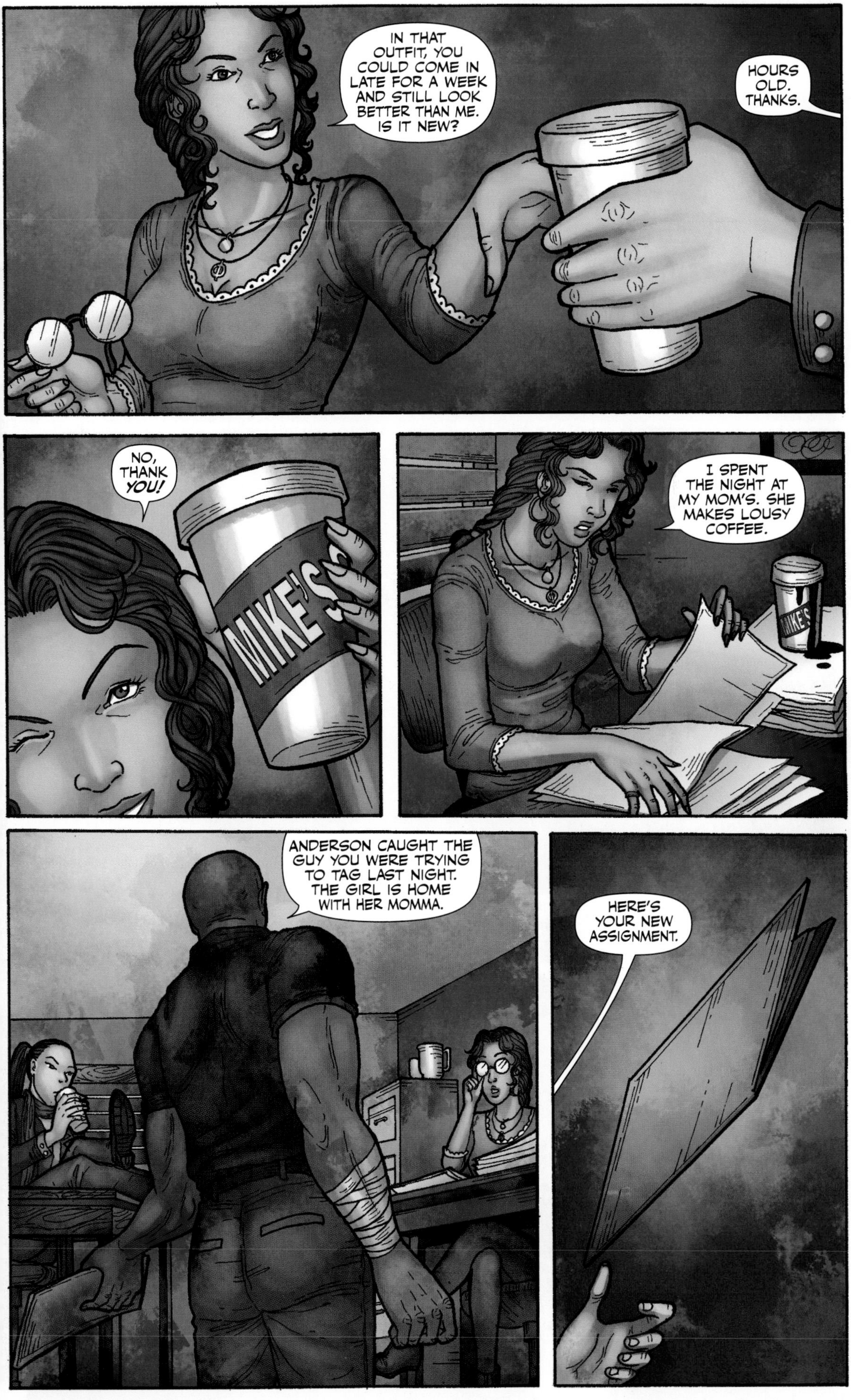
IN THAT OUTFIT, YOU COULD COME IN LATE FOR A WEEK AND STILL LOOK BETTER THAN ME. IS IT NEW?
HOURS OLD. THANKS.
NO, THANK *YOU!*
MIKE'S
I SPENT THE NIGHT AT MY MOM'S. SHE MAKES LOUSY COFFEE.
MIKE'S
ANDERSON CAUGHT THE GUY YOU WERE TRYING TO TAG LAST NIGHT. THE GIRL IS HOME WITH HER MOMMA.
HERE'S YOUR NEW ASSIGNMENT.

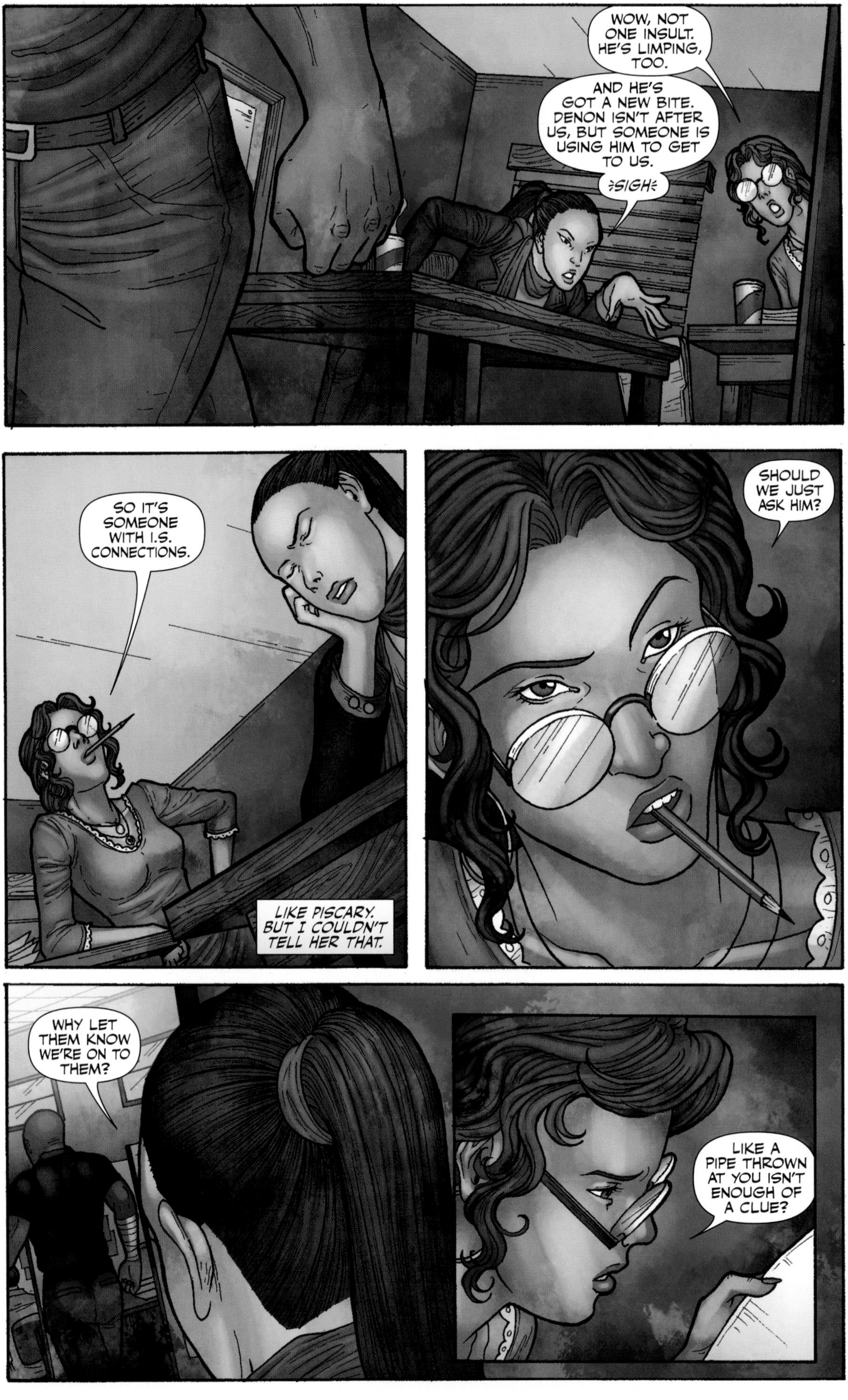
WOW, NOT ONE INSULT. HE'S LIMPING, TOO.
AND HE'S GOT A NEW BITE. DENON ISN'T AFTER US, BUT SOMEONE IS USING HIM TO GET TO US.
SIGH
SO IT'S SOMEONE WITH I.S. CONNECTIONS.
LIKE PISCARY. BUT I COULDN'T TELL HER THAT.
SHOULD WE JUST ASK HIM?
WHY LET THEM KNOW WE'RE ON TO THEM?
LIKE A PIPE THROWN AT YOU ISN'T ENOUGH OF A CLUE?

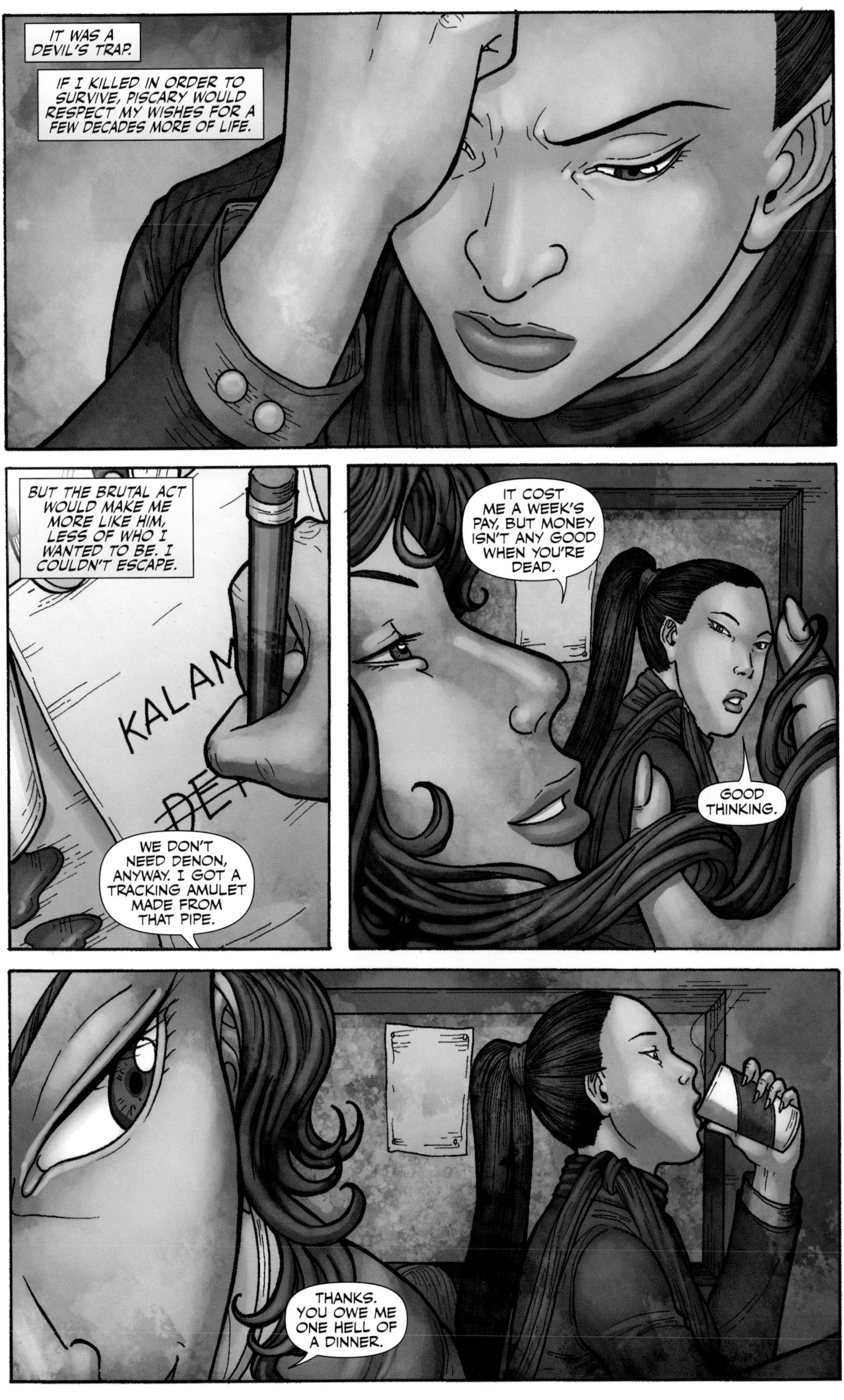
IT WAS A DEVIL'S TRAP.
IF I KILLED IN ORDER TO SURVIVE, PISCARY WOULD RESPECT MY WISHES FOR A FEW DECADES MORE OF LIFE.
BUT THE BRUTAL ACT WOULD MAKE ME MORE LIKE HIM, LESS OF WHO I WANTED TO BE. I COULDN'T ESCAPE.
KALAM
WE DON'T NEED DENON, ANYWAY. I GOT A TRACKING AMULET MADE FROM THAT PIPE.
IT COST ME A WEEK'S PAY, BUT MONEY ISN'T ANY GOOD WHEN YOU'RE DEAD.
GOOD THINKING.
THANKS. YOU OWE ME ONE HELL OF A DINNER.

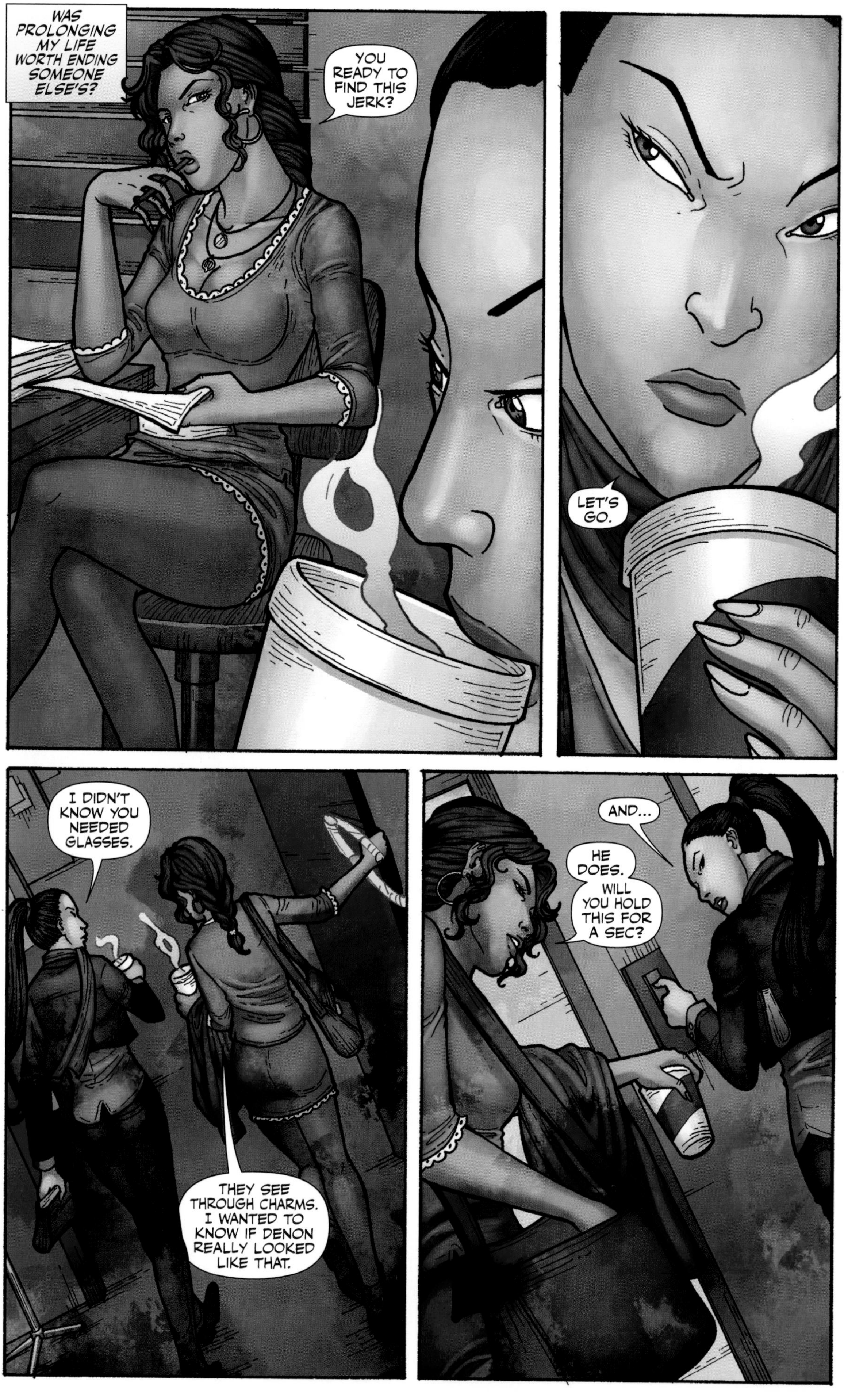
WAS PROLONGING MY LIFE WORTH ENDING SOMEONE ELSE'S?
YOU READY TO FIND THIS JERK?
LET'S GO.
I DIDN'T KNOW YOU NEEDED GLASSES.
THEY SEE THROUGH CHARMS. I WANTED TO KNOW IF DENON REALLY LOOKED LIKE THAT.
AND...
HE DOES.
WILL YOU HOLD THIS FOR A SEC?

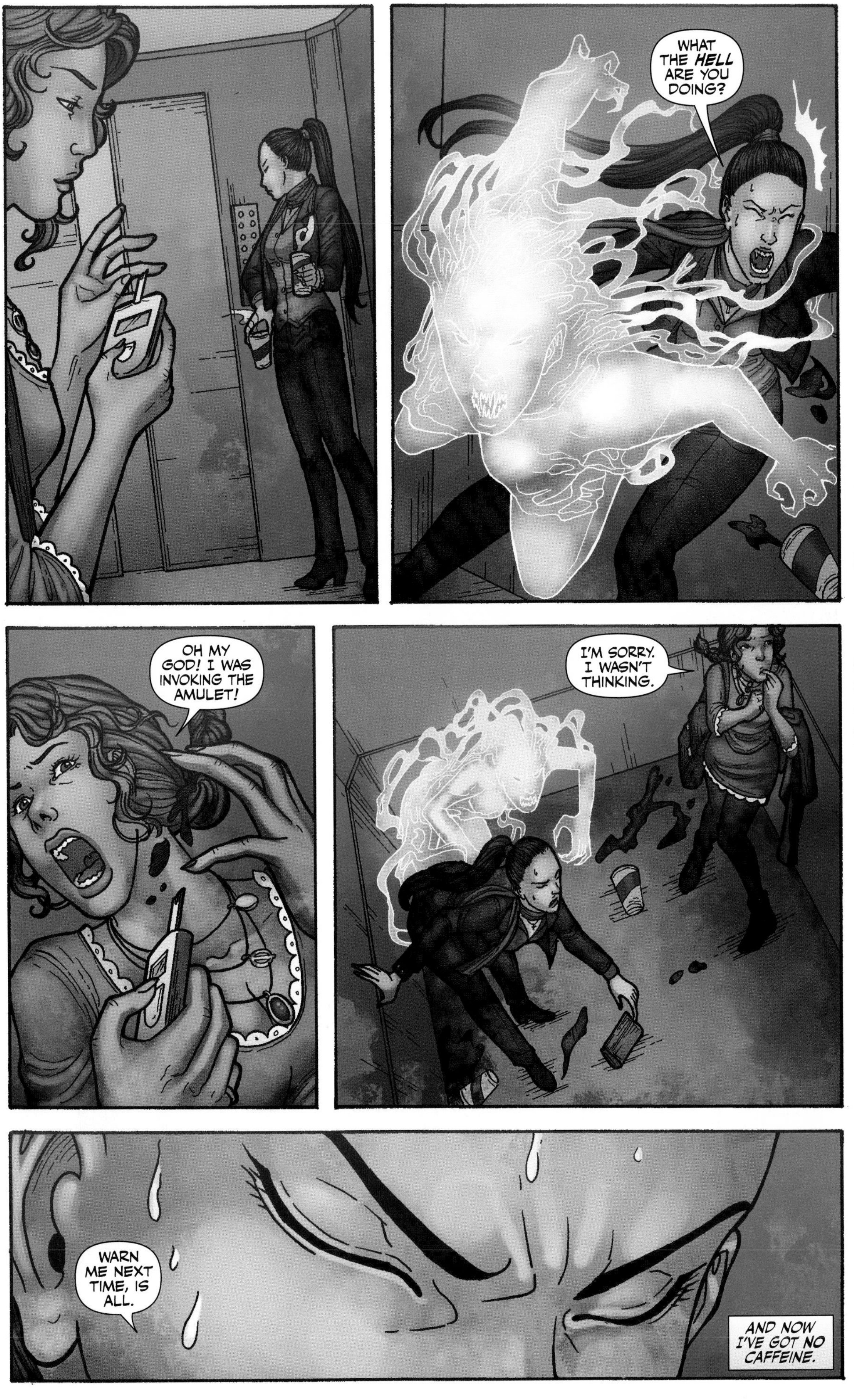
WHAT THE HELL ARE YOU DOING?
OH MY GOD! I WAS INVOKING THE AMULET!
I'M SORRY. I WASN'T THINKING.
WARN ME NEXT TIME, IS ALL.
AND NOW I'VE GOT NO CAFFEINE.

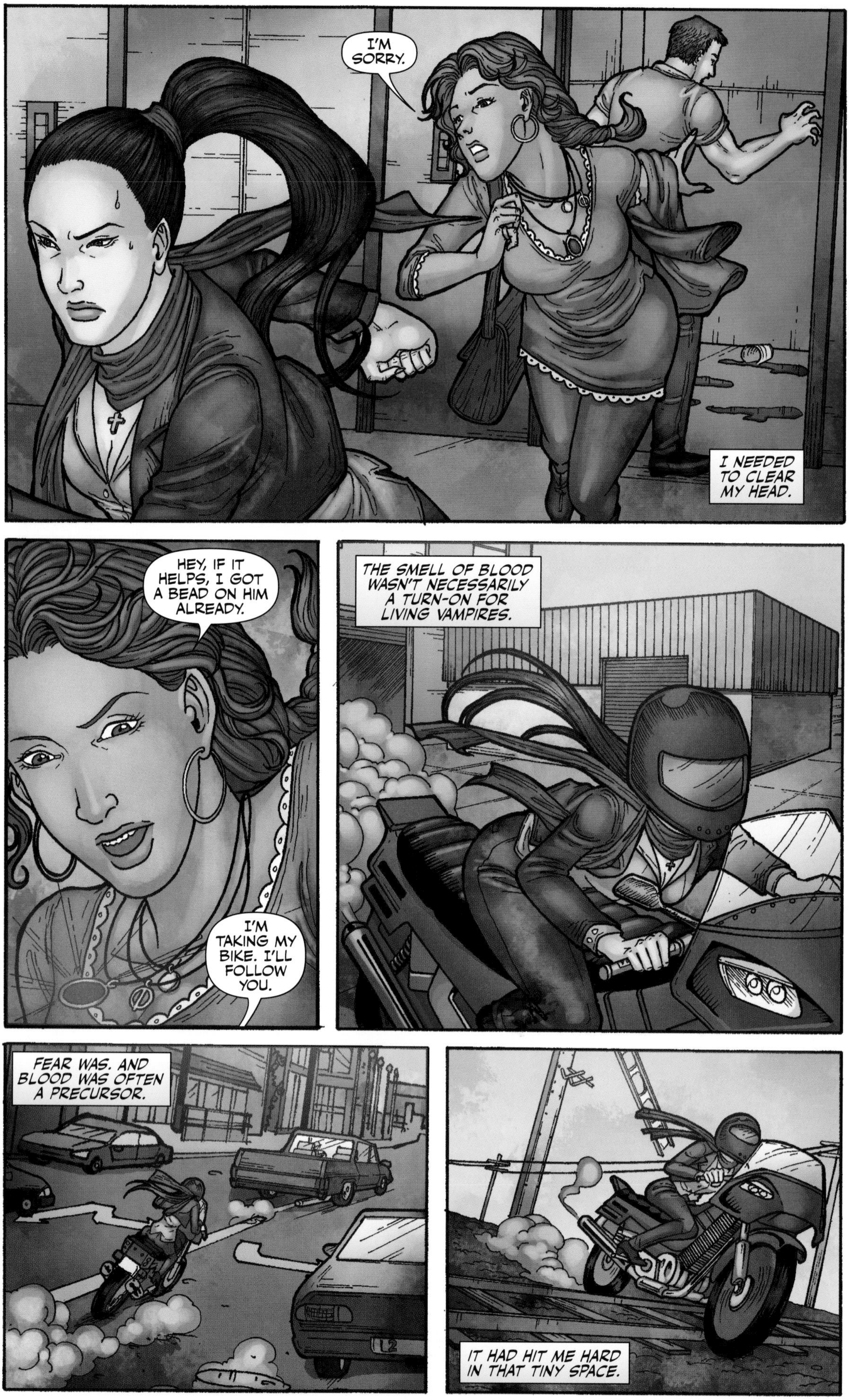
I'M SORRY.
I NEEDED TO CLEAR MY HEAD.
HEY, IF IT HELPS, I GOT A BEAD ON HIM ALREADY.
I'M TAKING MY BIKE. I'LL FOLLOW YOU.
THE SMELL OF BLOOD WASN'T NECESSARILY A TURN-ON FOR LIVING VAMPIRES.
FEAR WAS. AND BLOOD WAS OFTEN A PRECURSOR.
IT HAD HIT ME HARD IN THAT TINY SPACE.

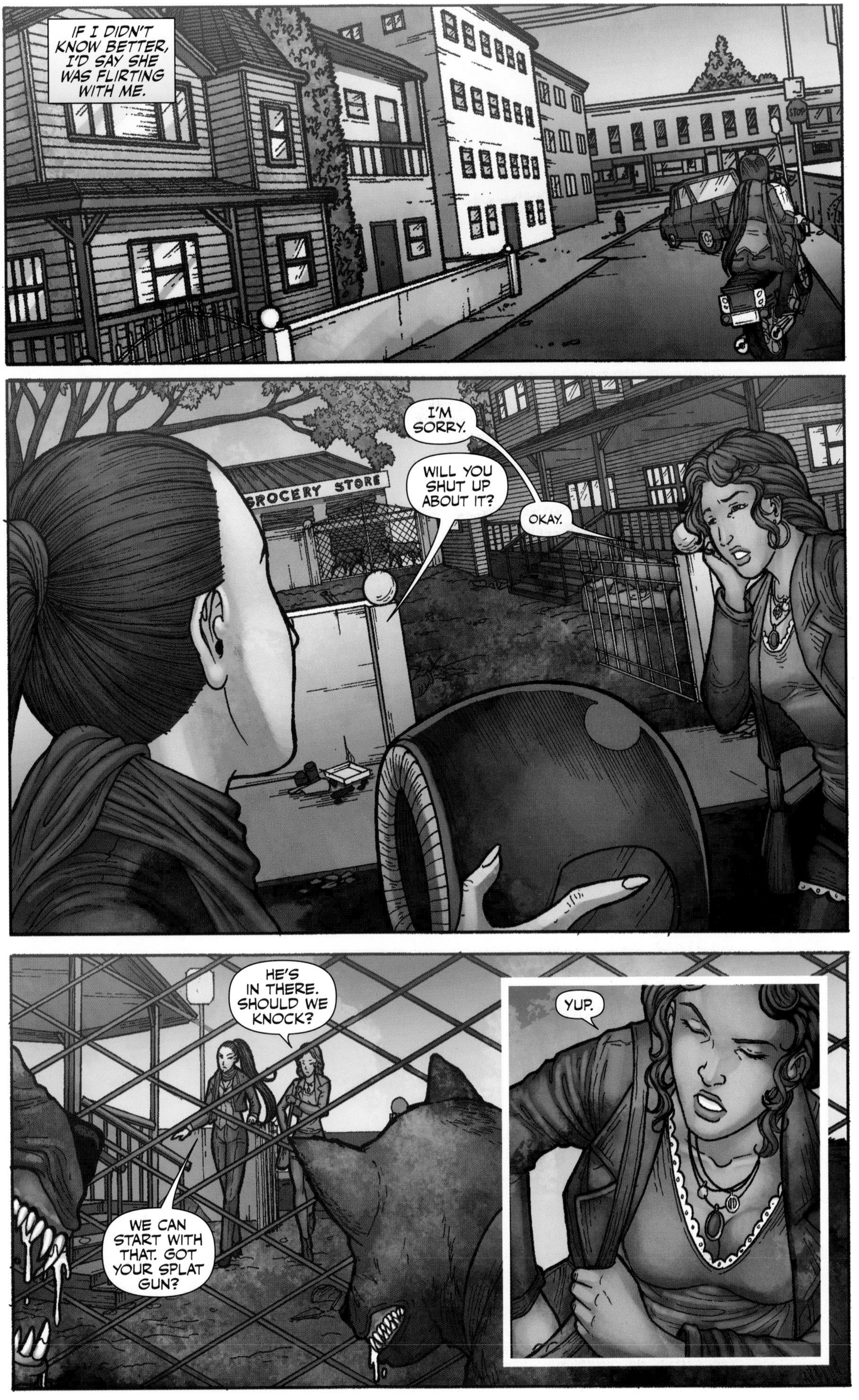
IF I DIDN'T KNOW BETTER, I'D SAY SHE WAS FLIRTING WITH ME.
GROCERY STORE
I'M SORRY.
WILL YOU SHUT UP ABOUT IT?
OKAY.
HE'S IN THERE. SHOULD WE KNOCK?
WE CAN START WITH THAT. GOT YOUR SPLAT GUN?
YUP.

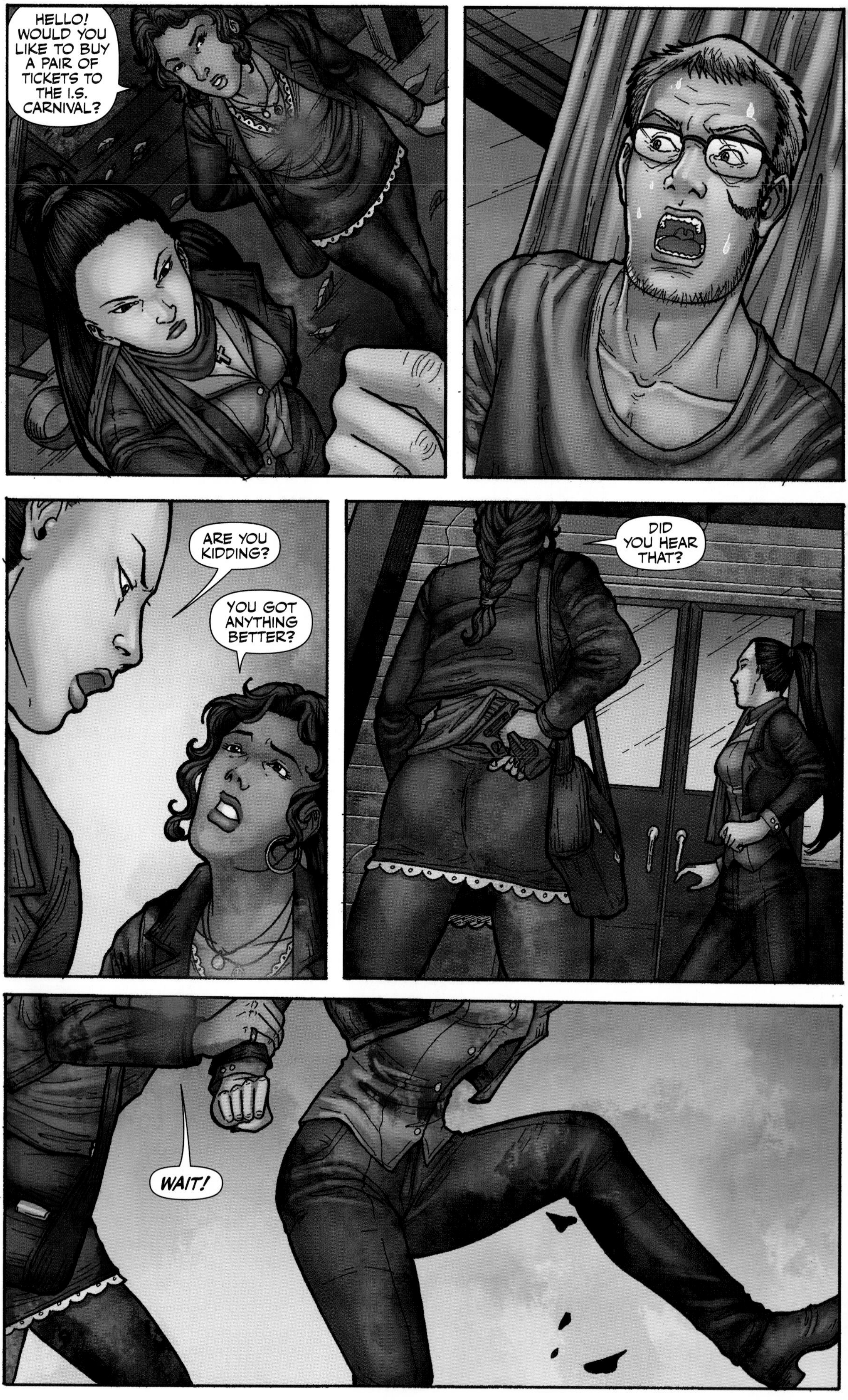

HELLO! WOULD YOU LIKE TO BUY A PAIR OF TICKETS TO THE I.S. CARNIVAL?
ARE YOU KIDDING?
YOU GOT ANYTHING BETTER?
DID YOU HEAR THAT?
WAIT!

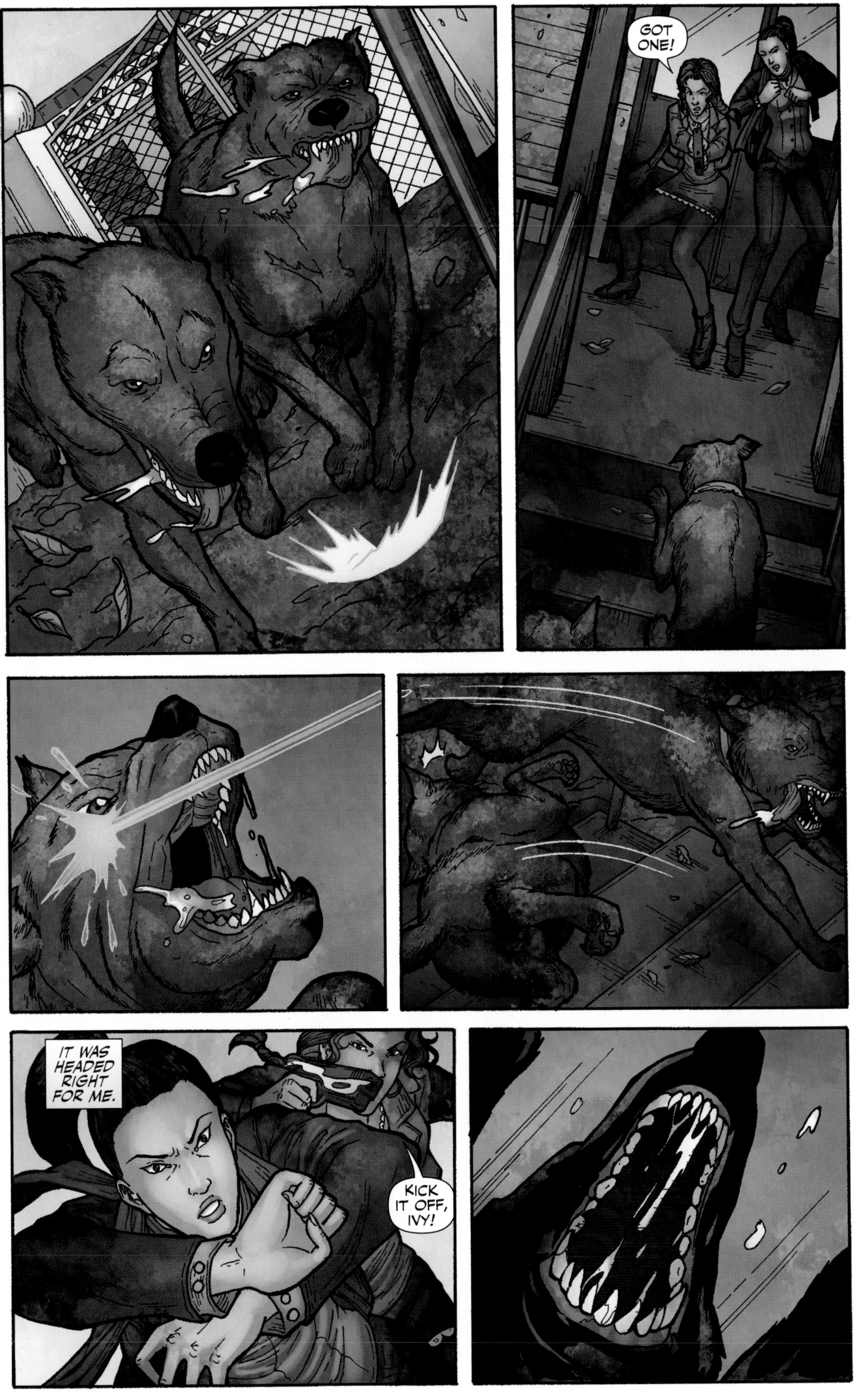

GOT ONE!
IT WAS HEADED RIGHT FOR ME.
KICK IT OFF, IVY!

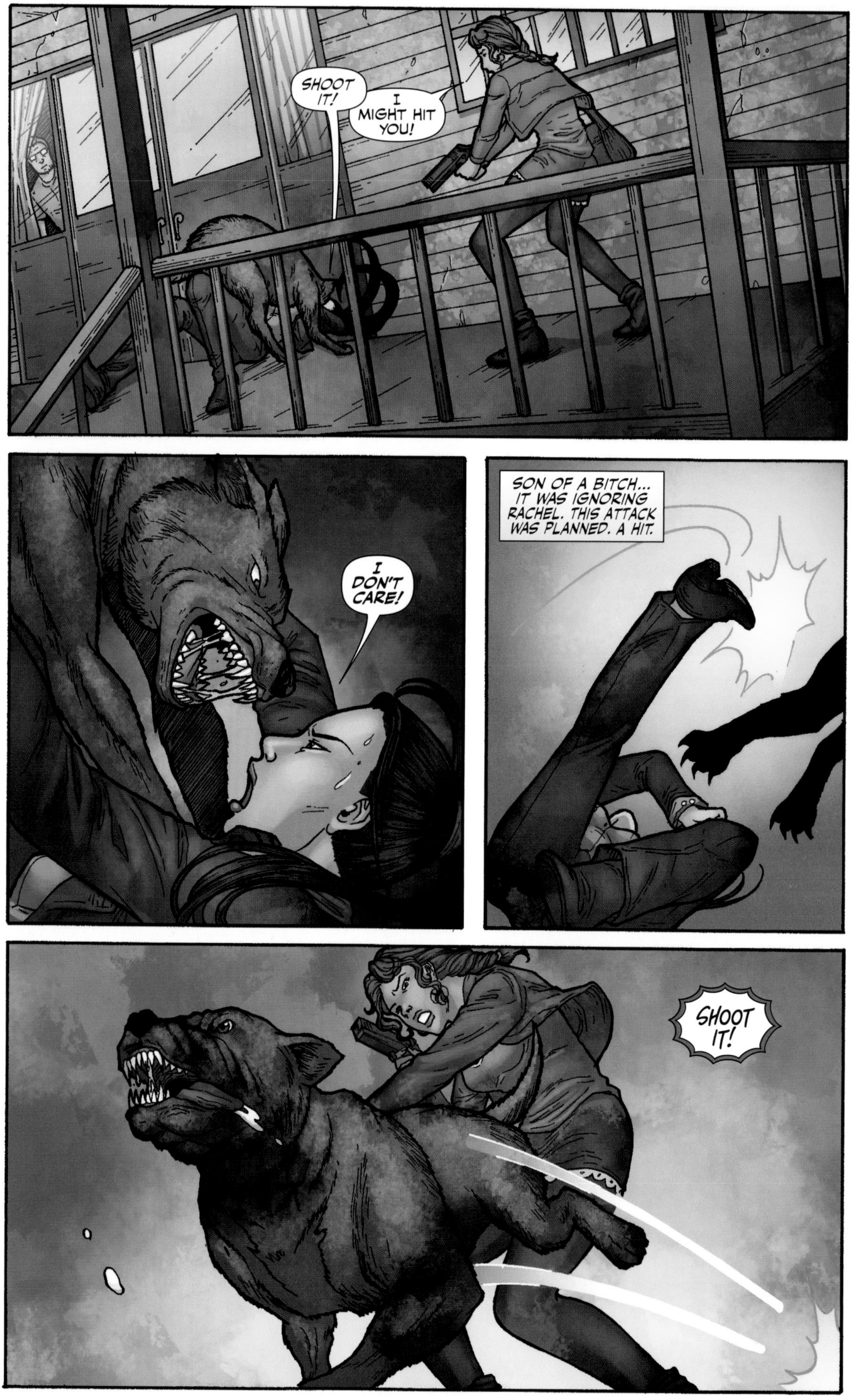
SHOOT IT!
I MIGHT HIT YOU!
I DON'T CARE!
SON OF A BITCH... IT WAS IGNORING RACHEL. THIS ATTACK WAS PLANNED. A HIT.
SHOOT IT!

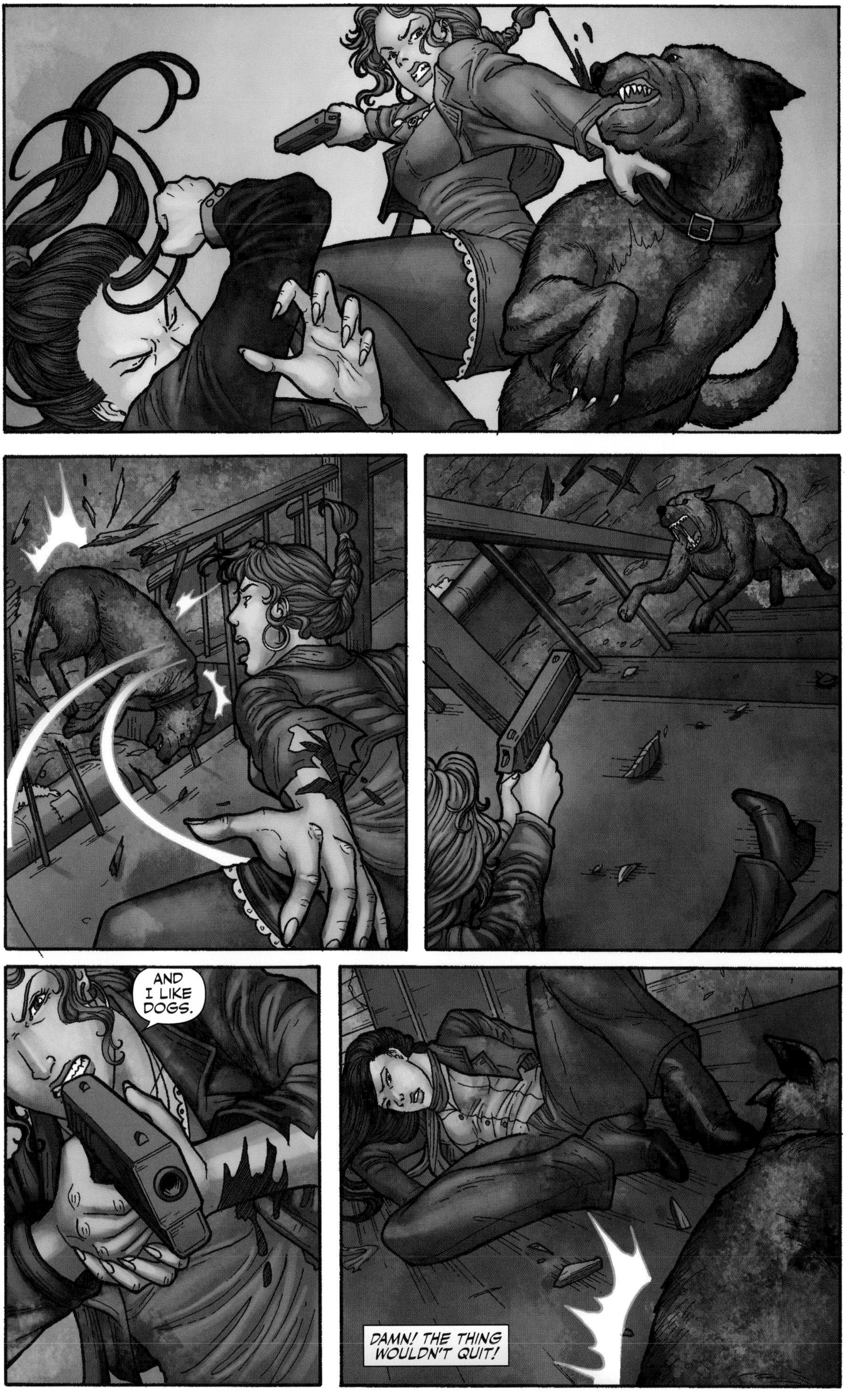
AND I LIKE DOGS.
DAMN! THE THING WOULDN'T QUIT!

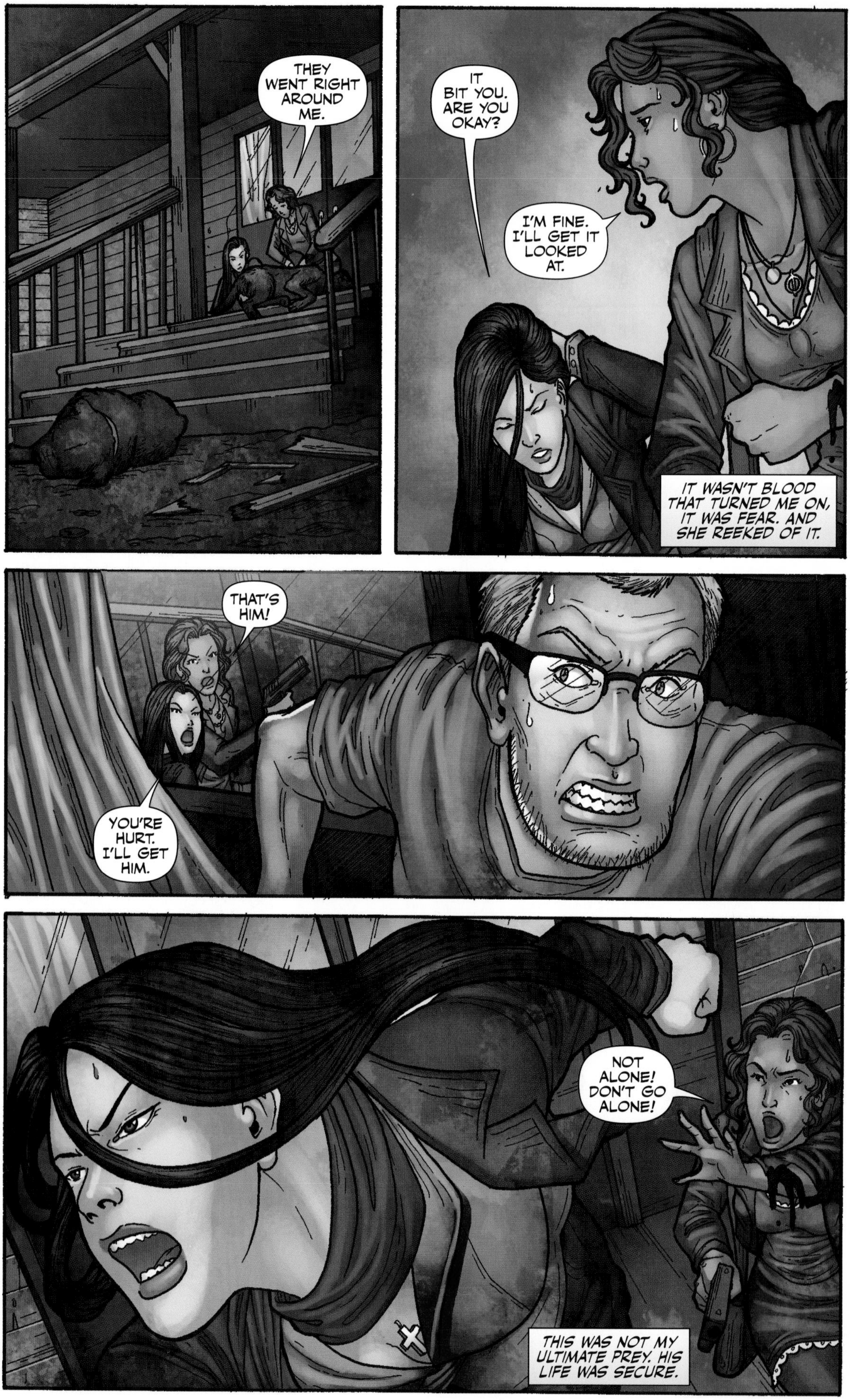
THEY WENT RIGHT AROUND ME.
IT BIT YOU. ARE YOU OKAY?
I'M FINE. I'LL GET IT LOOKED AT.
IT WASN'T BLOOD THAT TURNED ME ON, IT WAS FEAR. AND SHE REEKED OF IT.
THAT'S HIM!
YOU'RE HURT. I'LL GET HIM.
NOT ALONE! DON'T GO ALONE!
THIS WAS NOT MY ULTIMATE PREY. HIS LIFE WAS SECURE.

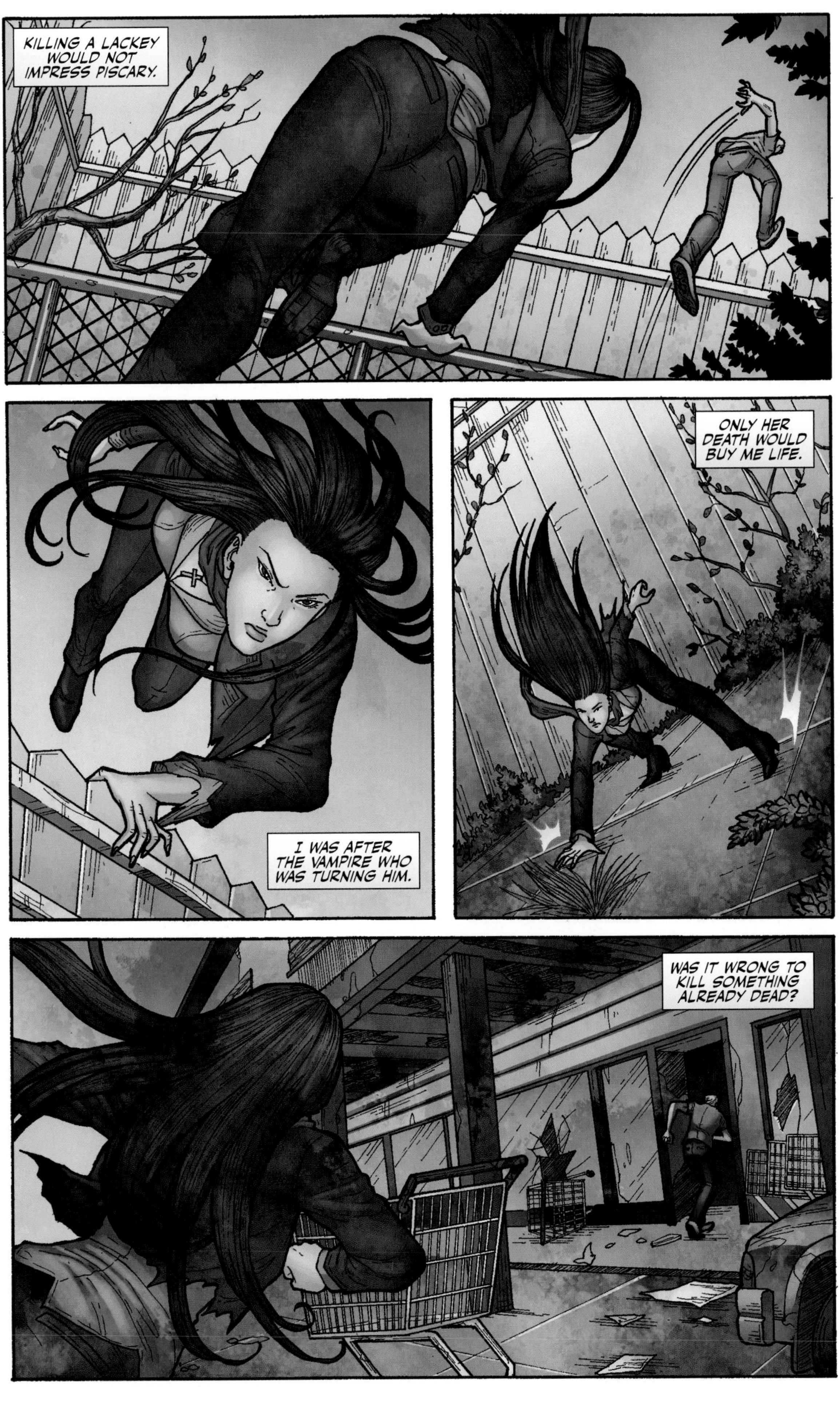

KILLING A LACKEY WOULD NOT IMPRESS PISCARY.
I WAS AFTER THE VAMPIRE WHO WAS TURNING HIM.
ONLY HER DEATH WOULD BUY ME LIFE.
WAS IT WRONG TO KILL SOMETHING ALREADY DEAD?

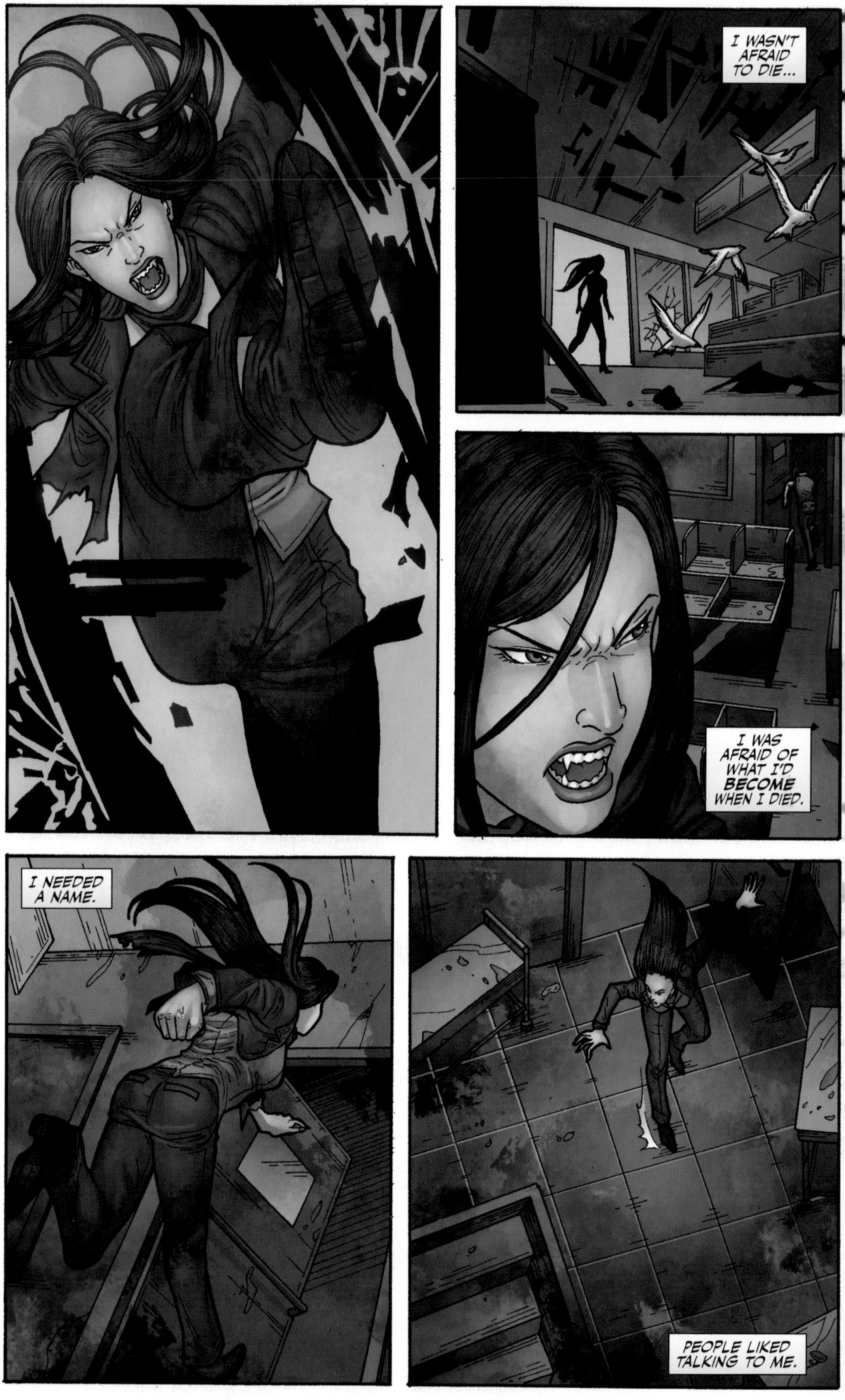

I WASN'T AFRAID TO DIE...
I WAS AFRAID OF WHAT I'D BECOME WHEN I DIED.
I NEEDED A NAME.
PEOPLE LIKED TALKING TO ME.

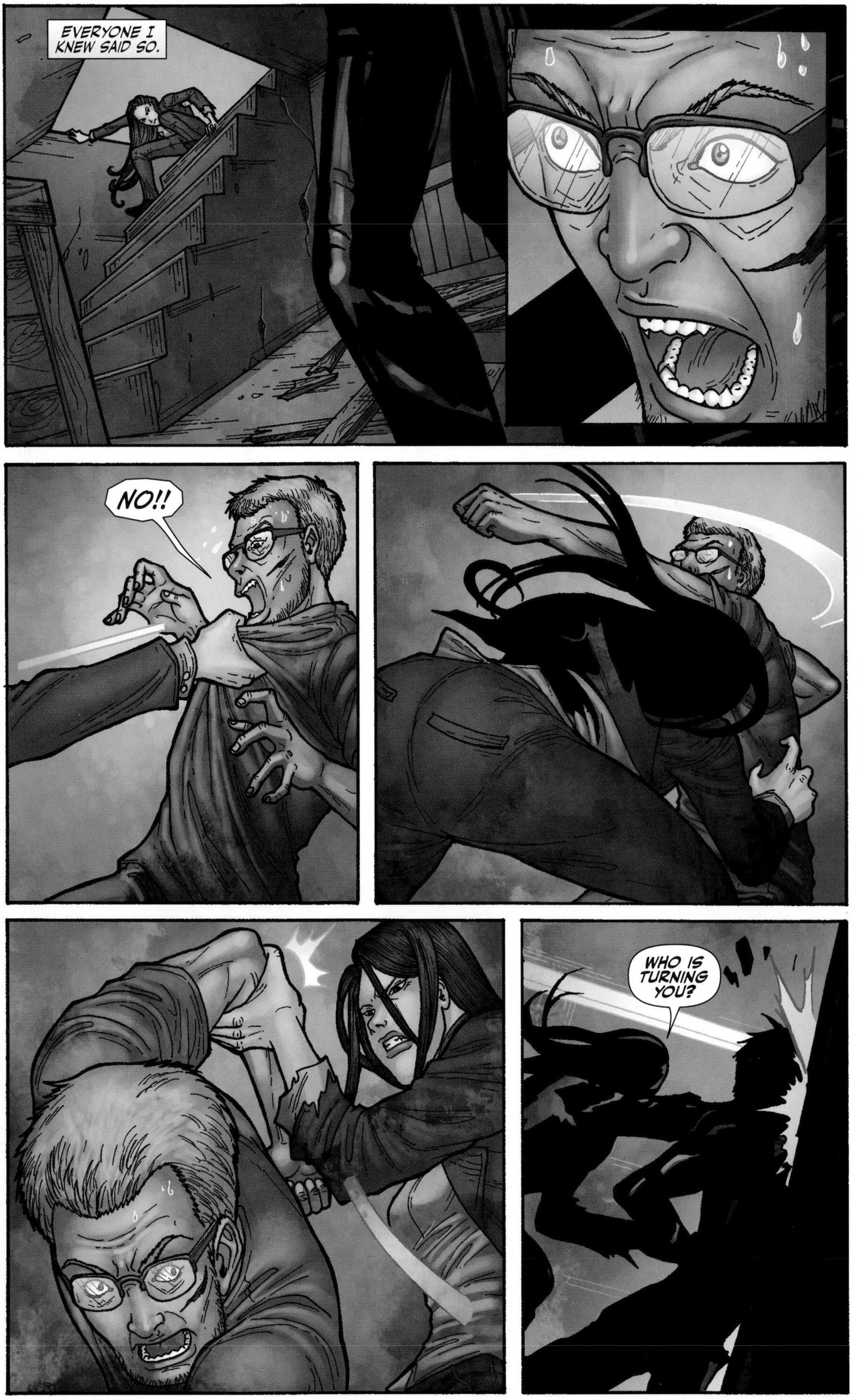
EVERYONE I KNEW SAID SO.
NO!!
WHO IS TURNING YOU?

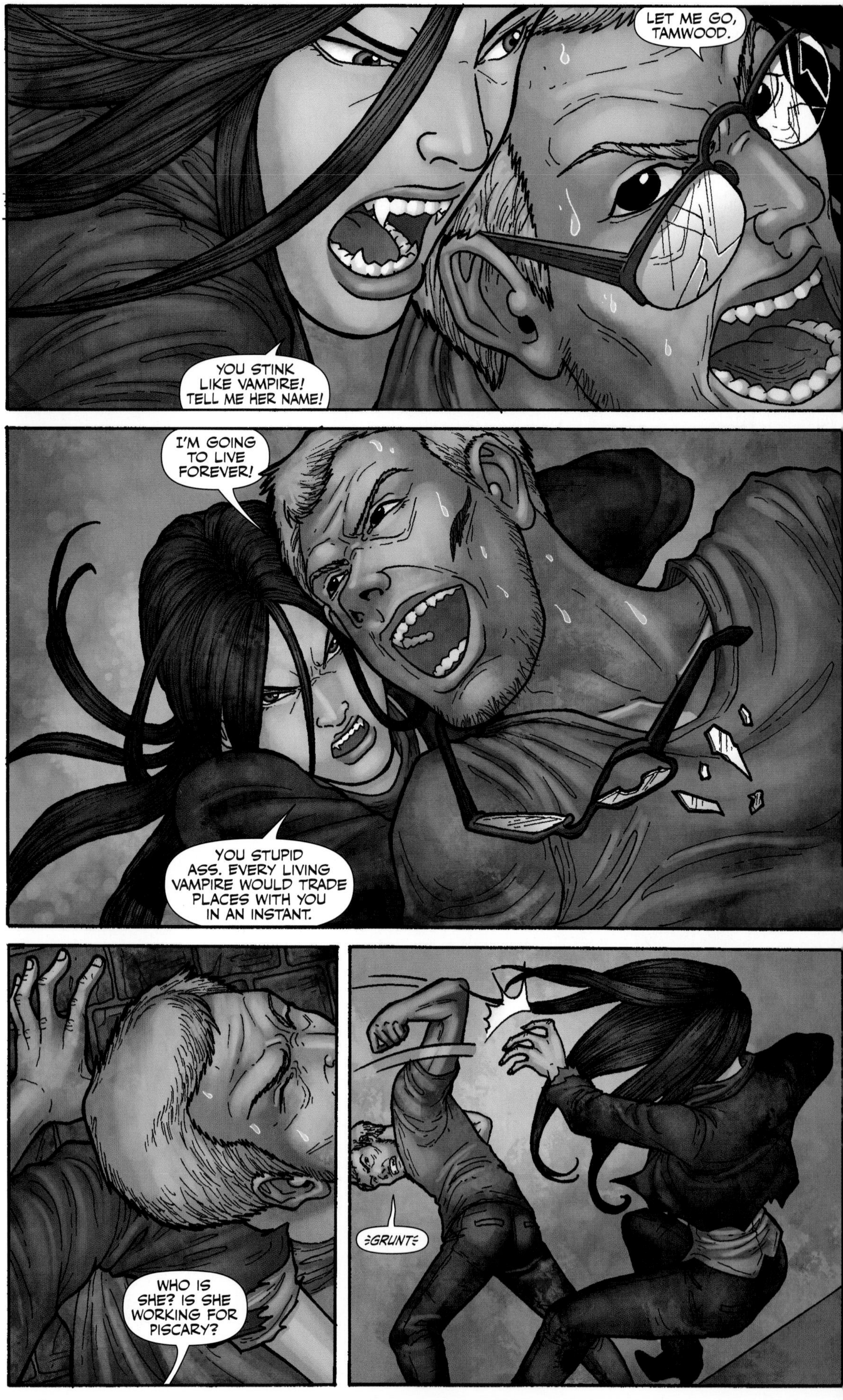
LET ME GO, TAMWOOD.
YOU STINK LIKE VAMPIRE! TELL ME HER NAME!
I'M GOING TO LIVE FOREVER!
YOU STUPID ASS. EVERY LIVING VAMPIRE WOULD TRADE PLACES WITH YOU IN AN INSTANT.
WHO IS SHE? IS SHE WORKING FOR PISCARY?
GRUNT

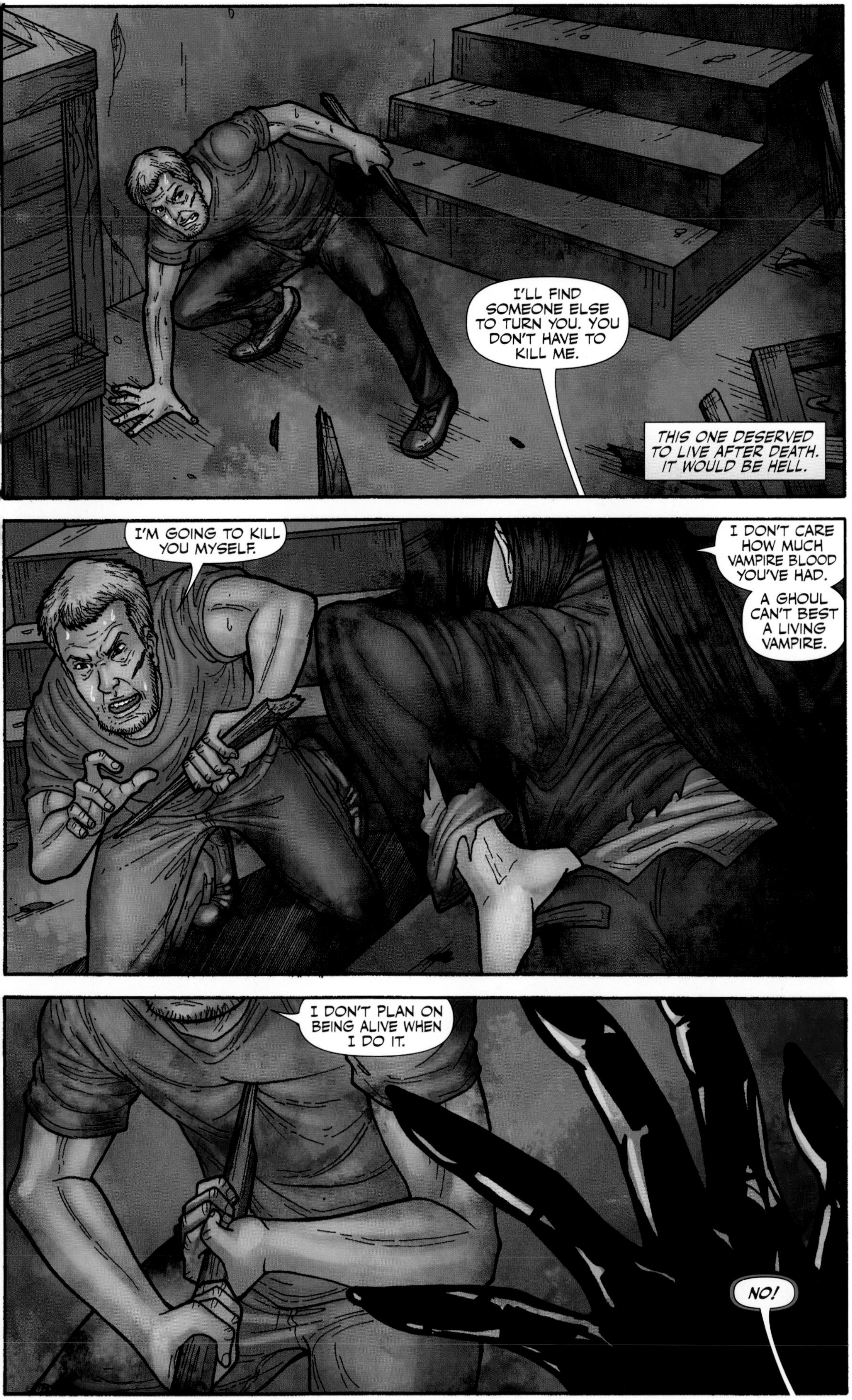
I'LL FIND SOMEONE ELSE TO TURN YOU. YOU DON'T HAVE TO KILL ME.
THIS ONE DESERVED TO LIVE AFTER DEATH. IT WOULD BE HELL.
I'M GOING TO KILL YOU MYSELF.
I DON'T CARE HOW MUCH VAMPIRE BLOOD YOU'VE HAD.
A GHOUL CAN'T BEST A LIVING VAMPIRE.
I DON'T PLAN ON BEING ALIVE WHEN I DO IT.
NO!

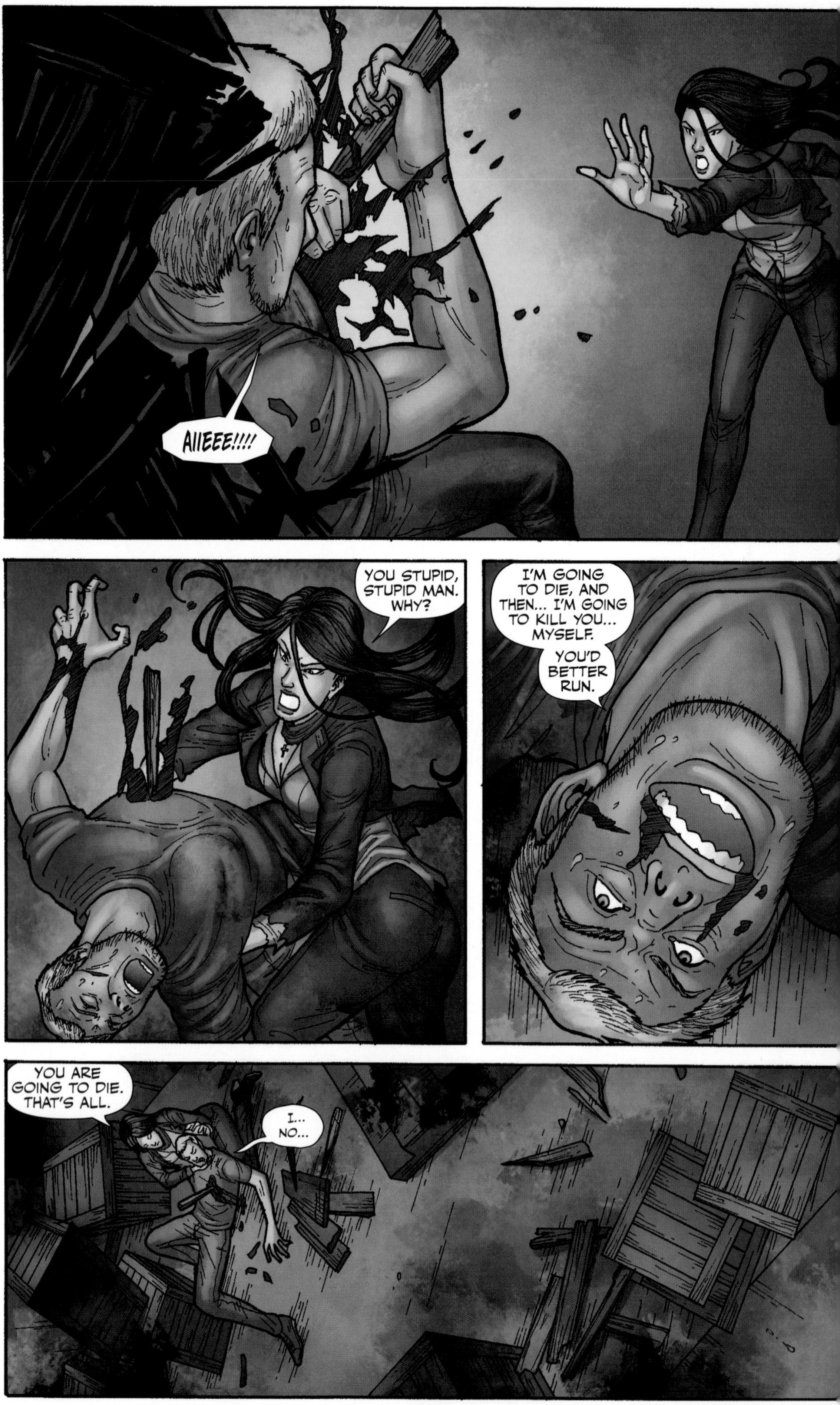
AIIEEE!!!!
YOU STUPID, STUPID MAN. WHY?
I'M GOING TO DIE, AND THEN... I'M GOING TO KILL YOU... MYSELF.
YOU'D BETTER RUN.
YOU ARE GOING TO DIE. THAT'S ALL.
I... NO...

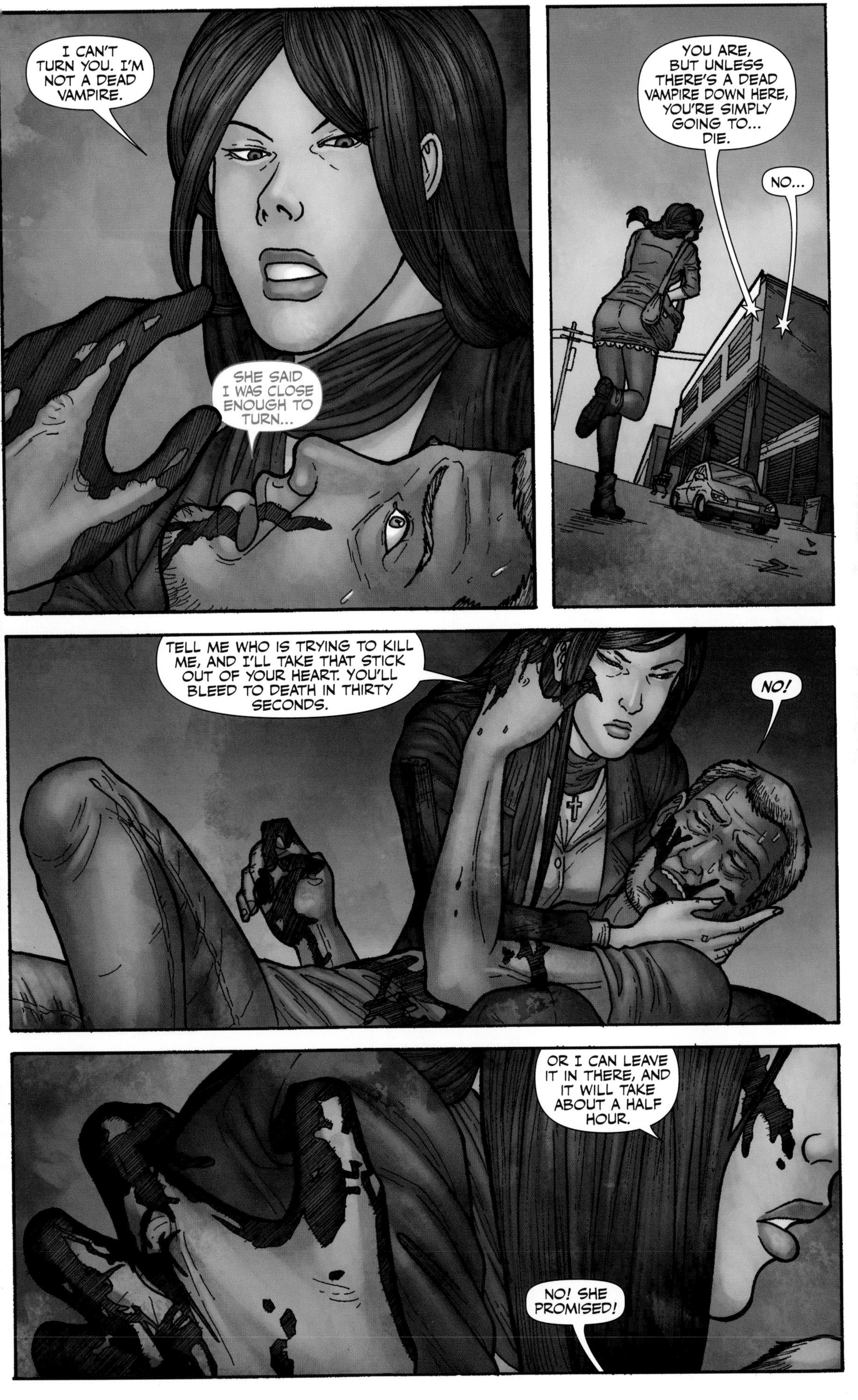
I CAN'T TURN YOU. I'M NOT A DEAD VAMPIRE.
SHE SAID I WAS CLOSE ENOUGH TO TURN...
YOU ARE, BUT UNLESS THERE'S A DEAD VAMPIRE DOWN HERE, YOU'RE SIMPLY GOING TO... DIE.
NO...
TELL ME WHO IS TRYING TO KILL ME, AND I'LL TAKE THAT STICK OUT OF YOUR HEART. YOU'LL BLEED TO DEATH IN THIRTY SECONDS.
NO!
OR I CAN LEAVE IT IN THERE, AND IT WILL TAKE ABOUT A HALF HOUR.
NO! SHE PROMISED!

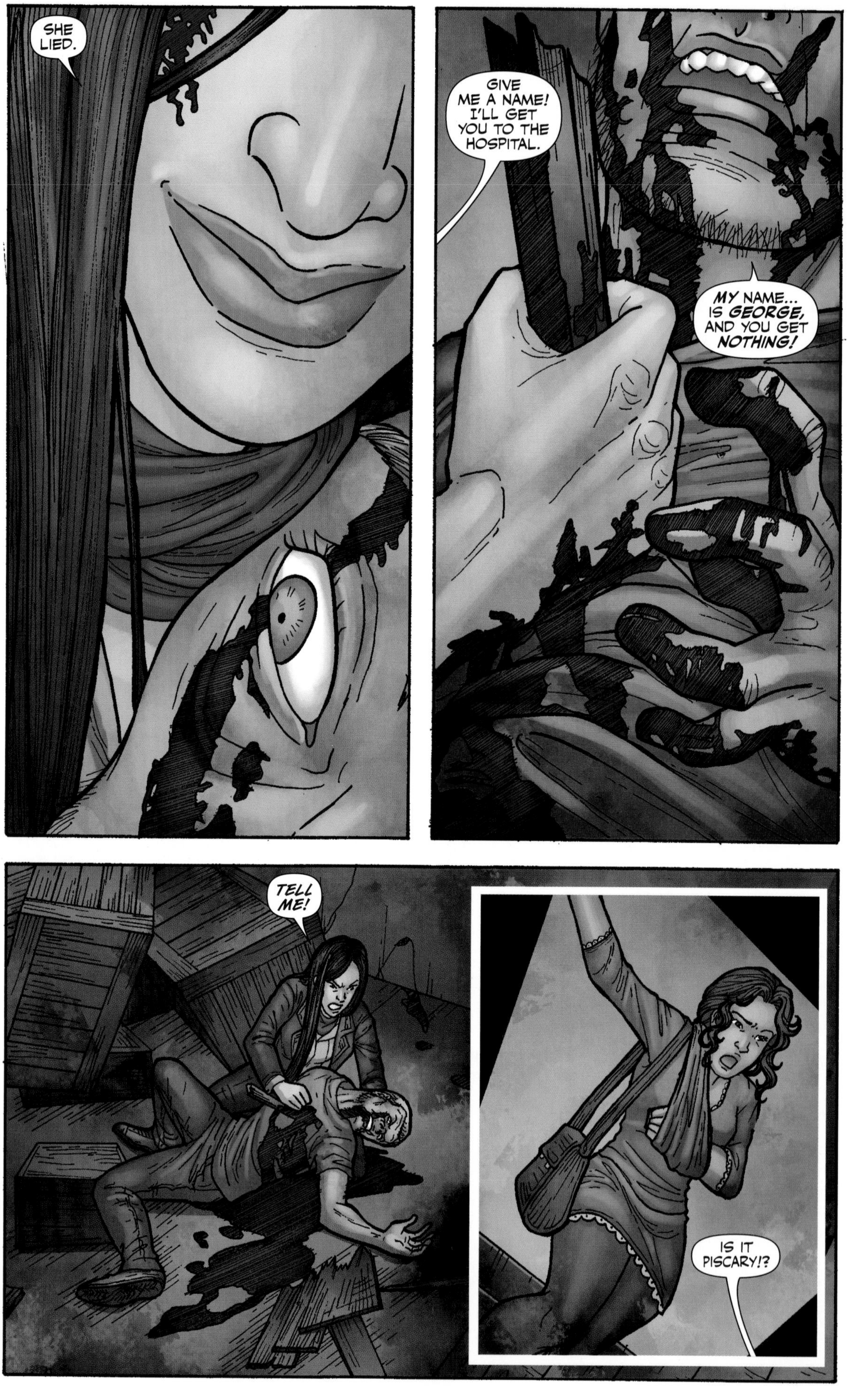
SHE LIED.
GIVE ME A NAME! I'LL GET YOU TO THE HOSPITAL.
MY NAME... IS GEORGE, AND YOU GET NOTHING!
TELL ME!
IS IT PISCARY!?

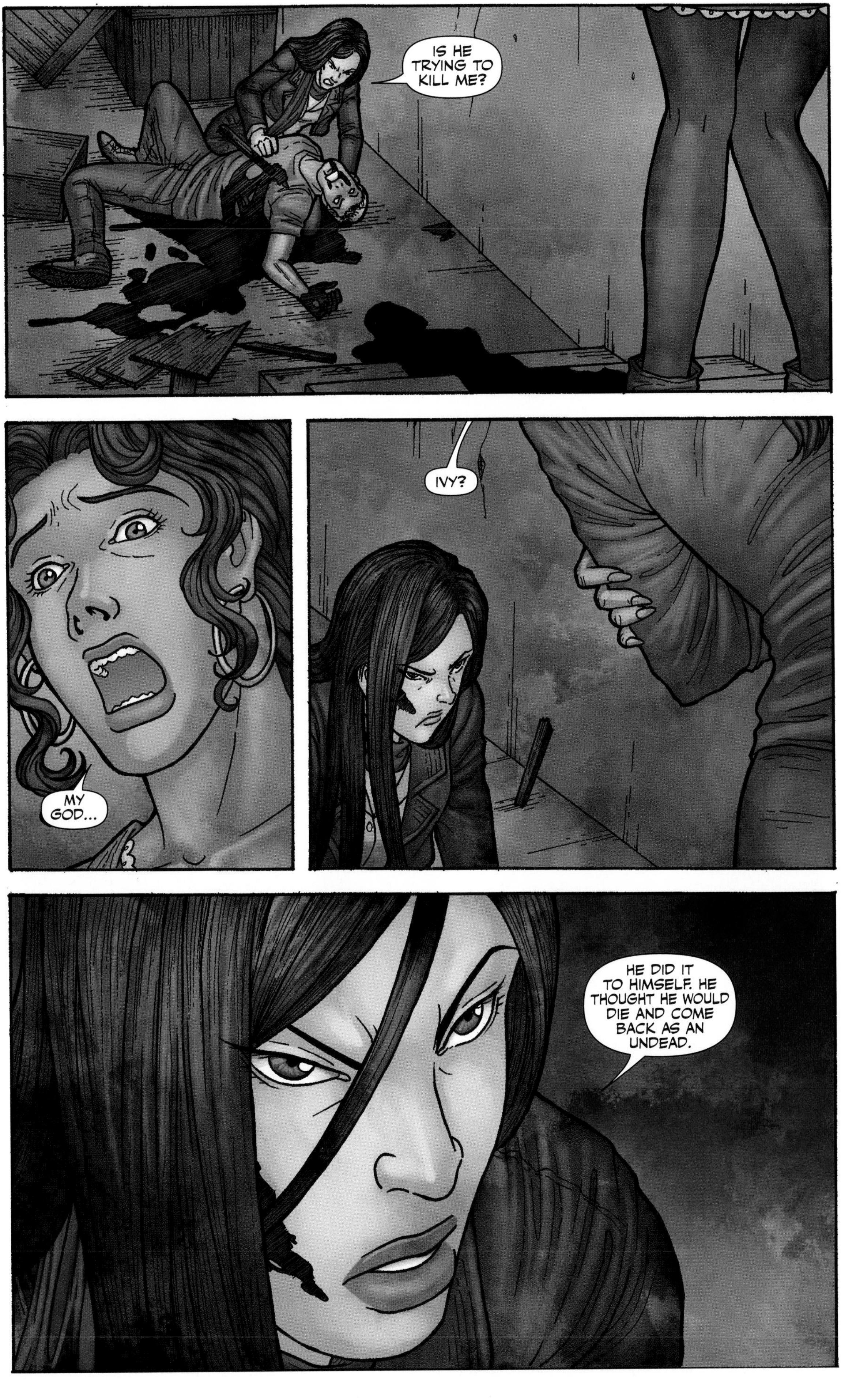
IS HE TRYING TO KILL ME?
MY GOD...
IVY?
HE DID IT TO HIMSELF. HE THOUGHT HE WOULD DIE AND COME BACK AS AN UNDEAD.

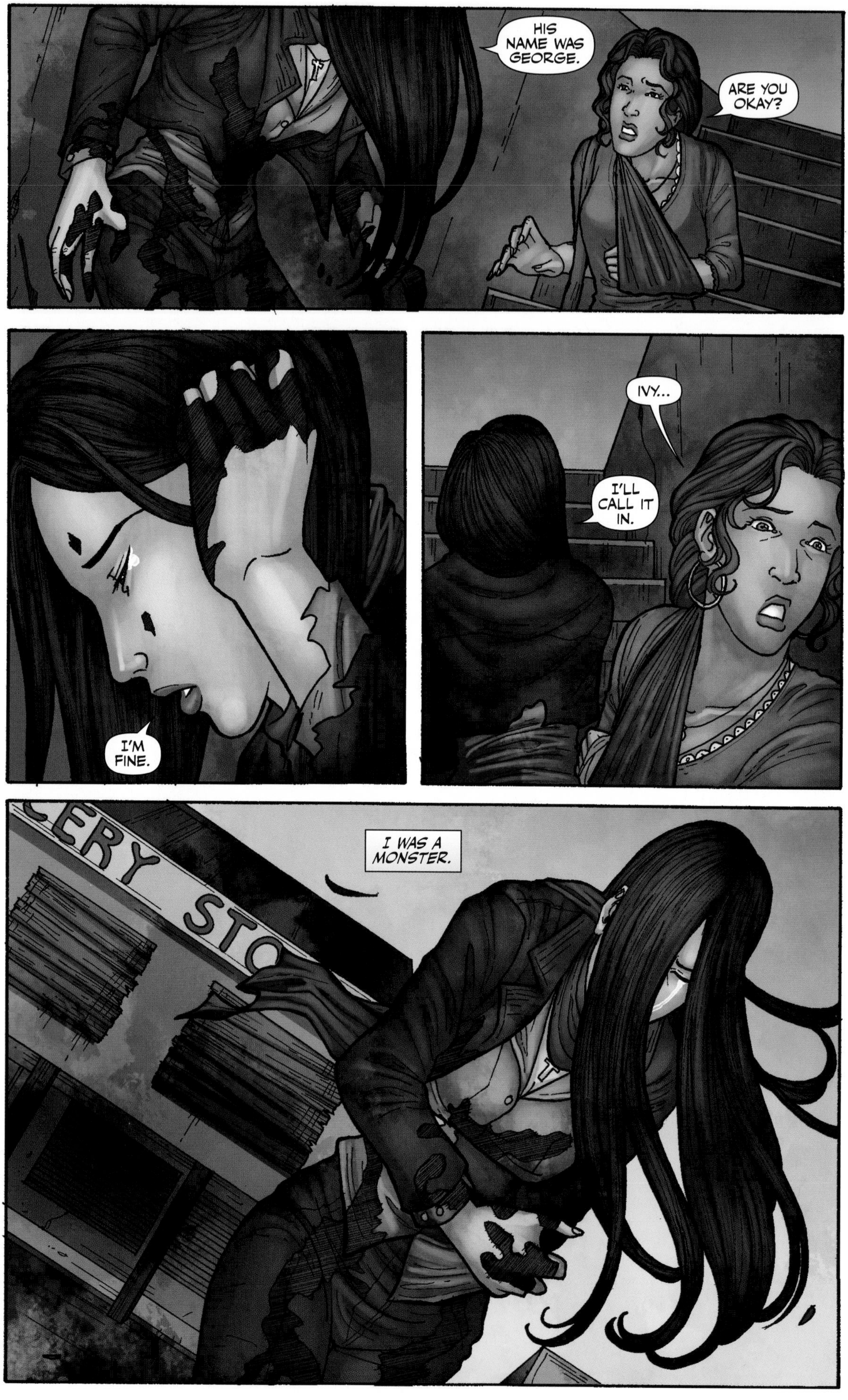
HIS NAME WAS GEORGE.
ARE YOU OKAY?
I'M FINE.
IVY...
I'LL CALL IT IN.
I WAS A MONSTER.
CERY STO

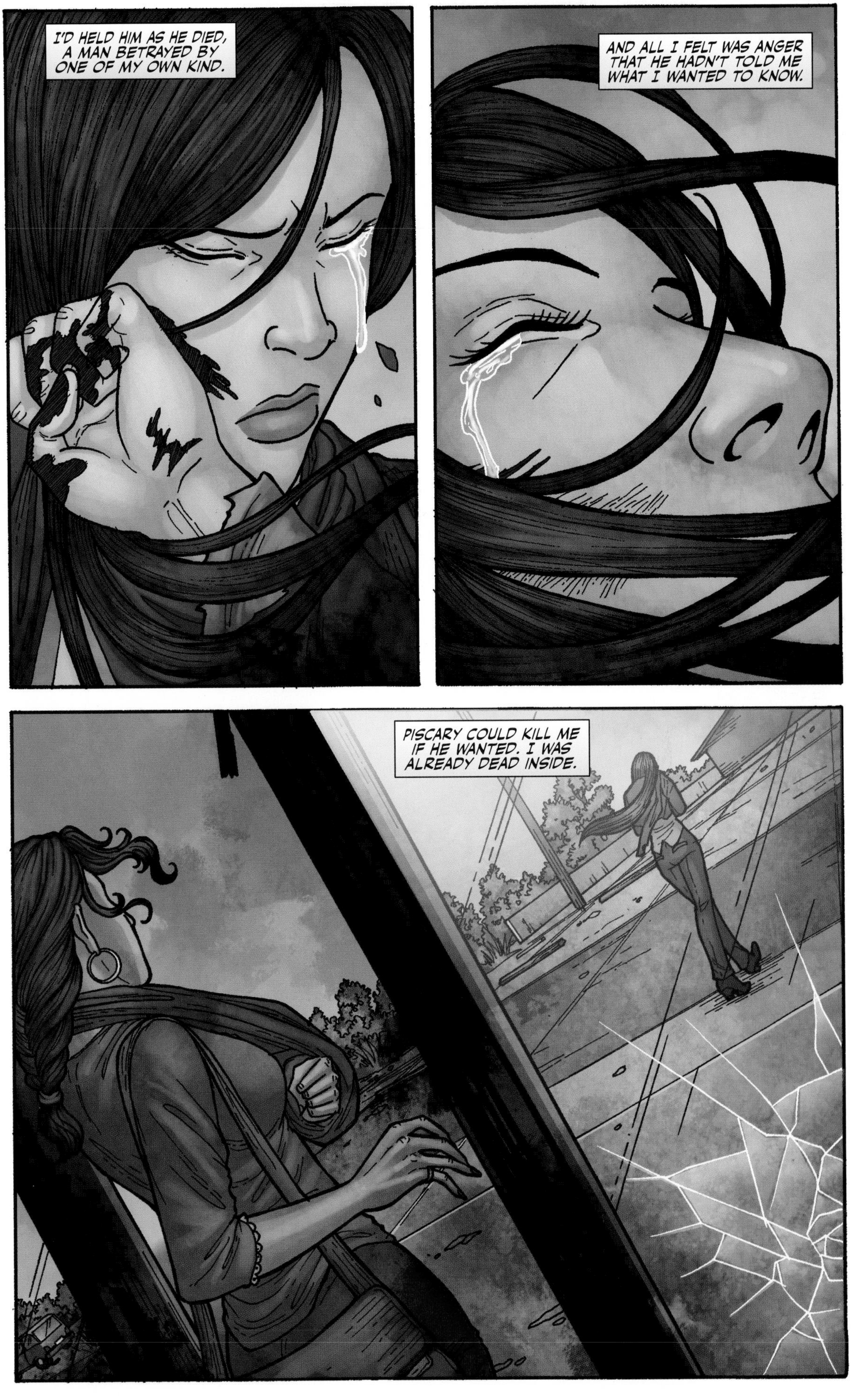
I'D HELD HIM AS HE DIED, A MAN BETRAYED BY ONE OF MY OWN KIND.
AND ALL I FELT WAS ANGER THAT HE HADN'T TOLD ME WHAT I WANTED TO KNOW.
PISCARY COULD KILL ME IF HE WANTED. I WAS ALREADY DEAD INSIDE.

CHAPTER 7

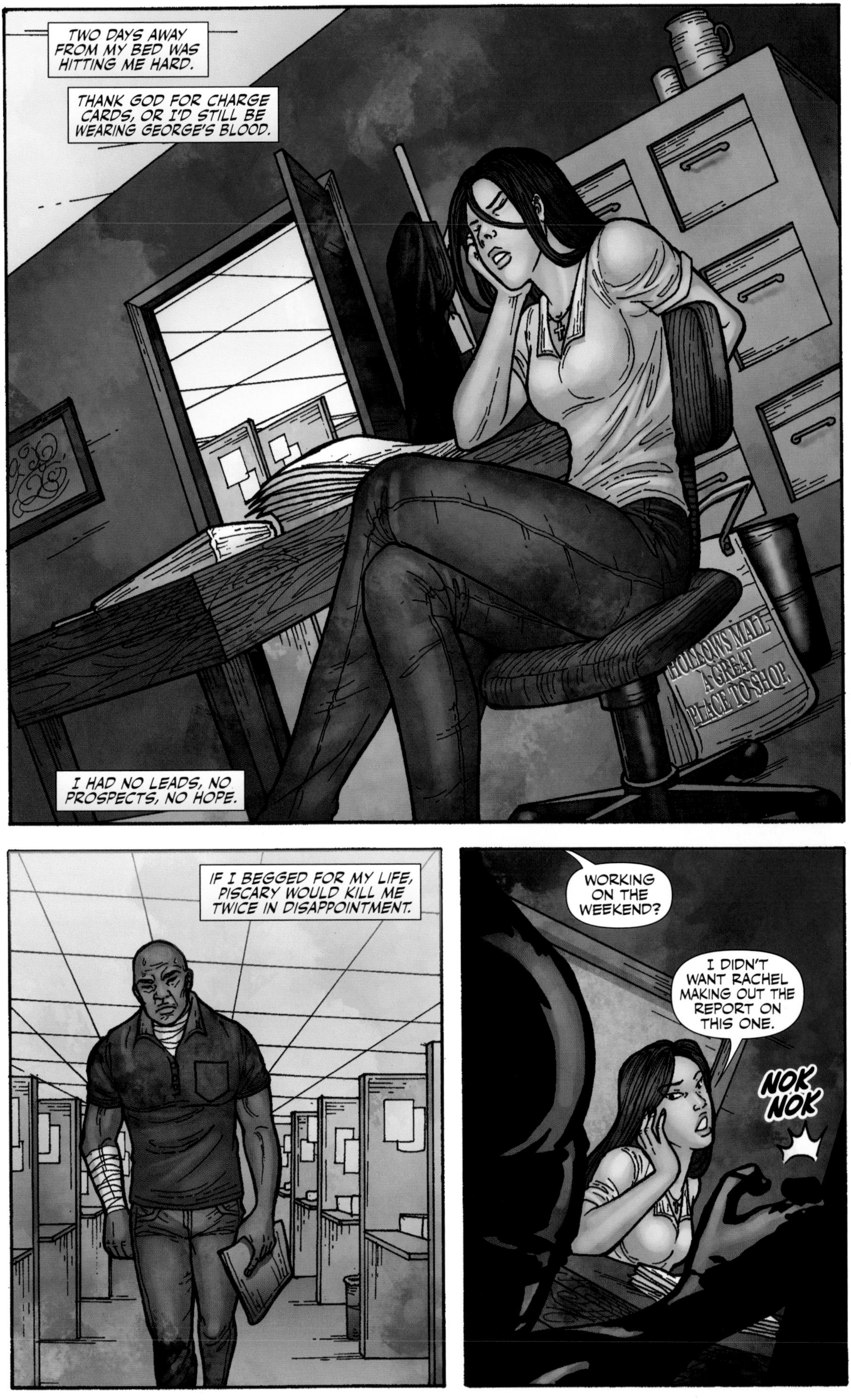
TWO DAYS AWAY FROM MY BED WAS HITTING ME HARD.
THANK GOD FOR CHARGE CARDS, OR I'D STILL BE WEARING GEORGE'S BLOOD.
HOLLOWS MALL A GREAT PLACE TO SHOP.
I HAD NO LEADS, NO PROSPECTS, NO HOPE.
IF I BEGGED FOR MY LIFE, PISCARY WOULD KILL ME TWICE IN DISAPPOINTMENT.
WORKING ON THE WEEKEND?
I DIDN'T WANT RACHEL MAKING OUT THE REPORT ON THIS ONE.
NOK NOK

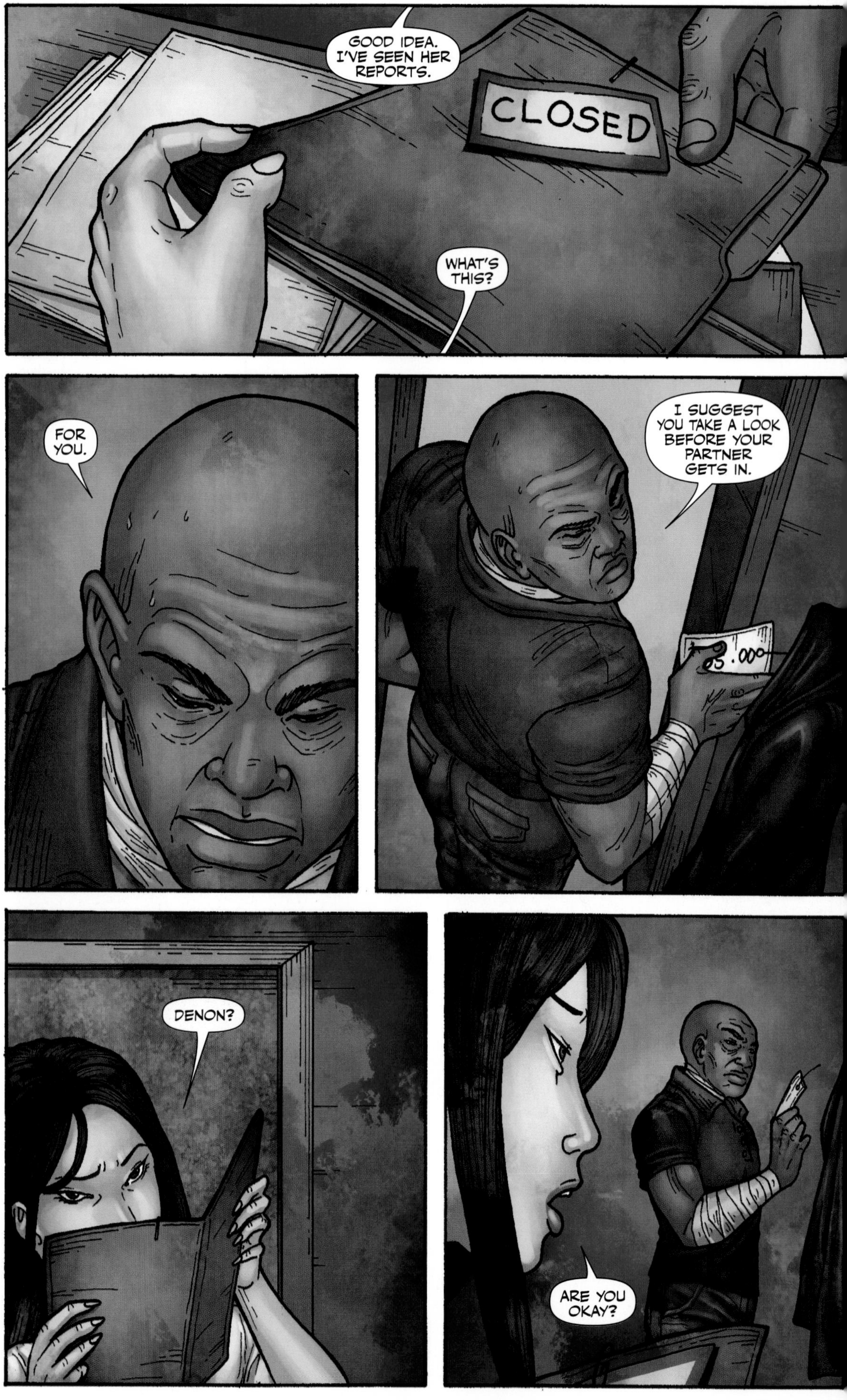
GOOD IDEA. I'VE SEEN HER REPORTS.
CLOSED
WHAT'S THIS?
FOR YOU.
I SUGGEST YOU TAKE A LOOK BEFORE YOUR PARTNER GETS IN.
DENON?
ARE YOU OKAY?

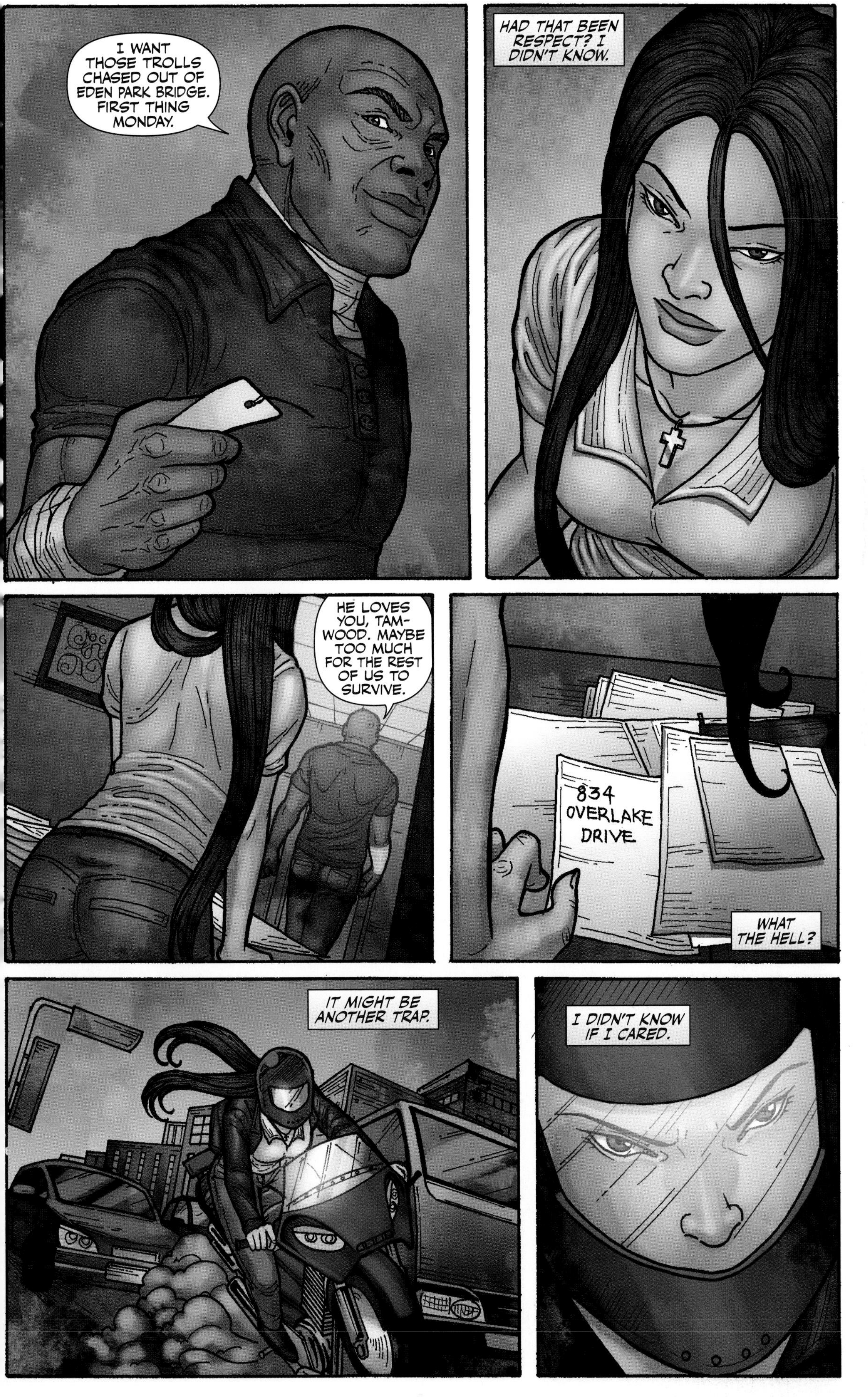
I WANT THOSE TROLLS CHASED OUT OF EDEN PARK BRIDGE. FIRST THING MONDAY.
HAD THAT BEEN RESPECT? I DIDN'T KNOW.
HE LOVES YOU, TAM-WOOD. MAYBE TOO MUCH FOR THE REST OF US TO SURVIVE.
834 OVERLAKE DRIVE
WHAT THE HELL?
IT MIGHT BE ANOTHER TRAP.
I DIDN'T KNOW IF I CARED.

IF IT WAS A HIT, IT WAS A GOOD ONE.

I NEVER HAD GOTTEN A LOOK INSIDE THE HOUSE.

I.S. WE'RE HERE TO SERVE YOU

CAUTION CAUTION CAUTION CAUTION CAUTION CAUTION CAUTION CAUTION CAUTION CAUTION CAUTION CAUTION CAU CAU CAUTION CAUTION CAU

DOGS WERE GONE... MOSTLY.

SOMETHING SMELLED DEAD.

CAUTION CAUTI

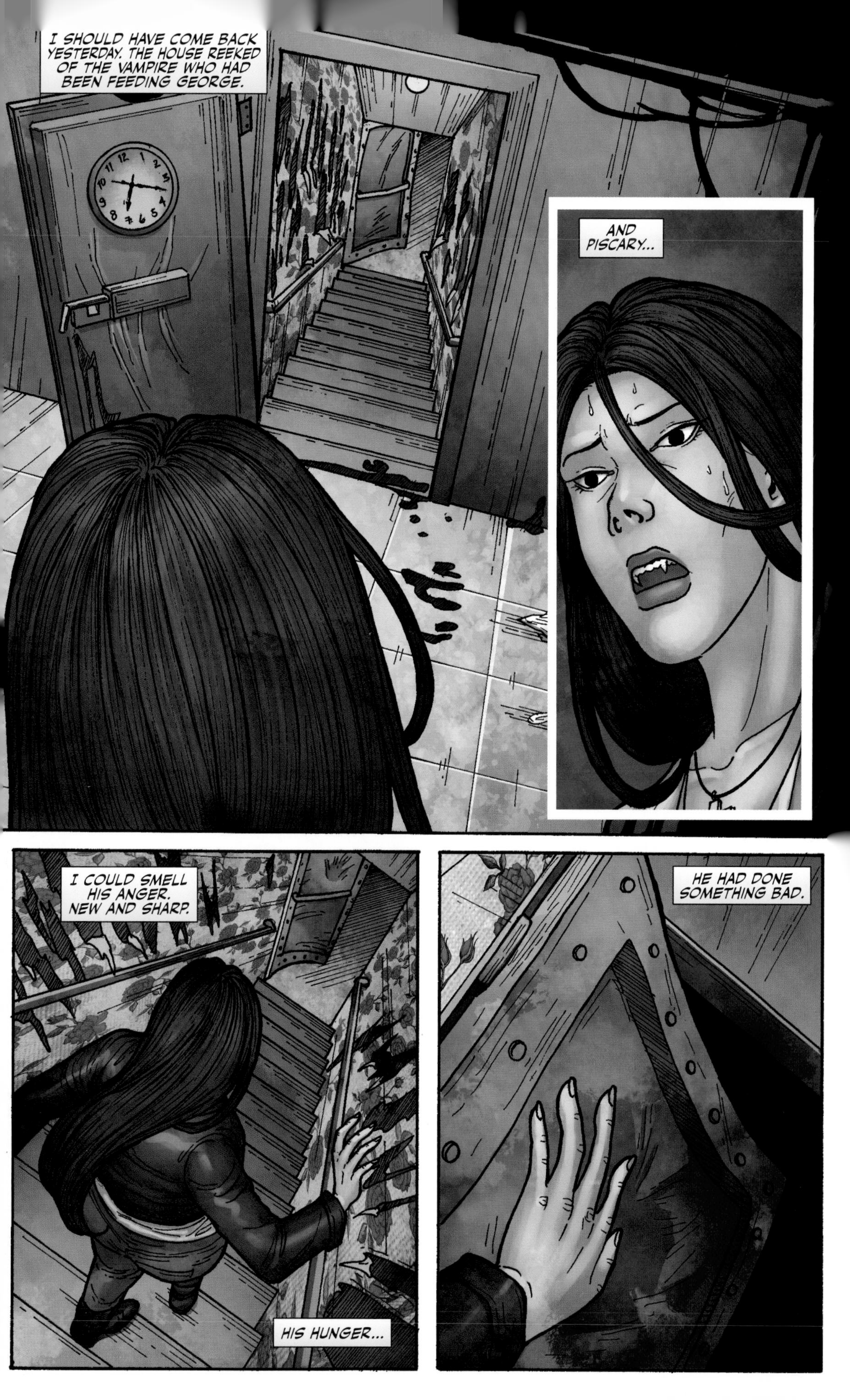
I SHOULD HAVE COME BACK YESTERDAY. THE HOUSE REEKED OF THE VAMPIRE WHO HAD BEEN FEEDING GEORGE.
AND PISCARY...
I COULD SMELL HIS ANGER. NEW AND SHARP.
HIS HUNGER...
HE HAD DONE SOMETHING BAD.

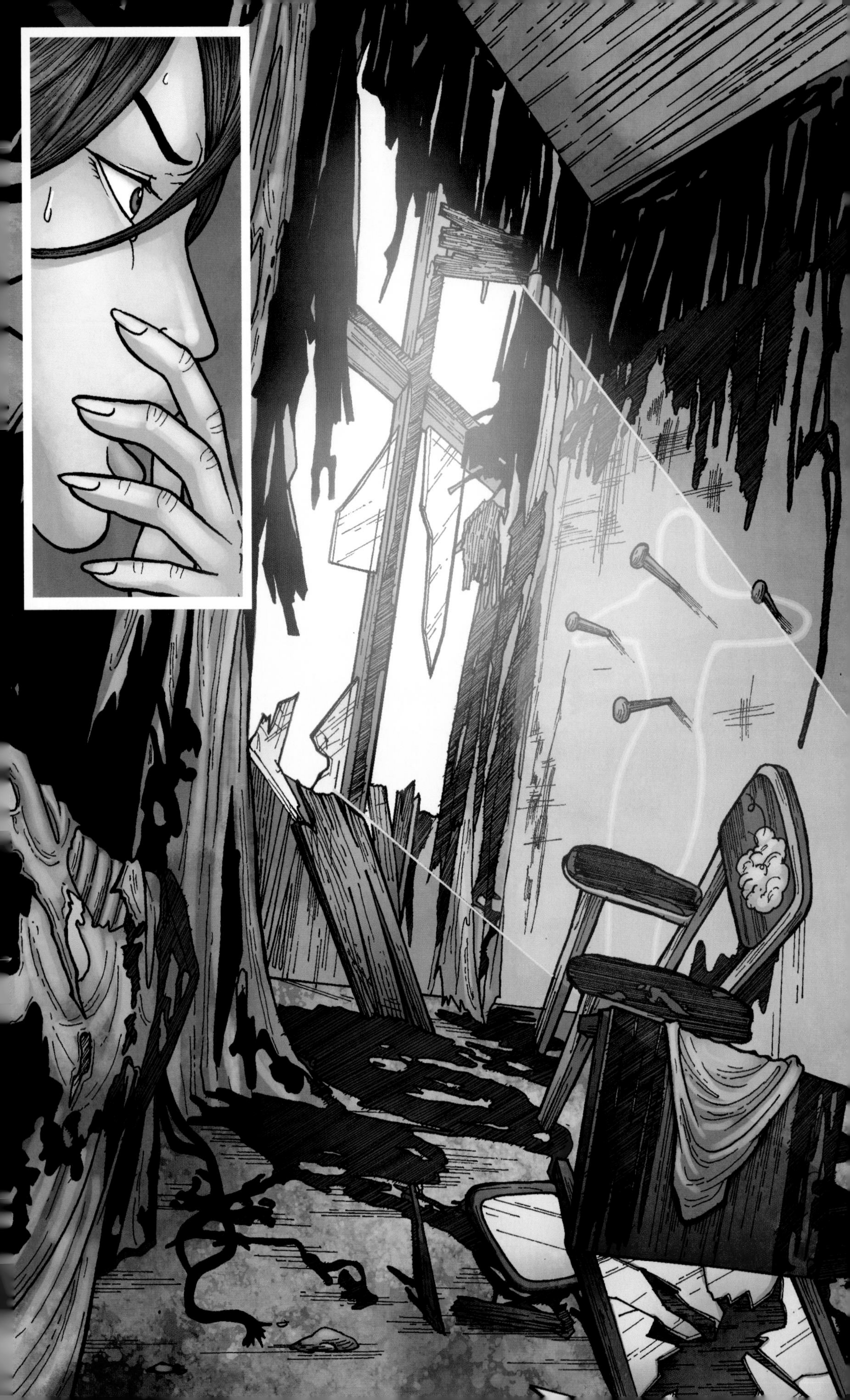

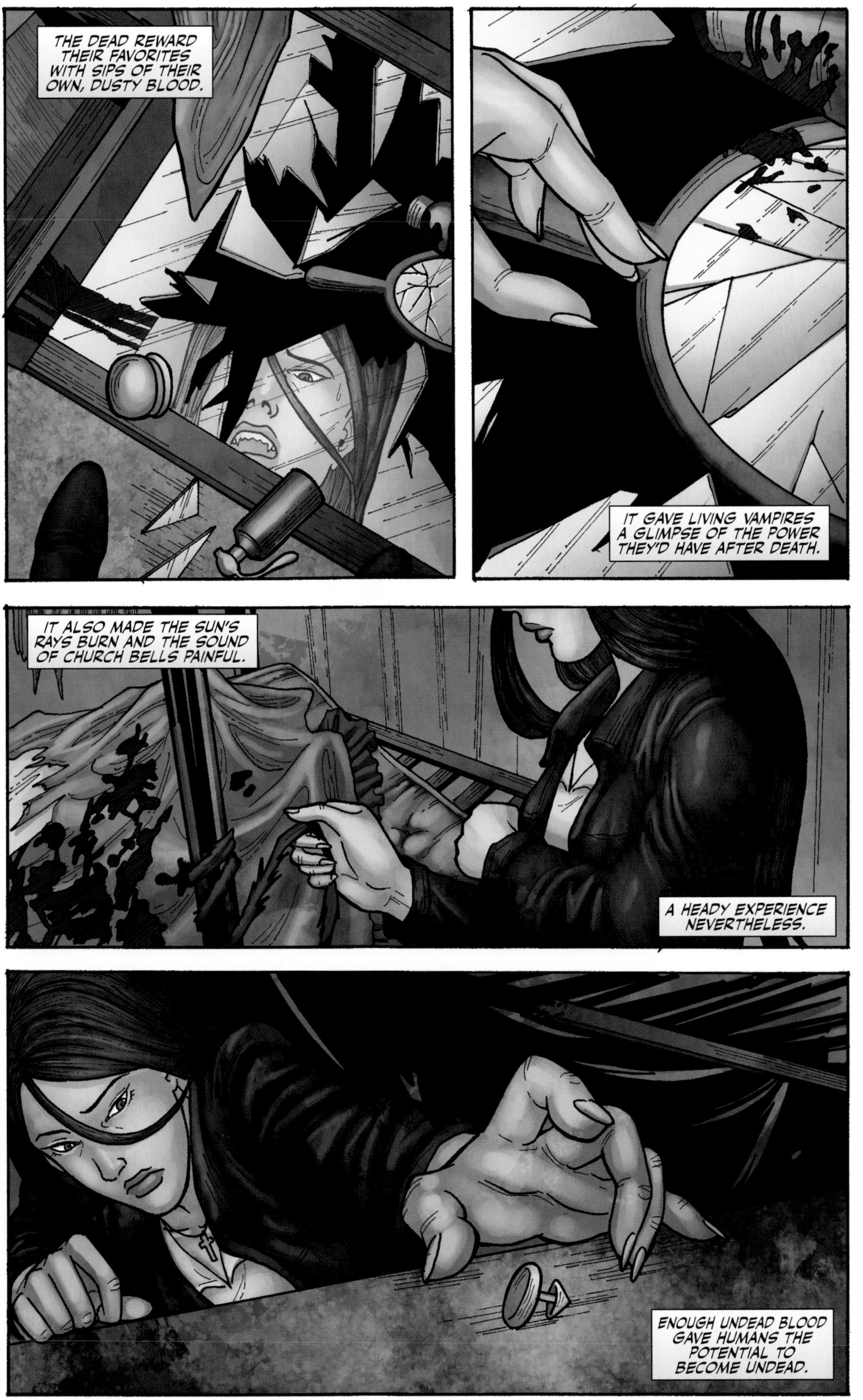
THE DEAD REWARD THEIR FAVORITES WITH SIPS OF THEIR OWN, DUSTY BLOOD.
IT GAVE LIVING VAMPIRES A GLIMPSE OF THE POWER THEY'D HAVE AFTER DEATH.
IT ALSO MADE THE SUN'S RAYS BURN AND THE SOUND OF CHURCH BELLS PAINFUL.
A HEADY EXPERIENCE NEVERTHELESS.
ENOUGH UNDEAD BLOOD GAVE HUMANS THE POTENTIAL TO BECOME UNDEAD.

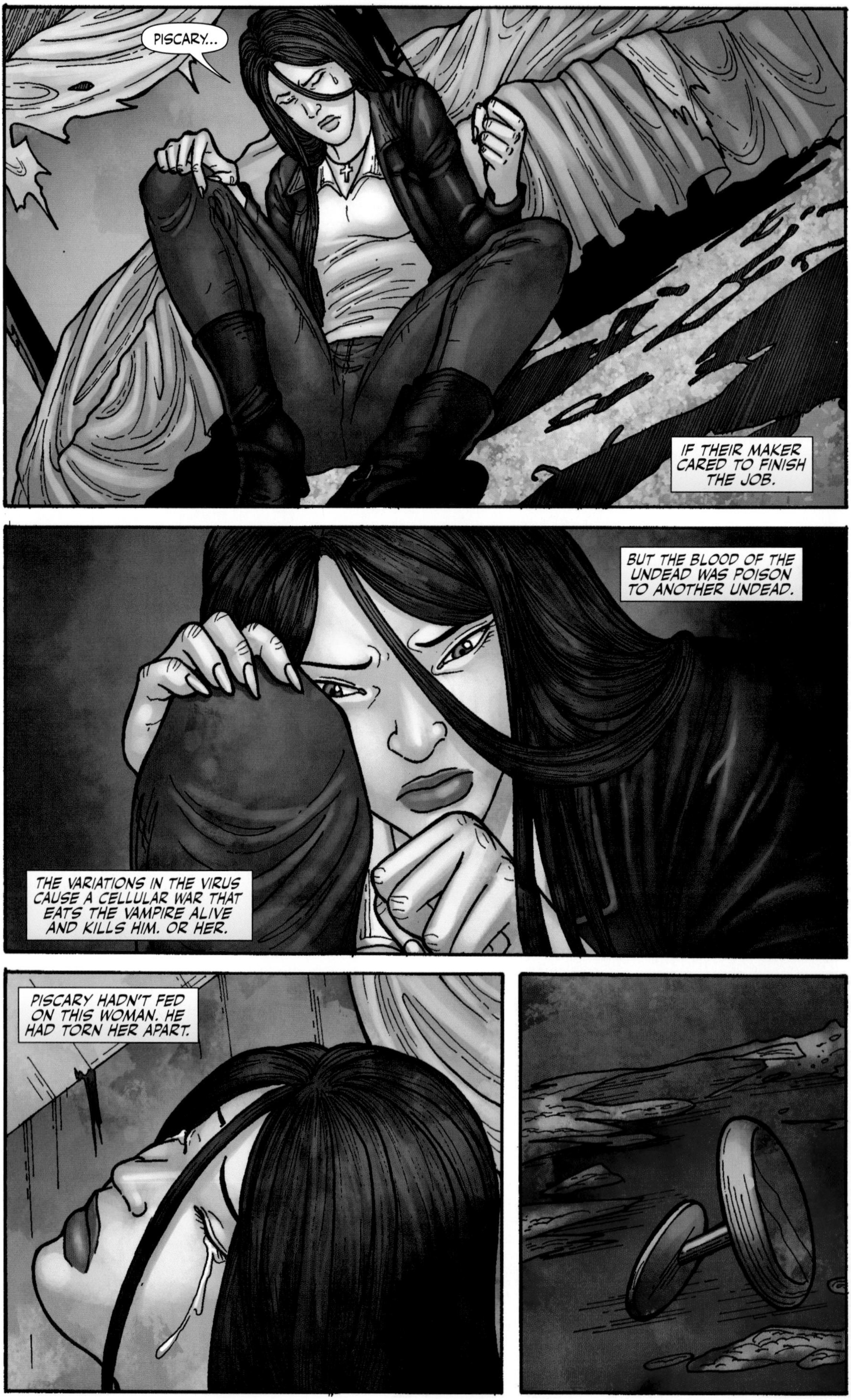
PISCARY...
IF THEIR MAKER CARED TO FINISH THE JOB.
BUT THE BLOOD OF THE UNDEAD WAS POISON TO ANOTHER UNDEAD.
THE VARIATIONS IN THE VIRUS CAUSE A CELLULAR WAR THAT EATS THE VAMPIRE ALIVE AND KILLS HIM. OR HER.
PISCARY HADN'T FED ON THIS WOMAN. HE HAD TORN HER APART.

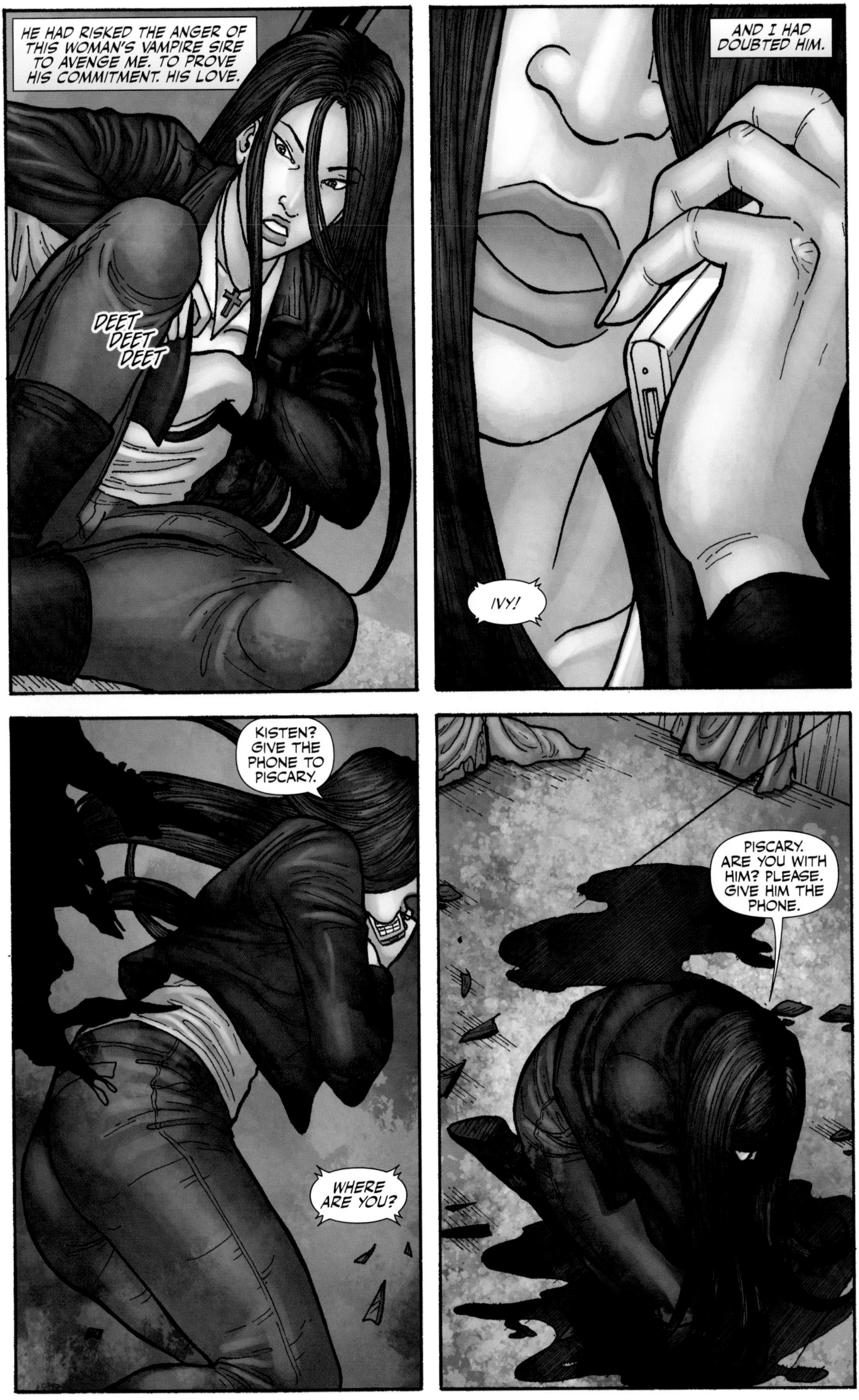

HE HAD RISKED THE ANGER OF THIS WOMAN'S VAMPIRE SIRE TO AVENGE ME. TO PROVE HIS COMMITMENT. HIS LOVE.
DEET DEET DEET
AND I HAD DOUBTED HIM.
IVY!
KISTEN? GIVE THE PHONE TO PISCARY.
WHERE ARE YOU?
PISCARY. ARE YOU WITH HIM? PLEASE. GIVE HIM THE PHONE.

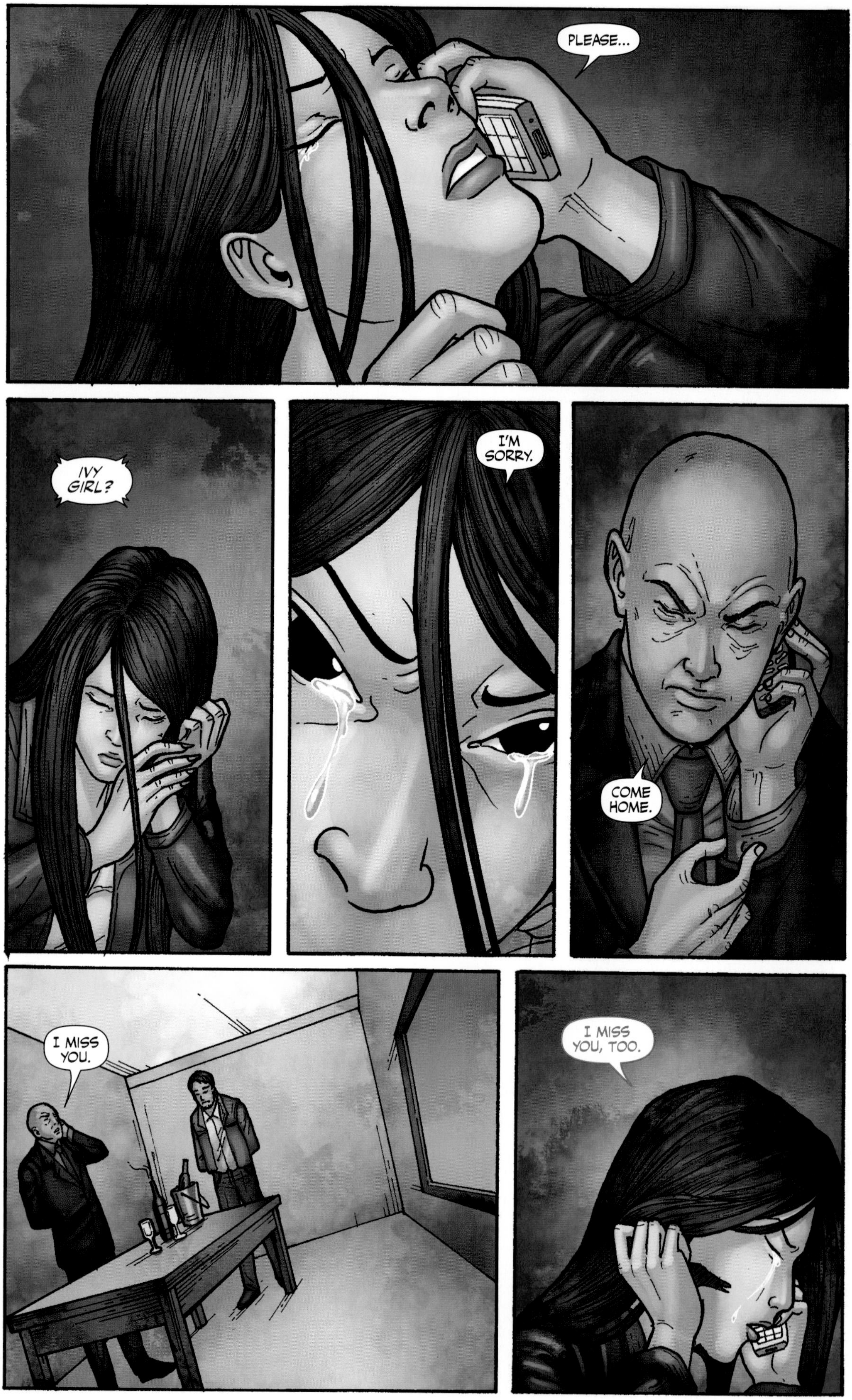
PLEASE...
IVY GIRL?
I'M SORRY.
COME HOME.
I MISS YOU.
I MISS YOU, TOO.

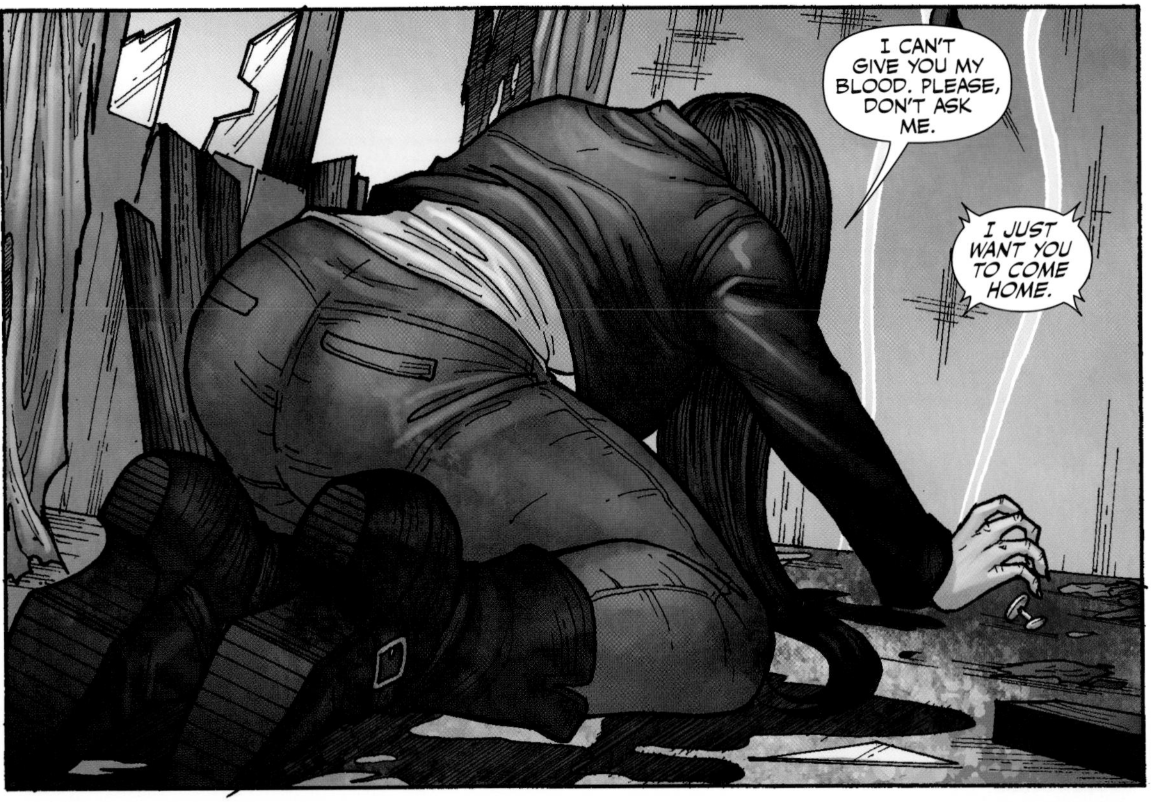
I CAN'T GIVE YOU MY BLOOD. PLEASE, DON'T ASK ME.
I JUST WANT YOU TO COME HOME.

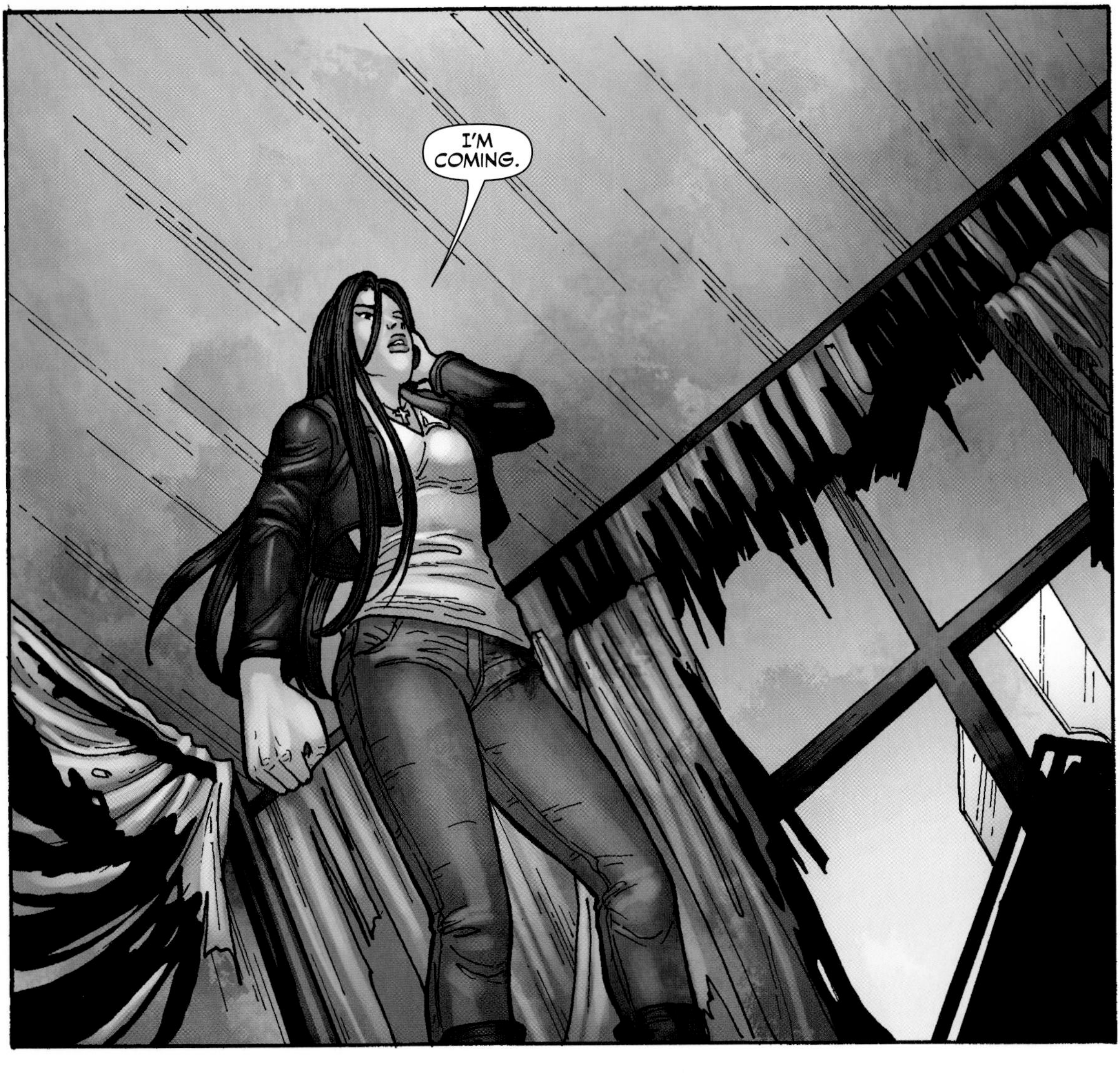
I'M COMING.

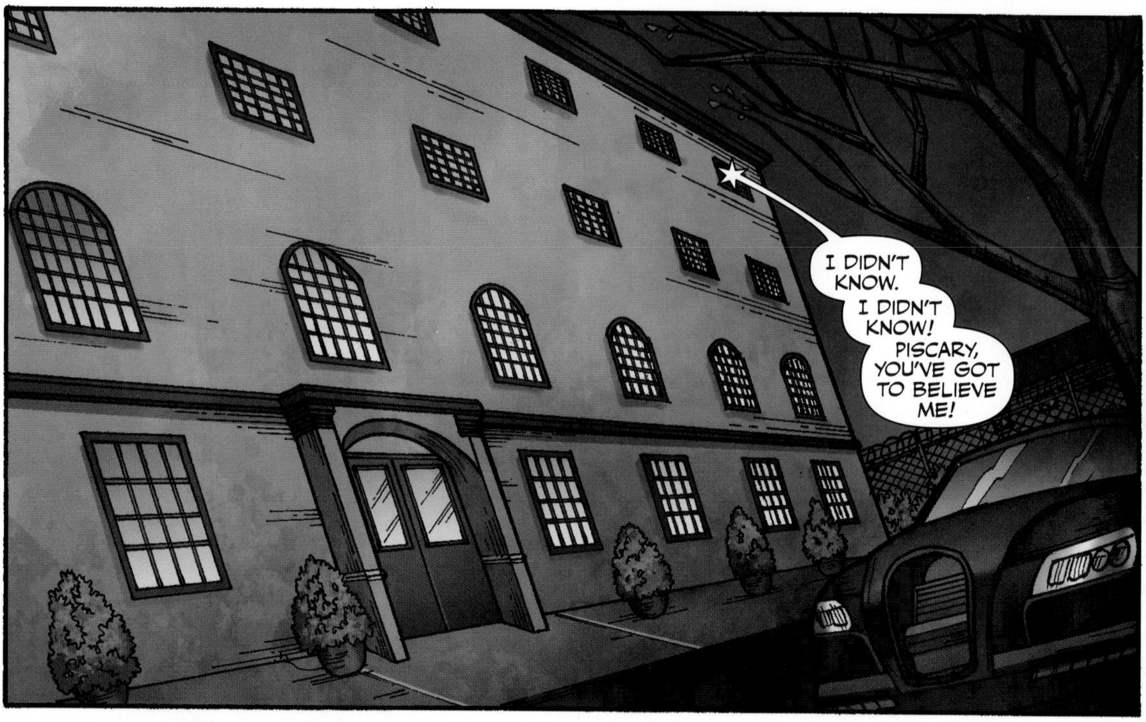
I DIDN'T KNOW.
I DIDN'T KNOW!
PISCARY, YOU'VE GOT TO BELIEVE ME!

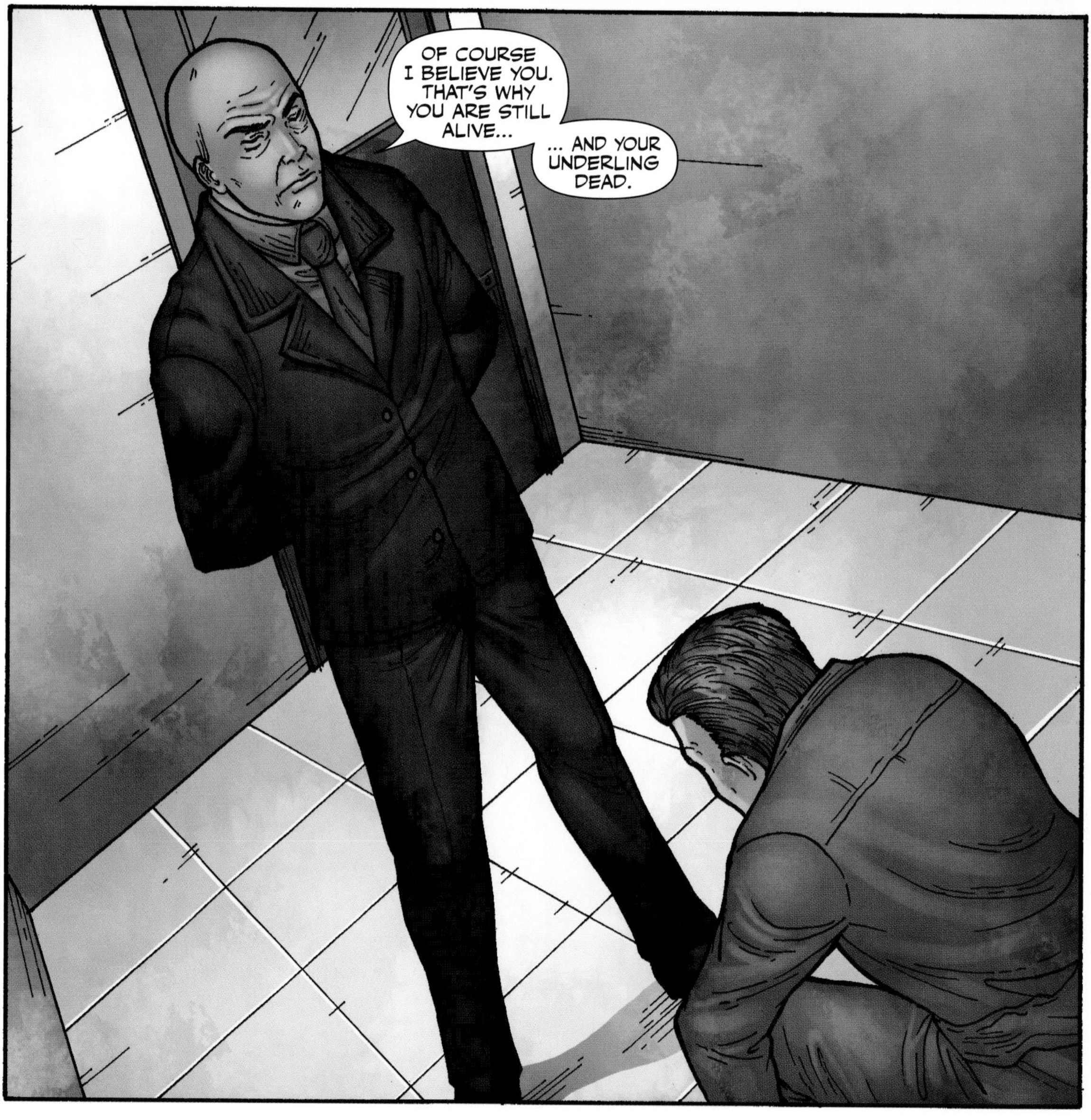
OF COURSE I BELIEVE YOU. THAT'S WHY YOU ARE STILL ALIVE...
... AND YOUR UNDERLING DEAD.

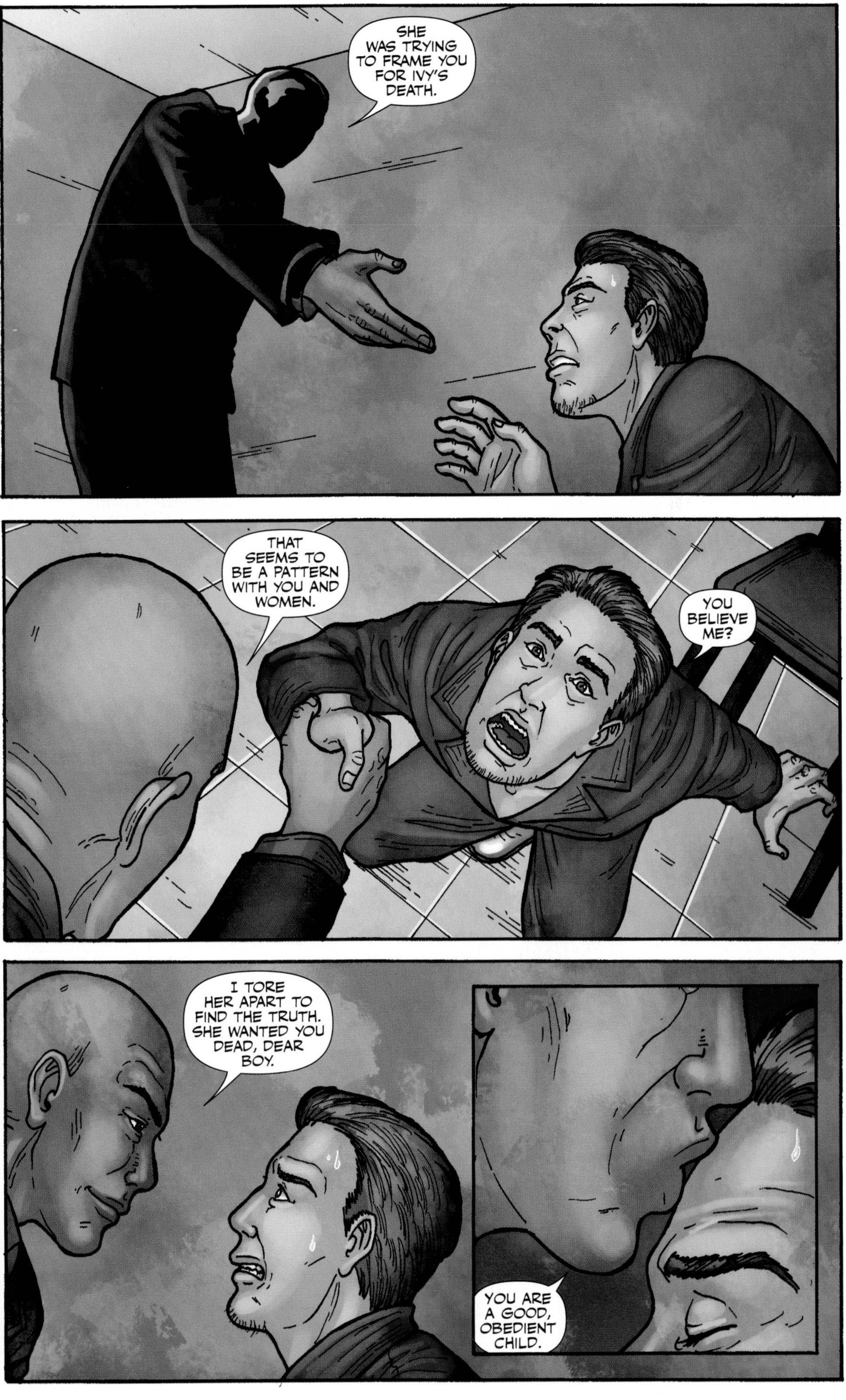
SHE WAS TRYING TO FRAME YOU FOR IVY'S DEATH.
THAT SEEMS TO BE A PATTERN WITH YOU AND WOMEN.
YOU BELIEVE ME?
I TORE HER APART TO FIND THE TRUTH. SHE WANTED YOU DEAD, DEAR BOY.
YOU ARE A GOOD, OBEDIENT CHILD.

CELESTE, WAS IT? SHE WITHSTOOD A GREAT DEAL OF PAIN, TRYING TO FRAME YOU.

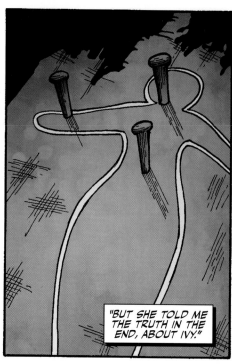

"BUT SHE TOLD ME THE TRUTH IN THE END, ABOUT IVY."

MY SWEET IVY GIRL.

YOU'LL NEVER HAVE HER.

IS THAT A THREAT?

A PREDICTION. AS YOU TRY TO BREED THE PERFECT MATE, YOU KEEP MAKING THE SAME MISTAKE.

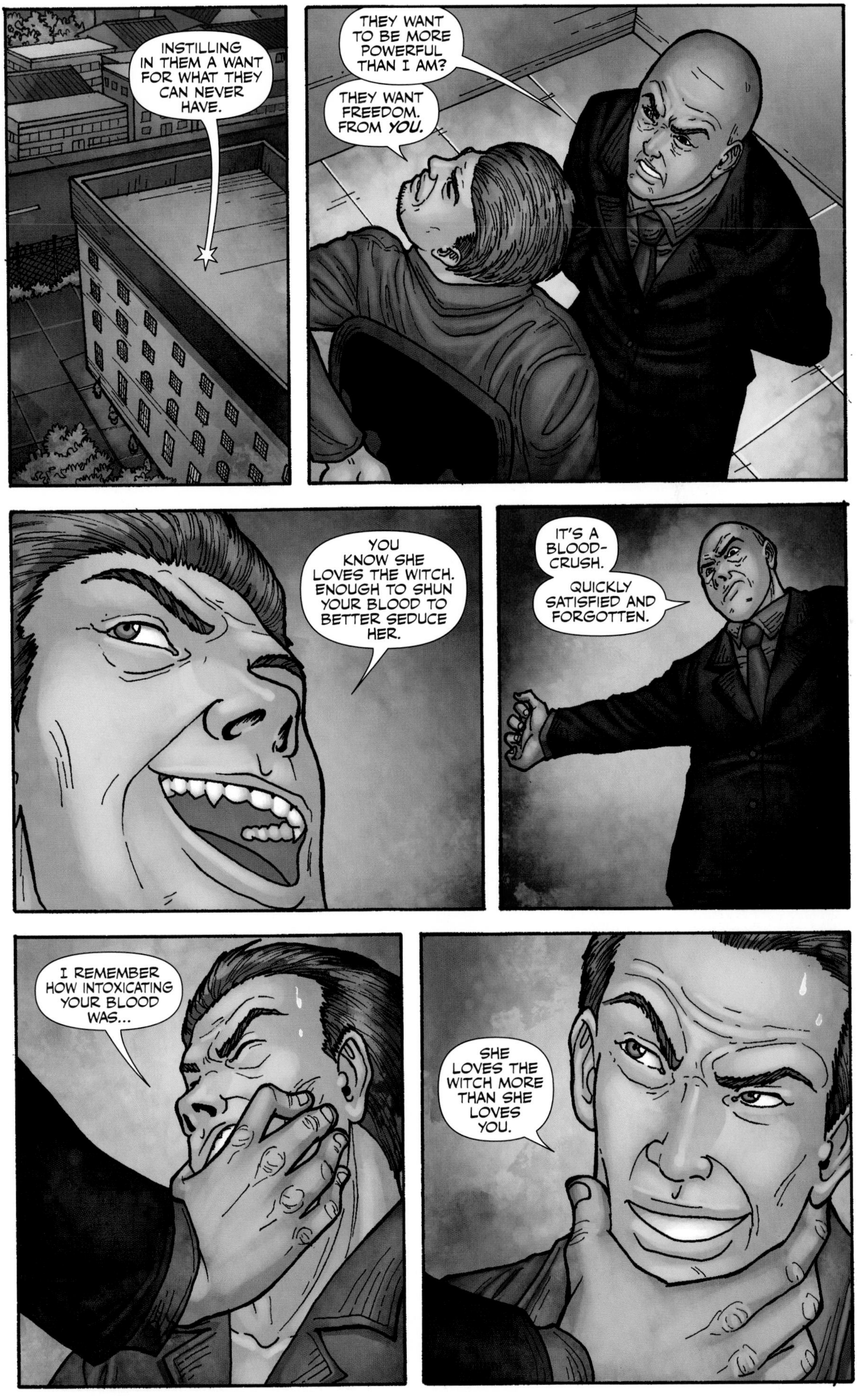
INSTILLING IN THEM A WANT FOR WHAT THEY CAN NEVER HAVE.
THEY WANT TO BE MORE POWERFUL THAN I AM?
THEY WANT FREEDOM. FROM *YOU.*
YOU KNOW SHE LOVES THE WITCH. ENOUGH TO SHUN YOUR BLOOD TO BETTER SEDUCE HER.
IT'S A BLOOD-CRUSH.
QUICKLY SATISFIED AND FORGOTTEN.
I REMEMBER HOW INTOXICATING YOUR BLOOD WAS...
SHE LOVES THE WITCH MORE THAN SHE LOVES YOU.

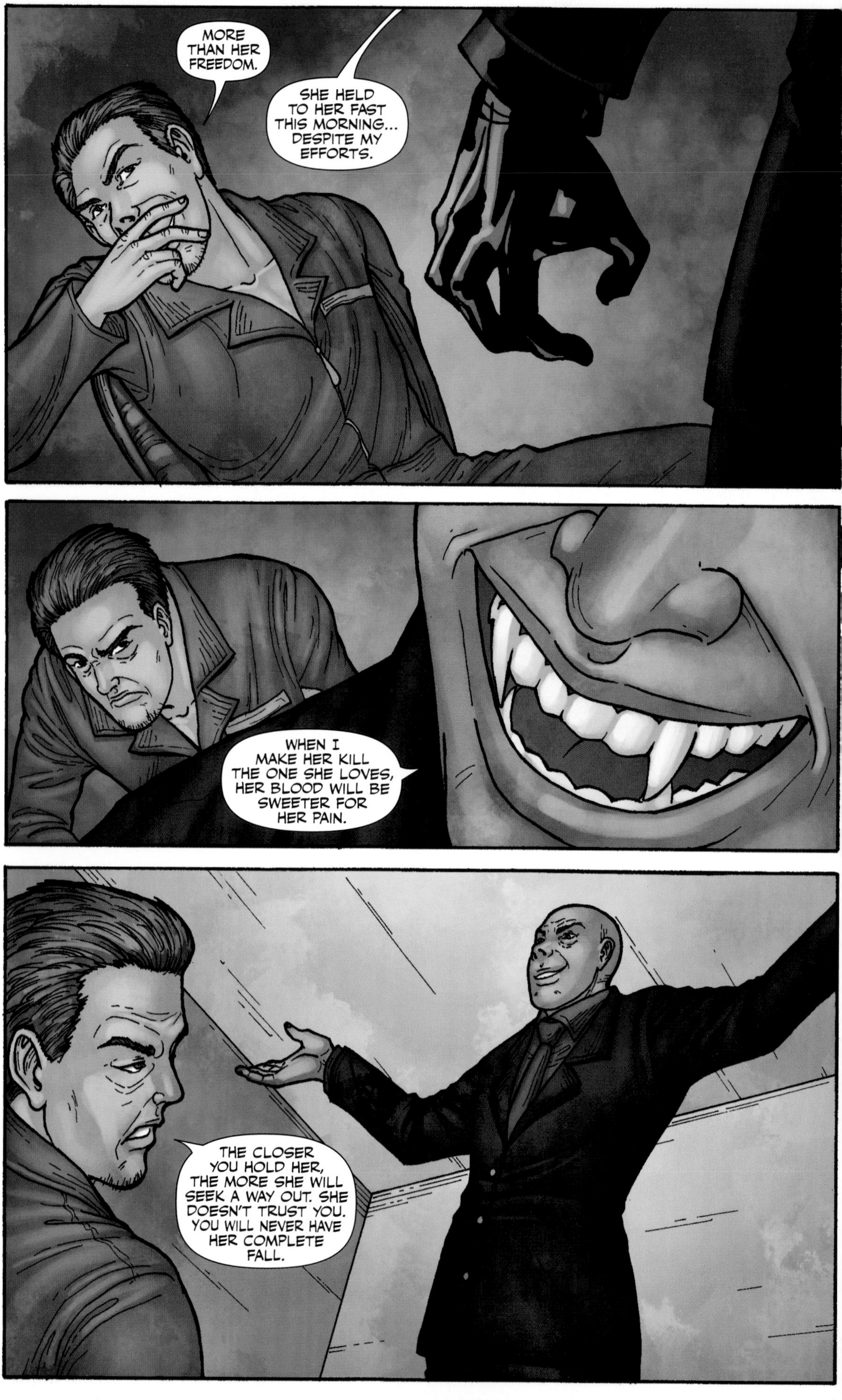
MORE THAN HER FREEDOM.
SHE HELD TO HER FAST THIS MORNING... DESPITE MY EFFORTS.
WHEN I MAKE HER KILL THE ONE SHE LOVES, HER BLOOD WILL BE SWEETER FOR HER PAIN.
THE CLOSER YOU HOLD HER, THE MORE SHE WILL SEEK A WAY OUT. SHE DOESN'T TRUST YOU. YOU WILL NEVER HAVE HER COMPLETE FALL.

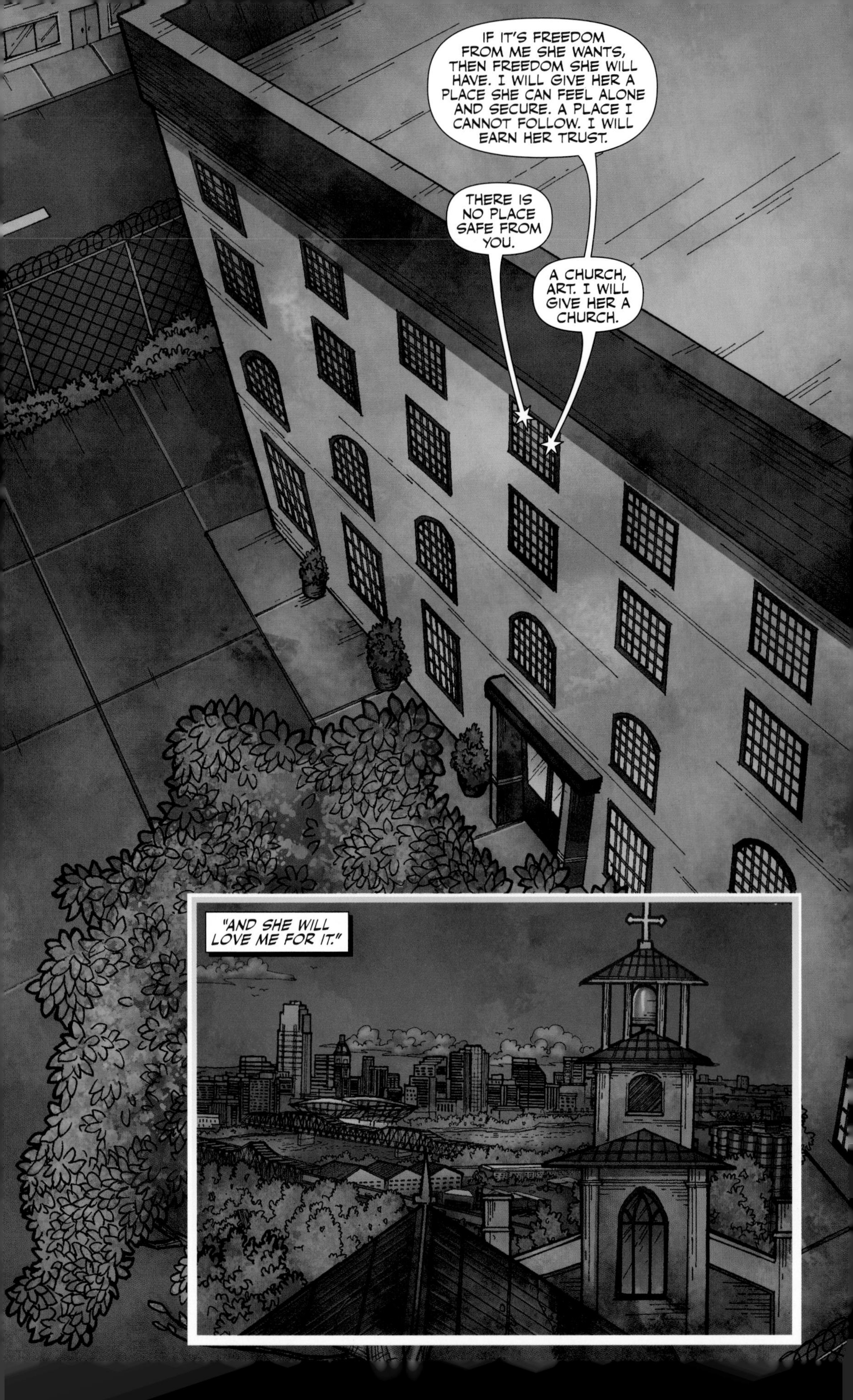
IF IT'S FREEDOM FROM ME SHE WANTS, THEN FREEDOM SHE WILL HAVE. I WILL GIVE HER A PLACE SHE CAN FEEL ALONE AND SECURE. A PLACE I CANNOT FOLLOW. I WILL EARN HER TRUST.
THERE IS NO PLACE SAFE FROM YOU.
A CHURCH, ART. I WILL GIVE HER A CHURCH.
"AND SHE WILL LOVE ME FOR IT."

About The Creators

KIM HARRISON was born and raised in the upper Midwest. In between working on the Hollows series starring witch Rachel Morgan and living vampire Ivy Tamwood, she is writing a young adult series starring Madison Avery. She is a member of both Romance Writers of America and Science Fiction and Fantasy Writers of America. When not at her desk, she is most likely to be found chasing down good chocolate, exquisite sushi, or the ultimate dog chew. (For her dog.) Her bestselling novels include *Dead Witch Walking; The Good, the Bad, and the Undead; Pale Demon;* and many more.

Penciller **GEMMA MAGNO** grew up at Morong, Rizal, Philippines. She was inspired to draw by watching anime and reading manga, and received a Presidential Award as Artist of the Year after winning several art competitions. Colorist **MAE HAO** was born in the Philippines and has assisted in projects published by Marvel, Dark Horse, and other publishers.

Artist's Sketchbook

A graphic novel is a collaborative project between author and artist. The characters, settings, and actions of the story are described by the writer—in this case, Kim Harrison herself—and executed by the artist. When the process goes smoothly, words and images meld to create a whole new kind of storytelling.

Since *Blood Crime* is the second graphic novel set in Kim's world of the Hollows, most of the characters and settings were already established. Artist Gemma Magno had only to follow the style of Pedro Maia's work in *Blood Work*. However, she did have the opportunity to create several new faces.

CELESTE AND GEORGE

Here are Kim's descriptions of these two characters, taken directly from her script. Gemma's interpretation of each was quickly approved.

Panel 1 [Top]—POV shift shown with darker, garish colors, harsher angles.

It's night. Feminine basement bedroom, lots of lace and pink. Canopy bed, with the covers strewn and pillows on floor. The table lamp on the night-stand has a lacy shawl over it to darken room. Curtains are closed on the one window, and no light is coming past them. Low ceiling, small windows up close to the top of the walls. Curtains pulled tight across them.

Kneeling on a fainting couch is George being bitten by a kneeling female vampire, the two of them twined about each other, the woman the domi-nant of the two. She is pale, in her early 30s, bright red lips and short black hair, like a flapper. She has an overdone necklace of metal links and a big stone. It's ugly. They are both still clothed, but there's a lot of skin showing, and her hand is beneath his shirt. Woman is wearing lace and a thin, lacy robe. George has a large bleeding gash on his neck, and he's pas-sive, his hands almost falling off the woman holding him up. His glasses are on a small table beside the fainting couch.

CELESTE

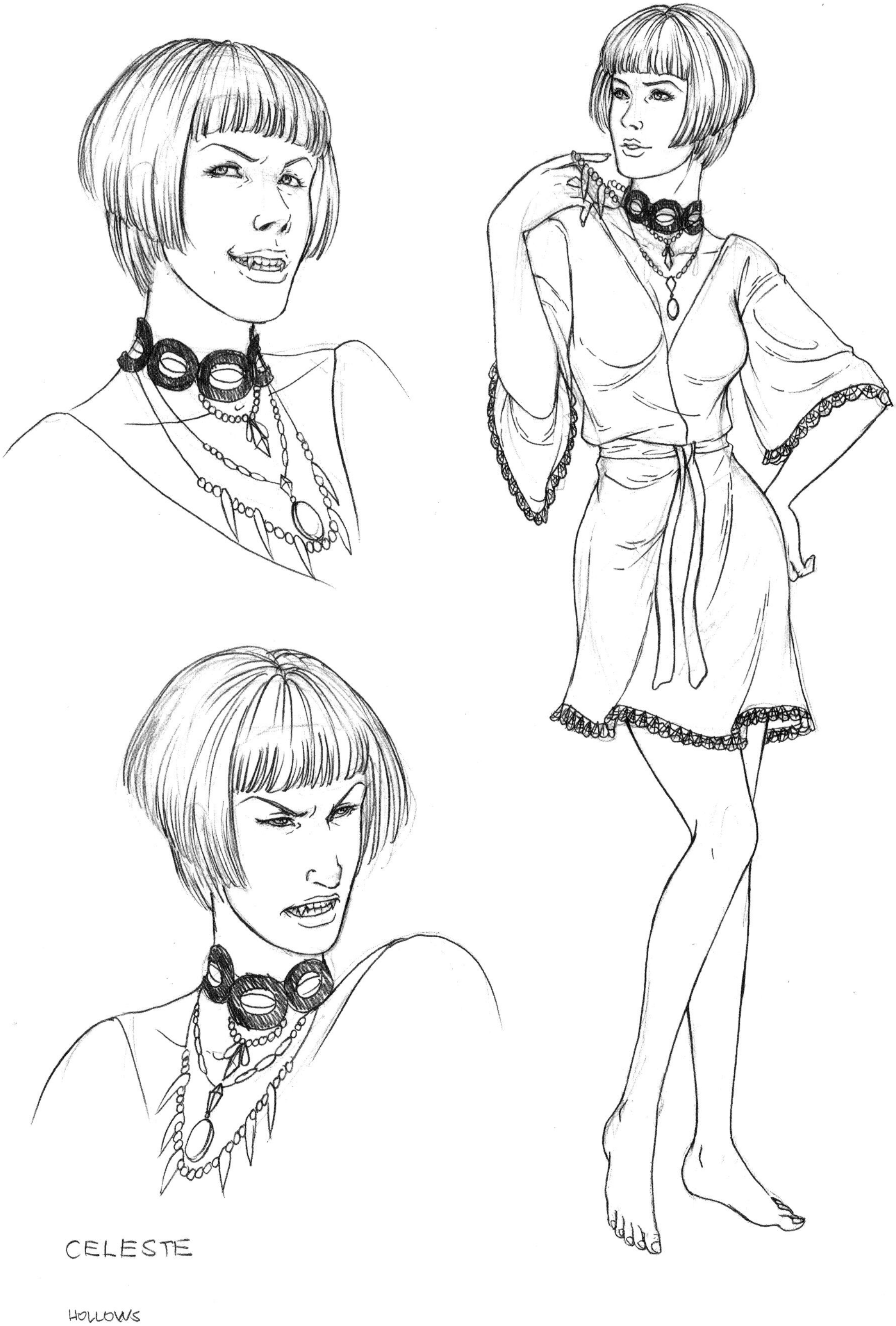
CELESTE
HOLLOWS

GEORGE

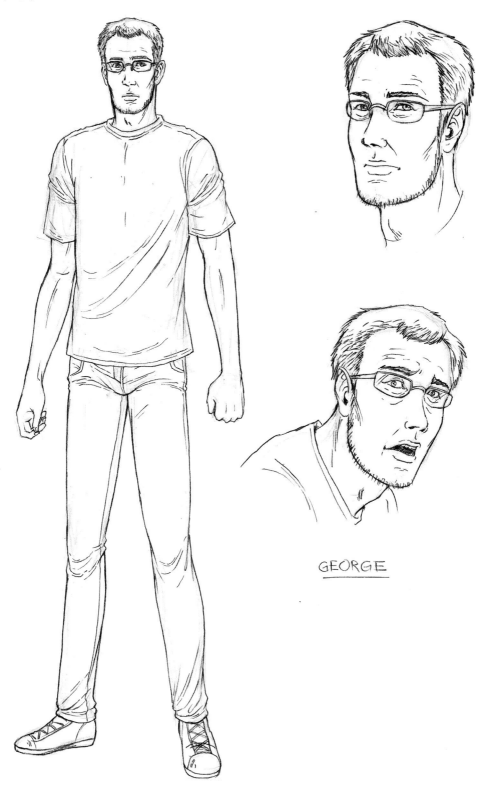

GEORGE

HOLLOWS

Here is the final art panel with the characters in place. Note how much the work of the colorist adds to the storytelling. Gemma Magno's job was to create the inked art. Then the pages went to colorist Mae Hao, whose task was to use color to communicate mood and personality.

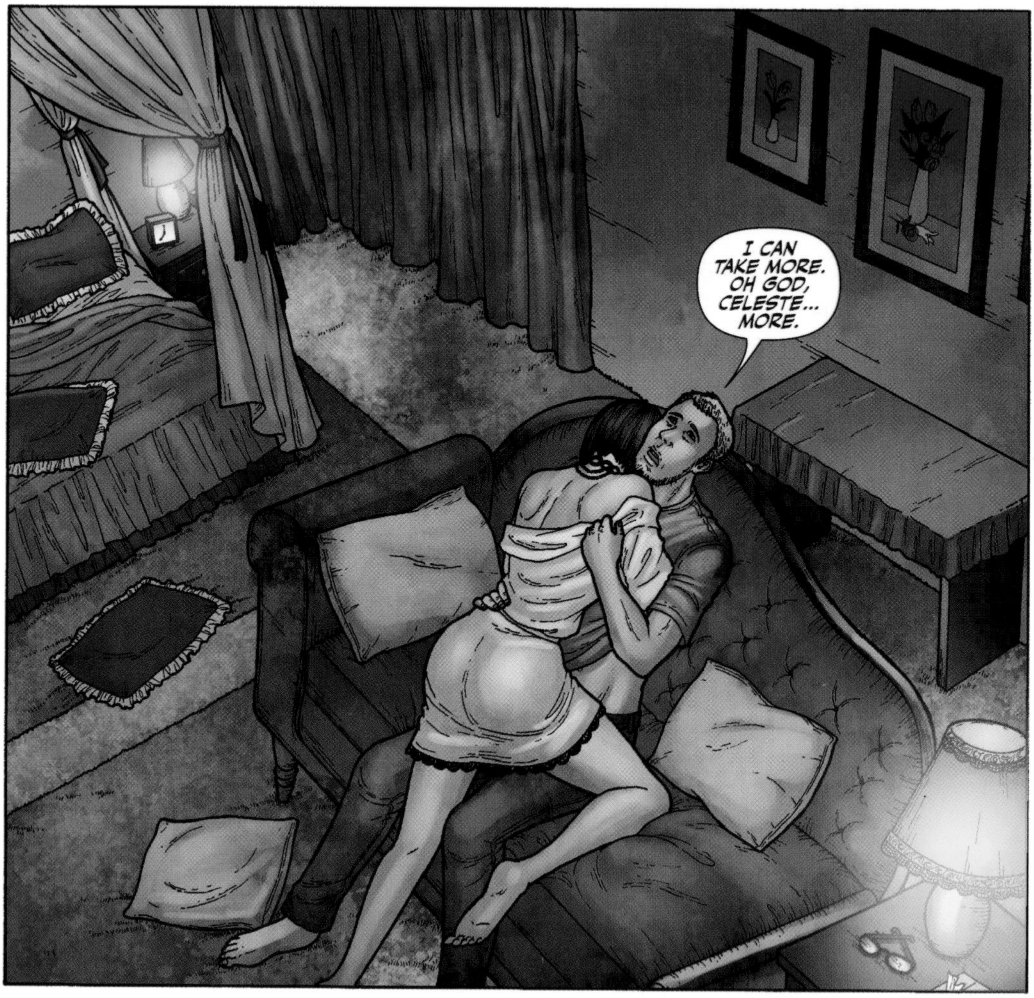
I CAN TAKE MORE. OH GOD, CELESTE... MORE.

ART

Kim was also quick to approve Gemma's sketch of Ivy's ex-boss, Art. Since he wears a prison jumpsuit throughout the book, he was easy to clothe!

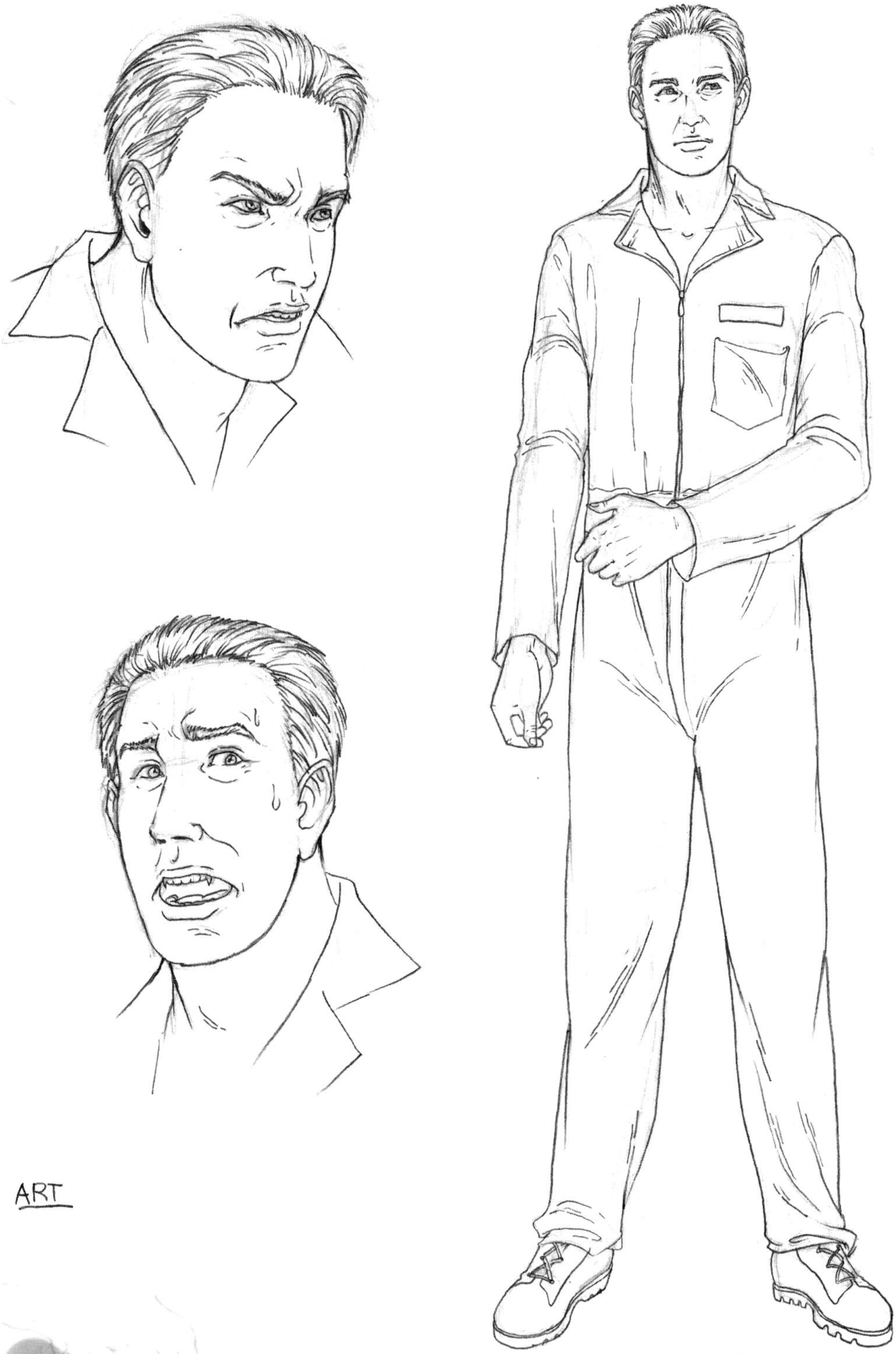
ART

THE ROUNDHOUSE KICK

Kim has what she refers to as "very dusty" first-degree black belts in both tae kwon do and hap-ki-do, and she had a clear image of what the fight scenes should look like early in the story. Gemma's first attempt at a roundhouse kick needed to be revised.

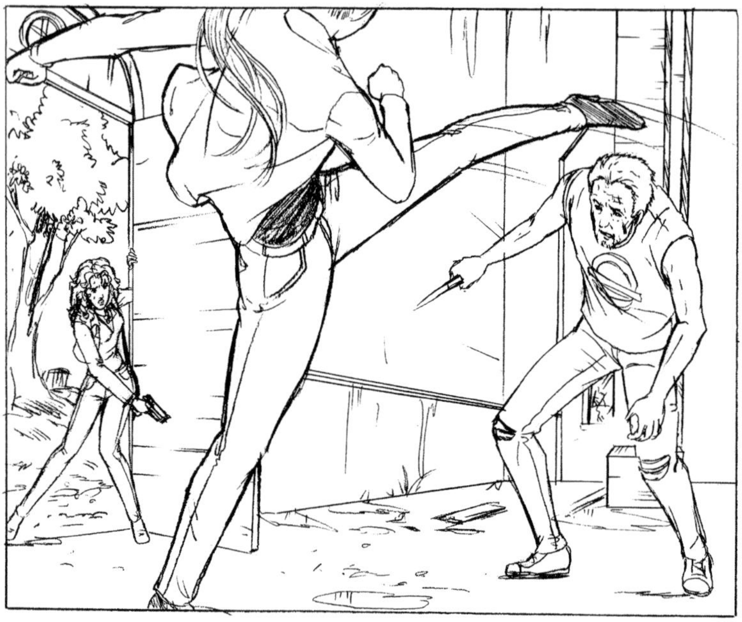

"A good kick has your hands in fists, held close to your chest and middle," Kim said. Gemma revised the art as follows.

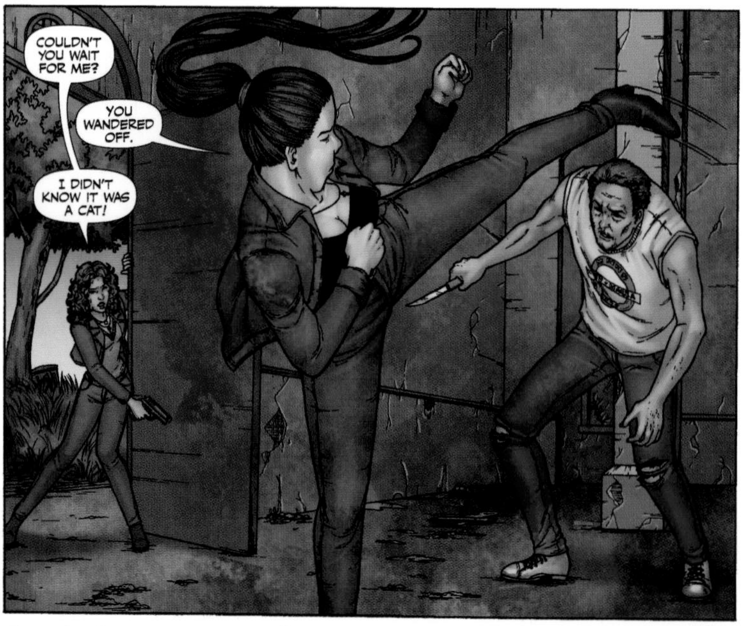
COULDN'T YOU WAIT FOR ME?
YOU WANDERED OFF.
I DIDN'T KNOW IT WAS A CAT!

PISCARY GOES TO THE PROM

Occasionally—though not often—colorist Mae Hao made a misstep. One example was putting Piscary in a baby blue suit for his faceoff with Art.

Kim requested that the suit be changed to black when she saw this first version: "I'm liking these colors except for the powder blue suit Piscary is wearing. Can it be changed to black or gray? I know all I said to the artist was make it a solid color, but it reminds me too much of Tim's prom tux. —laugh—"

(As Kim's readers may know, Tim is her husband. Alas, no photograph of the prom tux appears here.)

From Script to Art

On the following pages, we show you a little behind-the-scenes magic: Kim Harrison's original script pages are presented alongside Gemma Magno's art. It's the perfect demonstration of the collaborative relationship between writer and artist in making a graphic novel. Kim's script gives precise directions for the panel layout for each page and detailed stage directions, to help the artist envision the world of the story. And the artist in turn brings her own interpretive flair to Kim's detailed script, resulting in a marvelous whole that's greater than the sum of its parts.

ORIGINAL SCRIPT: PAGE 30

Panel 1 [Top]—Piscary is holding both her wrists and is bowed over one, kissing it. He's not angry. Ivy is now begging, her back hunched as she tries to pull away. Ivy's hunger shadow is scared, trying to get away from Piscary's shadow. Piscary's shadow is laughing, gripping Ivy's shadow so hard it's bleeding.

IVY: Please . . .

CAPTION: . . . but he was listening.

Panel 2 [Middle]—Both the characters and their shadows are showing here, if possible. Piscary is pulling her closer again. His eyes are black, and he looks evil. Ivy's expression is one of breathless hope. Piscary's shadow is tearing gaping holes in Ivy's shadow with long claws. Ivy's shadow is kneeling, begging for mercy.

PISCARY: I've given Rachel to you.

PISCARY: If someone is trying to kill her, I'll find out who.

Panel 3 [Bottom Left]—Piscary is holding Ivy close, his face hidden by her neck as he kisses her there. Ivy's eyes are closed, but she's clearly enjoying it, her hands gripping Piscary's shoulders. Piscary's shadow is biting Ivy's shadow, and Ivy's shadow is arching for more.

CAPTION: It wasn't him? But he had lied to me before. . .

Panel 4 [Bottom Right]—Close up of Piscary nuzzling Ivy's neck, his fangs almost touching her skin. If you can get Ivy's hands clenched on his shoulder, all the better.

PISCARY: Stay with me tonight . . .

IVY: Oh, God . . .

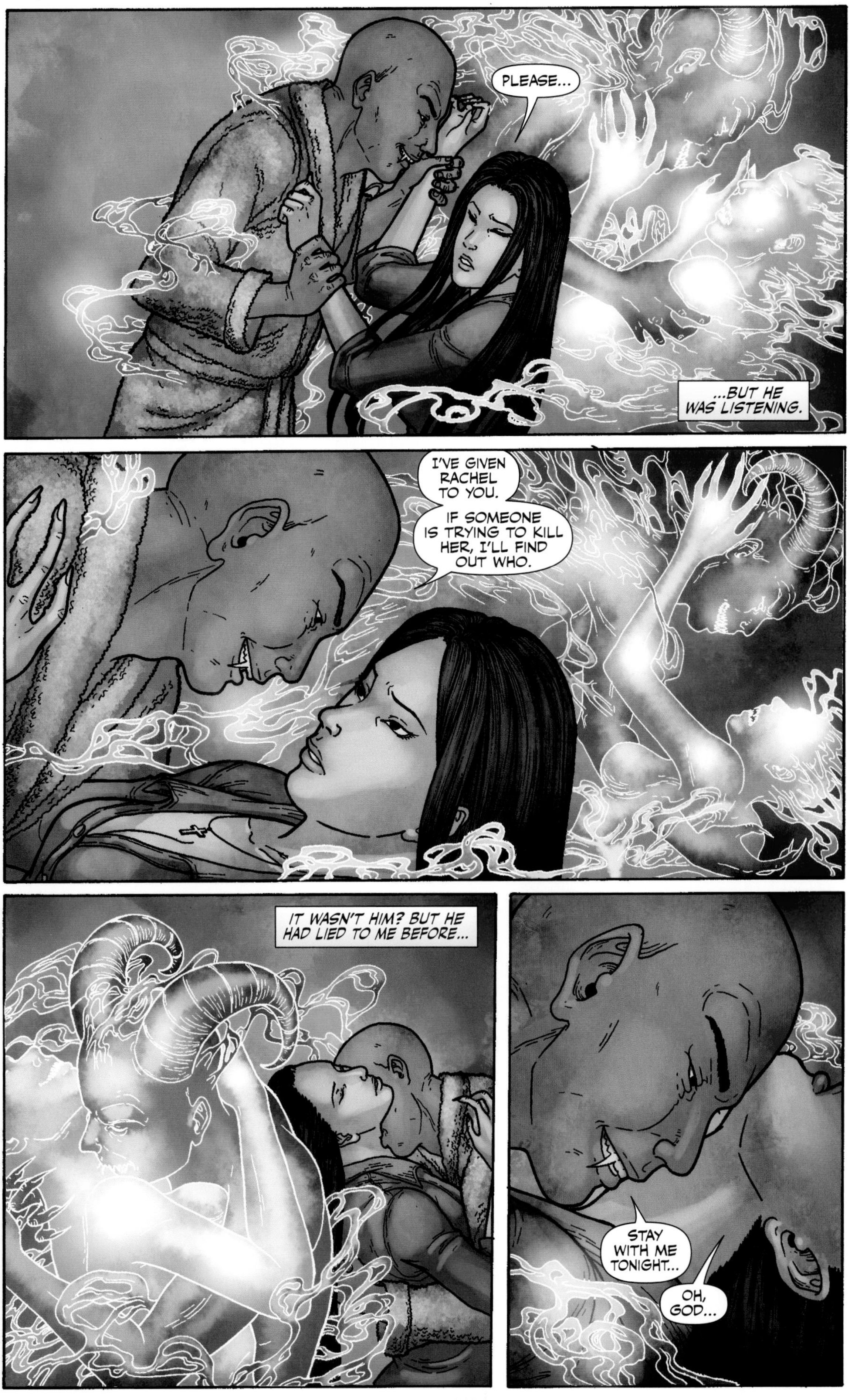
PLEASE...
...BUT HE WAS LISTENING.
I'VE GIVEN RACHEL TO YOU.
IF SOMEONE IS TRYING TO KILL HER, I'LL FIND OUT WHO.
IT WASN'T HIM? BUT HE HAD LIED TO ME BEFORE...
STAY WITH ME TONIGHT...
OH, GOD...

ORIGINAL SCRIPT: PAGE 94

Panel 1 [Upper Left]—Close up of Rachel to show her anger.

RACHEL: Did you know you put your hands in your pockets when you lie?

Panel 2 [Upper Right]—Rachel shining the light right on Ivy. Ivy has come closer, looking almost sheepish and squinting in the bright light and dripping from rain. There's a gleam of light on the stairway at the back wall.

IVY: I'll work on that. Thanks.

RACHEL: Stupid vamp! I ought to just—

Panel 3 [MIDDLE]—Rachel spinning to the stairway, droplets of rain flinging from her. Her expression is alarmed. Her gun is aimed, and a puff of air shows it has been fired. The flashlight is falling. Ivy is in a half crouch.

Panel 4 [BOTTOM]—The flashlight is rolling on floor. Rachel is jerking Ivy toward her. Ivy is surprised, and her hair is in her face as she falls forward, arms outstretched.

RACHEL: Look out!

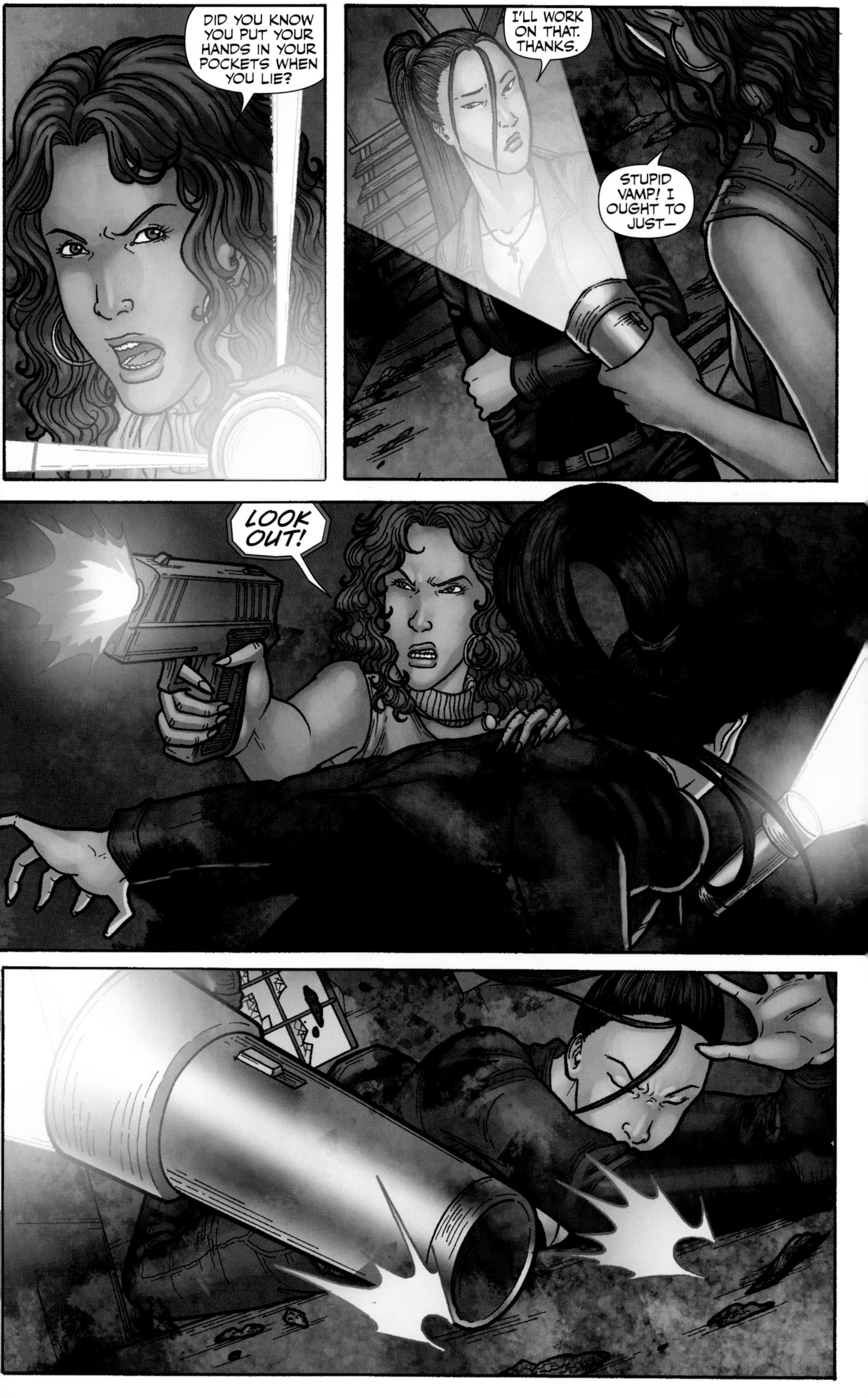
DID YOU KNOW YOU PUT YOUR HANDS IN YOUR POCKETS WHEN YOU LIE?
I'LL WORK ON THAT. THANKS.
STUPID VAMP! I OUGHT TO JUST—
LOOK OUT!

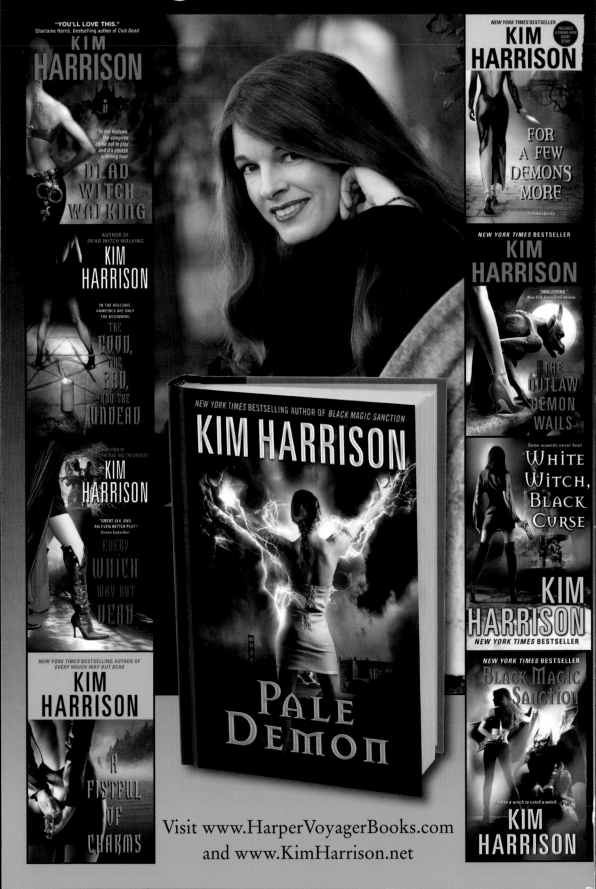